This exclusive One Spirit edition brings together three more thought-provoking inspiring works by internationally acclaimed author Paulo Coelho. *The Valkyries* is a story that asks why it is that we destroy the things we love most. Here Coelho confronts his past during a forty-day quest he and his wife take into the starkly beautiful and sometimes dangerous Mojave Desert, where they encounter the Valkyries, strange warrior women who travel the desert on motorcycles. A masterful blend of the exotic locales, dramatic adventure, and stark storytelling for which Coelho's fictional works are renowned, this true-life adventure story brings a poignant message about letting go of the past and believing in the future.

Crafted with masterful prose and clarity of vision, *The Fifth Mountain* is Coelho's inspiring story of the biblical prophet Elijah. Fleeing his homeland from persecution in the ninth century B.C., twenty-three-year-old Elijah takes refuge with a young widow and her son in the beautiful town of Akbar. Already struggling to maintain his sanity in a world fraught with tyranny and war, he is now forced to choose between his newly discovered love and his overwhelming sense of duty. Evoking the drama and intrigue of the colorful world of the Middle East, Coelho turns the trials of Elijah into an intensely moving account of a man's soul-shattering trial of faith.

Veronika Decides to Die is a dazzling portrait of a young woman at the crossroads of despair and liberation. Twenty-four-year-old Veronika appears to have everything—youth, beauty, boyfriends and a loving family, a fulfilling job—but something is missing in her life. So, one cold November morning Veronika decides to die. She takes a handful of sleeping pills expecting never to wake up. But she does—at a mental hospital where she is told that she has only days to live. Based on events in Coelho's own life, this poetic, exuberant novel questions the meaning of madness and celebrates individuals who do not fit into patterns society considers to be normal.

PAULO COELHO's books have sold more than thirty million copies and have been translated into fifty-one languages. Besides the works in this volume he is als̲ ̲ ̲ ̲ ̲ ̲ ̲ ̲ *The Alchemist, The Pilgrimage, By the River Piedra I* ̲ ̲ ̲ ̲ ̲ ̲ ̲ ̲ ̲ ̲ ̲ ̲ ̲ ̲ ̲ *Light: A Manual.* He lives in Ri̲ ̲ ̲ ̲

The Valkyries

The Fifth Mountain

Veronika Decides to Die

The Valkyries

The Fifth Mountain

Veronika Decides to Die

Paulo Coelho

One Spirit · New York

The Valkyries

An Encounter with Angels

Translated by Alan R. Clarke

And an angel descended
where they were
and the glory of the Lord
shone all about them.

Luke 2:9

Prologue

"Something that is of great importance to me?" J. thought for a few moments before responding. "Magic."

"No, something else," Paulo insisted.

"Women," J. said. "Magic and women."

Paulo laughed.

"They're important to me, too," he said. "Although marriage has slowed me down a bit."

It was J.'s turn to laugh.

"A bit," he said. "Just a bit."

Paulo filled his master's glass with wine. It had been four months since they had seen each other, and this was a quite special night. Paulo wanted to talk for a while longer, build the suspense, before giving J. the package he had brought.

"I used to imagine the great masters as people who were far removed from the world," he said to J. "If you had answered me that way a few years ago, I think I would have abandoned my apprenticeship."

"You should have done that," J. said, sipping at his wine. "And I would have found a beautiful woman disciple to take your place."

They drank the entire bottle of wine as they sat talking in the restaurant located on the top floor of J.'s hotel. They spoke of work, magic, and women. J. was euphoric about the huge contract he had just negotiated for the Dutch multinational for which he worked. And Paulo was excited about the package he had brought with him.

"Let's have another bottle," Paulo said.

"In honor of what?"

"Your coming to Rio de Janeiro. . . . The beautiful view from the window over there. . . . And the present I've brought you."

J. looked out the window to see Copacabana beach sparkling below. "The view deserves a toast," he said, signaling to the waiter.

When they were halfway through the second bottle, Paulo placed the package on the table.

Looking at J., he said, "If you were to ask me what is important to me, I would say: my master. It was he who taught me to understand that love is the only thing that never fails. He who had the patience to lead me along the intricate paths of magic. He who had the courage and dignity, despite his powers, to present himself always as a person with some doubts and with certain weaknesses. He who helped me to understand the forces that can transform our lives."

"We've had a lot of wine," J. said. "I don't want to get serious."

"I'm not talking about serious things. I'm talking about joyful things. I'm talking about love."

He pushed the package to J.'s side of the table. "Open it."

"What is his?"

"A way of saying thank you. And of passing on to others all the love you taught me."

J. opened the package. It contained almost two hundred typed pages, on the first of which was written *"The Alchemist."*

Paulo's eyes were gleaming.

"It's a new book," he said. "Look at the next page."

There was an inscription written in longhand: "For J., the alchemist who knows and uses the secrets of the Great Work."

Paulo had anxiously awaited this moment. He had been able to keep completely secret the fact that he was writing a new book, even though he knew that J. had really liked his previous book.

"This is the original manuscript," Paulo continued. "I'd like you to read it before I send it to the publisher."

He tried to read the expression in his master's eyes, but they were impenetrable.

"I have meetings all day tomorrow, J. said, "so I'll be able to read it only at night. Let's have lunch two days from now."

Paulo had been expecting a different reaction. He thought that J. would be happy, and moved by the inscription.

"Let's do that," said Paulo, hiding his disappointment. "I'll be back in two days."

J. called for the check. They walked silently to the elevator. J. pushed the button for the eleventh floor.

When the elevator stopped at his floor, J. pushed the Emergency button to hold the door open. Then he approached Paulo and said, "May the Lamb of God protect you," making a sign on the forehead of his disciple.

Paulo embraced his master and said good night. Resetting the button, J. stepped out of the elevator.

"Why didn't you make copies of the original?" he asked, as the door began to close.

"In order to give God the chance to make it disappear, if that was his will."

"Wise decision," Paulo heard J. say as the door closed. "I hope that the literary critics never discover where it is."

They met two days later, at the same restaurant.

J. began, "There are certain secrets of alchemy described in your book. Secrets I never discussed with you. And you presented them quite correctly."

Paulo was delighted. This was just what he wanted to hear.

"Well, I've been studying," he explained.

"No, you haven't been studying," J. said. "Yet what you've written about is correct."

"I can't fool him," Paulo thought. "I'd like him to think I'm dedicated, but I can't fool him."

He looked outside. The sun was glaring, and the beach was crowded.

"What do you see in that immense sky?" J. asked.

"Clouds."

"No," J. said. "You see the soul of the rivers. Rivers that have just been reborn in the sea. They will rise to the sky, and remain there until, for whatever reason, they once again become rain and fall to earth.

"The rivers return to the mountains, but carry with them the wisdom of the sea."

J. poured himself some mineral water. He didn't usually drink during the day.

"That is how you discovered those secrets we had never discussed, J. said. "You are a river. You have already run down to the sea, and you know its wisdom. You have died and been reborn many times. All you have to do is remember."

Paulo was happy. It was a kind of praise: His master said that he had "discovered secrets." But he was unable to ask openly which secrets they were.

"I have a new task for you," J. said. Silently, he thought, *It has to do with your book. Because I know it's very important to you, and it doesn't deserve to be destroyed.* But Paulo didn't need to hear about that.

One week later, J. and Paulo walked together through the airport. Paulo wanted to know more about the task that his master had assigned him the week before, but J. carefully avoided conversation. They sat down at a table in the cafeteria.

"We were able to have dinner together only twice during my stay here in Rio," J. began, "and this is our third. It's in observance of the saying 'Anything that occurs once can never occur again. But, should it happen twice, it will surely happen a third time.'"

J. was trying to avoid the subject, but Paulo persevered. He knew now that his master had liked the book's dedication, because he had overheard a conversation between J. and the receptionist at the hotel. And later, one of J.'s friends had referred to Paulo as "the book's author."

He must have told a number of people about it—there was, after all, only one copy of the original. *Vanity of vanities,* he said to himself. He thanked God for having given him a master so human.

"I want to ask you about the task," Paulo said once again. "I don't want to ask 'how' or 'where,' because I know you won't tell me."

"Well, that's one thing you've learned in all this time," J. laughed.

"In one of our conversations," Paulo continued, "you told me about a man named Gene, who was able to do what you are now asking of me. I'm going to look for him."

"Did I give you his address?"

"You mentioned that he lived in the United States, in the California desert. It shouldn't be too hard to get there."

"No, it isn't."

As they spoke, Paulo became aware that the voice on the public address system was continually announcing flight departures. He began to feel tense, fearing there wouldn't be enough time to complete their conversation.

"Even though I don't want to know 'how' or 'where,' you taught me that there is a question we should always ask as we undertake something. I'm asking you that question now: Why? Why must I do this?"

"Because people always kill the things they love," J. replied.

As Paulo pondered the mystery of this answer, once again he heard a departure announced.

"That's my plane," J. said. "I have to go."

"But I don't understand your answer to my question."

Asking Paulo to pay the bill, J. quickly wrote something on a paper napkin.

Placing the napkin on the table in front of his disciple, J. said, "During the last century, a man wrote about what I've just said to you. But it's been true for many generations."

Paulo picked up the napkin. For a fraction of a second, he thought it might contain a magic formula. But it was a verse from a poem.

> And each man kills the thing he loves,
> By all let this be heard,
> Some do it with a bitter look,
> Some with a flattering word,
> The coward does it with a kiss,
> The brave man with a sword.

The waiter came with the change, but Paulo didn't notice. He couldn't stop looking at those terrible words.

"And so, the task," J. said after a long silence. "It's needed to break that curse."

"One way or another," Paulo said slowly, "I have wound up destroying what I've loved. I've seen my dreams fall apart just when I seemed about to achieve them. I always thought that was just the way life was. My life and everyone else's."

"The curse can be broken," J. repeated, "if you complete the task."

They walked through the noisy airport in silence. J. was thinking about the books that his disciple had written. He thought about Chris, Paulo's wife. He knew that Paulo was being drawn toward the magical initiation that appears at one time or another in everyone's life.

He knew that Paulo was on the brink of seeing one of his greatest dreams realized.

And this meant danger, because J.'s disciple was like all human beings: He was going to find that he did not necessarily deserve all that he had received.

But he didn't tell Paulo any of this.

"The women of your country are beautiful," J. said with a smile, as they arrived at the passport control line. "I hope I can come back."

But Paulo spoke seriously.

"So that's what the task is for," he said, as his master handed over his passport for stamping. "To break the curse."

And J. answered, just as seriously. "It's for love. For victory. And for the glory of God."

THEY HAD BEEN DRIVING FOR ALMOST SIX HOURS. FOR THE hundredth time, he asked the woman at his side if they were on the right road.

For the hundredth time, she looked at the map. Yes, they were going the right way, even though their surroundings were green, and a river ran nearby, and there were trees along the road.

"I think we should stop at a gas station and check," she said.

They drove on without speaking, listening to old songs on the radio. Chris knew that it wasn't necessary to stop at a gas station, because they were on the right road—even if the scenery around them was completely different from what they had expected. But she knew her husband well. Paulo was nervous and uncertain, thinking that she was misreading the map. He would feel better if they stopped and asked.

"What are we doing here?"

"I have a task to perform," he answered.

"Strange task," she said.

Very strange, he thought. *To speak to his guardian angel.*

"Okay," she said after a while, "you're here to speak to your guardian angel. Meanwhile, how about talking a bit with me?"

But he said nothing, concentrating on the road, thinking again that she had made a mistake about the route. *No point in insisting*, she thought. She was hoping they would come upon a gas station soon.

They had headed out on their journey straight from Los Angeles International Airport. She was afraid that Paulo was tired, and might fall asleep at the wheel. They didn't seem to be anywhere near their destination.

I should have married an engineer, she said to herself.

She had never gotten used to his life—taking off suddenly, looking for sacred pathways, swords, conversing with angels, doing everything possible to move further along the path to magic.

He has always wanted to leave everything behind.

She remembered their first date. They had slept together, and within a week she had moved her art work table into his apartment. Their friends said that Paulo was a sorcerer, and one night Chris had telephoned the minister of the Protestant church she attended, asking him to say a prayer.

But during that first year, he had said not one word about magic. He was working at a recording studio, and that seemed to be all he was concerned about.

The following year, life was the same. He quit his job and went to work at another studio.

During their third year together, he quit his job again (a mania for leaving everything behind!) and decided to write scripts for T V. She found it strange, the way he changed jobs every year—but he was writing, earning money, and they were living well.

Then, at the end of their third year together, he decided—once again—to quit his job. He gave no explanation, saying only that he was fed up with what he was doing, that it didn't make sense to keep quitting his jobs, changing one for another. He needed to discover what it was that he wanted. They had put some money aside, and had decided to do some traveling.

In a car, Chris thought, *just like we're doing now.*

Chris had met J. for the first time in Amsterdam, when they were having coffee at a cafe in the Brower Hotel, looking out at the Singel canal. Paulo had turned pale when he saw the tall, white-haired man dressed in a business suit. Despite his anxiety, he finally worked up the courage to approach the older man's table.

That night, when Paulo and Chris were alone again, he drank an entire bottle of wine. He wasn't a good drinker, and became drunk. Only then did he reveal what she already knew: that for seven years he had dedicated himself to learning magic. Then, for some reason—which he never explained, although she asked about it a number of times—he had given it all up.

"I had a vision of J. two months ago, when we visited Dachau," Paulo said.

Chris remembered that day. Paulo had wept. He said that he was being called but didn't know how to respond.

"Should I go back to magic?" he had asked.

"Yes, you should," she had answered, but she wasn't sure.

Since Amsterdam, everything had changed. There were rituals, exercises, practices. There were long trips with J., with no defined date of return. There were long meetings with strange women, and men who had an aura of sensuality about them. There were challenges and tests, long nights when he didn't sleep, and long weekends when he never left the house.

But Paulo was much happier, and he no longer thought about quitting his job. Together they had founded a small publishing house, and he was doing something he'd dreamed of for a long time: writing books.

Finally, a gas station. As a young Native American woman filled the tank, Paulo and Chris took a stroll.

Paulo looked at the map and confirmed the route. Yes, they were on the right road.

Now he can relax. Now he'll talk a bit, Chris thought.

"Did J. say you were to meet with your angel here?" she asked hesitantly.

"No," he replied.

Great, he gave me an answer, she thought, as she looked out at the brilliant green vegetation, lit by the setting sun. If she hadn't checked the map so often, she too would have doubted this was the right road. The map said that they should be at their destination in another six miles or so, but the scenery seemed to be telling them they had a long way to go.

"I didn't have to come here," Paulo continued. "Any place would do. But I have a contact here."

Of course. Paulo always had contacts. He referred to such people as members of the Tradition; but when Chris described them in her diary, she referred to them as the

"Conspiracy." Among them were sorcerers and witch doctors—the kind of people one has nightmares about.

"Someone who speaks with angels?"

"I'm not sure. One time, J. referred—just in passing—to a master of the Tradition who lives here, and who knows how to communicate with the angels. But that might just be a rumor."

He might have been speaking seriously, but Chris knew that he might also have just selected a place at random, one of the many places where he had "contacts." A place that was far from their daily life, and where he could concentrate better on the Extraordinary.

"How are you going to speak to your angel?"

"I don't know," he replied.

What a strange way to live, thought Chris. She looked at her husband as he walked over to pay the bill. All she knew was that he felt he had to speak with the angels, and that was that! Drop everything, jump on a plane, fly for twelve hours from Brazil to Los Angeles, drive for six hours to this gas station, arm himself with enough patience to remain here for forty days: all of this in order to speak—or rather, try to speak—with his guardian angel!

He laughed at her, and she smiled back. After all, this wasn't all that bad. They had their occasional daily irritations—paying bills, cashing checks, paying courtesy calls, accepting some tough times.

But they still believed in angels.

"We'll do it," she said.

"Thanks for the 'we,'" he answered with a smile. "But I'm the magus around here."

THE WOMAN AT THE STATION HAD SAID THEY WERE GOING in the right direction—about ten more minutes. They drove in silence. Paulo turned the radio off. There was a small elevation, but only when they reached the top did they realize how high up they were. They had been climbing steadily for six hours, without realizing it.

But they were there.

He parked on the shoulder and turned off the motor. Chris looked back in the direction from which they had come to see if it was true: Yes, she could see green trees, plants, vegetation.

But there in front of them, extending from horizon to horizon, was the Mojave Desert: the enormous desert that spreads into many states and into Mexico, the desert she had seen so many times in Westerns when she was a child, the desert that had places with strange names like the Rainbow Forest and Death Valley.

It's pink, Chris thought, but she didn't say anything. He was staring out at its immensity, trying to determine where the angels dwelt.

If you stand in the middle of the main park, you can see where the town of Borrego Springs begins and where it ends. But there are three hotels for the winter tourists who come there for the sun.

They left their luggage in the room and went to a Mexican restaurant for dinner. The waiter stood nearby for some time, trying to determine what language they were speaking. Finally, when he couldn't figure it out, he asked. When they said they were from Brazil, he said he had never met a Brazilian before.

"Well, now you've met two," Paulo laughed.

By the next day, the entire town will have heard about it, he thought. *There's not much news in Borrego Springs.*

After their meal, they walked about the town, hand in hand. Paulo wanted to wander out into the desert, get the feel of it, breathe in the air of the Mojave. So they meandered over the desert's rocky floor for a half hour, at last stopping to look back at the few distant lights of Borrego Springs.

There in the desert, the heavens were clear. They sat on the ground and made their separate wishes on the falling stars. There was no moon, and the constellations stood out brilliantly.

"Have you ever had the feeling, at certain moments in your life, that someone was observing what you were doing?" Paulo asked Chris.

"How did you know that?"

"I just know. There are moments when, without really knowing it, we are aware of the presence of angels."

Chris thought back to her adolescence. In those days, she had had that feeling very strongly.

"At such moments," he continued, "we begin to create a kind of film in which we are the main character, and we are certain that someone is observing our actions.

"But then, as we get older, we begin to think that such things are ridiculous. We think of it as having been just a child's fantasy of being a movie actor. We forget that, at those moments in which we are presenting ourselves before an invisible audience, the sensation of being observed was very strong."

He paused for a moment.

"When I look up at the night sky, that feeling often returns, and my question is always the same: Who is out there watching us?"

"And who is it?"

"Angels. God's messengers."

She stared up at the heavens, wanting to believe what he had said.

"All religions, and every person who has ever witnessed the Extraordinary, speak of angels," Paulo went on. "The universe is populated with angels. It's they who give us hope. Like the one who announced that the Messiah had been born. They also bring death, like the exterminating angel that traveled through Egypt destroying all those who did not display the right sign at their door. Angels with flaming swords in their hands can prevent us from entering into paradise. Or they can invite us in, as the angel did to Mary.

"Angels remove the seals placed on prohibited books, and they sound the trumpets on the day of Final Judgment. They bring the light, as Michael did, or darkness, as Lucifer did."

Hesitantly, Chris asked, "Do they have wings?"

"Well, I haven't seen an angel yet," he answered. "But I wondered about that, too. I asked J. about it."

That's good, she thought. *At least I'm not the only one who has simple questions about the angels.*

"J. said that they take whatever form a person imagines they have. Because they are God's thoughts in live form, and they need to adapt to our wisdom and our knowledge. They know that if they don't, we'll be unable to see them."

Paulo closed his eyes.

"Imagine your angel, and you will feel its presence right now, right here."

They fell quiet, lying there on the floor of the desert. There was not a sound to be heard, and Chris began once again to feel like she was in a film, playing to an invisible audience. The more intensely she concentrated, the more certain she was that all around her there was a strong presence, friendly and generous. She began to imagine her angel, dressed in blue, with golden hair and immense white wings—exactly as she had pictured her angel as a child.

Paulo was imagining his angel, as well. He had already immersed himself many times in the invisible world that surrounded them, so it was not a new experience for him. But now, since J. had assigned him this task, he felt that his angel was much more present—as if the angels made themselves available only to those who believed in their existence. He knew, though, that whether one believed in them or not, they were always there—messengers of life, of death, of hell, and of paradise.

He dressed his angel in a long robe, embroidered in gold. And he also gave his angel wings.

THE HOTEL WATCHMAN, EATING HIS BREAKFAST, TURNED TO them as they came in.

"I wouldn't go out into the desert at night again," he said.

This really is a small town, Chris thought. *Everybody knows what you're doing.*

"It's dangerous in the desert at night," the guard explained. "That's when the coyotes come out, and the snakes. They can't stand the heat of the day, so they do their hunting after the sun goes down."

"We were looking for our angels," Paulo said.

The watchman thought that the man didn't speak English very well. What he had said didn't make sense. Angels! Perhaps he'd meant something else.

The two finished their coffee quickly. Paulo's "contact" had set their meeting for early in the morning.

CHRIS WAS SURPRISED WHEN SHE SAW GENE FOR THE first time. He was quite young, certainly not more than twenty, and he lived in a trailer out in the desert, several miles from Borrego Springs.

"This is a master of the Conspiracy?" she whispered to Paulo, when the youth had gone to fetch some iced tea.

But Gene was back before Paulo could respond. They sat under an awning that extended along the side of the trailer.

They talked about the rituals of the Templars, about reincarnation, about Sufi magic, about the Catholic church in Latin America. The boy seemed to know a great deal, and it was amusing to listen to their conversation—they sounded like fans discussing a popular sport, defending certain tactics and criticizing others.

They spoke of everything—except angels.

The heat of the day was intensifying. They drank more tea as Gene, smiling agreeably, told them of the marvels of the desert. He warned them that novices should never go into it at night, and that it would be smart to avoid the hottest hours of the day, as well.

"The desert is made of mornings and afternoons," he said. "The other times are risky."

Chris listened to their conversation for as long as she could. But she had awakened early, and the sun was getting stronger and stronger. She decided she'd close her eyes and take a quick nap.

WHEN SHE AWOKE, THE SOUND OF THEIR VOICES WAS coming from a different place. The two men were at the rear of the trailer.

"Why did you bring your wife?" she heard Gene ask in a guarded tone.

"Because I was coming to the desert," Paulo answered, also whispering.

Gene laughed.

"But you're missing what's best about the desert. The solitude."

What a cheeky kid, Chris thought.

"Tell me about the Valkyries you mentioned," Paulo said.

"They can help you to find your angel," replied Gene. "They're the ones who instructed me. But the Valkyries are jealous and tough. They try to follow the same rules as the angels—and, you know, in the kingdom of the angels, there is no good and no evil."

"Not as we understand them," Paulo countered.

Chris had no idea what they meant by "Valkyries." She had a vague memory of having heard the name in the title of an opera.

"Was it difficult for you to see your angel?"

"A better word would be *anguishing.* It happened all of a sudden, back in the days when the Valkyries came through here. I decided I'd learn the process just for the fun of it, because at that point, I didn't yet understand the language of the desert, and I was upset about everything that was happening to me.

"My angel appeared on that third mountain peak. I was up there just wandering and listening to music on my Walkman. In those days, I had already mastered the second mind."

What the hell is the "second mind"? Chris wondered.

"Was it your father who taught it to you?"

"No. And when I asked him why he had never told me about the angels, he told me that some things are so important that you have to learn about them on your own."

They were silent for a moment.

"If you meet with the Valkyries, there's something that will make it easier for you to get along with them," Gene said.

"What's that?"

The young man laughed.

"You'll find out. But it would have been a lot better if you hadn't brought your wife along."

"Did your angel have wings?" Paulo asked.

Before Gene could answer, Chris had arisen from her folding chair, come around the trailer, and now stood before them.

"Why is he making such a big thing about your coming here alone?" she asked, speaking Portuguese. "Do you want me to leave?"

Gene went on with what he was saying to Paulo, paying no attention whatsoever to Chris's interruption. She waited for Paulo's answer—but she might just as well have been invisible.

"Give me the keys to the car," she said, at the limit of her patience.

"What does your wife want?" Gene finally asked.

"She wants to know what the 'second mind' is."

Damn! Nine years we've been together, and this stranger already knows all about us!

Gene stood up.

"Sit down, close your eyes, and I will show you what the second mind is," he said.

"I didn't come here to the desert to learn about magic or converse with angels," Chris said. "I came only to be with my husband."

"Sit down," Gene insisted, smiling.

She looked at Paulo for a fraction of a second, but was unable to determine what he was thinking.

I respect their world, but it has nothing to do with me, she thought. Although all their friends thought that she had become completely involved in her husband's lifestyle, the fact was that she and he had spoken very little of it to one another. She was used to going with him to certain places, and had once even carried his sword for purposes of a ceremony. She knew the Road to Santiago, and had—because of their relationship—learned quite a bit about sexual magic. But that was all. J. had never proposed that he teach her anything.

"What should I do?" she asked Paulo.

"Whatever you think," he answered.

I love you, she thought. If she were to learn something about his world, there was no doubt it would bring them even closer. She went back to her chair, sat down, and closed her eyes.

"What are you thinking about?" Gene asked her.

"About what you two were discussing. About Paulo traveling by himself. About the second mind. Whether his angel has wings. And why this should interest me at all. I mean, I don't think I've ever spoken to angels."

"No, no. I want to know whether you're thinking about something else. Something beyond your control."

She felt his hands touching both sides of her head.

"Relax. Relax." His voice was gentle. "What are you thinking?"

There were sounds. And voices. It was only now that she realized what she was thinking, although it had been there for almost an entire day.

"A melody," she answered. "I've been singing this melody to myself ever since I heard it yesterday on the radio on our way here."

It was true, she had been humming the melody incessantly. To the end, and then once again, and then from start to finish again. She couldn't get it out of her mind.

Gene asked that she open her eyes.

"That's the second mind," he said. "It's your second mind that's humming the song. It can do that with anything. If you're in love with someone, you can have that person inside your head. The same thing happens with someone you want to forget about. But the second mind is a tough thing to deal with. It's at work regardless of whether you want it to be or not."

He laughed.

"A song! We're always impassioned about something. And it's not always a song. Have you ever had someone you loved stick in your mind? It's really terrible when that happens. You travel, you try to forget, but your second mind keeps saying: 'Oh, he would really love that!' 'Oh, if only he were here.'"

Chris was astonished. She had never thought of such a thing as a second mind.

She had two minds. Functioning at the same time.

GENE CAME TO HER SIDE.

"Close your eyes again," he said. "And try to remember the horizon you were looking at."

She tried to recall it. "I can't," she said, her eyes still closed. "I wasn't looking at the horizon. I know that it's all around me, but I wasn't looking at it."

"Open your eyes and look at it."

Chris looked out at the horizon. She saw mountains, rocks, stones, and sparse and spindly vegetation. A sun that shone brighter and brighter seemed to pierce her sunglasses and burn into her eyes.

"You are here," Gene said, now with a serious tone of voice. "Try to understand that you are here, and that the things that surround you change you—in the same way that you change them."

Chris stared at the desert.

"In order to penetrate the invisible world and develop your powers, you have to live in the present, the *here and now*. In order to live in the present, you have to control your second mind. And look at the horizon."

Gene asked her to concentrate on the melody that she had been humming. It was "When I Fall in Love." She didn't know the words, and had been making them up, or just singing a ta-de-dum.

Chris concentrated. In a few moments, the melody disappeared. She was now completely alert, listening only to Gene's words.

But Gene seemed to have nothing more to say.

"I have to be alone now," he said. "Come back in two days."

PAULO AND CHRIS LOCKED THEMSELVES INSIDE THEIR AIR-conditioned hotel room, unwilling to confront the 110 degrees of the midday desert. No books to read, nothing to do. They tried taking a nap, but couldn't sleep.

"Let's explore the desert," Paulo said.

"It's too hot out there. Gene said it was even dangerous. Let's do it tomorrow."

Paulo didn't answer. He was certain he could turn the fact that he was locked into his hotel room into a learning experience. He tried to make sense of everything that happened in his life, and used conversation only as means for discharging tension.

But it was impossible; trying to find a meaning in everything meant he had to remain alert and tense. Paulo never relaxed, and Chris had often asked herself when he would tire of his intensity.

"Who is Gene?"

"His father is a powerful magus, and he wants Gene to maintain the family tradition—like engineers who want their children to follow in their footsteps."

"He's young, but he wants to act mature," Chris commented. "And he's giving up the best years of his life out here in the desert."

"Everything has its price. If Gene goes through all this—and doesn't abandon the Tradition—he'll be the first in a line of young masters to be integrated into a world that the older masters, although they understand it, no longer know how to explain."

Paulo lay down and started to read the only book available, *The Guide to Lodging in the Mojave Desert*. He didn't want to tell his wife that, in addition to what he had already told her, there was another reason that Gene was here: He was powerful in the paranormal processes, and had been prepared by the Tradition to be ready to act when the gates to paradise opened.

Chris wanted to talk. She felt anxious cooped up in the hotel room, and had decided not to "make sense of everything," as her husband did. She was not there to seek a place within a community of the elite.

"I didn't really understand what Gene was trying to teach me," she said. "The solitude and the desert can increase your contact with the invisible world. But I think it causes us to lose contact with other people."

"He probably has a girlfriend or two around here," Paulo said, wanting to avoid conversation.

If I have to spend another thirty-nine days locked up with Paulo, I'll commit suicide, she promised herself.

THAT AFTERNOON, THEY WENT TO A COFFEE SHOP ACROSS the street from the hotel. Paulo chose a table by the window. They ordered ice cream. Chris had spent several hours studying her second mind, and had learned to control it much better than before, but her appetite was never subject to control.

Paulo said, "I want you to pay close attention to the people who pass by."

She did as Paulo had asked. In the next half hour, only five people passed by.

"What did you see?"

She described the people in detail—their clothing, approximate age, what they were carrying. But apparently that wasn't what he wanted to hear. He insisted on more, trying to get a better answer, but couldn't do so.

"Okay," he said. "I'm going to tell you what it was that I wanted you to notice: All the people who passed by in the street were looking down."

They waited for some time before another person walked by. Paulo was right.

"Gene asked you to look to the horizon. Try that."

"What do you mean?"

"All of us create a kind of 'magic space' around us. Usually it's a circle with about a fifteen-foot radius, and we pay attention to what goes on within it. It doesn't matter whether it's people, tables, telephones, or windows; we try to maintain control over that small world that we, ourselves, create.

"A magus, though, always looks much further. We expand that 'magic space' and try to control a great many more things. They call it 'looking at the horizon.'"

"Well, why should I do that?"

"Because you're here. If you do it, you'll see how much things change."

When they left the coffee shop, she started to pay attention to things in the distance. She noticed the mountains, the occasional cloud that appeared as the sun began to set, and—in a strange way—she seemed to be seeing the air about her.

"Everything Gene told you is important," Paulo said. "He has already seen and talked with his angel, and he is using you as a means of instructing me. He knows the power of his words, and he knows that advice not heeded is returned to its giver, losing its energy. He needs to be sure that you are interested in what he tells you."

"Well, why doesn't he show these things directly to you?"

"Because there is an unwritten rule in the Tradition: A master never teaches another master's disciple. And he knows I am J.'s disciple. But since he wants to be of help to me, he is using you for that purpose."

"Is that why you brought me here?"

"No. It was because I was afraid of being alone in the desert."

He could have said it was because he loves me, she thought. *That would have been more truthful.*

33

THEY STOPPED THE CAR ON THE SHOULDER OF THE narrow dirt road. Two days had passed, and they were to meet Gene that night—Gene, who had told her always to look to the horizon. She was excited about their meeting.

But it was still morning. And the days in the desert were long.

She looked out at the horizon: mountains that suddenly sprang up millions of years ago, crossing the desert in a long *cordillera*. Although the earthquakes that created them had occurred long ago, one could still see how the earth's surface had buckled—the ground still climbed smoothly toward the mountains, and then, at a certain altitude, a kind of wound opened, out of which rocks sprang, pointing to the sky.

Between the mountains and the car was a rocky valley with sparse vegetation: thorn bushes, cacti, and yucca. Life that insisted on surviving in an environment that didn't support it. And an immense white expanse the size of five football fields stood out in the middle of it all. It reflected the morning sun, and resembled a field of snow.

"Salt. A salt lake."

Yes. This desert must once have been the bed of an ocean. Once a year, seagulls from the Pacific Ocean flew the hundreds of miles to this desert to eat the species of shrimp that appeared when the rains began. Human beings may forget their origins, but nature, never.

"It must be about three miles from here," Chris said.

Paulo checked his watch. It was still early. They had looked to the horizon and it had shown them a salt lake. One hour's walk there, another to return, no risk of the midday sun.

Each placed a canteen of water on their belt. Paulo put his cigarettes and a Bible in a small bag. When they arrived at the lake, he was going to suggest that they read a passage from it, chosen at random.

THEY BEGAN TO WALK. CHRIS KEPT HER EYES FIXED on the horizon whenever possible. Although it was a simple thing to be doing, something strange was happening: She felt better, freer, as if her internal energy had been increased. For the first time in many years, she regretted not having taken a more intense interest in Paulo's "Conspiracy." She had always imagined difficult rituals that only those who were prepared and disciplined could perform.

They walked at a leisurely pace for half an hour. The lake appeared to have shifted its location; it always seemed to be at the same distance from them.

They walked for another hour. They must already have covered four miles or so, but the lake appeared to be only a bit closer.

It was no longer early morning, and the heat of the sun was building.

Paulo looked back. He could see the car, a tiny red point in the distance but still visible—impossible to become lost. And when he looked at the car, he saw something else that was important.

"Let's stop here," he said.

They left the path they were taking and walked to a boulder. They huddled in close to it, because it cast only a very small shadow. In the desert, shadows appear only early in the morning or late in the afternoon, and then only near the rocks.

"Our calculation was wrong," he said.

Chris had already noticed that. She was surprised, because Paulo was good at estimating distances, and he had trusted her guess of three or four miles.

"I know how we went wrong," he said. "There's nothing in the desert to base comparisons on. We're used to calculating distance based on the size of things. We know the approximate size of a tree, or a telephone pole, or a house. They help us to decide whether things are near or far away."

Here, there was no point of reference. There were rocks they'd never seen, mountains whose size they could not estimate, and only the sparse vegetation. Paulo had realized this as he looked back at the car. And he could see that they had walked more than four miles.

"Let's rest a while, and then we'll go back."

That's all right, Chris thought. She was fascinated with the idea of continuing to look out at the horizon. It was a completely new experience for her.

"This business of looking at the horizon, Paulo . . ." Chris paused.

He waited, knowing that she would continue. He knew that she was worried that she might say something silly, or find some esoteric meaning in things, as many do who know only a little about the path.

"It seems as if . . . I don't know . . . I can't explain it . . . as if my soul has grown."

Yes, Paulo thought. *She's on the right track.*

"Before, I looked in the distance, and things in the distance seemed really *far,* you know? They seemed not to be a part of my world. Because I was used to looking only at things that were close, the things around me.

"But, two days ago, I got used to looking into the distance. And I saw that besides tables, chairs, and objects, my world also included the mountains, clouds, the sky. And my soul—my soul seems to have eyes that it uses to touch those things."

Wow! That's a great way of saying it, Paulo thought.

"My soul seems to have grown," Chris repeated.

He opened the bag, took out his cigarettes, and lit one before speaking.

"Anyone can see that. But we're always looking at the things that are closest to us. Looking down and inward. So our power diminishes, and using your term, our soul shrinks.

"Because our soul includes nothing but ourselves. It doesn't include oceans, mountains, other people; it doesn't even include the walls of the houses where we live."

Paulo liked the expression "My soul has grown." If he had been talking with another member of the Tradition, there's no doubt that he would have heard much more complicated explanations, such as "My consciousness expanded." But the term his wife had used was more exact.

He finished his cigarette. There was no point in insisting that they make it to the lake; the temperature would soon reach 110 in the shade. The car was far away, but visible, and in an hour and a half they'd be back to it.

They started walking. Surrounded by the desert, by the huge horizon, a feeling of freedom began to grow in their souls.

"Let's take off our clothes," Paulo said.

"But someone might be watching," Chris said automatically.

Paulo laughed. They could see for miles around them. The day before, when they had been out walking all morning and afternoon, only two cars had passed—and, even then, they had heard the sound of their approach long before the cars had appeared. The desert was the sun, the wind, and the silence.

"Only our angels are watching," he answered. "And they've already seen us naked many times."

He took off his shorts and his shirt and the canteen, placing them all in the bag.

Chris struggled to keep from laughing. She took her clothes off too, and in a few moments they were two people crossing the Mojave in their sneakers, their hats, and their sunglasses—one of them carrying a bag. Anyone watching would find it hilarious.

THEY WALKED FOR HALF AN HOUR. THE CAR WAS STILL just a point on the horizon, but—in contrast to the lake—it was growing in size as they approached it. They would be there in a short while.

Suddenly, Chris felt tremendously tired.

"Let's rest for a few minutes," she said.

Paulo stopped immediately, saying, "I can't carry this bag anymore. I'm really tired."

How could he not be able to carry the bag? Even with everything it held, it couldn't weigh more than six or seven pounds.

"You have to carry it. The water's in there."

Right, he had to carry it.

"Well then, let's get going," he said irritably.

Everything was so romantic just a few minutes ago, thought Chris. And now he was irritated. Well, forget it. She was tired, too.

They walked a bit farther, and their exhaustion worsened. If it were up to her, nothing more would be said—she didn't want to make things worse.

What a dope, she thought. To get angry in the midst of such beauty, and right after they had been talking about such interesting things as . . .

She couldn't remember, but it wasn't important. She was too tired to think now.

Paulo stopped and put the bag down in the sand.

"Let's rest," he said.

He didn't seem irritated now. He must be getting tired, too. Just like her.

There was no shade. But she needed to rest.

They sat down on the hot sand. The fact that they were naked and that the ground burned their skin didn't matter. They had to stop. Just for a while.

She remembered what they had been discussing: horizons. She noticed that now, even without wanting to, she had the feeling that her soul had grown. And it seemed like her second mind had stopped working altogether. She didn't think of melodies or repetitious things, and she didn't even care if someone was watching them walk naked across the desert.

Nothing was important. She felt relaxed, unworried, free.

They sat there for a few minutes in silence. It was hot, but the sun didn't bother them. If it started to, they had plenty of water.

He stood up first.

"I think we had better keep walking. It's not far to the car now. We'll rest in the air-conditioning when we get there."

She was sleepy. She just wanted to nap for a bit. But she got up, anyway.

They walked a bit farther, and now the car was getting close. Not more than ten minutes to walk.

"Since we're so close, let's sleep for a while. Five minutes."

Sleep for five minutes? Why would he say that? Was he reading her mind? There couldn't be any problem with sleeping for just five minutes. They could get a good tan, as if they'd been to the beach.

They sat down again. They had been walking for half an hour, not counting their pauses. Why couldn't they just sleep for five minutes or so?

They heard the sound of a motor. Half an hour earlier, she would have leaped up and dressed in a hurry. But now, so what? It didn't matter at all. Let anyone look who wants to look. It didn't make any difference to her. She just wanted to sleep.

Paulo and Chris watched calmly as a truck drove down the road, passed their car, and stopped just beyond. A man got out and walked toward the vehicle. He looked inside, then walked around the car, examining everything.

Might be a thief, Paulo thought. He imagined the guy stealing the car, leaving them both stranded in the desert with no way to get back. The key was in the ignition—he hadn't taken it with him for fear of losing it.

But they were in the Mojave Desert. In New York, maybe. But here—no one stole cars here.

Chris looked out at the desert. It was golden and beautiful. Golden. Different from the pinkness of the desert at sundown.

An agreeable feeling of relaxation permeated her entire body. The sun didn't bother her—people didn't know how lovely the desert could be during the day!

The man gave up his inspection of the car, and placed his hand above his eyes. He was looking for them.

She was naked . . . and he would surely see that. So what? Paulo didn't seem worried, either.

The man began walking toward them. The feeling of lightness and euphoria was increasing, but exhaustion kept them from moving. The desert was golden and beautiful. Everything was serene, at peace—the angels, yes, the angels would appear before long. That was what they had come to the desert for—to talk with their angels!

She was naked, and she was not ashamed.

The man stopped when he reached them. What language was he speaking? They couldn't understand what he was saying.

Paulo tried to concentrate on what he was hearing, and realized that the man was speaking English. After all, they were in the United States.

"Come with me," the man said.

"We want to rest," Paulo said. "Five minutes."

The man picked up the bag and opened it.

"Put this on," he said to Chris, handing her clothing to her.

She forced herself to get up, and did as he said. She was too tired to argue.

He ordered Paulo to do the same, and Paulo was also too tired to argue. The man saw the canteens filled with water, opened one of them, filled the cap, and ordered them to drink.

They weren't thirsty. But they did as the man said. They were quite calm, and completely at peace with the world—and they had no desire to argue.

They would do anything they were told to do, obey any order, so long as they were left in peace.

"Let's walk," the man said.

They couldn't even think. They sat there gazing at the desert. They would do anything so long as the stranger left them alone.

But the man escorted them to the car, told them to get in, and started the engine. "I wonder where he's taking us," Paulo thought. But he wasn't worried—the world was at peace, and the only thing he wanted to do was sleep. Surely his angel would appear before long.

PAULO AWOKE WITH HIS STOMACH CHURNING, AND A tremendous need to vomit.

"Lie still for a while longer."

Someone was speaking to him, but in his head there was only confusion. He still remembered the golden paradise where all had been serene and peaceful.

He tried to move, and felt as if thousands of needles were sticking into his head.

I think I'll go back to sleep, he thought. But he couldn't—the needles wouldn't allow it. And his stomach was still turning over.

"I want to throw up," he said.

When he opened his eyes, he saw that he was sitting in a kind of mini-market: He could see several refrigerator cabinets with soft drinks and shelves with foodstuffs. The sight of the food made him feel nauseated again. Then he noticed nearby a man he had never seen before.

The man helped him to get up. In addition to the imaginary needles in his head, Paulo realized that he had another in his arm. Only this one was real.

The man held the needle in place and helped Paulo to the bathroom, where he vomited some water, nothing more.

"What's happening? What's this needle for?"

It was Chris, speaking Portuguese. He returned to the store and saw that she was sitting up, too, with a needle in her arm.

Paulo felt a little better now, and no longer needed the man's support. He helped Chris up and to the bathroom, where she vomited.

"I'm going to use your car to get back to mine," the stranger said. "I'll leave the keys in the ignition. You can get a ride to it when you're ready."

Paulo was starting to remember what had happened, but the nausea had returned, and he had to vomit again.

When he came back, the man had left, but a boy of seventeen or eighteen was there.

"Just another hour," the boy said. "The solution will be used up then, and you can go."

"What time is it?"

The boy told them. Paulo struggled to get up—he had an appointment, and there was no way he was going to miss it.

"I have to meet with Gene," he said to Chris.

"Sit down," the boy said. "Not until the solution is used up."

The comment was unnecessary. Paulo no longer had either the strength or desire to walk even to the door.

I've missed the meeting, he thought. But at this point, nothing mattered. The less he thought about, the better.

"FIFTEEN MINUTES," GENE SAID. "THAT'S ALL IT TAKES, and without even realizing what's happening, you die."

They were back at the old trailer. It was the afternoon of the next day, and the entire scene was bathed in pink. Nothing like the desert of the previous day—golden, peaceful, nausea, vomiting.

They hadn't been able to eat or sleep for twenty-four hours—they threw up everything they tried to eat. But now that strange sensation was passing.

"It's good that your horizon had been expanded. And that you were thinking about angels. An angel appeared."

Paulo thought it would be better to have said "Your soul had grown." Besides, the guy who had appeared wasn't an angel—he had an old truck, and he spoke English.

"Let's get going," said Gene, asking Paulo to start the car. He took the passenger seat, with no show of ceremony. And Chris, grumbling in Portuguese, climbed into the back.

Gene began to give instructions—take that road there, go for a few miles, drive fast so that the car gets cool inside, turn off the air-conditioning so the motor doesn't overheat. Several times they drove off the narrow dirt road into the desert. But Gene knew what he was doing. He wasn't going to make the same mistakes they had.

"What happened yesterday?" Chris asked for the hundredth time. She knew that Gene wanted her to ask. He might already have seen his guardian angel, but he acted like any other young man his age.

"Sunstroke," he finally explained. "Haven't either of you ever seen a film about the desert?"

Of course they had. Thirsty men, dragging themselves across the sand in search of a drop of water.

"We didn't feel thirsty at all. The two canteens were filled with water."

"That's not what I'm talking about," the American interrupted. "I mean your clothing."

The clothing! The Arabs with their long robes, and several hoods—one on top of the other. Of course, how stupid we were! Paulo had already heard about that, and he'd already walked across three other deserts ... and he had never felt the desire to take his clothes off. But here, that morning, after the frustration of the lake that they seemed never to reach.... *How could I have had such a stupid idea?* he thought.

"When you took off your clothes, the water in your bodies began to evaporate immediately. You can't even perspire, because the climate is so dry. In fifteen minutes, you were both already dehydrated. No thirst or anything—just a slight feeling of disorientation."

"And the exhaustion?"

"That exhaustion is death arriving."

I sure didn't know it was death arriving, Chris said to herself.

If someday she had to choose an easy way to leave the world behind, she would come back and take off her clothing in the middle of the desert.

"Most people who die in the desert die with water in their canteen. The dehydration is so rapid that we feel as if we've drunk an entire bottle of whiskey, or taken an overdose of some tranquilizer." He suggested that, starting now, they drink water periodically—even if they weren't thirsty—because their bodies needed the water.

"But an angel did appear," Gene said.

Before Paulo could say what he was thinking, Gene ordered him to stop at the foot of a cliff.

"Let's get out here and go the rest of the way on foot."

They began to walk along a narrow path that led to the top of the cliff. Before they had gone far, Gene realized he had forgotten the flashlight from the car. He went back, picked it up, and sat on the hood of the car for some time, staring out at the desert.

Chris is right; solitude does strange things to people. He's behaving strangely, Paulo thought as he watched the youth down below.

But, a few seconds later, Gene had climbed the narrow path again, and they pushed on.

In forty minutes, with no great difficulty, they had reached the top. There was some sparse vegetation there, and Gene asked that they sit down facing north. His attitude, usually expansive, had changed—he seemed more distant, and looked as if he were concentrating hard.

"You've both come here in search of angels," he said, sitting down at their side.

"That's what I came for," Paulo said. "And I know that you have spoken with one."

"Forget about my angel. Many people in this desert have already seen or conversed with their angel. So have a lot of people in cities, or at sea, or in the mountains."

There was a tone of impatience in his voice.

"Think about *your* guardian angels," he continued. "Because my angel is here, and I can see him. This is my holy place."

Both Paulo and Chris thought back to their first night in the desert. And they imagined their angels once again, with their raiment and their wings.

"You must always have a holy place. Mine once was a small apartment, and at another time, a square in the middle of Los Angeles. Now it's here. A sacred hymn opens a gate to heaven, and heaven appears."

They both looked around at Gene's holy place: the rocks, the hard ground, the desert plants. Perhaps snakes and coyotes passed through here at night, too.

Gene appeared to be in a trance.

"It was here that I was first able to see my angel, although I knew that the angel was everywhere, and that the angel's face is the face of the desert I live in, or of the city where I lived for eighteen years.

"I was able to talk with my angel because I had faith that the angel existed. And because I loved my angel."

Neither Chris nor Paulo dared ask what they had talked about.

Gene went on, "Everyone can make contact with four different kinds of entities in the invisible world: the elementals, the disembodied spirits, the saints, and the angels.

"The elementals are the vibrations of things in nature—fire, earth, water, and air—and we make contact with them using rituals. These are pure forces—like earthquakes, lightning, or volcanoes. Because we need to understand them as 'beings,' they traditionally appear in the form of dwarfs, fairies, or salamanders. But all one can do is use the power of the elementals—we never learn anything from them."

Why is he saying all this? Paulo thought. *Has he forgotten that I'm a master of magic, too?*

Gene continued his explanation, "The disembodied spirits are those that wander between one life and another, and we make contact with them by means of a medium. Some are great masters—but all that they teach us we can learn on earth, because that's where they learned what they know. Better, then, to let them wander in the direction of their next step, to look out at the horizon, and to take from *here* the same wisdom as they did."

    Paulo must know all about this, Chris thought. *He's probably talking to me.*

YES, GENE WAS SPEAKING TO CHRIS—IT WAS BECAUSE she was here that he was here. There was nothing he could teach Paulo, twenty years older than he and more experienced, and who, on his own, would surely find the way to talk with his angel. Paulo was one of J.'s disciples—and the things Gene had heard about J.! At their first meeting, Gene had tried in various ways to get the Brazilian to talk, but the woman had made it impossible. He was unable to learn anything about the techniques, the processes, or the rituals used by J.

That first meeting had been deeply disappointing for him. He thought that the Brazilian might be using J.'s name without the master's knowledge. Or—who knows?—perhaps J. had made a mistake for the first time in his selection of a disciple. And if that were the case, the entire Tradition would soon know about it. But that night of their meeting, he had dreamed of his guardian angel.

And his angel had asked that he initiate the woman into the path of magic. Just initiate her: Her husband would do the rest.

In the dream, he argued that he had already taught her about the second mind, and had asked that she look out at the horizon. The angel said that Gene should pay attention to the man, but that he should take care of the woman. And then the angel disappeared.

Gene was trained to be disciplined. So he was now doing what the angel had commanded—and he hoped that it was being observed up above.

"After the disembodied spirits," he continued, "the saints appear. These are the true masters. They lived among us at one time, and are now closer to the light. The great teachings of the saints are their lives here on earth. Contained in them are all we need to know, and all we have to do is imitate them."

"How do we invoke the saints?" Chris asked.

"Through prayer," Paulo answered, cutting Gene off.

He wasn't jealous—although it was clear to him that the American wanted to impress Chris. *He respects the Tradition. He's going to use my wife as a means of reaching me. But why is he being so basic, talking about things that I already know so well?* he thought.

"We invoke the saints through constant prayer," Paulo continued. "And when they are near, everything changes. Miracles happen."

Gene couldn't help but notice the Brazilian's hostile, almost aggressive tone of voice. But he wasn't going to say anything about his dream of the angel, because he didn't owe this man anything.

"Finally," Gene said, "there are the angels."

THEY MADE THE RETURN TRIP IN AWKWARD SILENCE, interrupted only when Gene had to indicate which turn should be taken. No one was interested in conversation—Paulo, because he thought that Gene had tricked him; Chris, because Paulo might be irritated at her comments, feeling that she was spoiling everything; and Gene, because he knew that the Brazilians were disappointed, and because of this, would not talk about J. and his techniques.

"You are wrong about one thing," Paulo said when they arrived at the trailer. "It was not an angel that we met up with yesterday. It was a guy driving a truck."

For a fraction of a second, Chris thought there would be no response—the hostility between the two men was growing stronger and stronger. The American turned and began to walk in the direction of his home, but suddenly he stopped.

"I want to tell you a story my father told me," he said. "A master and his disciple were walking together in the desert. The master was teaching his charge that he could always trust in God, since he was aware of everything.

"Night fell, and they decided to pitch camp. The master raised the tent, and the disciple was given the assignment of tethering the horses to a rock. But, as he stood by the rock, he thought to himself: *The master is testing me. He said that God is aware of everything, and then asked me to tie up the horses. He wants to see whether or not I believe in God.*

"Instead of tethering the animals, he said a long prayer, and left the fate of the horses in God's hands.

"Next day, when they awoke, the horses were gone. Disappointed, the disciple complained to the master, saying that he no longer believed in him, since God had not taken care of everything, and had forgotten to watch over the horses.

"'You are wrong,' the master answered. 'God wanted to take care of the horses. But in order to do so, he needed to make use of your hands to tether them to the stone.'"

THE YOUNG MAN LIT A SMALL GAS LANTERN THAT WAS hanging outside the trailer. The light dimmed the brilliance of the stars somewhat.

"When we begin to think about our angels, they begin to manifest themselves. Their presence becomes closer and closer, more real. But, at the beginning, angels show themselves as they have done throughout our life: through others.

"Your angel used that man. He must have been caused to leave his home early—something must have changed in his routine, altering everything so that he could be there just at the moment that you needed him. That is a miracle. Do not try to regard it as a common event."

Paulo said nothing.

"Look," Gene explained. "When we were climbing the mountain, I forgot the flashlight," Gene went on. "You probably noticed that I was back at the car for quite a while. Whenever I forget something on leaving the house, I feel that my guardian angel is in action, causing me to lose a few seconds—and this short time interval may signify important things. It may allow me to avoid an accident, or cause me to run into someone I need to see.

"So, after I get what I've forgotten, I always sit down and count to twenty. That way, the angel has time to take action. An angel uses many instruments."

Gene asked Paulo to wait where he was for a few moments. He entered the trailer, and returned with a map. "The last time I saw the Valkyries, it was here."

He pointed to a place on the map. Chris realized that the animosity between the two seemed to have lessened.

"Take care of her," Gene said. "It's a good thing that she came with you."

"I think so," Paulo said. "Thank you for everything."

And they said good-bye.

"WHAT A FOOL I'VE BEEN," PAULO SAID, PUNCHING THE steering wheel as they drove away.

"What do you mean, a fool? I thought you were jealous!"

But Paulo was laughing, in a good mood.

"Four processes! And he only said three! It's through the fourth process that you converse with your angel!"

He looked at Chris, and his eyes were gleaming with the joy of discovery.

"The fourth process: channeling!"

ALMOST TEN DAYS IN THE DESERT. THEY STOPPED AT ONE place where the ground had opened in a series of wounds, as if prehistoric rivers had run through there, dozens of them, leaving long, deep arroyos that were becoming larger through the action of the sun.

In those parts, not even the scorpions could survive, much less snakes, coyotes, or the ever-present tumbleweed. The desert was full of such places, known as badlands.

The two entered into one of the immense wounds. The earthen walls were high, and all that could be seen was a tortuous path, with no beginning or end.

They were no longer irresponsible adventurers, feeling that nothing could harm them. The desert had its laws, and killed those who did not respect them. They had learned what the laws were—the sound of the rattlesnake, the hours that it was safe to be out there, the precautions. Before entering the badlands, they had left a note in the car saying where they were going. Even if it were only for half an hour, and it appeared to be unnecessary, ridiculous, a car might stop, and someone would see the note and know what direction they had taken. They had to facilitate the instruments of their guardian angels.

They were looking for the Valkyries. Not there, at the end of the world—because nothing living could survive for long in those badlands. There—well, this was just training. For Chris.

But they knew that the Valkyries were nearby, because they saw the signs. They lived in the desert, never staying for long in one place—but they left signs.

Paulo and Chris had found some clues. At the beginning, they had stopped at one small town after another, asking about the Valkyries, and no one had ever heard of them. The directions Gene had given them were of no use—they had probably long ago passed by the spot on the map he had shown them. But one day, in a bar, they met a boy who remembered having read something about them. He described the way the Valkyries dressed, and the signs they left.

They began to ask others about women who were dressed that way. Some responded with obvious disapproval, saying the Valkyries had passed by a month ago, a week ago, three days ago.

Finally, they had reached a place that seemed to be just a day's travel from where the Valkyries should be.

THE SUN WAS ALREADY NEAR THE HORIZON—OR THEY would not have risked being out in the desert. The earthen walls cast shadows. It was the perfect place.

Chris couldn't stand to repeat the whole thing yet again. But she had to—she hadn't yet achieved any meaningful results.

"Sit there. With your back to the sun."

She did as Paulo said. And then, automatically, she began to relax. She sat cross-legged, with her eyes closed—but she could feel the entire desert surrounding her. Her soul had been swelling during these days in the desert, and she knew that her world had expanded. It was more vast than it had been two weeks earlier.

"Concentrate on your second mind," he said.

Chris sensed an inhibited tone in his voice. He could not act toward her in the same way as he did with other disciples—after all, she knew his faults and weaknesses. But Paulo made a supreme effort to act as a master would, and she respected him for that.

She concentrated on her second mind. She allowed all thoughts to come to mind—and, as always, they were absurd thoughts for someone who was in the middle of the desert. For the past three days, whenever she had tried the exercise, she realized that her automatic thinking was very much concerned with whom she should invite to her birthday celebration—three months from now.

But Paulo had asked that she not be concerned about that. That she allow her concerns to flow freely.

"Let's start from the beginning again," he said.

"I'm thinking about my party."

"Don't fight your thoughts. They are stronger than you are," Paulo said for the thousandth time. "If you want to rid yourself of them, accept them. Think about what they want you to think about until they grow tired."

She went over her list of invitations. She rejected some. She substituted others. This was the first step: Pay attention to the second mind until it grew tired.

Now, the birthday celebration disappeared more quickly than before. But she was still composing the list. It was unbelievable how a subject like that could demand her attention for so many days, occupy hours when she could be thinking of more interesting things.

"Think until you are tired. Then, when you are tired, open the channel."

Paulo walked away from his wife and leaned against the wall. Gene was an expert, and took very seriously the business of not being able to teach anything to the disciple of another master. But, through Chris, he had given Paulo all of the clues that he needed.

The fourth way of communicating with the invisible world was channeling.

Channeling! How many times had he seen people in their cars in the midst of a traffic snarl, talking to themselves, without realizing that they were performing one of the most sophisticated of the magical processes! But, because of its extreme simplicity, all one need do is sit in a quiet place and be attentive to the thoughts that emerge from the bottom of one's mind.

Channeling has generally been considered a superficial practice. Nothing of the kind! Since the beginnings of humanity, people have known that, if they wanted to enter into contact with God, they had to make room in their soul. They had to allow their spiritual energy to manifest itself, and to create a bridge between the visible and the invisible.

How can one create such a bridge? Various mystical processes address the importance of "not being." Relax, allow the mind to become empty, and surprise yourself with the great treasure that begins to flow from your soul. The word inspiration means exactly that: the bringing in of air, allowing oneself to drink from an unknown source.

Channeling required no loss of awareness during the contact with the spirits; it was a more natural process for a person to use in order to plunge into the unknown. It allowed for contact with the Holy Spirit, with the soul of the world, with the enlightened masters. No ritual was needed, no incorporation, nothing. Every human being knew, subconsciously, that there was a bridge available to the invisible, a bridge one could cross without fear.

And everyone tried to do so, even without being aware of it. Everyone surprised themselves, saying things they had never thought before, giving advice of the "I don't know why I'm saying this" type, doing certain things that didn't appear to make sense.

And everyone liked to spend time observing nature's miracles—a thunderstorm, a sunset—ready to enter into contact with the universal wisdom, think about things that were truly important.

But at such times, the invisible wall would appear: the second mind.

The second mind was there, barring the entrance, with its repetitive ideas, its unimportant problems, its melodies, its financial problems, its unresolved passions.

He stood and approached Chris.

"Be patient, and listen to everything your second mind has to say. Don't respond. Don't argue. It will get tired."

Once again, Chris went over the invitation list, even though she had already lost interest in it. When she finished, she put a period to it.

And she opened her eyes.

There she was, in that wound in the earth. She felt the still air that surrounded her.

"Open the channel. Begin to speak."

Speak!

She had always been fearful of speaking out, of seeming

ridiculous, stupid. Fearful of learning what others thought of what she said, because they always seemed more capable, more intelligent. Always seemed to have an answer for everything.

But now she was here, and she had to have the courage even to say things that made no sense, that were absurd. Paulo had explained that this was one way of channeling: speak. Conquer your second mind, and allow the universe to do what it wanted with it.

She began to move her head back and forth, wanting to do all that, and suddenly she wanted to make strange noises. And she did so. It wasn't ridiculous. She was free to do as she pleased.

She had no idea where these things came from—but they were coming from within, from the bottom of her soul, and manifesting themselves. From time to time, her second mind returned with its concerns, and Chris tried to organize them, but that's the way it had to be—no logic, no censure, but rather the joy of a warrior entering into an unknown world. She needed to speak the pure language of the heart.

Paulo listened in silence, and Chris felt his presence. She was totally aware, but free. She could not concern herself with what he was thinking—she had to continue to speak, making the gestures that came to her, singing the strange melodies. Yes, everything must make some kind of sense, because she had never heard these sounds before, these melodies, these words and movements. It was difficult, and she had the fear that she was fantasizing things, wanting to appear to be more in contact with the Invisible than she really was. But she overcame her fear of the ridiculous, and went on.

Today, something different was happening. She was no longer doing what she did out of obligation, as in the first days. She was enjoying herself. And she began to feel secure. A wave of security washed back and forth, and Chris tried desperately to go with it.

In order to keep the wave close to her, she had to speak. Say anything that came to mind.

"I see the earth." Her voice was hesitant, calm, even though her second mind made an appearance from time to time, saying that Paulo must be finding all of this ridiculous. "We are in a safe place, we can stay here tonight, lie here and look up at the stars and talk of angels. There are no scorpions, no snakes, no coyotes.

"The planet set aside certain places for itself. It tells us to go away. In those places, without the millions of life forms that walk on its surface, the earth is able to be alone. She also needs her solitude, for she needs to understand herself."

Why am I saying that? He's going to think I'm showing off. I'm aware!

Paulo looked around. The dry bed of the river seemed gentle, smooth. But it inspired a terror of total solitude, of the complete absence of life.

"Say a prayer," Chris went on. Her second mind was no longer able to make her feel ridiculous.

But suddenly, she felt fear. Fear of not knowing which prayer, of not knowing how to continue.

And when she felt the fear, her second mind returned—and the ridicule, the shame, the concern about Paulo returned with it. After all, he was the Magus—he knew more than she, and must think all of this was phony.

She took a deep breath. She concentrated on the present, on the earth where nothing grew, on the sun that was already hidden. Bit by bit, the wave of security came back—like a miracle.

"Say a prayer," she repeated.

And it is going to echo
clearly
against the sky
when I come along
making my noise

She sat there in silence for a while, sensing that she had given her all, and that the channeling had ended. Then she turned to him.

"I went very far today. It's never happened that way."

Paulo caressed her face and kissed her. She didn't know whether he was doing that out of pity or pride.

"Let's go," he said. "Let's respect the earth's desire."

"Maybe he is saying that to give me a stimulus, to get me to try to continue channeling," she thought. But she was certain—something had happened. She hadn't invented all that.

"The prayer?" she asked, fearful of his answer.

"It's an ancient indigenous chant. From the Ojibway shamans."

She was proud of her husband's knowledge, even though he said it didn't count for much.

"How can these things happen?"

Paulo remembered J., discussing in his book the secrets of alchemy: "The clouds are rivers that already know the sea." But he wasn't inclined to explain. He was feeling tense, irritable, and didn't know exactly why he was staying on in the desert; after all, he already knew how to converse with his guardian angel.

"Did you see the film *Psycho*?" Paulo asked Chris when they arrived back at the car.

Chris nodded her head.

"The lead actress dies in the bathroom early on in the film. In the desert, I learned how one converses with the angels by the third day. Meanwhile, I promised myself that I would spend forty days here, and now I can't change my mind."

"Well, there's still the Valkyries."

"The Valkyries! I can live without them!"

He's afraid that he won't succeed in finding them, Chris thought.

"I already know how to converse with the angels, and that's what's important." Paulo's tone of voice was hostile.

"I've been thinking about that," Chris answered. "You already know, *but you don't want to try.*"

That's my problem, Paulo said to himself as he started the car. *I need some strong emotions. I need a challenge.*

He looked over at Chris. She was busy reading The *Desert Survival Manual* they had bought in one of the towns they had passed through. They drove off through yet another of the immense desert flats that seemed to have no end.

It's not just a problem of spiritual search, he continued thinking, as he alternated between looking at Chris and watching the road. He loved his wife, but he was getting fed up with marriage. He needed some strong passion in his love, in his work, in almost everything he did in his life. And that went against one of nature's most important laws: Every movement needs to pause at times.

He knew that if he continued the way he was, nothing in his life would last for very long. He was beginning to understand what J. had meant when he said that people wind up killing what they love most.

TWO DAYS LATER, THEY REACHED GRINGO PASS, A PLACE with only one motel, a mini-market, and the U.S. customs building. The Mexican border was only a few yards from the center of town, and the two took snapshots of each other with one foot in each country.

At the mini-market, they asked about the Valkyries, and the woman who owned the luncheonette said she had seen "that bunch of lesbians" that morning, but that they had moved on.

"Did they cross into Mexico?" Paulo asked.

"No, no. They took the road to Tucson."

They went back to the motel, and sat down on the verandah. The car was parked directly in front of them.

"Look how dirty the car's become," Paulo said after a few minutes. "I think I'll wash it."

"The owner of the motel wouldn't like to find out people are using water for washing their car. We're in the desert, remember?"

Paulo didn't answer. He stood up, took a roll of paper towels from the car, and began to wipe away at the dust. Chris remained seated.

He's upset. He can't sit still, she thought. "I've got something serious to tell you," she said.

"You've done your work very well, don't worry," he answered, as he used up one paper towel after another.

"That's just what I wanted to talk to you about," Chris

insisted. "I didn't come here to do work. I came because I thought our marriage was beginning to fall apart."

She feels the same way I do, he thought. But he continued with his cleaning.

"I've always respected your spiritual search, but I have mine, too," Chris said. "And I'm going to go on with it. I want you to understand that. I'm going to continue attending mass."

"I go to church, too."

"But what you're doing here is different, you know? You chose this way of communicating with God, and I've chosen a different one."

"I know that. I don't want to change."

"But meanwhile"—she took a deep breath, not knowing what his response would be—"meanwhile, something is happening to me. I want to speak to my angel, too."

She stood and went over to him. She began to gather the paper towels scattered on the ground.

"Do me a favor," she said, looking directly into her husband's eyes. "Don't leave me in the middle of the road."

THERE WAS A SMALL DINER NEXT TO THE GAS STATION.

They sat near the window. It was early in the morning, and the world was still quiet. Outside was the desert, the immense, packed surface . . . and silence.

Chris missed Borrego Springs, Gringo Pass, and Indio. In those places, the desert had a face: mountains, valleys, stories of pioneers and conquistadors.

Here, though, the immense emptiness was all there was to see. And the sun. The sun that before long would color the world yellow, raise the temperature to 115 in the shade, and make life impossible.

The man behind the counter took their order. He was Chinese, and spoke with a strong accent—he could not have been here for very long. Chris imagined how many times the world had turned to bring the Chinese man to this luncheonette in the middle of the American desert.

They asked for coffee, bacon, and toast, and sat there in silence.

Chris looked at the man's eyes—they appeared to gaze to the horizon, the eyes of one whose soul had grown.

But no, he was not engaged in a holy exercise, or trying to develop his spiritual side. His was the gaze of boredom. He wasn't seeing anything—not the desert, not the road, and not even the two customers who had come in so early in the morning. He limited himself to the motions required—put the coffee in the coffeemaker, fry the eggs, say, "Can I help you?" or "Thank you." The meaning of his life appeared to have been left behind, or to have disappeared in the immensity of the treeless desert.

The coffee came. They began to sip it, in no hurry. They had nowhere to go.

Paulo looked at the car outside. It had done no good at all to have cleaned it two days before. It was covered with dust once again.

They heard a sound in the distance. In a few minutes, the first truck of the day would drive past. The man behind the counter might put his boredom and eggs and bacon aside, and go outside to try to find something, wanting to be a part of the world that was on the move, the world that passed by his diner. It was the only thing he could do; watch from a distance as the world went by. He probably no longer even dreamed of leaving the luncheonette behind and hitching a ride on one of the trucks to somewhere else. He was addicted to silence and emptiness.

The sound grew louder, but it didn't seem to be that of a truck engine. For a moment, Paulo's heart was filled with hope. But it was only a hope, nothing more. He tried not to think about it. The sound came closer and closer, and Chris turned to see what was happening outside.

Paulo stared at his coffee, afraid she might perceive his anxiety.

The windows of the restaurant rattled slightly with the

noise. The counterman tried to ignore it—he knew the sound, and he didn't like it.

But Chris was fascinated. The horizon lit up with metallic reflections of the sun. The thundering engines seemed to shake the plants, the asphalt, the roof, and the windows of the restaurant.

With a roar, the Valkyries swept into the gas station. And the straight road, the flat desert, the tumbleweed, the Chinese man, and the two Brazilians in search of their angels, all felt their presence.

THE WOMEN, ON THEIR POWERFUL MOTORCYCLES, SPUN one way and then the other, dangerously close to one another, their machines shimmering in the hot air, their gloved hands toying skillfully with danger. They shouted out, as if to awaken the desert, to say they were alive and happy because it was morning.

Fear gripped Paulo's heart. Maybe they wouldn't stop there, maybe they were only trying to remind the counterman that life, joy, and skill still existed.

All at once, the rumbling stopped.

The Valkyries dismounted, shaking the desert from their bodies. They pounded the dust from their black leathers, and removed the colorful bandannas that they wore over their faces like bandits to keep the desert out of their lungs.

Then they entered the luncheonette.

Eight women.

They asked for nothing. The counterman seemed to know what they wanted—he was already placing eggs, bacon, and bread on the hot grill. Even with all the commotion, he continued to appear to be the obedient servant.

"Why is the radio turned off?" asked one of them.

The counterman turned it on.

"Louder!" said another.

Like a robot, he turned the radio to its loudest setting. The forgotten diner was suddenly transformed into a Manhattan disco. Some of the women kept time with the music by clapping their hands, while others carried on shouted conversations amidst the clamor.

But Chris, watching, saw that one of them moved not at all—the oldest of them, the one with long, curly red hair. She didn't enter into the conversation or the clapping of hands. She took no interest in the breakfast being prepared.

Intently, she stared at Paulo. And Paulo, resting his chin on his left hand, met the woman's gaze.

Chris felt a stab in her heart. *Why is he sitting like that?* Something very strange was happening. Perhaps the fact that she had been looking out at the horizon for so many days— or had been training so hard at the channeling—was changing the way she saw what went on around her. She had been having premonitions, and now they were manifesting.

She pretended not to notice that the two were eyeing each other. But her heart was giving her some inexplicable signals—and she couldn't tell whether they were good signals or bad.

Gene was right, Paulo thought. *It is easy to make contact with them.*

Slowly, the other Valkyries were beginning to perceive what was happening. First, they looked at the eldest, and then, following her gaze, turned to the table where Paulo and Chris were seated. Their conversation was silenced, and they no longer swayed in time to the music.

"Turn it off," the eldest said to the counterman.

As always, he obeyed. Now the only sound that could be heard was the sizzling of the eggs and bacon on the grill.

As her friends watched, the red-haired woman walked to the couple's table and simply stood there, looking at them. Then, without preamble, she spoke.

"Where did you get that ring?" she asked Paulo.

"At the same shop where you bought your brooch," he answered.

It was only then that Chris saw the metal brooch pinned to the leather jacket. It was made in the same design as the ring that Paulo wore on the ring finger of his left hand.

That's why he was resting his chin on his left hand.

She had already seen many rings in the Tradition of the Moon—of every color, metal and carved—always in the form of a serpent, the symbol of wisdom. But never had she seen one like the one her husband wore. J. had given Paulo that ring in 1982, when they were in Norway, saying that he was thereby completing "the Tradition of the Moon, a cycle that was interrupted by fear." And now, in the middle of the desert—a woman with a brooch of the same design.

"What do you want?" the redhead asked.

Paulo stood up, and the two stared at each other, face-to-face. Chris's heart was beating wildly—she was certain that it wasn't jealousy.

"What do you want?" she asked again.

"To speak with my angel. And something else."

She seized Paulo's hand and ran her fingers over his ring. Softening a bit, she seemed to become more feminine.

"If you bought that ring at the same place I did, you must know how it's made," she said, her eyes fixed on the serpents. "If not, then sell it to me. It's a beautiful piece."

It was simply a silver ring carved into two serpents. Each had two heads, and the design was quite simple.

Paulo said nothing.

"You don't know how to converse with angels, and this ring isn't yours," said the Valkyrie.

"I do know. Through channeling."

"Right," said the woman. "That's all that's required."

"I told you that there was something else I wanted."

"What is it?"

"Gene saw his angel. I want to see mine. I want to speak to my angel, face-to-face."

"Gene?" The woman's eyes searched the past, trying to recall who Gene was, where he lived.

"Yes, now I remember," she said. "He lives in the desert. Because that's where he met his angel."

"No. He is studying to become a master."

"This business of seeing your angel is just a myth. It's enough to converse with them."

Paulo stepped closer to the Valkyrie.

Chris knew the trick her husband was using: He called it "destabilization." Normally, two people converse at arm's length. When one of them approaches the other too closely, the other's thinking becomes disorganized.

"I want to see my angel." He was quite close to the woman, and he was staring at her.

"What for?" The Valkyrie appeared to be intimidated. The trick was working.

"Because I'm desperately in need of help. I have won important things for myself, but I am going to destroy them, because I tell myself that they have lost their meaning. I know it's not true. I know they are still important, and that if I destroy them, I'll be destroying myself, as well."

He maintained a neutral tone of voice, showing no emotion.

"When I learned that channeling was all that was needed in order to speak with my angel, I lost interest. It was no longer a challenge, but rather something I knew very well. I realized that my path to magic was about to end; the unknown was becoming too familiar to me."

Chris was shocked: Why was he making this confession in such a public place, in front of people whom he had never seen before?

"In order to continue along my path, I need something more," he finished. "I need mountains that are taller and taller."

The Valkyrie said nothing for a moment.

"If I teach you how to see your angel," she said, "your

desire to seek out taller and taller mountains may disappear. And that's not always a good thing."

"No, that will never disappear," Paulo replied. "What will vanish is the idea that the mountains I've conquered are too small. I will be able to keep alive my love for what I've accomplished. That's what my master was trying to say to me."

Maybe he's talking about our marriage, too, Chris thought.

The Valkyrie held out her hand to Paulo.

"My name is M.," she said.

"My name is S.," Paulo answered.

Chris was startled. Paulo had given his magic name! Very few people knew that secret, since the only way to cause a certain kind of evil to a magus is by using his magic name. Only those who were completely trustworthy were allowed to know the name.

Paulo had just met this woman. He couldn't trust her that much.

"But you can call me Valhalla," the red-haired woman continued.

That's the name of the Vikings' paradise, Paulo thought, and he told her his given name in return.

The redhead appeared to relax a bit. For the first time, she looked at Chris, seated at the table.

"In order to see an angel, three things are needed," said the Valkyrie, turning back to Paulo as if Chris didn't exist.

"And, in addition to those three things, courage is needed. A woman's courage, not a man's."

Paulo made it appear that he was paying no attention.

"Tomorrow, we will be near Tucson," Valhalla said. "Come to see us at noon, if your ring is authentic."

Paulo got the map out of the car, and Valhalla showed him the place where they should meet. One of the other Valkyries told Valhalla that her breakfast was getting cold. She turned back to her place at the counter and asked the man to turn on the radio again.

For a long time, Paulo and Chris sat over their coffee, watching the Valkyries eat.

Finally, the women got up and began to leave. As Valhalla reached the door, Paulo called out, "What are the three conditions for conversing with one's angel?"

Quietly, the redhead replied: "Break a pact. Accept forgiveness. And make a bet."

PAULO AND CHRIS LOOKED OUT AT THE CITY BELOW. FOR the first time in almost three weeks, they were in a real hotel—room service, bar, and breakfast in bed.

It was six in the evening, the hour in which they had gotten into the habit of practicing their channeling exercises. But Paulo was fast asleep.

Chris knew that the meeting that morning at the diner had changed everything; if she wanted to talk to her angel, she would have to do it on her own.

They had spoken little during the trip to Tucson. She had asked him only why he had divulged his magic name. Paulo answered that Valhalla had given him hers, and he could do no less.

Perhaps he was telling the truth, perhaps this was what he believed, but Chris wondered. She was a woman, and she saw things that men don't. She thought that Paulo might want to talk to her later that night.

Chris called the desk clerk and asked where the nearest bookstore was located. There was none nearby, he said; she would have to drive. She thought about it for a few moments, and then got the car keys. They were in a big city; if Paulo awoke, he would think that she had gone exploring.

SHE BECAME LOST IN THE TRAFFIC SEVERAL TIMES, BUT eventually found a huge shopping mall. One of the shops made keys, and she had a copy made of the keys to the car.

She wanted to have one, just to be secure.

In a bookstore, she leafed through a volume until she found what she was looking for:

VALKYRIES: the nymphs at Wotan's palace.

She had no idea who Wotan was, but that wasn't important.

Messengers of the gods, they led heroes to their death—and then to paradise.

Messengers. *Like the angels,* she thought. Death and paradise. Also like the angels.

They excite combatants with the love that their charm excites in their hearts, and through the example of bravery at the battlefront, mounted on steeds as fast as the clouds and as deafening as a thunderstorm.

They couldn't have chosen a better name, she thought.

At the same time, they symbolize both the inebriation of courage and rest for the warrior, the adventure of love in battle, encounter, and loss.

Right, absolutely. Paulo would want to talk to her.

THEY WENT DOWN TO HAVE DINNER AT THEIR OWN hotel—even though Paulo had tried to insist that they walk a bit, get to know this large city built in the middle of the desert. But Chris said she was tired, wanted to get to bed early, enjoy the comforts.

They made small talk throughout the meal. Paulo was exaggeratedly attentive. Chris knew that her husband was waiting for the right moment. So she made it appear that she was interested in everything he said, and showed enthusiasm when he said that Tucson had the most complete desert museum in the world.

In his enthusiasm, he mentioned that the museum included live coyotes, snakes, and scorpions, with a great deal of information concerning them. They could spend the entire day there.

She said she'd like very much to see it.

"You could go tomorrow morning," Paulo said.

"But Valhalla mentioned noontime."

"You don't have to be there."

"It's a strange hour," she answered. "No one spends much time in the desert at high noon. We learned that—in the worst way possible."

Paulo had thought it strange, too. But he didn't want to miss the chance; he was afraid Valhalla might change her mind, despite the ring and everything else.

He changed the subject, and Chris could sense her husband's anxiety. They went back to small talk for a time. They drank an entire bottle of wine, and she was sleepy. Paulo suggested they go right up.

"I don't know if you should go tomorrow," he said.

She had already tasted of everything—the meal, the place, Paulo's anxiety. She was enjoying the chance of confirming for herself that she really knew this man well. But now it was getting late, and it was time to give him a definite answer.

"I'm going with you. No matter what."

He was irritated. He told her that she was jealous, and that she was spoiling his process.

"Jealous of whom?"

"Of the Valkyries. Of Valhalla."

"That's crazy."

"But this is *my* quest. I brought you with me because I wanted you at my side. But there are certain things I have to do alone."

"I want to go with you," she said.

"Magic has never been important to you before. Why now?"

"Because I began the journey. And I've asked that I not be abandoned in the middle of the road," she answered, putting the matter to rest.

The silence was complete.

Everyone was wearing sunglasses against the blinding sun. Everyone—except Chris and Valhalla. Chris had removed hers so that Valhalla would know that she was looking directly into her eyes.

Chris had been bearing up under the woman's gaze for some time.

The minutes passed, and no one spoke. The only word that had been spoken the entire time had been Paulo's hello when they had arrived at the meeting place. His greeting had not been returned. Valhalla simply approached Chris and stood directly before her.

And, since that moment, nothing else had happened.

We must have been doing this for twenty minutes, Chris thought, but she didn't know how much time had actually elapsed. The glare of the sun, the heat, and the silence confused her.

She tried to distract herself a bit. They were at the foot of a mountain—wonderful, the desert once again contained mountains! Behind Valhalla, an entrance had been carved into the stone. Chris tried to imagine what the door led to, and found that she wasn't able to think clearly—just as on the day they had returned from the salt lake.

No one was perspiring—the dryness of the air was so great that all moisture evaporated immediately, as Gene had said. Chris knew that they were rapidly dehydrating—even though she had drunk as much water as possible, and even though she had prepared for the noonday desert. And even though she wasn't nude.

The other Valkyries had formed a semicircle; they wore their kerchiefs on their heads, in the manner of gypsies or pirates. Valhalla alone was bareheaded—her kerchief encircled her neck. The sun seemed not to bother her.

She is dismissing me with her eyes, Chris thought.

She knew this could not continue forever. There was a limit. She didn't know what that limit was, nor how or when she would know, but very soon, the sun would begin to be damaging. Meanwhile, everyone continued immobile—and all of this had happened because of her. Because she had insisted on coming along. *Messengers of the gods, they lead the heroes to death and to paradise.*

She had made a bad mistake, but now it was too late. She had come because her angel had required that she do so; her angel had said that Paulo was going to need her that afternoon.

No, no, it wasn't a mistake. My angel insisted that I be here, she thought.

Her angel—she was conversing with her angel! Nobody knew it, not even Paulo.

She began to feel dizzy, and she was certain she would faint soon. But she was going to see it through—it was no longer just a matter of being at her husband's side, or obeying her angel, or being jealous. Now it was a woman's pride— face-to-face with another woman.

"Put your glasses on," Valhalla said. "This sun could blind you."

"You're not wearing glasses," she answered. "And you're not afraid."

Valhalla gave a signal, and suddenly, the blazing light of the sun was multiplied a dozen times.

The Valkyries were using the mirrors on their motorcycles to reflect the sun directly into Chris's eyes. She saw a gleaming semicircle, knitted her brows, and kept her gaze upon Valhalla.

But she could no longer see clearly. The woman's image appeared to grow and grow, and the confusion in her mind increased. She felt she was about to fall, and at that moment, leather-covered arms came to her support.

Paulo watched Valhalla catch Chris in her arms. All of this could have been avoided. He could have insisted that she remain at the hotel—no matter what she was thinking. From the moment that he had first seen the brooch, he had known which tradition the Valkyries came from.

They had also seen his ring, and they knew that he had been tested in many ways. That it would be difficult to frighten him. But they would do everything possible to test the fiber of any stranger who entered their group. Even if that stranger was his wife.

But they could not prevent Chris, nor anyone else, from learning what they wanted to learn. They had taken a vow: Everything that was hidden had to be revealed. Chris was now being tested in the first great virtue of those who seek the spiritual path: courage.

The Valkyrie looked at Paulo. "Help me."

Paulo helped her support his wife. They took her to the car and laid her down on the backseat.

"Don't worry. She'll come around very quickly. With a serious headache."

He wasn't worried. He was proud.

Valhalla went to her cycle and brought a canteen. Paulo noted that she had already donned her sunglasses—she must have reached her limit, as well.

She bathed Chris's forehead in water, and dabbed some on her wrists and behind her ears. She opened her eyes, blinked several times, and sat up.

"Break a pact," she said, looking at the Valkyrie.

"You are an interesting woman," Valhalla said, passing her hand across Chris's face. "Put your glasses on."

Valhalla caressed Chris's hair. And even though both were now wearing dark glasses, Paulo knew they were staring at each other.

THEY WALKED TO THE STRANGE DOOR IN THE MOUNTAIN.

Valhalla turned to the other Valkyries. "For love. For victory. And for the glory of God."

The same phrase J. had used. The words of those who know angels.

The Valkyries started their engines, blowing up a cloud of dust. The women did the same maneuvers they had at the gas station—passing closely by each other—and, minutes later, they had disappeared around the mountain.

Valhalla turned to Chris and Paulo.

"Let's go in," she said.

There was no door, just a grate. On it hung a sign:

DANGER

THE FEDERAL GOVERNMENT

PROHIBITS ENTRY

VIOLATORS WILL BE PROSECUTED

"Don't believe it," said the Valkyrie. "They're not going to spend any time guarding this."

It was an old, abandoned gold mine. Valhalla, carrying a lantern, began to move forward carefully, so as not to bump her head on the passage beams. Paulo noticed that here and there the floor had collapsed. It might have been dangerous, but now wasn't the time to think about it.

As they went deeper, the temperature fell, and it even became pleasant. He was worried about a lack of air, but

Valhalla was moving along as if she knew the place well—she must have been there many times, and she was still alive. Now wasn't the time to think about that, either.

After walking for ten minutes or so, the Valkyrie halted. They sat on the floor of the passage, and she placed the lantern in the middle of their circle.

"Angels," she said. "Angels are visible to those who accept the light. And break the pact with the darkness."

"I have no pact with the darkness," Paulo responded. "I had one. But no longer."

"I'm not talking about a pact with Lucifer, or with Satan, or with..." She began to speak the names of various demons, and her face looked strange.

"Don't say those names," Paulo interrupted. "God is in the words, and the devil as well."

Valhalla laughed. "It looks as if you've learned the lesson. Now, break the pact."

"I have no pact with evil," Paulo repeated.

"I'm talking about your pact with defeat."

Paulo thought of what J. had said—about destroying what we love most. But J. had said nothing about pacts; he knew Paulo well enough to know that his pact with evil had been broken a long time ago. The silence within the mine was worse than in the desert. Not a sound was heard, except Valhalla's voice—which sounded different.

"We have a contract, you and I: not to win when victory is possible," she insisted.

"I have never made any such pact," Paulo said for the third time.

"Everyone has. At some point in our lives, we all enter into such an agreement. That's why there is an angel with a burning sword at the gates to paradise. To allow entry only to those who have broken that pact."

Yes, she's right, thought Chris. *Everyone has made this pact.*

"Do you find me attractive?" Valhalla asked, once again changing the tone of her voice.

"You are a beautiful woman," Paulo answered.

"One day, when I was still an adolescent, I saw my best friend crying. We were inseparable, and we loved each other completely, and I asked what had happened. When I insisted on knowing, she told me that her boyfriend was in love with me. I didn't know that, and that day I made the pact. Without really knowing why, I began to gain weight, to take poor care of myself, to become unattractive. Because—unconsciously—I felt that my beauty was a curse, and had caused suffering for my best friend.

"Before long, I had destroyed all meaning in my life because I just didn't care about myself anymore. I reached the point that everything about my life became unbearable: I thought about dying."

Valhalla laughed.

"As you can see, I broke the pact."

"True," Paulo said.

"Yes, it is true," Chris said. "You are lovely."

"We are in the heart of the mountain," the Valkyrie continued. "Outside, the sun is shining, and here there is only darkness. But the temperature is pleasant, we can sleep, we have nothing to worry about. This is the darkness of the pact."

She raised her hand to the zipper of her leather jacket.

"Break the pact," she said. "For the glory of God. For love. And for victory."

She began to lower the zipper slowly. She wore nothing beneath the jacket.

The light from the lantern caused a medallion between her breasts to gleam.

"Take it," she said.

Paulo touched the medallion. The archangel Michael.

"Take it from around my neck."

He removed the medallion and held it in his hands.

"Both of you, hold the medallion."

Suddenly, Chris blurted out, "I don't need to see my angel! I don't need to. Just speaking will do."

Paulo held the medallion in his hand.

"I've already begun talking with my angel," Chris went on, more quietly. "I know that I can, and that's good enough."

Paulo didn't believe her. But Valhalla knew that it was the truth. She had read it in her eyes when they were outside. She also knew that her angel wanted her to be there with her husband.

Nevertheless, she had to test her courage. It was the rule of the Tradition.

"All right," the Valkyrie said. With a rapid movement, she blew out the lantern. The darkness was total.

"Put the cord around your neck," she said to Paulo. "And hold the medallion with both hands joined, in prayer."

Paulo did as he was told. He was fearful of a darkness so complete, and he was remembering things he would rather not think about.

He felt Valhalla approaching him from behind. Her hands touched his head.

The darkness seemed almost solid. Nothing, not a scintilla of light, entered there.

Valhalla began to pray in a strange language. At first, he tried to identify the words she was saying. Then, as her fingers moved across his head, Paulo felt the medallion growing hot. He concentrated on the heat in his hands.

The darkness was changing. Various scenes from his life began to pass before him. Light and shadow, light and shadow, and—suddenly, he was once again in darkness.

"I don't want to remember that . . ." he pleaded with the Valkyrie.

"Remember! Whatever it is, try to remember every minute of it."

The darkness brought terror to him, the terror he had experienced fourteen years earlier.

When he woke up, he found a note on the coffee table: "I love you. I'll be right back." At the bottom, she had written the date: "25 May 1974."

Funny. To put the date on a love note.

He had awakened a bit dizzy, still startled by the dream. In it, the director of the recording studio was offering him a job. He didn't need a job: The director actually functioned more like his employee—his and his partner's. Their records were at the top of the charts, selling thousands of copies, and letters were arriving from all corners of Brazil, from people wanting to know what the Alternative Society was.

All you have to do is listen to the words of the song, *he thought to himself. It wasn't really a song—it was a mantra from a magic ritual, with the words of the Beast of the Apocalypse being read in the background in a low voice. Whoever sang the song would be invoking the forces of darkness. And everyone was singing it.*

He and his partner had done the whole thing. The royalties they earned were being used to buy a lot near Rio de Janeiro. There they would recreate what, almost one hundred years earlier, the Beast had tried to establish in Cefalu, Sicily. But the Beast was expelled by the Italian authorities. The Beast had erred on many points—he had not gathered a sufficient number of disciples, and he did not know how to earn money. The Beast told everyone that his number was 666, and that he had come to create a world where the strong would be served by the weak, and the only law was that everyone do as they desired. But the Beast didn't know how to spread the ideas—few people had taken the Beast's words seriously.

He and his partner, Raul Seixas, well, they were completely different! Raul sang, and the entire country listened. They were young, and they were earning money. Yes, it was true that Brazil was in the hands of a military dictatorship, but the government was concerned about guerrillas. They couldn't waste their time with a rock singer. Just the opposite: The authorities felt that rock music kept the country's youth away from communism.

He drank his coffee standing at the window. He was going to take a walk, and meet later with his partner. It didn't bother him at all that nobody knew who he was, while his friend was famous. What mattered was that they were earning money, and this would allow them to put their ideas into practice. People from the world of music, and the world of magic—ah, they knew! His anonymity with regard to the general public was even rather funny—more than once, he had had the pleasure of hearing someone comment on his work—without knowing that the author was listening nearby.

He donned his sneakers. As he was tying the laces, he felt dizzy.

He raised his head. The apartment seemed darker than it should have been. The sun was shining outside, and he had just left the window. Something was burning—an electrical appliance, maybe, because the stove was disconnected. He looked throughout the apartment. Nothing.

The air was heavy. He decided to go out right away—without tying his sneakers, he started to leave, but realized that he really wasn't feeling well.

Could be something I ate, *he said to himself. But when he ate something that was off, his entire body usually gave him a signal, and he knew that. He wasn't nauseated, didn't feel like vomiting. Just a kind of dizziness that didn't seem to want to pass.*

Dark. The darkness grew; it seemed like a gray cloud around him. He felt the dizziness again. Yes, it had to be something he had eaten—Or maybe an acid flashback, he thought. But he hadn't tried LSD in five years. The delayed effects had disappeared after the first six months, and never returned.

He was frightened, he had to get out.

He opened the door—the dizziness was coming and going, and he might get worse out in the street. Better to stay home and wait. The note was there on the table—she would be home shortly—he could wait. They could go together to the pharmacy or to a doctor, although he hated doctors. It couldn't be anything serious. No one has a heart attack at age twenty-six.

No one.

He sat down on the couch. He needed some distraction. He shouldn't think about her, or the time would pass even more slowly. He tried to read the paper, but the dizziness, the lightheadedness, came and went, stronger each time. Something was pulling him into a black hole that appeared to have formed in the middle of the room. He began to hear noises—laughing, voices, things breaking. That had never happened—never! Whenever he had taken anything, he knew he was drugged, knew it was a hallucination and would pass with time. But this—this was terribly real!

No, no, it couldn't be real. The reality was the rugs, the curtains, the bookshelves, the coffee table with the leftovers of bread on it. He made an effort to concentrate on the scene surrounding him, but the feeling of a black hole in front of him, the voices, the laughter, all continued.

None of this was happening. Definitely! He had practiced magic for six years. Performed all the rituals. He knew it was nothing more than suggestion. A psychological effect that was playing on his imagination. Nothing more.

His panic was increasing, and the dizziness was more pronounced— pulling to the outside of his body, toward a dark world, toward that laughter, those voices, those noises—real!

I cannot let myself be afraid. Fear will make it come back. He tried to control himself, went to the sink and bathed his face. He felt a bit better, the feeling seemed to have passed. He put his sneakers on and tried to forget about it. He toyed with the idea of telling his partner he had entered into a trance, had been in contact with demons.

But he had only to think about that, and the dizziness returned— more strongly.

"I'll be right back," the note said, and she hadn't come!

I never achieved concrete results in the astral plane, *he thought. He had never seen anything. No angels, no devils, no spirits of the dead. The Beast wrote in his diary that he was able to make things materialize, but he was lying, the Beast had never gotten that far. He knew that. The Beast had failed. He liked the Beast's ideas because they were rebellious, chic. And very few people had ever heard them. And people are always more respectful of those who speak of things no one understands. As for the rest—Hare Krishna, Children of God, the Church of Satan, Maharishi—everyone knew about those. The Beast—the Beast was just for the chosen few! "The law of the powerful," one of his books talked about. The Beast was on the cover of* Sgt. Pepper's Lonely Hearts Club Band, *one of the Beatles's best known records—and almost no one knew it. Maybe not even the Beatles knew what they were doing when they placed that photograph there.*

The phone rang. It might be his girlfriend. But if she had written, "I'll be right back," why would she be phoning?

Only if something was happening.

That's why she hadn't come. The intervals between bouts of dizziness were growing shorter and shorter, and everything was turning black again. He knew—something was telling him—that he couldn't let that feeling take him over. Something terrible might happen—he might enter into that darkness and never return. He had to maintain control at any cost—he needed to occupy his mind, or that thing would dominate him.

The phone. He concentrated on the phone. Speak, converse, think of other things, take his mind off that darkness, the phone was a miracle, a solution. He knew it. He knew that somehow he couldn't surrender. He had to answer the phone.

"Hello?"

It was a woman's voice. But it wasn't his girlfriend—it was Argelia.

"Paulo?"

He didn't answer.

"Paulo, can you hear me? I need you to come over to my house! Something strange is going on!"

"What's happening?"

"You know, Paulo! Explain it to me, for God's sake!"

He hung up before he heard something he didn't want to hear. It wasn't a delayed drug effect. It wasn't a symptom of insanity. It wasn't a heart attack. It was real. Argelia had participated in the rituals, and "that" was happening to her, too.

He panicked. He sat there without thinking for a few minutes, and the darkness began to take him over, coming closer and closer, causing him to step to the edge of the lake of death.

He was going to die—for everything he had done without believing, for the many people he had involved without knowing it, for so much evil spread about in the name of what was good. He would die, and the Darkness would go on, because it was manifesting itself now, before his very eyes, demonstrating that things really worked, collecting what was owed for the time in which it had been used, and he had to pay—because he didn't want to know what the price was before, thought it was for free, that everything was a lie or just suggestion!

His years in the Jesuit school came back to him, and he prayed for the strength needed to get back to a church, ask forgiveness, pray that at least God would save his soul. He had to be able to do it. He found that as long as he could keep his mind busy, he was able to dominate the dizziness, at least partly. He needed time to get to the church . . . What a ridiculous idea!

He looked at the bookcase, and resolved that he would calculate how many records he owned—after all, he had always put that task off! Yes, it was important to know the exact number of records, and he began to count: one, two, three . . . he did it! He was able to overcome the dizziness, the black hole that was pulling him in. He counted all of the records—and then counted them again, to make certain he was correct. Now the books. He had to count in order to know how many books he had. Did he have more books than records? He began to count. The dizziness halted, and he had so many books. And magazines. And alternative newspapers. He would count everything, write it down, really know how many things he owned. It was so important.

He was counting the silverware when he heard the key turn in the lock. She was here, finally. But he couldn't allow himself to be distracted—he couldn't even talk about what was happening; any moment now, it was all going to stop. He was certain of it.

She went straight to the kitchen, and hugged him, crying.

"Help me! Something strange is happening. You know what it is, help me!"

He didn't want to lose his count of the silverware—that was his salvation. Keep the mind busy. Better if she hadn't arrived—it didn't help. And she thought the same as Argelia—that he knew everything, that he knew how to stop it.

"Keep your mind busy!" he shouted, as if he were possessed. "Count how many records you have! And how many books!"

She looked at him without understanding what he was talking about. Like a robot, she walked to the bookcase.

But she didn't get there. She suddenly threw herself to the floor.

"I want my mother . . ." she said, over and over. "I want my mother . . ."

He did too. He wanted to phone his parents, ask for help—his parents whom he never saw, who belonged to a middle-class world he had abandoned long ago. He tried to go on with the silverware count, but she was there, crying like a child, pulling at her hair.

That was too much. He was responsible for what was happening, because he loved her, and had taught her the rituals, guaranteed that she could get what she wanted, that things were improving day by day (although he never for a moment believed what he was saying!). Now she was there, begging for help, trusting in him——and he had no idea what to do.

For a moment, he thought of issuing an order, but he had already lost his silverware count, and the black hole came back suddenly with even greater strength.

"You help me," he said. "I don't know what to do."

And he began to cry.

He was crying out of fear, as when he was a child. He wanted his parents, as she did. He was bathed in a cold sweat, and was certain he would die. He seized her hand, and her hands were cold, too, even though her clothing was soaked in perspiration. He went to the bathroom to wash his face——as he used to do when the effects of the drugs were really strong. Maybe it would work with regard to "that," too. The hallway seemed immense, the thing was stronger now——he was no longer counting records, books, pencils, silverware. There was no place to hide.

"Running water."

The thought came from some far corner of his mind, some place that the darkness had not seemed to penetrate. Running water! Yes, there was a power in darkness, in delirium, in madness——but there were other things!

"Running water," he said to her, as he bathed his face. "Running water keeps the evil away."

She heard the certainty in his voice. He knew, he knew everything. He would save her.

He turned the shower on, and they both huddled under it—with their clothing, their documents, their money. The cold water moistened their bodies, and, for the first time since he had awakened, he experienced a sense of relief. The dizziness vanished. They stayed for two or three hours under the spray, without speaking, shivering from fear and the cold. They stepped out only once, to phone Argelia and tell her to do the same thing. The dizziness returned, and they had to flee back into the shower. There, everything seemed calm, but they needed desperately to understand what was happening.

"I never believed it," he said.

She looked at him, not understanding. Two years earlier, they had been two hippies, without a cent to their name, and now his songs were being heard all over the country. He was at the peak of success—even though few people knew his name; and he had been saying that it was all the result of the rituals, the occult studies, the power of magic.

"I never believed it," he continued. "Or I never would have walked those paths! I never would have risked myself, or you."

"Do something, for the love of God!" she said. "We can't stay here in the shower forever!"

He left the shower again, checking whether the dizziness and the black hole were still there. He went to the bookcase and came back with the Bible. He had a Bible in the house only so that he could read from the Revelation to John, be certain about the reign of the Beast. He had done everything as called for by the Beast's followers—and, in his heart, he had believed none of it.

"Let's pray to God," he said. He felt ridiculous, demoralized before this woman whom he had tried to impress for all those years. He was weak, he

was going to die. He had to humiliate himself, beg for forgiveness. What was most important now was the saving of his soul. In the end, everything was true.

He embraced the Bible, and recited prayers he had learned as a child—Our Father, Hail Mary, the Creed. She refused at the beginning, and then recited them with him.

Then he opened the book at random. The water poured down on the pages, but he was able to read the story of someone who had asked something of Jesus, and Jesus said that he must maintain the faith. The man answered: "Lord, I believe—help me in my incredulity."

"Lord, I believe, help me in my incredulity!" he shouted through the sound of the falling water.

"Lord, I believe, help me in my incredulity!" he said in a whisper, through his sobs.

He began to feel strangely calm. If the terrible evil they had experienced really existed, then it was true that the kingdom of heaven did, as well, and along with it, everything else that he had learned and then denied throughout his life.

"The eternal life exists," he said, knowing that he would never again believe in those words. "I don't care if I die. You cannot fear death, either."

"I'm not afraid," she answered. "I'm not afraid, but I think it's unfair. It's a pity."

They were only twenty-six. It really was a pity.

"We have been through everything someone our age could have experienced," he answered. "Most people haven't even come close."

"That's true," she said. "We can die."

He lifted his face, and the sound of the water in his ears seemed like thunder. He was no longer crying, nor afraid; he was only paying the price for his insolence.

"Lord, I believe, help me in my incredulity," he repeated. "We want to make an exchange. We offer you anything, absolutely anything, in return for the salvation of our souls. We offer our lives, or everything we own. Please accept, my lord."

She looked at him with contempt. The man she had admired so. The powerful, mysterious, courageous man she had so admired, who had convinced so many people with regard to the Alternative Society, who had preached about a world where anything was allowed, where the strong ruled over the weak. That man was there, crying, screaming for his mother, praying like a child, and saying that he had always been courageous—because he had believed in nothing.

He turned, and said they should both look up and make the exchange. She did so. She had lost her man, her faith, and her hope. She had nothing else to lose.

He placed his hand on the faucet, and slowly shut it down. Now they could die; God had forgiven them.

The stream of water turned to droplets, and then there was complete silence. Soaked to the bone, they looked at each other. The dizziness, the black hole, the laughter, and the noises, all had disappeared.

HE WAS LYING IN A WOMAN'S LAP, CRYING. HER HAND WAS caressing his head.

"I made that pact," he said tearfully.

"No," the woman answered. "It was a trade."

Paulo clutched the archangel medallion. Yes, there had been a trade—and the punishment was severe. Two days after that morning in 1974, they were imprisoned by the Brazilian political police and accused of subversion based on the Alternative Society. He was placed in a dark cell, similar to the black hole he had seen in his living room. He was threatened with death, and he gave in, but it was a trade. When he was released, he split up with his partner and was expelled from the world of music for a long time. No one would give him a job. But it was a trade.

Other members of the group had not made the trade. They survived in the "black hole," and regarded him as a coward. He lost his friends, his security, his desire to go on living. For years, he was afraid to go out into the street—the dizziness might return, the police could appear again. And, even worse, after his release from prison he never saw his girlfriend again. At times, he regretted the trade—it would have been better to have died than to have to live that way. But now it was too late to go back.

"There was a pact," Valhalla said. "What was it?"

"I promised I would abandon my dreams."

For seven years, he paid the price for the trade. But God

was generous, and allowed him to rebuild his life. The director of the recording studio, the same person he had dreamed about that May morning, gave him a job and became his only friend. He went back to composing, but every time his work brought some success, something wound up happening, and everything went down the drain.

He remembered J's words: People destroy what they love.

"I always figured it was part of the bargain," he said.

"No," Valhalla said. "God was severe, but you were more severe than he was."

"I promised that I would never grow again. I thought that I could no longer trust myself."

The Valkyrie held his head to her bare breasts.

"Tell me about the dread," she said. "The dread that I saw when we met at the luncheonette."

"The terror . . ." He didn't know how to begin, because he felt he would sound absurd. "The terror doesn't allow me to sleep at night, or rest during the day."

Now Chris understood her angel. She had to be here, hearing this, because he would never have told her . . .

". . . and now I have a wife that I love, I found J., I walked the holy Road to Santiago, I've written books. I'm being faithful to my dreams again, and that's where the dread comes from. Because everything is going the way I would like it to, and I know that soon it will all be destroyed." It was terrible to say that. He had never said it to anyone—not even himself.

He knew that Chris was there, hearing it all. And he was ashamed.

"That's the way it was with the songs," he said, forcing himself to go on. "That's the way it's been with everything I've done since then. Nothing has lasted more than two years."

He felt Valhalla's hands removing the medallion from around his neck. He stood. He didn't want her to light the lantern, because he lacked the courage to confront Chris.

But Valhalla lit the lantern, and the three made their way out in silence.

"We two are going out first, and you come along later," Valhalla said to Paulo as they were reaching the end of the tunnel.

Paulo was certain that, just as with his girlfriend of fourteen years earlier, Chris would never again trust him.

"Today, I believe in what I'm doing," he tried to say before the other two left. It sounded like a plea for forgiveness, like self-justification.

No one answered. After a few more steps, Valhalla extinguished the lantern. There was now sufficient light for them to see.

"From the moment that you set foot outside," the Valkyrie said, "promise, in the name of the archangel Michael, that never again—never again—will you raise your hand against yourself."

"I'm afraid to say that," he answered. "Because I don't know how to comply."

"You have no choice, if you want to see your angel."

"I didn't realize what I was doing to myself. I might continue with the same kind of self-betrayal."

"Now you know," Valhalla said. "And the truth gives you freedom."

Paulo nodded his head.

"You will still have many problems in your life, some of them normal, some of them difficult. But, from now on, only God's hand will be responsible for everything—you will interfere no more."

"I promise in the name of Saint Michael."

The women went out. He waited a moment, and then began to walk. He had been in the darkness long enough.

THE RAYS OF LIGHT, REFLECTING FROM THE STONE WALLS, showed the way. There was the grated door, a door leading to a prohibited kingdom. A door that frightened him. Because out there was the kingdom of light, and he had been living for years in the darkness. A door that appeared to be closed— but, for anyone who approached it, it was open.

The door to the light was there in front of him. He wanted to pass through. He could see the golden light of the sun outside, but he decided not to put on his sunglasses. He needed the light. And he knew that the archangel Michael was at his side, sweeping away the darkness with his lance.

For years he had believed in the implacable hand of God, in his punishment. But it was his own hand, not God's, that had wrought such destruction. Never, for the rest of his life, would he do that again.

"Break the pact," he said to the darkness of the mine and to the desert light. "God has the right to destroy me. I do not."

He thought of the books he had written, and was happy. The year would end without any problem—because the pact had been broken. There was no doubt that problems would arise in his work, in love, and along the path to magic—serious problems or passing problems, as Valhalla had said. But from now on, he would battle side by side with his guardian angel.

You must have made a tremendous effort, he said to his angel. *And, in the end, I spoiled everything, and you couldn't understand it.*

His angel was listening. The angel knew about the pact, too, and was happy at not having to devote efforts to keeping Paulo from destroying himself.

Paulo found the door and passed through it. The sun blinded him for a moment, but he kept his eyes open—he needed the light. He saw the figures of Valhalla and Chris approaching. "Put your hand on his shoulder," Valhalla said to Chris. "Be a witness."

Chris obeyed.

Valhalla took a few drops of water from her canteen and made a cross on his forehead—as if baptizing him. Then she knelt, and told them to kneel as well.

"In the name of the archangel Michael, the pact was known in heaven. In the name of the archangel Michael, the pact was broken."

She placed the medallion on his forehead, and asked that he repeat her words:

Sainted angel of the Lord,
My zealous guardian . . .

The prayer from childhood echoed from the walls of the mountain, and spread throughout that part of the desert.

If I trust in you,
The divine piety
Will rule me always, and guard,
Govern, and enlighten.
Amen.
"Amen," said Chris.
"Amen," he repeated.

PEOPLE WERE APPROACHING THEM CURIOUSLY.

"They're lesbians," said one.

"They're crazy," said another.

The Valkyries paid no attention, but continued with what they were doing. They had tied one kerchief to another, forming a kind of rope. They sat on the ground in a circle— their arms resting on their knees, holding the joined kerchiefs.

Valhalla was in the middle, on foot. People continued to arrive. When a small multitude had formed, the Valkyries began to chant a psalm.

By the rivers of Babylon,
There we sat down, yea, and wept.
We hung our harps upon the willows
In the midst of it.

The people watched, understanding none of it. It was not the first time these women had appeared in the city. They had been there before, speaking of strange things—although certain words were similar to those uttered by television preachers.

"Have courage." Valhalla's voice rang out clearly and strongly. "Open your heart, and listen to what your dreams tell you. Follow those dreams, because only a person who is not ashamed can manifest the glory of God."

"The desert's made them crazy," a woman said.

Some people left immediately. They were fed up with preaching.

"There is no sin but the lack of love," Valhalla continued. "Have courage, be capable of loving, even if love appears to be a treacherous and terrible thing. Be happy in love. Be joyful in victory. Follow the dictates of your heart."

"That's impossible," someone in the crowd said. "People have obligations."

Valhalla turned in the direction of the voice. She was doing it—people were paying attention! Different from five years earlier, when no one came near them during their appearances in the city.

"We have children. We have husbands and wives. People have to earn a living," another person said.

"Well, meet your obligations. But obligations never prevented anyone from following their dreams. Remember that you are a manifestation of the absolute, and do only those things in your lives that are *worth the effort*. Only those who do that will understand the great transformations that are yet to be seen."

The Conspiracy, Chris thought, as she listened. She remembered the time long ago when she had sung in the plaza with others from her church, to save people from sin. In those days, no one spoke of a New Age—they spoke of the coming of Christ, of punishment and hell. There was no Conspiracy, such as now.

She walked through the crowd and found Paulo. He was sitting on a bench, far from the gathering.

"How long are we going to travel with them?" she asked.

"Until Valhalla teaches me how to see angels."

"But we've been here for almost a month."

"She cannot refuse me. She swore on the Tradition. She has to keep her vow."

The crowd was growing in size. Chris was thinking how difficult it must be to talk to the people gathered there.

"They're not going to take the Valkyries seriously," she said. "Not with the way they're dressed, and with those motorcycles."

"They have been fighting for some very old ideas," Paulo said. "Nowadays, soldiers dress in camouflage. They disguise themselves, and they hide. But the old warriors dressed in colorful outfits, much more obvious on the field of battle.

"They wanted the enemy to see them. They took pride in battle."

"Why are they doing this? Why preach in public parks and in bars and in the middle of the desert? Why are they helping us to speak to our angels?"

He lit a cigarette. "You joke about a Conspiracy, but you're right," he said. "There is a Conspiracy."

She laughed. No, no, there was no Conspiracy. She had used that term because her husband's friends acted like secret agents, always careful not to discuss certain things when others were present, always changing the subject—although they had sworn, all of them had, that there was nothing occult in the Tradition.

But Paulo seemed to be serious.

"The gates to Paradise have been reopened," he said. "God banished the angel with the burning sword who was at the gate. For some time—no one is certain for how long—anyone could enter, since it was obvious that the gates were open."

As he was speaking to Chris, Paulo recalled the abandoned gold mine. Up until that day—a week ago—he had chosen to remain outside of paradise.

"What guarantees entry?"

"Faith. And the Tradition," he answered.

They walked over to an ice cream wagon and bought cones. Valhalla continued to speak, and her sermon appeared to be endless. Before long, she might even try to get the spectators to participate, at which point it would probably end.

"Does everyone know that the gates are open?" Chris asked.

"Some people have noticed—and they are calling the others. But there's a problem."

Paulo pointed to a monument in the middle of the square. "Let's suppose that paradise is there. And every person on earth is here in the plaza. Each of them has their own path for arriving there.

"That's why people talk with their angels. Because only

the angels know the best path. It does no good to seek advice about it from others."

"Follow your dreams, and take your risks," they heard Valhalla saying.

"What will this world be like?"

"It will be only for those who enter into paradise," Paulo answered. "The world of the 'Conspiracy.' The world of people who are able to see the transformations that are occurring, of people who have the courage to pursue their dreams and listen to angels. A world for all those who believe in that world."

A murmur arose from the crowd, and Chris knew that the play had begun. She wanted to move forward to observe, but what Paulo was saying was more important.

"For centuries, we wept on the banks of the rivers of Babylon," Paulo continued. "We hung up our harps, we were prohibited from singing, we were persecuted and massacred. But we never forgot that there was a promised land. The Tradition survived everything.

"We learned how to fight, and we were strengthened by the battle. People are once again speaking of the spiritual world that only a few years ago was seen as something that only ignorant, complacent people believed in. There is an invisible thread that unites all those on the side of the light—like those joined kerchiefs of the Valkyries. And this thread is becoming a strong, shining rope, anchored by the angels. A handrail that is perceived by those who are most sensitive, and that will support us. Because we are many, and we are spread all over the earth. All of us moved by the same faith."

She said, "It's a world that has so many names, isn't it? New Age, Sixth Golden Age, Seventh Beam, and so on."

"But it's all the same world. I'll guarantee you."

Chris looked at Valhalla, there in the plaza, speaking of angels.

"Well, why is she trying to convince others?"

"No, no, she's not trying to convince them of anything. We all came from Paradise, we have spread throughout the world, and now we're returning there. Valhalla is asking these people to pay the price of that return."

Chris remembered the afternoon in the mine. "Sometimes it's a very high price."

"It may be. But there are people who are willing to pay it. They know that what Valhalla is saying is true, because it brings back something they had forgotten. All of them still carry in their soul memories and visions of Paradise. Years may go by without their remembering—until something happens: the birth of a child, a serious loss, a feeling of imminent danger, a sunset, a book, a song . . . or a group of women dressed in leather, speaking of God. Anything. Suddenly, these people remember.

"That's what Valhalla is doing. Reminding them that a place exists. Some of them are listening, others aren't—those who aren't will pass by the gates without seeing that they're open."

"But she's talking about this new world."

"Those are just the words she uses. Actually, they have retrieved their harps from the willows, and are playing them again—and millions of people all over the world are singing of the joys of the Promised Land. No one is alone anymore."

They heard the sound of motorcycles. The play was over. Paulo began to walk toward the car.

"Why didn't you ever tell me about all this?" she asked.

"Because you already knew."

Yes, she had known. But only now did she remember.

The Valkyries rode from city to city on their motorcycles, with their trappings, their kerchiefs, and their strange outfits. And they spoke of God.

Paulo and Chris went with them. When they made camp on the outskirts of a city, the couple stayed in hotels. When they stopped in the middle of the desert, they slept in the car. They made a campfire, and the dangers of the desert receded—the animals did not approach. As they dropped off to sleep, they could look up at the stars and hear the howls of the coyotes in the distance.

Ever since the afternoon at the mine, Paulo had been practicing the channeling process. He was afraid that Chris might think that he hadn't really known what he had tried to teach her.

"I know J.," she said, when the subject came up. "You don't have to prove your knowledge to me."

"My girlfriend back in those days also knew the person who was teaching me," he answered.

They sat down together every afternoon, working at the destruction of their second minds; they prayed for their angels, and tried to invoke their presence.

"I believe in this new world," he said to Chris, when they had completed yet another exercise in channeling.

"I know you believe in it. Or you wouldn't have done the things you've done during your lifetime."

"But, even so, I don't know whether the things I do are really correct."

"Give yourself some credit," she answered. "You're doing the best you can—very few people would travel so far to find their angel. And don't forget, you broke the pact."

The pact he had broken in the mine: J. was going to be happy about that! Although Paulo was almost certain that he already knew everything, J. hadn't tried to argue Paulo out of this trip to the desert.

When the two had completed their channeling exercises, they talked for hours about angels. But only between themselves—Valhalla never again spoke of the matter.

ONE AFTERNOON, AFTER THEIR CONVERSATION, HE WENT TO talk with Valhalla.

"You know the Tradition," he said. "You cannot interrupt a process once you have begun it."

"I'm not interrupting anything," she answered.

"But soon I'll have to go back to Brazil. And I haven't yet accepted forgiveness, nor made a bet."

"I'm not interrupting the process," she said again.

She suggested that they take a walk out in the desert. When they reached a certain point, they sat down together and watched the sunset, and talked about rituals and ceremonies. Valhalla asked about J.'s teaching methods, and Paulo wanted to know what the results were of her preaching in the desert.

"I'm preparing the path," she said casually. "I am doing my part, and I expect to do it right through to the end. Then, I'll know what the next step is."

"How are you going to know when the time comes to stop?"

Valhalla pointed to the horizon. "We have to make eleven trips through the desert, pass through the same places eleven times and repeat the same things eleven times. That's all I was told to do."

"Your master said that?"

"No, the archangel Michael."

"And what trip is this?"

"This is the tenth."

The Valkyrie put her head on Paulo's shoulder, and they sat in silence for a long time. He had a desire to caress her, put her head in his lap, as she had done for him at the abandoned mine. She was a warrior, but she, too, needed to rest.

He thought about it for some time, but decided against it. And the two returned to the camp.

AS THE DAYS PASSED, PAULO BEGAN TO SUSPECT THAT Valhalla was teaching him everything he needed to know—but that, as Gene had done, she was doing it without directly showing him the path. He began to observe closely what the Valkyries did; he thought he might perceive some clue, some teaching, a new practice. And, when Valhalla called him to go with her at day's end—something she did every day now—he decided that he would discuss things with her.

"There's nothing that prevents you from teaching me directly," he said. "You are not a master. It's not like it is with Gene, or J., or even with me—people who know two Traditions."

"Yes, I am a master. I learned through revelation. You're right that I don't pronounce curses, and I don't participate in covens, nor am I a member of any secret societies. But I know many things that you don't know, because the archangel Michael taught them to me."

"Well, that's why I'm here. To learn."

The two were seated in the sand, leaning against some rocks.

"I need affection," she said. "I really need affection."

Paulo shifted his position, and Valhalla laid her head in his lap. They sat there for some time, looking out at the horizon.

It was Paulo who spoke first. He didn't want to raise the subject, but felt he had to.

"I'm going away soon, you know."

He awaited her reaction. She said nothing.

"I have to learn how to see my angel. I feel as if you have been trying to teach me, but that I'm not seeing it."

"No. My teachings are as clear as the desert sun."

Paulo caressed the hair that covered his lap.

"You have a beautiful wife," Valhalla said.

Paulo understood the comment, and took his hands away.

When he had rejoined Chris that night, he told her what Valhalla had said about her. Chris smiled, but said nothing.

THEY CONTINUED TO TRAVEL WITH THE VALKYRIES.
Even after Valhalla's comment—about the clarity of her
teachings—Paulo continued to pay close attention to everything the Valkyries did. But the routine varied little: travel
along, speak in public places, perform the rituals he already
knew, and move on.

And make love. They made love to men they met along
the way. Usually they were groups on motorcycles, bold
enough to approach the Valkyries. When this happened,
there was a tacit agreement that Valhalla would have the right
to first choice. If she wasn't interested, any of the others could
approach the newcomer.

The men never knew this. They were made to feel that
they were with the woman they had chosen—but the choice
had been made much earlier. By the women.

The Valkyries drank beer and talked of God. They performed sacred rituals, and made love out among the rocks. In the
larger cities, they went to some public place to perform their miracle play—getting those who were in the audience to participate.

At the end, they asked for contributions. Valhalla never
played a role, but she directed everything that was happening.
Afterward, she would pass her kerchief around, and she
always received money.

Every afternoon, before Valhalla called Paulo to walk
with her in the desert, he and Chris practiced their channeling and talked with their angels. Although the channel was

not yet completely opened, they felt the presence of constant protection, of love and peace. They heard phrases that made little sense, they had some intuitions, and many times the only sensation was one of joy—nothing more. But they knew they were speaking to their angels, and that the angels were happy at this.

Yes, the angels were happy, because they had been contacted again. Any person who resolved to speak with them would discover that it was not the first time. They had already conversed with them when they were children—the angels had appeared in the form of "secret friends," and had been their companions in long conversations and in play, protecting them from evil and from danger.

And every child had spoken with their guardian angel— until that day when their parents noticed that the child was talking to people who "didn't exist." Then they became intrigued, blamed it on excessive childish imagination, consulted with educators and psychologists, and came to the conclusion that the child should give up that sort of behavior.

The parents always insisted on telling their children that their secret friends didn't exist—perhaps because they had forgotten that they too had spoken to their angel at one time. Or, who knows, perhaps they thought they lived in a world where there was no longer any place for angels. Disenchanted, the angels had returned to God's side, knowing that they could no longer impose their presence.

But a new world was beginning. The angels knew where the gates to Paradise were, and they would conduct all who believed in them to those gates. Perhaps they needn't even believe—it was enough that they *needed* angels, and the angels would return gladly.

PAULO SPENT HIS NIGHTS TRYING TO UNDERSTAND WHY
Valhalla was doing as she did—putting things off.

Chris knew the answer. And the Valkyries knew the
answer, as well—even though none of them said anything
about it.

Chris was waiting for the blow to fall. Sooner or later it
was going to happen. That's why Valhalla had not left them,
had not taught them what else they needed to know about
meeting with their angel.

ONE AFTERNOON, IMMENSE MOUNTAIN FORMATIONS BEGAN to appear off to the right side of the road as they drove. Soon, to the left, mountains and canyons could be seen, and a gigantic salt flat, gleaming in the sun, extended from one side to the other.

They had arrived at Death Valley.

The Valkyries made camp close to Furnace Creek—the only place for miles around where there was water. Chris and Paulo decided to stay with the group, because the only hotel for miles was filled.

That night, the entire group sat around the campfire, chatting about men and motorcycles, and—for the first time in many days—angels. As they always did before sleeping, the Valkyries knotted together their kerchiefs, held the long cord that was formed, and once again repeated the psalm that sang of the rivers of Babylon and of the harps hanging in the willow trees. They could never forget that they were warriors.

When the ritual was over, silence fell over the encampment, and everyone made their sleeping arrangements. Except Valhalla.

She walked some distance from the camp, and gazed for a long time at the moon. She asked the archangel Michael to continue to appear to her, to continue to provide her with valuable advice, and to help her to maintain a firm hand.

"You won in your battles with the other angels," she prayed. "Teach me to win. That I not disperse this flock of eight people, so that one day we might be thousands, millions. Forgive my errors, and fill my heart with enthusiasm. Grant me the strength to be both man and woman, both hard and soft.

"May my word be your lance.

"May my love be your scale."

She made the sign of the cross, and fell silent, listening to the howl of a coyote in the distance. She was wakeful, and began to think back on her life. She remembered when she had been just an employee at the Chase Manhattan Bank, and when her life amounted to nothing more than her husband and her two children.

"Then I saw my angel," she said to the silent desert. "The angel appeared to me, enveloped in light, and asked that I take on this mission. I was not forced, there were no threats, nor any promise of reward. My angel simply asked."

She had left the next day, and went straight to the Mojave Desert. She began preaching alone, speaking of the open gates to Paradise. Her husband divorced her and won custody of the children. She didn't really understand clearly why she had accepted this mission, but every time she wept out of pain and solitude, her angel told her stories of other women who had accepted messages from God: the Virgin Mary, Saint Theresa, and Joan of Arc. The angel said that all the world needed was an example. People who were capable of following their dreams and of fighting for their ideas.

She lived for almost a year outside Las Vegas. She exhausted the little money she had been able to pull together, went hungry, and slept outdoors. Until one day, a poem came into her hands.

The poem told the story of a saint, Maria Egipciaca. She was traveling to Jerusalem, and had no money to pay for her passage across a river. The boatman, eyeing the attractive woman, suggested to her that, although she had no money, she did have her body. Maria Egipciaca surrendered herself to the boatman. When she arrived at Jerusalem, an angel appeared and blessed her for what she had done. And, although today almost no one remembers her, she was canonized by the church following her death.

Valhalla interpreted the story as a sign. She preached in God's name during the day, and twice a week went to the casinos, became the lover of wealthy men, and was able to put together some money. She never asked her angel whether she was doing the right thing—and her angel said nothing.

Little by little, led by the invisible hands of other angels, her companions began to arrive.

"One more trip," she said again, aloud, to the silent desert. "Only one more trip to complete my mission, and then I can get back to the world. I have no idea what awaits me, but I want to get back. I need love, affection. I need someone who can protect me here on earth, just as my angel protects me in heaven. I have done my part; I have no regrets, even though it was awfully hard."

She made the sign of the cross again, and returned to the encampment.

SHE SAW THAT THE BRAZILIAN COUPLE WAS STILL SEATED by the campfire, gazing at the flames.

"How many days until your fortieth?" she asked Paulo.

"Eleven."

"Well then, tomorrow night, at ten o'clock, in Golden Canyon, I will make you accept forgiveness. The Ritual That Demolishes Rituals."

Paulo was astonished. She was right! The answer had been under his nose the whole time!

"Using what?" he asked.

"Using hatred," Valhalla answered.

"That's fine," he said, trying to conceal his surprise. But Valhalla knew that Paulo had never used hatred in the Ritual That Demolishes Rituals.

She left the couple and went to where Rotha, the youngest of the Valkyries, was sleeping. She affectionately caressed the girl's face to awaken her—Rotha might have been making contact with the angels that appear in one's sleep, and Valhalla didn't want to interrupt the conversation. Rotha finally opened her eyes.

"Tomorrow night, you are going to learn how to accept forgiveness," Valhalla said. "And then you will be able to see your angel."

"But I'm already a Valkyrie."

"Of course. And even if you are not able to see your angel, you will still be a Valkyrie."

Rotha smiled. She was twenty-three, and was proud to be roaming the desert with Valhalla.

"Don't wear your leather outfit tomorrow. Not from the moment the sun rises until the end of the Ritual That Demolishes Rituals."

She embraced her with great affection. "Go back to sleep," she said.

Paulo and Chris continued to sit by the fire for another half hour. Then they arranged some of their clothing as pillows, and prepared to sleep. They had thought about purchasing sleeping bags at every large city they had passed through, but they couldn't bring themselves to shop around. More than anything, they always hoped to find a hotel somewhere. So, when it was necessary to camp out with the Valkyries, they either had to sleep in the car or near the fire. Their hair had already been scorched several times by blowing sparks—but nothing any more serious had happened until now.

"What did she mean?" Chris asked as they lay there.

"Nothing important." He had had a couple of beers, and was sleepy.

But Chris pressed the matter. She wanted an answer.

"Everything in life is a ritual," Paulo said. "For witches as much as for those who have never heard of witchcraft. Both are always trying to perform their rituals to perfection."

Chris knew that those on the magical path had their rituals. And she understood, as well, that there were rituals in everyday life—marriages, baptisms, graduations.

"No, no. I'm not talking about those obvious rituals," he went on impatiently. He wanted to sleep, but she pretended not to have sensed his irritation. "I'm saying that everything is a ritual. Just as a mass is a great ritual, composed of various parts, the everyday experience of any person is, also.

"A carefully elaborate ritual that the person tries to perform precisely, because he or she is afraid that—if any part is left out—everything will go wrong. The name of that ritual is *Routine*."

He decided to sit up. He was groggy because of the beers he had drunk, and if he continued to lie down, he would be unable to complete his explanation.

"When we are young, we don't take anything too seriously. But slowly, this set of daily rituals becomes solidified, and takes us over. Once things have begun to go along pretty much as we imagined they would, we don't dare risk altering the ritual. We like to complain, but we are reassured by the fact that each day is more or less like every other. At least there is no unexpected danger.

"That way, we are able to avoid any inner or outer growth, except for the kinds that are provided for within the ritual: so many children, such and such a kind of promotion, this and that kind of financial success. When the ritual becomes consolidated, the person becomes a slave."

"Does that happen sometimes with those on the path?"

"Of course. They use the ritual to make contact with the invisible world, to destroy the second mind, and to enter into the Extraordinary. But, for us too, the terrain we conquer becomes familiar. And we feel the need to seek out new territories. But any magus is fearful of changing the ritual. It's a fear of the unknown, or a fear that other rituals won't function as well—but it is an irrational fear, a strong one, that never disappears without some help."

"And what is the Ritual That Demolishes Rituals?"

"Since a magus is unable to change their rituals, the Tradition decides to change the magus. It's a kind of Sacred Theater in which the magus has to play a different character."

He lay down again, turned on his side, and pretended to sleep. Chris might ask for further explanations. She might want to know why Valhalla had mentioned hatred.

Negative emotions were never invoked in the sacred theater. On the contrary, people who participated in that kind of theater tried to work with the good, and to assume characters that were strong, enlightened. That way, they were able to convince themselves that they were better people than they had thought, and—when they believed that—their lives changed.

To work with negative emotions would mean the same thing. He would wind up convincing himself that he was worse than he had imagined.

THEY SPENT THE AFTERNOON OF THE FOLLOWING DAY
exploring Golden Canyon, a series of ravines with tortuous
curves and walls about twenty feet high. At the moment that
the sun set, while they were doing their channeling exercise,
they saw how the place had acquired its name: The brilliant
minerals embedded in the rock reflected the rays of the sun,
causing the walls to appear to be carved out of gold.

"Tonight there will be a full moon," Paulo said.

They had already seen the full desert moon, and it was an
extraordinary spectacle.

"I awoke today thinking about a passage in the Bible," he
continued. "It's from Solomon: 'It is good that you retain
this, and that you not take away your hand from it; for whoever fears the Lord will emerge from everything unscathed.'"

"A strange message," Chris said.

"Very strange."

"My angel is speaking to me more and more," she told him.
"I'm beginning to understand the words. I understand perfectly
well what you were talking about in the mine, because I never
believed that this communication with my angel could happen."

That made Paulo feel pleased. And together they contemplated afternoon's end. This time, Valhalla had not
appeared for their walk in the desert.

The glistening stones they had seen that afternoon were
no longer apparent. The moon cast a strange, phantasmagor-
ical light into the ravine. They could hear their own footsteps

in the sand, as they walked along in silence, alert to any sound they might hear. They didn't know where the Valkyries were meeting.

They came almost to the end point, where the fissure widened to form a small clearing. No sign of them.

Chris broke the silence. "Maybe they decided against it."

She knew that Valhalla was going to prolong the game as long as possible. But Chris wanted it to be over.

"The animals are on the prowl. I'm afraid of the snakes," she said. "Let's go back."

But Paulo was looking upward.

"Look," he said. "They haven't decided against it."

Chris followed his gaze. At the top of the rocks that formed the right wall of the ravine, the figure of a woman was looking down at them.

She felt a shiver.

The figure of another woman appeared. And another. Chris went to the middle of the clearing; she could see three more women on the other side.

Two were missing.

"WELCOME TO THE THEATER!" VALHALLA'S VOICE ECHOED from the stone walls. "The audience is already here, and they await the spectacle!"

That was how Valhalla had always begun her plays in the city parks.

But I'm not part of the spectacle, Chris thought. *Maybe I should climb up there with them.*

"Here, the price of admission is paid upon leaving," the voice continued, repeating what was always said in the city squares. "It may be a high price, or we might return what is paid. Do you want to take the risk?"

"Yes, I do," Paulo answered.

"What is all this?" Chris suddenly shouted. "Why such dramatics, why so much ritual, why all of this just to see an angel? Isn't it enough to speak with the angel? Why don't you do as everyone else does: simplify the way we make contact with God and with what is sacred in this world?"

There was no response. Paulo felt that Chris was ruining everything.

"The Ritual That Demolishes Rituals," said one of the Valkyries from high in the rocks.

"Silence!" Valhalla shouted. "The audience gets to speak only when this is over! Applaud or boo—but pay the admission!"

Valhalla finally appeared. She wore her kerchief knotted around her forehead, Indian-style. She usually wore it that way when she was saying her prayers at day's end. It was her crown.

She brought with her a barefoot girl, wearing Bermudas and blouse. When they had come closer, and the moonlight illuminated their faces, Chris saw that it was one of the Valkyries—the youngest of the group. Without her leather outfit and her aggressive air, she seemed only a child.

Valhalla placed her in front of Paulo, and traced a large square around them. At each of its corners, she stopped and spoke a few words. Paulo and Rotha repeated the words in Latin—the young woman made several errors, and had to begin again.

She doesn't even know what she's saying, Chris thought. Neither the square nor the words were a part of what usually happened at the performances in the city.

When Valhalla had completed the inscription of the square, she asked that the two approach her. They remained within the square, while she stood outside.

Valhalla turned to Paulo, looked deep into his eyes, and handed him the long leather belt she usually wore around her waist.

"Warrior, you are imprisoned within your destiny by the power of these lines and of these sacred names. Warrior, victorious in battle, you are now in your castle, and you will receive your reward."

In his mind, Paulo created the walls of the castle. From that moment on, the ravine, the Valkyries, Chris, Valhalla, and everything else ceased to be of importance.

He was an actor in the sacred theater. The Ritual That Demolishes Rituals.

"Prisoner," Valhalla said to the girl, "your defeat has been humiliating. You were unable to defend your army with honor. The Valkyries will come down from heaven to recover your body when you are dead. But until then, you will receive the punishment that the loser deserves."

With an abrupt gesture, she tore open the girl's blouse.

"Let the spectacle begin! This, oh warrior, is your trophy!"

He seized the girl violently. She fell awkwardly, cutting her chin, and it bled.

Paulo knelt at her side. In his hand, he clutched Valhalla's belt, and it seemed to have an energy of its own. It frightened him, and for a few moments he left the imaginary walls of the castle and returned to the ravine.

"She's really hurt," Paulo said. "She needs some help."

"Warrior, that is your trophy!" Valhalla repeated, stepping away. "The woman who knows the secret you are after. Extract that secret from her, or give it up forever."

"Not for ourselves, Lord, not for ourselves, but for the glory of your name," he said in a low voice, repeating the motto of the Templars. He had to make a quick decision. He recalled the

time when he believed in nothing, thinking all of this was simply dramatics—but even then, things were transformed, and the truth emerged.

He was faced with the Ritual That Demolishes Rituals. A sacred moment in the life of a magus.

"Sed nomini Tuo de Gloriam," he said again. And in the moment that followed, he dressed himself in the role suggested by Valhalla. The Ritual That Demolishes Rituals began to unfold. Nothing else was important—only that unknown path, that frightened woman at his feet, and a secret that had to be won from her. He strode around his victim, and thought of those times when morality was different—when taking possession of a woman was a rule of combat. Men had risked their lives in war for gold and women.

"I won!" he screamed at the girl. "And you lost!"

He knelt and seized her by the hair. Her eyes stared into his.

"It is we who will win," the girl said.

He threw her violently to the ground again.

"The rule of victory is to win."

"All of you think you won," the prisoner continued. "You won only a battle. It is we who will win the war."

Who was this woman who dared to speak to him this way? She had a lovely body—but that could wait. He had to learn the secret he had sought for so long.

"Teach me how to see my angel," he said, trying to keep his voice calm. "Then you will be set free."

"I am free."

"No. You don't know the rules of victory," he said. "That's why we defeated all of you."

The woman seemed to become confused. "Tell me about those rules," she said. "And I will tell you the secret about your angel."

The prisoner was making a trade. He could torture her, destroy her. There she was, fallen at his feet—yet she was proposing a trade. Perhaps she wouldn't confess under torture. Better to make the trade. He would tell her about the five rules of victory, since she was never going to leave there alive.

"The morality rule: You have to fight on the side that is in the right, and that's why we won. The weather rule: A war in the rain is different from a war in the sun; a battle in the winter is different from a battle in the summer."

He could fool her now. But he wasn't able to invent false rules on the spot. The woman would notice his hesitancy.

"The space rule," he continued. "A war in a ravine is different from a war in the field. The choice rule: The warrior knows how to choose who should give advice, and who will remain at his side in combat. A chieftain cannot be surrounded by cowards or traitors."

He thought for a moment about whether he should continue. But he had already told her four of the rules.

"The strategy rule," he said finally. "The way in which the battle is planned."

That was all of it. The girl's eyes gleamed.

"Now tell me about the angels."

She looked at him, saying nothing. She had learned the formula, even though it was too late. Those valiant warriors never lost a battle—and legend had it that they used five rules of victory. Now she knew what they were.

She knew it would do her no good, but at least she could die in peace. She deserved the punishment she was to receive.

"Tell me about the angels," the warrior said again.

"No! I won't tell you about the angels."

The warrior's eyes changed, and she was delighted. He would show no mercy. The only thing that frightened her was that the warrior might be governed by the rule of morality, and spare her life. She wasn't deserving of that. She was guilty—dozens, hundreds of sins accumulated during her short life. She had disappointed her parents, disappointed men who had grown close to her. Deceived the warriors who had fought at her side. She had allowed herself to be taken prisoner—she was weak. She deserved to be punished.

"Hatred!" they heard a distant woman's voice say. "The secret of the ritual is hatred!"

"We made a trade," the warrior repeated, and now his voice was as cold as steel. "I lived up to my side."

"You are not going to let me leave alive," she said. "But at least I got what I wanted. Even though it's of no use to me."

"Hatred!" The voice of the woman was beginning to

have an effect on him. He was allowing his worst feelings to surface. Hatred was permeating the warrior's heart.

"You are going to suffer." he said. "The worst tortures anyone has ever experienced."

"I will suffer."

"I deserve this," she thought. She deserved the pain and the punishment. She deserved death. Ever since she was a child, she had refused to fight—she didn't believe that she was capable of it. She accepted everything from others, suffered in silence the injustices to which she fell victim. She wanted everyone to see that she was a good girl. That she was sensitive in her heart, and able to help everyone. She wanted to be liked at any cost. God had given her a good life, and she had not been able to make use of it. Instead, she begged that others love her, lived her life as others wanted her to, all in order to show that she was kindhearted and able to please everyone.

She had been unfair to God, had thrown her life away. Now she needed an executioner who would dispatch her quickly to hell.

The warrior felt the belt becoming alive in his hand. For a moment, his eyes met those of his prisoner.

He was waiting for her to change her mind, beg his forgiveness. Instead, the prisoner winced as she awaited the blow.

Suddenly, everything disappeared except his rage at having been tricked by his prisoner. The hatred came in waves, and he was beginning to see how capable he was of cruelty. He had always been wrong, he had always allowed his heart to give in at the very moment when he should have meted out justice. He had always forgiven—not because he was a good person, but because he was a coward. He was afraid that he couldn't see such things through to the end.

Valhalla looked at Chris, and Chris returned her stare. The moonlight prevented each from seeing clearly into the eyes of the other. And that was a good thing, because each was afraid to reveal what she was feeling.

"For God's sake!" the prisoner screamed again, before the blow was delivered.

The warrior halted his stroke in midair.

But the enemy had arrived.

"Enough," said Valhalla. "That's enough."

Paulo's eyes were glazed. He grabbed Valhalla by the shoulders.

"I feel this hatred!" he shouted. "I'm not making it up! I've let some demons loose that I wasn't even aware of!"

Valhalla took the belt from his hand, and went to see whether Rotha was injured.

She was crying, her head between her knees.

"It was all true," she said, embracing Valhalla. "I provoked him, and I used him as my instrument of punishment. I wanted him to destroy me, to put me to death. My parents blamed me, my brothers and sisters blamed me. All I've ever done in life was wrong."

"Go and put on another blouse," said Valhalla.

Rotha stood up, trying to arrange her torn clothing.

"I want to stay this way," she said.

Valhalla hesitated for a moment, but said nothing. She walked to the wall of the canyon and began to climb. At the top, she was surrounded by three Valkyries, and she gave a signal that the others climb up, as well.

Chris, Rotha, and Paulo climbed the wall in silence. The moonlight showed them the way; with the many handholds in the rocks, it was not a difficult ascent. At the top, they could look out at a vast plain riven by arroyos.

Valhalla told Paulo and the girl to come together again, face to face, embracing.

"Did I hurt you?" Paulo asked. He was horrified with himself.

Rotha shook her head. She was ashamed—she would never succeed at becoming a woman like those who surrounded her. She was too weak.

Valhalla knotted together the kerchiefs of two of the Valkyries. She slipped them through the belt loops of the man and woman, binding them to each other. From where she stood, Chris could see that the moon formed a halo around the couple. It would have been a beautiful scene—if it were not for all that had happened. If that man and woman were not so distant from each other—or so close.

"I am unworthy of seeing my angel," Rotha said to Valhalla. "I am weak, and my heart is filled with shame."

"I am unworthy of seeing my angel," Paulo said, so that all could hear. "I have hatred in my heart."

"I have loved many," Rotha said. "But spurned true love."

"I have nourished hatred for years, and avenged myself over things that were unimportant," Paulo continued. "I was always forgiven by my friends, but never learned how to forgive them in return."

Valhalla turned to face the moon.

"We are here, archangel. The Lord's will be done. Our inheritance is hatred and fear, humiliation and shame. The Lord's will be done.

"Why was it not enough simply to close the gates to Paradise? Did you also have to cause us to carry hell in our hearts? But, if that is the will of the Lord, you must know that all of humanity has been doing his will for generations and generations."

Then Valhalla began to stride in circles around the couple, chanting.

"THIS IS THE PREFACE, THE SALUTATION.

"Praised be Our Lord Jesus Christ, forever may he be praised.

"Guilty warriors are speaking to You.

"Those who have always used the best weapons they have—against themselves.

"Those who deem themselves unworthy of blessings. Those who believe that happiness is not for them. Those who suffer more greatly than others do.

"Those who arrived at the gates of freedom, gazed at paradise, and said to themselves: 'We should not enter. We are not deserving.' They are speaking to You.

"Those who one day experienced the judgment of others, and concluded that most of them were right. They are speaking to You.

"Those who judge and condemn themselves. They are speaking to You."

ONE OF THE VALKYRIES HANDED THE BELT TO VALHALLA, and she raised it toward heaven.

"This is the first element: Air.

"Here is the belt. If we are that way, punish us.

"Punish us because we are different. Because we have dared to dream, and to believe in those things no one else any longer believes in.

"Punish us because we challenged what exists, what everyone else accepts, what most others want to remain unchanged.

"Punish us because we speak of faith, and we feel hopeless. We speak of love, but we receive neither the affection nor the comfort we feel we deserve. We speak of freedom, and we are prisoners to our own guilt.

"Lord, even were I to raise this belt high, high enough to touch the stars, I would not touch your hand.

"Because your hand covers our heads. And it caresses us, and you say to us: 'Suffer no more. I have already suffered enough.'

"You say to us: 'Like you, I dreamed, and I believed in a new world. I spoke of love, and at the same time, asked our Father to end my ordeal. I challenged what was. What the majority cared not to change. I thought I was wrong when I performed my first miracle: changing water to wine, simply to enliven a party. I felt the hard stare of others, and I shouted, "Father, Father, why have you forsaken me?"'

"'They have already used the belt on me. You need suffer no more.'"

VALHALLA THREW THE BELT TO THE GROUND, AND scattered sand to the wind.

"This is the second element: Earth.

"We are a part of this world, Lord. And this world is filled with our fears.

"We will write our sins in the sand, and it will be the desert wind's task to scatter them.

"Keep our hands strong, keep us from ceasing to struggle, even though we judge ourselves unworthy of going into battle.

"Make use of our lives, nourish our dreams. If we are made of the Earth, the Earth is also made of us. Everything is only one thing.

"Teach us and use us. We are forever yours.

"The Law was reduced to one commandment: 'Love your neighbor as yourself.'

"If we love, the world changes. The light of love scatters the darkness of guilt.

"Keep us strong in love. Make us accept for ourselves the love of God.

"Show us our love for ourselves.

"Require us to seek out the love of others. Even with fear of rejection, of severe glances, of the hardness of heart of some—do not permit us ever to give up our quest for love."

ONE OF THE VALKYRIES HELD OUT A TORCH TO VALHALLA.
She lit it, and held up the blazing torch to heaven

"This is the third element: Fire.

"You say, Lord: 'I came to set fire to the Earth. And I am watchful that the fire grow.'

"May the fire of love grow in our hearts.

"May the fire of transformation glow in our movements.

"May the fire of purification burn away our sins.

"May the fire of justice guide our steps.

"May the fire of wisdom illuminate our path.

"May the fire that spreads over the Earth never be extinguished. It has returned, and we carry it within us.

"Prior generations passed on their sins to succeeding ones. Thus has it been, down to our fathers.

"Now, though, we will pass forward the torch of your fire.

"We are warriors of the light, this light that we carry with pride.

"The fire that, when kindled for the first time, showed us our faults and our sins. We were surprised and frightened, and we felt ourselves to be incapable.

"But it was the fire of love. And it consumed what was bad in us when we accepted it.

"It showed us that we are neither better nor worse than those who frowned at us.

"And for this we accept forgiveness. There is no more guilt, and we can return to paradise. And we will bring with us the fire that will burn on earth."

VALHALLA INSERTED THE TORCH INTO A CREVICE IN THE rocks. Then she opened her canteen and spilled a few drops of water on Paulo's and Rotha's heads.

"This is the fourth element: Water.

"You said: 'Whoever drinks of this water will never thirst.'

"Well then, we are drinking this water. We wash away our sins, for love of the transformation that is going to shake the Earth.

"We will hear what the angels say, we will be messengers of their words.

"We will do battle with the best weapons and the speediest of horses.

"The gates are open. We are worthy to enter."

"Lord Jesus Christ, who said to his apostles, 'My peace I leave you, my peace I give you,' do not look at our sins, but at the faith that animates your assembly."

Chris knew that passage. It was similar to one used in the Catholic service.

"Lamb of God, who takes away the sins of the world, have pity on us," Valhalla concluded, untying the kerchiefs that joined Paulo and Rotha.

"You are free."

Then Valhalla approached Paulo.

The sting, thought Chris. *Now comes the serpent's sting. It's the payment. She's in love. If the Valkyrie tells him what the price is, he will pay with pleasure. And I won't be able to say a thing—because I'm just an ordinary woman, and I know nothing about the laws in the world of angels. None of them knows that I have already died many times here in the desert, and been reborn so many times, as well. They don't know that I have been speaking to my angel, and that my soul has grown. They're used to me, and they know how I think. I love him. She is only enamored.*

"Now, it's you and me, Valkyrie! The Ritual That Demolishes Rituals!"

Chris's scream echoed out over the sinister desert, bathed in the light of the moon.

Valhalla was expecting the scream. She had already dealt with guilt, and knew that what she wanted was no crime.

Only a caprice. She was entitled to cultivate her caprices—her angel had taught her that such things took no one away from God, or from the sacred task each person had to perform in their life.

She remembered the first time she had seen Chris, at the luncheonette. A shiver had coursed through her body, and strange intuitions—intuitions she was unable to understand—had taken hold of her. *The same thing must have happened to her,* she thought.

Paulo? She had completed her mission with him. And, although he didn't know it, the price she had charged was high—as they had traveled through the desert, she had learned many rituals that J. used only with his disciples. He had told her everything.

She also desired him as a man. Not for what he was, but for what he knew. A caprice, and her angel forgave capriciousness.

She looked again at Chris, and thought, *This is my tenth round. I too need to change. This woman is an instrument of the angels.*

Never taking her eyes from Chris, the Valkyrie said, "The Ritual That Demolishes Rituals. May God tell us what our characters should be!"

She had accepted the challenge. Her moment for growth had arrived.

The two women began to walk around the circumference of an imaginary circle, like cowboys of the old West before a gunfight. Not a sound could be heard—it was as if time had stopped.

The other Valkyries understood what was happening because they were all women, accustomed to fighting for love. And they would do so through to the ultimate consequences, using every trick and artifice. They would do so for love, the justification for their lives and their dreams.

Chris's character began to emerge. She donned the leather outfit, and tied the kerchief around her head. Between her breasts shone the medallion of the archangel Michael. She had dressed herself as a strong character, as the woman she admired and would like to be: She was Valhalla.

Chris gestured with her head, and the two stood still. Valhalla felt as though she were standing before a mirror.

Looking at Chris, she could see herself. She knew the arts of war by heart, but had forgotten the lessons of love. She knew the five rules of victory, and had slept with every man she desired, but she had forgotten the art of love.

She regarded herself as reflected by this other person; she had enough power to defeat her. But her own character was emerging, taking form, and this character, although it was also possessed of sufficient power, was not used to this type of battle.

She had transformed herself into a woman in love, who marched with her man, carrying his sword when necessary, and protecting him from all danger. She was a strong woman, although she appeared to be a weak one. She was a person who walked the path of love, regarding it as the only possible road to wisdom. A path where mysteries were revealed through surrender and forgiveness. She was seeing it with such clarity!

Valhalla had assumed the character of Chris.

And Chris saw herself, reflected in the other.

Chris began to walk slowly toward the precipice. Valhalla did the same, and both approached the abyss. A fall from there would be fatal. But they were women who would recognize no limits. Chris stopped at the very edge, allowing time for Valhalla to do so, as well.

The floor of the desert was thirty feet below, and the moon was thousands of miles above. Between the moon and the desert floor, two women confronted each other.

"He is my man. Don't covet him merely out of capriciousness. You don't love him," Chris said.

Valhalla didn't respond.

"I'm going to take one more step," Chris continued. "I'll survive. I'm a courageous woman."

"I'll do it with you," answered Valhalla.

"Don't. You know about love now. It's a huge world, and you will have to spend the rest of your life trying to understand it."

"I will step back if you will. You know about your strength now. Your horizon now extends to mountains, valleys, and deserts. Your soul has grown large, and will continue to grow. You've discovered your courage, and that's enough."

"Enough, if what I taught you is sufficient to pay the price you were going to charge me."

A long silence. Then the Valkyrie walked over to Chris. And kissed her.

"I accept that as the price," she said. "Thank you for what you have taught me."

Chris removed the watch from her wrist. It was all she had to offer.

"Thank you for what you taught me, too," she said. "Now I know about my strength. I would never have learned about it, though, unless I had come to know a strange, beautiful, powerful woman."

With great tenderness, she placed the watch on Valhalla's wrist.

THE SUN SHONE DOWN ON DEATH VALLEY. THE Valkyries tied their kerchiefs around their faces, leaving only their eyes exposed.

Valhalla approached the couple. "You cannot go with us. You have to talk to your angel."

"There's one thing left," Paulo said. "The bet."

"Bets and pacts are made with the angels. Or with the devils."

"I still don't know how to see my angel," he answered.

"You have already broken a pact. You have already accepted forgiveness. The bet you must make with your angel."

The other women's motorcycles roared. She placed the kerchief across her face, mounted her bike, and turned to Chris.

"I will always be a part of you," Chris said. "And you will always be a part of me."

Valhalla removed a glove and threw it to Chris. Then she revved her engine and the cycles sped away, leaving behind a gigantic cloud of dust.

A MAN AND A WOMAN WERE TRAVELING ACROSS THE desert. On some days, they stopped at cities with thousands of inhabitants, and on others, in towns with just one motel, a restaurant, and a gas station. They kept to themselves—and each afternoon they walked out through the rocks and the sand, feeling as if they had returned to the place where the first star was about to be born. And there, they talked with their angels.

They heard voices, gave advice to one another, and remembered things that seemed to have been completely forgotten sometime in the past.

She had completed her communication with the protection and wisdom of her angel, and was now gazing at the desert sunset.

He sat there, waiting. He wanted his angel to descend and appear in blazing glory. He had done everything right, and now he had simply to wait.

He waited one, two, three hours. He rose only when night had completely fallen; he found his wife, and they returned to the city.

They had dinner, and returned to the hotel. She went to bed and pretended to sleep, while he stared into space.

She got out of bed in the middle of the night, and went to where he sat, asking him to come to bed. She said that she was afraid of sleeping alone because of a bad dream. He lay down beside her, quietly.

"You are already communicating with your angel," he had grown used to saying at such times. "I've heard you speaking when you are channeling. You say things you would never say in ordinary life. Wise things. Your angel is here."

He caressed her, but continued to lie there in silence. She asked herself if his sadness was really because of the angel, or perhaps had to do with some lost love.

This question remained locked inside.

Paulo was thinking about the woman who had left, but that wasn't what made him disconsolate. Time was passing, and soon he would have to return to his own country. He would meet again with the man who had taught him that angels exist.

That man, Paulo imagined, *will tell me that I did enough. That I broke a pact that needed to be broken, that I accepted forgiveness that I should have accepted long ago. Yes, that man will continue to teach me about the path to wisdom and love, and I will get closer and closer to my angel. I'll speak with my angel every day, giving thanks for protection and asking for help. And that man will tell me that it is sufficient.*

Yes, because J. had taught him from the beginning that there are frontiers. That it was necessary to go as far as possible—but that there were certain times when one had to accept the mystery, and understand that each person had his own gift. Some knew how to cure, others possessed words of wisdom, while others conversed with spirits. It was through the sum of such gifts that God could demonstrate his glory, using humankind as his instrument. The gates to paradise would be open to those who had resolved that they would pass through them. The world was in the hands of those who had the courage to dream—and to realize their dreams.

Each to their own talent. Each to their own gift.

But none of that consoled Paulo. He knew that Gene had seen his angel. That Valhalla had seen her angel. That many others had written books and stories and reports telling of their meetings with their angels.

And he had not been able to see his own.

IN SIX MORE DAYS, THEY WOULD HAVE TO LEAVE THE desert. They stopped in a small city called Ajo, where most of the inhabitants were elderly. It was a place that had known its moments of glory—when the mine there had brought jobs, prosperity, and hope to the inhabitants. But, for some reason—unknown to any of them—the company had sold its houses to the employees and closed the mine.

Paulo and Chris sat in a restaurant, drinking coffee and waiting for the cool evening to arrive. An old woman asked if she could sit with them.

"All of our children have gone away," she told them. "No one is left except the old-timers. Some day, the entire city will disappear, and all our work, everything we built, will no longer mean a thing."

It had been a long time since anyone had even passed through the place. The old woman was happy to have some-one to talk to.

"People come here, build, and hope that what they are doing is important," she continued. "But overnight, they find that they are demanding more of the Earth than it has to give. So, they abandon everything and move on, without thinking about the fact that they have involved others in their dream—others who, weaker than they, have to stay behind. Like with the ghost towns out there in the desert."

Maybe that's what's happening to me, Paulo thought. *I brought myself here, and I've abandoned myself.*

He recalled that once an animal trainer had told him how he was able to keep his elephants under control. The animals, as infants, were bound by chains to a log. They would try to escape, but could not. They tried throughout their entire infancy, but the log was stronger than they were.

So they became accustomed to captivity. And when they were huge and strong, all the trainer had to do was place the chain around one of their legs and anchor it anywhere—even to a twig—and they would not attempt to escape. They were prisoners of their past.

The long hours of daylight seemed to have no end. The sky caught fire, the Earth baked, and they had to wait, wait, wait—until the color of the desert changed again to softer tones of pink. That was when he could leave the city, try his channeling, and once again await the appearance of his angel.

"Someone once said that the earth produces enough to satisfy needs, but not enough to satisfy greed," the old woman continued.

"Do you believe in angels?" Paulo asked her.

The woman was astonished at the question. But that was all that Paulo wanted to talk about.

"When you're old, and death isn't too far off, you begin to believe in anything," she said. "But I don't know if I believe in angels."

"They exist."

"Have you ever seen one?" There was a mixture of incredulity and hope in her eyes.

"I talk with my guardian angel."

"Does your angel have wings?"

It was the question everyone asked. Yet he had forgotten to ask it of Valhalla.

"I don't know. I haven't seen my angel yet."

The woman considered whether she should get up and leave. The solitude of the desert made some people strange. But maybe this man was joking with her, just passing the time.

She wanted to ask where the couple came from, and what they were doing in a place like Ajo. She hadn't been able to identify their strange accent.

Maybe they're from Mexico, she thought. But they didn't look like Mexicans. She would ask when the opportunity arose.

"I don't know if you two are fooling around with me," she said, "but, as I said, I'm getting close to death. I suppose I could last another five or ten years. Maybe even twenty. But at my age, you certainly realize you're going to die."

"I know that I'm going to die, too," Chris said.

"No, not like an old person does. For you, it's a remote idea. It might happen some day. For us, it's something that could happen tomorrow. That's why many elderly people spend the time remaining to them looking only in one direction: the past. It's not that they're so fond of their memories, but they know that looking in that direction they won't see anything to be feared.

"Very few old people look to the future, and I'm one of them. When we look into the future, we see what it holds for us: death."

Paulo didn't say anything. You can't say anything new about awareness of death to those who practice magic, but he knew the woman would leave the table if she knew that he was a magus.

"That's why I'd like to believe that you both are serious. That angels really exist."

"Death is an angel," Paulo said. "I have seen it twice in this incarnation, but very briefly. There wasn't enough time to see its face. But I know people who have seen, and I know others that were oppressed by Death, and later told me about it. They said that Death has a handsome face, and a gentle touch."

The old woman stared at Paulo. She wanted to believe him.

"Does Death have wings?"

"This angel is made of light," he answered. "When the moment comes, Death assumes the form that is easiest for you to deal with."

The old woman thought about that. Then she stood up.

"I'm not afraid anymore. I have prayed, and asked that

the angel of death have wings when it comes to me. My heart tells me that my wish will be granted."

She kissed them both. It was no longer important to her where they came from.

"It was my angel that sent you both. Thank you so much."

Paulo remembered Gene. He too had been an angel's instrument. Thinking of Gene, Paulo realized that he and Chris had also served as the instruments of an angel.

AT SUNSET, THEY WENT TO A MOUNTAIN NOT FAR FROM AJO. They sat facing the east, waiting for the first star to appear. When that occurred, they would initiate their channeling activity.

They called this process Contemplation of the Angel. It was the first ceremony they had created after the Ritual That Demolishes Rituals had swept the others away.

"I never asked," Chris said as they waited. "Why it is that you want to see your angel?"

"Well, you've already explained to me a number of times that it didn't matter at all to you."

His voice had a sarcastic tone. She pretended not to notice.

"Okay. But it's important for you. Can you tell me why?"

"I've already explained that. The day of our meeting with Valhalla."

"You don't need a miracle," she insisted. "You're just being capricious."

"There's nothing capricious in the spiritual world. Either you accept it, or you don't."

"So? Haven't you accepted this, your world? Or was everything you said a lie?"

She must be thinking of that story in the mine, Paulo thought. It was a difficult question to answer, but he was bound to try.

"I've already witnessed a number of miracles," he began. "Many miracles. You and I have even witnessed some together. We watched J. create openings in the clouds, fill the darkness with light, move objects from one place to another.

"You've seen me read people's minds, cause the wind to blow, perform rituals involving power. I've seen magic function many times in my life—both for evil and for good. I have no doubts about it."

He paused. "But we have also become used to miracles. And we always want to see others. Faith is a difficult conquest, and it requires daily combat in order to be maintained."

It was time for the star to appear, and he had to end his explanation. But Chris interrupted.

"It's been that way with our marriage, too," she said. "And I'm exhausted."

"I don't understand. I'm speaking about the spiritual world."

"The only reason I'm able to understand what you're saying is because I know your love," she said. "We've been together for a long time. But after the first two years of joy and passion, every day began to be a challenge for me. It's been very difficult to keep the flames of our love alive."

She regretted having brought up the subject—but now she was going to see it through.

"Once you told me that the world was divided into the farmers, who love the Earth and the harvest, and the hunters, who love the dark forests and conquest. You said I was a farmer, like J. That I walked the path of wisdom, achieved through contemplation. And you said I was married to a hunter."

Her thoughts were pushing their way out, and she couldn't stop herself. She was afraid the star might appear before she had finished.

"And I am married to a hunter. I know that, and its been very difficult being married to you! You're like Valhalla, like the Valkyries. They never rest. They deal only in the strong emotions of the hunt, of taking risks. Of the darkness of night and the taking of prisoners. At the beginning, I didn't think I'd be able to live with that. I, who was looking for a life like everybody else's, married to a magus! A magus whose world is governed by laws I don't even know—a person who feels he is alive only when he is facing challenges."

She looked into his eyes.

"Isn't J. a much more powerful magus than you are?"

"Much wiser," Paulo answered. "Much more experienced. He follows the path of the farmer, and it is on that path that he finds his power. I'll be able to achieve my power only by following the path of the hunter."

"Well then, why did he accept you as a disciple?"

Paulo laughed. "For the same reason that you chose me as a husband. Because we're different from one another."

"Valhalla, you, and all your friends think only in terms of the Conspiracy. Nothing else is important—you're all fixated on this business of changes, of a new world to come. I believe in that new world, too—but, God, does it have to be this way?"

"What way?"

She thought for a minute. She didn't know exactly what he was getting at. "This way that always involves conspiracies."

"That's *your* word for it."

"But I know it's true. And you confirmed it."

"I said that the gates of paradise are open, for a certain time, to all who desire to enter. But I also said that each person has his or her own path—and only one's angel can say which is the correct one."

Why am I acting this way? What's going on with me? she thought. She remembered the engravings she had seen as a child, of angels leading children to the edge of an abyss. She was surprised at what she had been saying here. She had fought many times with him, but she had never spoken about magic in the way that she was now.

Yet her soul had grown during these forty days in the desert, she had learned about her second mind, she had crossed swords with a powerful woman. She had died many times, and was stronger each time she was reborn.

The hunt actually gave me great pleasure, she thought.

Yes. That's what was driving her crazy. Because, since the day she had challenged Valhalla to the duel, she had had the feeling that she had wasted her entire previous life.

No, she thought. *I can't accept that. I know J. He is a farmer-type, and an enlightened person. I spoke with my angel before Paulo did. I know how to speak to my angel as well as Valhalla does—even though the language is still a bit strange.*

But she was apprehensive. Perhaps she had been wrong in choosing how she wanted to live her life. *I've got to keep talking,* she thought. *I have to convince myself that I didn't make the wrong choice.*

"You need yet another miracle," she said. "And you will always need yet another. You will never be satisfied, and you will never understand that the kingdom of heaven cannot be conquered by force."

God, make his angel appear, because it's so important to him! Make me be wrong, Lord.

"You're not even giving me a chance to talk," he said.

But at that moment, the first star appeared on the horizon.

It was time for channeling.

THEY SAT DOWN, AND, AFTER A BRIEF PERIOD OF RELAXING, began to concentrate on the second mind. Chris couldn't stop thinking about Paulo's last comment—she really hadn't permitted him to talk.

Now it was too late. She had to allow her second mind to recite its boring problems. To voice the same concerns, over and over. Her second mind that night wanted to get at her heart. It was saying she had chosen the wrong path, and had found her true destiny only when she had experimented with the Valhalla character.

It was telling her that it was too late to change, that her life had been a failure, that she would spend the rest of her life following her husband—without experiencing the pleasures of the dark forest and the taking of prisoners.

It was telling her she had chosen the wrong husband—that she would have been better off marrying a farmer-type. It was telling her that Paulo had other women, and that those women were hunter-types that he met on the night of the full moon, and at secret magic rituals. It was telling her that she should leave him, so that he could be happy with a woman who was his equal.

She argued several times—saying that it wasn't important that she knew there were other women, that she wouldn't leave him on that account. Because love isn't logical or rational. But her second mind came back at her—so she decided not to argue. She would just listen quietly until the conversation went silent and died out.

Then a kind of fog began to envelop her thinking. The channeling had begun. An indescribable sensation of peace took hold of her, as if the wings of her angel were covering the entire desert, preventing anything bad from happening. Whenever she did her channeling, she felt a great love for herself and for the universe.

She kept her eyes open, so as not to lose her awareness, but the cathedrals began to appear. They emerged, enveloped in mist, immense churches she had never visited, but that existed somewhere in the world. During her early days of channeling, she'd had only confused impressions, indigenous songs blending with meaningless words; but now her angel was showing her cathedrals. That seemed to make some sort of sense, although she couldn't quite understand it.

In the beginning, they had only been trying to begin a conversation. With each day that passed, she was able to understand her angel better. Soon, there would be a level of communication as clear as the one she enjoyed with anyone who spoke her own language. It was only a matter of time.

THE ALARM ON PAULO'S WATCH SOUNDED. TWENTY MINUTES had passed. The channeling was over.

She looked at him, knowing what was going to happen now. He would sit there without saying a word, sad and disappointed. His angel hadn't appeared. They would return to the small motel in Ajo, and he would take a walk while she tried to sleep.

She waited until he stood, and then stood up, as well. But there was a strange gleam in his eye.

"I will see my angel," he said. "I know I will. I made the bet."

"The bet, you will have to make with your angel," Valhalla had said. She had never said, *"The bet, you will have to make with your angel, when he appears."* Yet, that's what Paulo had understood her to mean. He had waited for an entire week for his angel to appear. He was ready to make any bet, because the angel was the light, and the light was what justified human existence. He trusted in that light, in the same way that, fourteen years earlier, he had doubted the darkness. In contrast with the traitorous experience with the darkness, the light established its rules beforehand—so that whoever accepted them was knowingly committing to love and compassion.

He had already met two of the three conditions, and almost failed with regard to the third—the simplest of them! But his angel's protection had prevailed, and, during the channeling . . . ah, how good it was to have learned to converse with the angels! Now he knew that he would be able to see his angel, because he had met the third condition.

"I broke a pact. I accepted forgiveness. And, today, I made a bet. I have faith, and I believe," he said. "I believe that Valhalla knows the method for seeing one's angel."

Paulo's eyes were shining. There would be no nocturnal walks, no insomnia tonight. He was absolutely certain that he was going to see his angel. Half an hour ago, he had asked for a miracle—but that was no longer important.

So that night it would be Chris's turn to be sleepless, and to walk the deserted streets of Ajo, imploring God to make a miracle, because the man she loved needed to see his angel. Her heart was squeezed more tightly than ever. Perhaps she preferred a Paulo who was in doubt. A Paulo who needed a miracle. A Paulo who appeared to have lost his faith. If his angel appeared, fine; if not, he could always blame Valhalla for having erred in her teaching. That way, he would not have to learn the most bitter lesson that God taught, when he closed the gates to paradise: the lesson of disappointment.

But instead, here was a man who seemed to have bet his life against the certainty that angels could be seen. And his only guarantee was the word of a woman who rode the desert, speaking of new worlds to come.

Perhaps Valhalla had never even seen an angel. Or maybe what worked for her didn't work for others—hadn't Paulo said that? Maybe he hadn't heeded his own words.

Chris's heart grew smaller and smaller as she saw the light in Paulo's eyes.

And at that moment, his entire face began to glow.

"Light!" he screamed. "Light!"

She turned. On the horizon, near where the first star had appeared, three lights shone in the sky.

"Light!" he said again. "The angel!"

Chris had a strong desire to kneel down and give thanks, because her prayer had been answered, and God had sent his army of angels.

Paulo's eyes filled with tears. The miracle had happened. He had made the right bet.

They heard a roar to their left, and another over their heads. Now there were five, six lights gleaming in the sky; the desert was alight.

For a moment she lost her voice. She, too, was seeing his angel! The bursts of sound were becoming stronger and stronger, passing to the left, passing to the right, over their heads, wild thunderbursts that didn't come from the sky, but from behind, from the side—and moved toward where the lights were.

The Valkyries! The true Valkyries, daughters of Wotan, galloping across the sky, carrying their warriors! She blocked her ears in fear.

She saw that Paulo was doing the same—but his eyes appeared to have lost their brilliance.

Immense balls of fire grew on the desert horizon, and they felt the ground shake under their feet. Thunder in the sky and on the Earth.

"Let's go," she said.

"There's no danger," he answered. "They're military planes. Far from here."

But the supersonic fighters broke the sound barrier close to where they stood, with a terrifying sound.

The two clung to each other as they watched the spectacle with fascination and terror. Now there were balls of fire on the horizon, and green lights. There were more than a dozen, falling slowly from the sky, illuminating the entire desert so that no one and nothing could remain hidden.

"It's just a military exercise," he reassured her. "The Air Force. There are a lot of bases around here. I've seen them on the map." Paulo had to shout to make himself heard. "But I wanted to believe they were angels."

They're the instruments of angels, she thought. *Angels of death.*

The yellow brilliance of the bombs falling on the horizon blended with the bright green lights falling slowly by parachute. Everything below was visible, and the planes were unerring as they dropped their mortal loads.

The exercise lasted for half an hour. And, just as suddenly as they had arrived, the planes disappeared, and silence returned to the desert. The last of the green lights came to earth and died. The ground no longer trembled, and they could see the stars again.

Paulo took a deep breath. He closed his eyes, and concentrated: *I won the bet. I'm absolutely sure I won the bet.* His second mind was coming and going, saying no, that it was all in his imagination, that his angel would not show himself. But he dug the nail of his index finger into his thumb until the pain was insupportable; pain always banishes nonsensical thinking.

"I will see my angel," he repeated, as they descended the mountain.

Her heart squeezed again. But she didn't want to allow him to see how she felt. The only way to change the subject quickly was to listen to what her second mind was saying, and to ask Paulo if it made sense.

"I want to ask you something," she said.

"Don't ask me about the miracle. It will happen or it won't. Let's not waste our energy discussing it."

"No, it's not about that."

She hesitated. Paulo was her husband. He knew her better than anyone did. She was fearful of his response, because what he said carried more weight than what others said. But she resolved that she would ask the question anyway; she couldn't stand keeping it inside.

Do you think I chose wrong?" she asked. "That I've wasted my life sowing seeds, content to watch the crops flourish around me instead of experiencing the strong emotions of the hunt?"

He walked along, looking up at the sky. He was still thinking about his bet, and about the planes.

"Often I look at people like J.," he said. "People like J., who are at peace, and through that peace, find communion with God. I look at you, able to talk with your angel before I was—even though it was I who came here to do that. I watch you sleeping so soundly, while I'm standing at the window, and I ask myself why the miracle I'm waiting so desperately for doesn't happen. And I ask myself: Did I choose the wrong path?"

He turned to her. "What do you think? Did I choose the wrong path?"

Chris took his hand in hers. "No. You would be very unhappy."

"And so would you if you had chosen mine."

"That's a good thing to remember."

BEFORE THE ALARM WENT OFF, HE SAT UP IN BED WITHOUT making a sound.

He looked outside, and it was still dark.

Chris was asleep. For a moment, he thought of waking her, and telling her where he was going. That she should say a prayer for him. But he decided against it. He could tell her everything when he returned. It wasn't as if he were heading for any place dangerous.

He switched on the light in the bathroom, and filled his canteen from the faucet. Then he drank as much water as he could swallow—he had no idea how long he would be out there.

He dressed, grabbed the map, and memorized his route. Then, he got ready to leave.

But he couldn't locate the key to the car. He looked in his pockets, in his knapsack, on the bedside table. He considered lighting the lamp—but no, it might awaken her, and the light from the bathroom was enough. He couldn't spend any more time looking—every minute spent here was a minute less that he could devote to waiting for his angel. Within four hours, the heat of the desert would be unbearable.

Chris hid the key, he thought. She was a different woman now—she was speaking to her angel, and her intuition had increased considerably. Perhaps she had guessed at what his plans were and was frightened.

Why would she be frightened? That night when he had seen her at the precipice with Valhalla, he and Chris had made a sacred agreement; they had promised that never again would they risk their lives in the desert. Several times, the angel of Death had passed close to them, and it wouldn't be smart to keep testing the patience of their guardian angel. Chris knew him well enough to know that he would never fail to keep a promise. That's why he was stealing away before the first rays of the sun were to be seen—to avoid the dangers of the night, and the dangers of the day.

Nevertheless, she was concerned, and had hidden the key.

He went to the bed, having decided to awaken her. And he stopped.

Yes, there was a reason. She wasn't worried about his safety, or about the risks he might take. She was fearful, but it was a different kind of fear—that her husband might be defeated. She knew that Paulo would try something. Only two days remained before they left the desert.

It was a good idea to do what you did, Chris, he thought, laughing to himself. *A defeat such as this would take two years to overcome, and for the whole time you would have to put up with me, spend sleepless nights with me, bear with my bad moods, suffer my frustration along with me. It would be much worse than these days I lived through, before I learned how to make my bet.*

He looked through her things; the key was in the security belt where she kept her passport and her money. Then he remembered his promise about safety—all this may have been a reminder. He had learned that you never go out into the desert without leaving at least some indication of your destination. Even though he knew that he would be back soon, and even knowing that his destination, after all, was not that far away—and that if anything were to happen, he could even return on foot—he decided not to run the risk. After all, he had promised.

He placed the map on the bathroom sink. And he used the can of pressurized shaving foam to make a circle around a location: Glorieta Canyon.

Using the same means, he sprayed a message on the mirror:

I WON'T MAKE ANY MISTAKES.

Then he put on his sneakers, and left.

When he was about to put the key into the ignition, he found he had left his own key there.

She must have had a copy made, he thought. *What did she think was going to happen? That I was going to abandon her in the middle of the desert?*

Then he recalled Gene's strange behavior when he had forgotten the flashlight in the car. Thanks to the matter of the key, Paulo had marked the place where he was heading. His angel was seeing to it that he took all the necessary precautions.

191

The streets of Borrego Springs were deserted. *Just like in the daytime,* he thought to himself. He remembered their first night there, when they had stretched out on the floor of the desert, trying to imagine what their angels would be like. Back then, all he wanted to do was talk to his.

He turned to the left, out of the city, and headed for Glorieta Canyon. The mountains were to his right—the mountains they had descended by car back when they had first arrived. Back then, he thought, and realized it hadn't been all that long ago. Only thirty-eight days.

But, as with Chris, his soul had died many times out there in the desert. He was pursuing a secret that he already knew, and had seen the sun turn into the eyes of death. He had met up with women who appeared to be angels and devils at the same time. He had reentered a darkness he thought he had forgotten. And he had discovered that, although he had spoken so often of Jesus, he had never completely accepted the Savior's forgiveness.

He had reencountered his wife—at the very moment when he believed he had lost her forever. Because (and Chris could never know it) he had fallen in love with Valhalla.

That was when he had learned the difference between infatuation and love. Like conversing with the angels, it was really very simple.

Valhalla was a fantasy. The warrior woman, the huntress. The woman who conversed with angels, and was ready to run any risk in order to surpass her limits. For her, Paulo was the man who wore the ring of the Tradition of the Moon, the magus who knew about the occult mysteries. The adventurer, capable of leaving everything behind to go out in search of angels. Each would always be fascinated by the other—so long as each remained exactly what the other imagined.

That's what infatuation is: the creation of an image of someone, without advising that someone as to what the image is.

But some day, when familiarity revealed the true identity of both, they would discover that behind the Magus and the Valkyrie there was a man and a woman. Each possessing powers, perhaps, each with some precious knowledge, maybe, but—they couldn't ignore the fact—each basically a man and a woman. Each with the agony and the ecstasy, the strength and the weakness of every other human being.

And when either of them demonstrated how they really were, the other would want to flee—because it would mean the end of the world they had created.

He found love on a cliff where two women had tried to stare each other down, with the full moon as a backdrop. And love meant dividing the world with someone. He knew one of the women well, and had shared his universe with her. They had seen the same mountains, and the same trees, although each had seen them differently. She knew his weaknesses, his moments of hatred, of despair. Yet she was there at his side.

They shared the same universe. And although often he had had the feeling that their universe contained no more secrets, he had discovered—that night in Death Valley—that the feeling was wrong.

He stopped the car. Ahead, a ravine pierced the mountain. He had chosen the place based on its name—actually, angels are present at all times and in all places. He got out, drank some more of the water that now he always carried in bottles in the trunk of the car, and fixed the canteen to his belt.

He was still thinking about Chris and Valhalla as he made his way to the ravine. *I think I'll probably be infatuated many more times,* he said to himself. He felt no guilt about it. Infatuation was a good thing. It gave spice to life, and added to its enjoyment.

But it was different from love. Love was worth everything, and couldn't be exchanged for anything.

He stopped at the mouth of the ravine and looked out over the valley. The horizon was shading to crimson. It was the first time he had seen the dawn out in the desert; even when they had slept out in the open, the sun was always up when he awoke.

What a beautiful sight I've been missing, he thought. The peaks of the mountains in the distance were gleaming, and pink streaks were creeping into the valley, coloring the stones and the plants that survived there virtually without water. He gazed at the scene for some time.

He was thinking of a book he had written, in which—at

a certain point—the shepherd, Santiago, climbs to the top of a mountain to look out over the desert. Except for the fact that Paulo was not atop a mountain, he was surprised at the similarity to what he had written about eight months earlier. He had also just realized the significance of the name of the city where he had disembarked in the United States.

Los Angeles. In Spanish: The Angels.

But this wasn't the time to be thinking of the signs he had seen along the way.

"This is your face, my guardian angel," he said aloud. "I see you. You have always been there before me, and never have I recognized you. I hear your voice. Every day I hear it more clearly. I know you exist, because they speak of you in all corners of the earth.

"Perhaps one man, or even an entire society, can be wrong. But all societies and all civilizations, everywhere on the planet, have always spoken of angels. Nowadays, children and the elderly and the prophets are listening. They will continue to speak of angels down through the centuries, because prophets, children, and old people will always exist."

A blue butterfly fluttered about him. It was his angel, responding.

"I broke a pact. I accepted forgiveness."

The butterfly drifted from one side to the other. He had seen numbers of white butterflies in the desert—but this one was blue. His angel was content.

"And I made a bet. That night, up on the mountain, I bet all of my faith in God, in life, in my work, in J. I bet everything I had. I bet that, when I opened my eyes, you would show yourself to me. I placed my entire life on one tray of the scales. I asked that you place your countenance on the other.

"And, when I opened my eyes, the desert was before me. For a few moments, I thought I had lost. But then—ah, how lovely the memory is—then, you spoke."

A streak of light appeared on the horizon. The sun was coming alive.

"Do you remember what you said? You said: 'Look around, this is my face. I am the place where you are. My mantle will cover you with the rays of the sun in daytime, and with the glow of the stars at night.' I heard your voice clearly!

"And then you said: 'Always need me.'"

His heart was content. He would wait for the sun to rise, and look for a long time at the face of his angel. Later, he would tell Chris of his bet. And tell her that seeing one's angel was even easier than speaking with him! One had only to believe that angels exist, only to need the angels. And they would show themselves, as brilliant as the rays of morning. And they would help, performing their task of protection and guidance, so that each generation would speak to the next of their presence—so that they would never be forgotten.

Write something, he heard a voice within him say.

Strange. He wasn't even trying to do his channeling. All he wanted to do was see his angel.

But some being within him was demanding that he write something. He tried to concentrate on the horizon and the desert, but that's all he could manage.

He went to the car and picked up a pen and some paper. He had had some experience with automatic writing, but had never gone deeply into it—J. had said that it wasn't for him. That he should seek out his true gift.

He sat down on the floor of the desert, pen in hand, and tried to relax. Before long, the pen would begin to move itself, would produce some strokes, and then words would follow. In order for this to happen, he had to lose a bit of his awareness, and allow something—a spirit or an angel—to take him over.

He surrendered completely, and accepted his role as instrument. But nothing happened. *Write something,* he heard the voice within him say again.

He was fearful. He wasn't going to be incorporated by some spirit. He was channeling, without meaning to—as if his angel were there, speaking to him. It wasn't automatic writing.

He took a different grip on the pen—now with firmness. The words began to emerge. And he wrote them down, without time even to think of what he was writing:

For Zion's sake, I will not hold my peace.
And for Jerusalem's sake, I will not rest,
Until her righteousness goes forth as brightness,
And her salvation, as a lamp that burns.

This had never happened before. He was *hearing* a voice within him, dictating the words:

You shall be called by a new name,
Which the mouth of the Lord will name.
You shall also be a crown of glory in the hand of the
  Lord,
And a royal diadem in the hand of your God.
You shall no longer be termed Forsaken,
Nor your land anymore be termed Desolate;
But you shall be called Hephzibah,
For the Lord delights in you, and your land shall be
  married.

He tried to converse with the voice. He asked to whom he should say this.

It has already been said, the voice answered. *It is simply being remembered.*

Paulo felt a lump in his throat. It was a miracle, and he gave thanks to God.

The golden globe of the sun was rising above the horizon.

He put down the pad and pen, stood up, and held out his hands in the direction of the light. He asked that all of that energy of hope—hope that a new day brings to millions of people on the face of the earth—would enter through his fingers and repose in his heart. He asked that he might always believe in the new world, in the angels, and in the open gates to paradise. He asked for protection by his angel and the Virgin Mary—for him, for all whom he loved, and for his work.

The butterfly came to him and, responding to a secret sign from his angel, landed on his left hand. He kept absolutely still, because he was in the presence of another miracle: His angel had responded.

He felt the universe stop at that moment: the sun, the butterfly, and the desert there before him.

And in the next moment, the air around him trembled. It wasn't the wind. It was a shock of air—the same as one feels when a car is passed by a bus at high speed.

A shiver of absolute terror ran up his spine.

SOMEONE WAS THERE.

"Do not turn around," he heard the voice say.

His heart was pounding, and he was beginning to feel dizzy. He knew it was fear. A terrible fear. He remained motionless, his arms extended before him, the butterfly poised on his hand.

I'm going to pass out, he thought.

"Do not pass out," the voice said.

He was trying to maintain control of himself, but his hands were cold, and he began to tremble. The butterfly flew away, and he lowered his arms.

"Kneel down," the voice said.

He knelt. He couldn't think. There was nowhere to go.

"Clear the ground,"

He did as the voice ordered. With his hands, he brushed a small area in the sand directly in front of him so that it was smooth. His heart continued to beat rapidly, and he was feeling more and more dizzy. He thought he might even have a heart attack.

"Look at the ground."

An intense light, almost as strong as the morning sun, shone on his left side. He didn't want to look directly at it, and wished only that everything would end quickly. For a moment, he recalled his childhood, when appearances of Our Lady had been described to children. He had passed many sleepless nights as a child, asking God never to order the

Virgin to appear to him—because the prospect was so frightening. Scary.

The same fright that he was experiencing now.

"Look at the ground," the voice insisted.

He looked down at the area he had just swept clear. And that was when the golden arm, as brilliant as the sun, appeared, and began to write in the sand.

"This is my name," the voice said.

The fearful dizziness continued. His heart was beating even faster.

"Believe," he heard the voice say. "The gates are open for a while."

He gathered every bit of strength he had remaining.

"I want to say something," he said aloud. The heat of the sun seemed to be restoring his strength.

He heard nothing. No answer.

An hour later, when Chris arrived—she had awakened the hotel owner, and demanded that he drive her there—he was still looking at the name in the sand.

THE TWO OTHERS WATCHED AS PAULO PREPARED THE cement.

"What a waste of water, out in the middle of the desert," Gene joked.

Chris asked him not to kid around, since her husband was still feeling the impact of his vision.

"I found where the passage came from," Gene said. "It's from Isaiah."

"Why that passage?" Chris asked.

"I have no idea. But I'm going to remember it."

"It speaks about a new world," she continued.

"Maybe that's why," Gene answered. "Maybe that's why."

Paulo called to them.

The three said a Hail Mary. Then Paulo climbed to the top of a boulder, spread the cement, and placed within it the image of Our Lady that he always carried with him.

"There. It's done."

"Maybe the guards will take it away when they find it here," Gene said. "They watch over the desert as if it were a flower garden."

"Maybe," Paulo said. "But the spot will still be marked. It will always be one of my sacred places."

"No," Gene said. "Sacred places are individual places. In this one, a text was dictated. A text that already existed. One that speaks of hope, and had already been forgotten."

Paulo didn't want to think about that now. He was still fearful.

"In this place, the energy of the soul of the world was felt," Gene said. "And it will be felt here forever. It is a place of power."

They gathered up the plastic sheeting in which Paulo had mixed the cement, placed it in the trunk of the car, and left to take Gene back to his old trailer.

"Paulo!" he said when they were saying their good-byes. "I think it would be good for you to know an old saying from the Tradition: *When God wants to drive a person insane, he grants that person's every wish.*"

"Could be," Paulo answered. "But it was worth it."

Epilogue

One afternoon, a year and a half after the angel's appearance, a letter arrived for me in Rio, from Los Angeles. It was from one of my Brazilian readers living in the United States, Rita de Freitas, and was in praise of *The Alchemist*.

On impulse, I wrote to her, asking that she go to a canyon near Borrego Springs to see whether the statue of Our Lady of Aparecida was still there.

After I had mailed the letter, I thought to myself: *That's pretty silly. This woman doesn't even know me. She's just a reader who wanted to say a few kind words, and she'll never do as I've asked. She's not going to get into her car, drive six hours into the desert, and see whether a small statue is still there.*

Just before Christmas in 1989, I received a letter from Rita, from which I have excerpted the following:

There have been some marvelous "coincidences." I had a week off from my job over the Thanksgiving holiday. My boyfriend (Andrea, an Italian musician) and I were planning on getting away to someplace different.

Then your letter arrived. And the place you mentioned was near an Indian reservation. We decided to go . . .

. . . On our third day there, we went to look for the canyon, and found it. It was on Thanksgiving Day. It was interesting, because we were driving very slowly, but saw no sign of the statue. We came to the end of a

canyon, stopped, and began climbing to the top of the cliff there. All we saw
were the footprints of coyotes.

At this point, we concluded that the statue couldn't any longer be
here . . .

As we were returning to the car, we saw some flowers among the rocks.
We stopped the car and got out. We saw some small candles burning, some
golden cloth with a butterfly woven into it, and a straw basket that had been
thrown aside. We decided that must have been the place where the statue had
been placed, but it was no longer there.

What was interesting was the fact that I'm sure none of that was there
when we had first passed by. We took a photograph—enclosed—and went
on our way.

When we were almost at the mouth of the canyon, we saw a woman
dressed in white. Her clothing seemed Arabian—turban, long tunic—and
she was walking in the middle of the road. Very strange—how could a
woman such as this appear out of nowhere, in the middle of the desert?

I was thinking: Could this be the woman who had placed those flowers and lighted the candles? There was no car to be seen, and I wondered
how she could have come there.

But I was so surprised that I couldn't bring myself to talk to her.

I examined the photo Rita had sent: It was exactly where
I had placed the statue.

It was Thanksgiving Day. And I'm certain that angels
were there that day.

I wrote this book in January/February 1992, shortly

after the end of the Third World War—where the battles were much more sophisticated than those fought with conventional arms. According to the Tradition, this war began in the 1950s, with the blockade of Berlin, and ended when the Berlin Wall fell. The victors divided up the defeated empire, as in a conventional war. The only thing that didn't occur was a nuclear holocaust—and this will never happen, because God's Work is too great to be destroyed by human beings.

Now, according to the Tradition, a new war will begin. An even more sophisticated war, survived by no one—because it is through its battles that man's growth will be completed. We will see the two armies—on one side, those who still believe in the human race, and know that our next step involves the growth of individual gifts. On the other side will be those who deny the future. Those who believe that life has a material ending, and—unfortunately—those who, although they have faith, believe that they discovered the path to enlightenment, and want the others to follow it with them.

That's why the angels have returned and must be attended. Only they can show us the way—no one else. We can share our experiences—as I have tried to share mine in this book—but there is no formula for this growth. God has generously made His wisdom and His love available to us, and it is easy, very easy, to find them. One has only to understand channeling—a process so simple that it was difficult for me to recognize and accept. Since the combat will take place for the most part in the astral plane, it will be our guardian angels who will wield the swords and shields, protecting us from danger, and guiding us to victory. But our responsibility is huge, as well: We, at this moment in history, must develop our own powers. We must believe that the universe doesn't end at the walls of our room. We must accept the signs, and follow our heart and our dreams.

We are responsible for everything that happens in this world. We are the warriors of the light. With the strength of our love and of our will, we can change our destiny, as well as the destiny of many others.

The day will come when the problem of hunger can be solved through the miracle of the multiplication of the bread. The day will come when love will be accepted by every heart, and the most terrible of human experiences—solitude, which is worse than hunger—will be banned from the face of the Earth. The day will come when those who knock at the gates will see them open; those who ask will receive; those who weep will be consoled.

For the planet Earth, that day is still a long way off. But for each of us, that day can be tomorrow. One has only to accept a simple fact: Love—of God and of others—shows us the way. Our defects, our dangerous depths, our suppressed hatreds, our moments of weakness and desperation—all are unimportant. If what we want to do is heal ourselves first, so that then we can go in search of our dreams, we will never reach paradise. If, on the other hand, we accept all that is wrong about us—and despite it, believe that we are deserving of a happy life—then we will have thrown open an immense window that will allow Love to enter. Little by little, our defects will disappear, because one who is happy can look at the world only with love—the force that regenerates everything that exists in the Universe.

In *The Brothers Karamazov*, Dostoyevsky tells us the story of the Grand Inquisitor, which I paraphrase here:

During the religious persecutions in Sevilla, when all who did not agree with the Church were thrown into prison, or burned at the stake, Christ returns to earth and mixes in with the multitudes. But the Grand Inquisitor notes his presence, and orders him jailed.

That night, he goes to visit Jesus in his cell. And he asks why Jesus has decided to return at that particular moment. "You are making things difficult for us," the Grand Inquisitor says. "After all, your ideals were lovely, but it is we who are capable of putting them into practice." He argues that, although the Inquisition might be judged in the future to have been severe, it is necessary, and that he is simply doing his job. There is no use talking of peace when man's heart is always at war; nor speaking of a better world when there is so much hatred in man's heart. There was no use in Jesus' having sacrificed himself in the name of the human race, when human beings still feel guilty. "You said that all people are equal, that each has the divine light within, but you forgot that people are insecure, and they need someone to guide them. Don't make our work more difficult than it is. Go away," says the Grand Inquisitor, having laid out all of his brilliant arguments.

When he is finished, there is silence in the cell. Then Jesus comes to the Grand Inquisitor, and kisses him on the cheek.

"You may be right," Jesus says. "But my love is stronger."

We are not alone. The world is changing, and we are a part of the transformation. The angels guide us and protect us. Despite all the injustice in the world, and despite the things that happen to us that we feel we don't deserve, and despite the fact that we sometimes feel incapable of changing what is wrong with people and with the world, and despite all of the Grand Inquisitor's arguments—love is even stronger, and it will help us to grow. Only then will we be able to understand the stars and miracles.

Author's Note

Anyone who has read *The Valkyries* will know that this book is very different from *The Pilgrimage* (previously published as *The Diary of a Magus*), *The Alchemist*, and *Brida*.

It was an extremely difficult book to write. First, because it deals with matters that require sensitivity on the part of the reader. Second, because I have already told this story to many people, and I feared that I might have exhausted my capacity to write it down. This fear remained with me from the first page to the last, but—thank God—it was only a fear.

The third and most important reason: In order to relate the events that took place, I had to reveal details from my personal life—my marriage, my relationships with others, and the fragile distance that separates the magical Tradition to which I belong from the person I am. As is true for any human being, exposing my weaknesses and my private life is not easy.

But—as was made quite clear in *The Pilgrimage*—the path to magic is the path of the common people. One can have a master, follow the esoteric Tradition, and possess the discipline needed to perform rituals; but the spiritual search is made up of many beginnings (thus the searcher is called an "initiate," someone who is always in the act of beginning something), and the only thing that matters—always—is the will to go on.

The Valkyries clearly presents the man that exists behind the magus, and this may disappoint those who are looking for "perfect beings," with their perfect truths regarding everything. But true seekers know that, regardless of our faults and defects, the spiritual path is stronger. God is love, generosity, and forgiveness; if we believe in this, we will never allow our weaknesses to paralyze us.

The events narrated in this book took place between September 5 and October 17, 1988. The sequential order of some of the events has been changed, and in two places I made use of fiction, only so that the reader could better grasp the matter at hand. But all of the essential events are true. The letter quoted in the Epilogue is on file at the Registry of Titles and Documents in Rio de Janeiro under number 478038.

Paulo Coelho

The Fifth Mountain

Translated by Clifford E. Landers

And he said, Verily I say unto you, No prophet is accepted in his own country.

But I tell you of a truth, many widows were in Israel in the days of Elias, when the heaven was shut up three years and six months, when great famine was throughout all the land;

But unto none of them was Elias sent, save unto Zarephath, a city of Sidon, unto a woman that was a widow.

Luke 4:24–26

ΠOTE FROM THE AUTHOR

◆ ◆ ◆

In my book *The Alchemist*, the central thesis lies in a phrase that King Melchizedek says to the shepherd boy Santiago: "When you want something, all the universe conspires in helping you to achieve it."

I believe this with all my heart. However, the act of living one's own destiny includes a series of stages that are far beyond our understanding, whose objective is always to take us back to the path of our Personal Legend—or to make us learn the lessons necessary to fulfill our own destiny. I think I can better illustrate what I am saying by relating an episode in my life.

On August 12, 1979, I went to sleep with a single certainty: at the age of thirty I was successfully making my way to the top of my career as a recording executive. I was working as artistic director for CBS in Brazil, and I had just been invited to the United

States to talk to the owners of the company, who would surely provide me with every opportunity to achieve all that I desired to do in my area. Of course my great dream—to be a writer—had been set aside, but what did that matter? After all, real life was very different from what I had imagined; there was no way to earn a living from literature in Brazil.

That night I made a decision: to abandon my dream. One had to adapt to circumstances and take advantage of opportunities. If my heart protested, I could deceive it by composing song lyrics whenever I wanted, and by doing some writing now and then for some newspaper. Besides, I was convinced that my life had taken a different path, but one no less exciting: a brilliant future awaited me in the world of the music multinationals.

When I woke up, I received a phone call from the president: I had just been fired, without further explanation. Although I knocked on various doors in the next two years, I never found a position again in that field.

When I finished writing *The Fifth Mountain*, I recalled that episode—and other manifestations of the unavoidable in my life. Whenever I thought myself the absolute master of a situation, something would happen to cast me down. I asked myself: why? Can it be that I'm condemned to always come close but never reach the finish line? Can God be so cruel that He would let me see the palm trees on the horizon only to have me die of thirst in the desert?

It took a long time to understand that it wasn't quite like

that. There are things that are brought into our lives to lead us back to the true path of our Personal Legend. Other things arise so we can apply all that we have learned. And, finally, some things come along to *teach* us.

In my book *The Pilgrimage*, I tried to show that these teachings need not be linked to pain and suffering; discipline and attentiveness alone are enough. Although this understanding has become an important blessing in my life, it still did not equip me to transit certain difficult moments that I experienced, even with total discipline and attentiveness.

One example is the case I have cited; I was a serious professional, made every effort to give the best there was in me, and had ideas that even today I consider worthwhile. But the unavoidable happened, at the very moment when I felt most secure and confident. I believe I am not alone in this experience; the unavoidable has touched the life of every human being on the face of the earth. Some have rebounded, others have given up—but all of us have felt the wings of tragedy brushing against us.

Why? To answer this question, I let Elijah lead me through the days and nights of Akbar.

PROLOGVE

❖ ❖ ❖

At the beginning of the year 870 B.C., a nation known as Phoenicia, which the Israelites called Lebanon, had marked almost three centuries of peace. Its inhabitants could take pride in their accomplishments; because they were not politically powerful, they had developed an enviable skill at negotiation as the only means of assuring survival in a world beset by constant war. An alliance made around the year 1000 B.C. with King Solomon of Israel had allowed the modernization of its merchant fleet and the expansion of trade. Since that time, Phoenicia had never stopped growing.

Its navigators had traveled to places as distant as Spain and the Atlantic Ocean, and there are theories—as yet unconfirmed—of their having left inscriptions in northeastern and southern Brazil. They carried glass, cedar, weapons, iron, and ivory. The inhabitants of the large cities such as Sidon, Tyre, and Byblos were familiar with numbers, astronomical calculations, the manufacture of wine, and for almost two hundred years had been using a set of characters for writing, which the Greeks knew as *alphabet*.

At the beginning of the year 870 B.C., a council of war was meeting in a distant place called Nineveh. A group of Assyrian generals had decided to send troops to conquer the nations located along the Mediterranean coast. Phoenicia had been selected as the first country to be invaded.

At the beginning of the year 870 B.C., two men hiding in a stable in Gilead, in Israel, expected to die in the next few hours.

PART I

PART 1

"I HAVE SERVED A LORD WHO NOW ABANDONS ME INTO the hands of my enemies," said Elijah.

"God is God," the Levite replied. "He did not tell Moses whether He was good or evil; He simply said: *I am.* He is everything that exists under the sun—the lightning bolt that destroys a house, and the hand of man that rebuilds it."

Talking was the only way to ward off fear; at any moment, soldiers would open the door to the stable where they were hiding, discover them both, and offer the only choice possible: worship Baal, the Phoenician god, or be executed. They were searching house by house, converting the prophets or executing them.

Perhaps the Levite would convert and escape death. But for Elijah there was no choice: everything was happening through his own fault, and Jezebel wanted his head under all circumstances.

"It was an angel of the Lord who obliged me to speak to King Ahab and warn him that it would not rain so long as Baal was worshiped in Israel," he said, almost in a plea for absolution for having heeded what the angel had told him. "But God acts slowly; when the drought begins to take hold, Princess Jezebel will already have destroyed all who remain loyal to the Lord."

The Levite said nothing. He was reflecting on whether he should convert to Baal or die in the name of the Lord.

"Who is God?" Elijah continued. "Is it He who holds the sword of the soldier, the sword that executes those who will not betray the faith of our patriarchs? Was it He who placed a foreign princess on our country's throne, so that all this misfortune could befall our generation? Does God kill the faithful, the innocent, those who follow the law of Moses?"

The Levite made his decision: he preferred to die. Then he began to laugh, for the idea of death frightened him no longer. He turned to the young prophet beside him and attempted to calm him. "Ask God, since you doubt His decisions," he said. "I have accepted my fate."

"The Lord cannot wish us to be massacred without mercy," insisted Elijah.

"God is all-powerful. If He limited Himself to doing only that which we call good, we could not call Him the Almighty; he would command only one part of the universe, and there would exist someone more powerful than He, watching and judging His acts. In that case, I would worship that more powerful someone."

"If He is all-powerful, why doesn't He spare the suffering of those who love Him? Why doesn't He save them, instead of giving might and glory to His enemies?"

"I don't know," said the Levite. "But a reason exists, and I hope to learn it soon."

"You have no answer to this question."

"No."

The two men fell silent. Elijah felt a cold sweat.

"You are terrified, but I have already accepted my fate," the Levite said. "I am going out, to bring an end to this agony. Each time I hear a scream out there, I suffer, imagining how it will be when my time comes. Since we've been locked in here, I have died a hundredfold, while I could have died just once. If I am to be beheaded, let it be as quickly as possible."

He was right. Elijah had heard the same screams, and he had suffered beyond his ability to withstand.

"I'm going with you. I weary of fighting for a few more hours of life."

He rose and opened the stable door, allowing the sun to enter and expose the two men hiding there.

◆

THE LEVITE took him by the arm, and they began to walk. If not for one then another scream, it would have seemed a normal day in a city like any other—a sun that barely tingled the skin, the breeze coming from a distant ocean to moderate the temperature, the dusty streets, the houses built of a mixture of clay and straw.

"Our souls are prisoners of the terror of death, and the day is beautiful," said the Levite. "Many times before, when I felt at peace with God and the world, the temperature was horrible, the desert wind filled my eyes with sand and did not permit me to see a hand's span before me. Not always does His plan agree with what we are or what we feel, but be assured that He has a reason for all of this."

"I admire your faith."

The Levite looked at the sky, as if reflecting briefly. Then he turned to Elijah. "Do not admire, and do not believe so much; it was a wager I made with myself. I wagered that God exists."

"You're a prophet," answered Elijah. "You too hear voices and know that there is a world beyond this world."

"It could be my imagination."

"You have seen God's signs," Elijah insisted, beginning to feel anxiety at his companion's words.

"It could be my imagination," was again the answer. "In actuality, the only concrete thing I have is my wager: I have told myself that everything comes from the Most High."

◆

THE STREET was deserted. Inside their houses, the people waited for Ahab's soldiers to complete the task that the foreign princess had demanded: executing the prophets of Israel. Elijah walked beside the Levite, feeling that behind each door and window was someone watching him—and blaming him for what had happened.

"I did not ask to be a prophet. Perhaps everything is merely the fruit of my own imagination," thought Elijah.

But, after what had occurred in the carpenter's shop, he knew it was not.

◆

SINCE CHILDHOOD, he had heard voices and spoken with angels. This was when he had been impelled by his father and mother to seek out a priest of Israel who, after asking many questions, identified Elijah as a *nabi*, a prophet, a "man of the spirit," one who "exalts himself with the word of God."

After speaking with him for many hours, the priest told his father and mother that whatever the boy might utter should be regarded as earnest.

When they left that place, his father and mother demanded that Elijah never tell anyone what he saw and heard; to be a prophet meant having ties to the government, and that was always dangerous.

In any case, Elijah had never heard anything that might interest priests or kings. He spoke only with his guardian angel and heard only advice about his own life; from time to time he had visions he could not understand—distant seas, mountains populated with strange beings, wheels with wings and eyes. As soon as the visions disappeared, he—obedient to his father and mother—made every effort to forget them as rapidly as possible.

For this reason, the voices and visions became more and more infrequent. His father and mother were pleased, and they did not raise the matter again. When he came of an age to sustain himself, they lent him money to open a small carpentry shop.

◆

NOW AND AGAIN, he would gaze respectfully upon the other prophets, who walked the streets of Gilead wearing their customary cloaks of skins and sashes of leather and saying that the Lord had singled them out to guide the Chosen People. Truly, such was not his destiny; never would he be capable of evoking a trance through dancing or self-flagellation, a common practice among those "exalted by the voice of God," because he was afraid of pain. Nor would he ever walk the streets of Gilead, proudly displaying the scars from injuries achieved during a state of ecstasy, for he was too shy.

Elijah considered himself a common man, one who dressed like the rest and who tortured only his soul, with the same fears and temptations of simple mortals. As his work in the carpentry shop went on, the voices ceased completely, for adults and workers have no time for such things. His father and mother were happy with their son, and life proceeded in harmony and peace.

The conversation with the priest, when he was still a child, came to be merely a remote memory. Elijah could not believe that Almighty God must talk with men to have His orders obeyed; what had happened in his childhood was only the fantasy of a boy with nothing to do. In Gilead, his native city, there were those thought by the inhabitants to be mad. They were unable to speak coherently and incapable of distinguishing the voice of the Lord from the delirium of insanity. They spent their lives in the streets, preaching the end of the world and living on the charity of others. Even so, none of the priests considered them "exalted by the voice of God."

Elijah concluded in the end that the priests would never be sure of what they were saying. The "exalted of God" were a consequence of a country uncertain of its way, where brother fought brother, where new governments appeared with regularity. Prophets and madmen were one and the same.

When he learned of his king's marriage to Jezebel, princess of Tyre, he had thought it of little significance. Other kings of Israel had done the same, and the result had been a lasting peace in the region and an ever more important trade with Lebanon. Elijah scarcely cared if the people of the neighboring country believed in gods that did not exist or dedicated themselves to strange religious practices such as worshiping animals and mountains; they were honest in their negotiations, and that was what mattered most.

Elijah went on buying the cedar they brought in and selling the products of his carpentry shop. Though they were somewhat haughty and liked to call themselves "Phoenicians" because of the different color of their skin, none of the merchants from Lebanon had ever tried to take advantage of the confusion that reigned in Israel. They paid a fair price for the merchandise and made no comment about the constant internal wars or the political problems facing the Israelites.

◆

AFTER ASCENDING to the throne, Jezebel had asked Ahab to replace the worship of the Lord with that of the gods of Lebanon.

That too had happened before. Elijah, though outraged at Ahab's compliance, continued to worship the God of Israel and to observe the laws of Moses. "It will pass," he thought. "Jezebel seduced Ahab, but she will not succeed in convincing the people."

But Jezebel was a woman unlike others; she believed that Baal had brought her into the world to convert peoples and nations. Astutely and patiently, she began rewarding those who deserted the Lord and accepted the new deities. Ahab ordered a temple built for Baal in Samaria and in it raised an altar. Pilgrimages began, and the worship of the gods of Lebanon spread to all parts.

"It will pass. It may take a generation, but it will pass," Elijah went on thinking.

◆

THEN SOMETHING he was not expecting took place. One afternoon, as he was finishing a table in his shop, everything around him grew dark and thousands of tiny lights began twinkling about him. His head began to ache as never before; he tried to sit but could not move a muscle.

It was not his imagination.

"I'm dying," he thought at that instant. "And now I'll discover where God sends us after death: to the heart of the firmament."

One of the lights shone more brightly, and suddenly, as if coming from everywhere at once:

"And the word of the Lord came unto him, saying: Tell Ahab, that as surely as the Lord God of Israel liveth, before whom thou standest, there shall not be dew nor rain these years, but according to My word."

The next moment, all returned to normal: the carpentry shop, the afternoon light, the voices of children playing in the street.

◆

ELIJAH DID NOT SLEEP that night. For the first time in many years, the sensations of his childhood came back to him; and it was not his guardian angel speaking but "something" larger and more powerful than he. He feared that if he failed to carry out the order he might be cursed in his trade.

By morning, he had decided to do as he had been asked. After all, he was only the messenger of something that did not concern him; once the task was done, the voices would not return to trouble him.

It was not difficult to arrange a meeting with King Ahab. Many generations before, with the ascension of King Samuel to the throne, the prophets had gained importance in commerce and in government. They could marry, have children, but they must always be at the Lord's disposal so that the rulers would never stray from the correct path. Tradition held that thanks to these "exalted of God" many battles had been won, and that Israel survived because its rulers, when they did stray from the path of righteousness, always had a prophet to lead them back to the way of the Lord.

Arriving at the palace, he told the king that a drought would assail the region until worship of the Phoenician gods was forsaken.

The sovereign gave little importance to his words, but Jezebel—who was at Ahab's side and listened attentively to what Elijah was saying—began to ask a series of questions about the message. Elijah told her of the vision, of the pain in his head, of the sensation that time had stopped as he listened to the angel. As he described what had happened, he was able to observe closely the princess of whom all were talking; she was one of the most beautiful women he had ever seen, with long, dark hair falling to the waist of a perfectly contoured body. Her green eyes, which shone in her dark face, remained fixed on Elijah's; he was unable to decipher what they meant, nor could he know the impact his words were causing.

He left convinced that he had carried out his mission and could go back to his work in the carpentry shop. On his way, he desired Jezebel, with all the ardor of his twenty-three years. And he asked God whether in the future he could find a woman from Lebanon, for they were beautiful with their dark skin and green eyes full of mystery.

◆

HE WORKED for the rest of the day and slept peacefully. The next morning he was awakened before dawn by the Levite; Jezebel had convinced the king that the prophets were a menace to the growth and expansion of Israel. Ahab's soldiers had orders to execute all who refused to abandon the sacred task that God had conferred upon them.

To Elijah alone, however, no right of choice had been given: he was to be killed.

He and the Levite spent two days hidden in the stable south of Gilead while 450 *nabi* were summarily executed. But most of the prophets, who roamed the streets flagellating themselves and preaching the end of the world for its corruption and lack of faith, had accepted conversion to the new religion.

◆

A SHARP SOUND, followed by a scream, broke into Elijah's thoughts. He turned in alarm to his companion.

"What was that?"

There was no answer; the Levite's body fell to the ground, an arrow piercing his chest.

Standing before him, a soldier fitted another arrow into his bow. Elijah looked about him: the street with doors and windows tightly shut, the sun shining in the heavens, a breeze coming from an ocean of which he had heard so much but had never seen. He thought of running, but he knew he would be overtaken before he reached the next corner.

"If I must die, let it not be from behind," he thought.

The soldier again raised his bow. To Elijah's surprise, he felt neither fear nor the instinct to survive, nor anything else; it was as if everything had been determined long ago, and the two of them—he and the soldier—were merely playing roles in a drama not of their own writing. He remembered his childhood, the mornings and afternoons in Gilead, the unfinished work he would leave in his carpentry shop. He thought of his mother and father, who had never desired their son to be a prophet. He thought of Jezebel's eyes and of King Ahab's smile.

He thought how stupid it was to die at twenty-three, without ever having known a woman's love.

The soldier's hand released the string, the arrow slashed through the air, hummed past his right ear to bury itself in the dusty ground behind him.

The soldier rearmed his bow and pointed it. But instead of firing, he fixed his eyes on Elijah's.

"I am the greatest archer in all King Ahab's armies," he said. "For seven years I have never erred a shot."

Elijah turned to the Levite's body.

"That arrow was meant for you." The soldier's bow was still taut, and his hands were trembling. "Elijah was the only prophet who must be killed; the others could choose the faith of Baal," he said.

"Then finish your task."

He was surprised at his own calmness. He had imagined death so often during the nights in the stable, and now he saw that he had suffered unnecessarily; in a few seconds all would be ended.

"I can't," said the soldier, his hands still trembling, the arrow changing directions at every instant. "Leave, get out of my presence, because I believe God deflected my arrow and will curse me if I kill you."

It was then, as he discovered that death could elude him, that the fear of death returned. There was still the possibility of seeing the ocean, of finding a wife, having children, and completing his work in the shop.

"Finish this here and now," he said. "At this moment I am calm. If you tarry, I will suffer over all that I am losing."

The soldier looked about him to make certain that no one had witnessed the scene. Then he lowered his bow, replaced the arrow in its quiver, and disappeared around the corner.

Elijah felt his legs begin to weaken; the terror had returned in all its intensity. He must flee at once, disappear from Gilead, never again have to meet face-to-face a soldier with a drawn bow and an arrow pointed at his heart. He had not chosen his destiny, nor had he sought out Ahab in order to boast to his neighbors that he could talk with the king. He was not responsible for the massacre of the prophets—nor even for, one afternoon, having seen time stop and the carpentry shop transformed into a dark hole filled with points of light.

Mimicking the soldier's gesture, he looked to all sides; the street was deserted. He thought of seeing if he could still save the Levite's life, but the terror quickly returned, and before anyone else could appear, Elijah fled.

HE WALKED FOR MANY HOURS, TAKING PATHS LONG since unused, until he arrived at the bank of the rivulet of Cherith. He felt shame at his cowardice but joy at being alive.

He drank a bit of water, sat, and only then realized the situation in which he found himself: the next day he would need to feed himself, and food was nowhere to be found in the desert.

He remembered the carpentry shop, his long years of work, and having been forced to leave it all behind. Some of his neighbors were friends, but he could not count on them; the story of his flight must have already spread throughout the city, and he was hated by all for having escaped while he sent true men of faith to martyrdom.

Whatever he had done in the past now lay in ruins—merely because he had elected to carry out the Lord's will. Tomorrow, and in the days, weeks, and months to come, the traders from Lebanon would knock on his door and someone would tell them the owner had fled, leaving behind a trail of innocent prophets' deaths. Perhaps they would add that he had tried to destroy the gods that protected heaven and earth; the story would quickly cross Israel's borders, and he could forget forever marrying a woman as beautiful as those in Lebanon.

◆

"THERE ARE the ships."

Yes, there were the ships. Criminals, prisoners of war, fugitives were usually accepted as mariners because it was a profession more dangerous than the army. In war, a soldier always had a chance to escape with his life; but the seas were an unknown, populated by monsters, and when a tragedy occurred, none were left to tell the story.

There were the ships, but they were controlled by Phoenician merchants. Elijah was not a criminal, a prisoner, or a fugitive but someone who had dared raise his voice against the god Baal. When they found him out, he would be killed and cast into the sea, for mariners believed that Baal and his gods governed the storms.

He could not go toward the ocean. Nor could he make his way north, for there lay Lebanon. He could not go east, where certain tribes of Israel were engaged in a war that had already lasted two generations.

◆

HE RECALLED the feeling of calm he had experienced in the
presence of the soldier; after all, what was death? Death was an
instant, nothing more. Even if he felt pain, it must pass at once,
and then the Lord of Hosts would receive him in His bosom.

He lay down on the ground and looked at the sky for a long
time. Like the Levite, he tried to make his wager. It was not a
wager about God's existence, for of that he had no doubt, but
about the reason for his own life.

He saw the mountains, the earth that soon would be beset
by a long drought, as the angel of the Lord had said, but for now
still had the coolness of many generations of rain. He saw the
rivulet of Cherith, whose waters in a short time would cease to
flow. He took his leave of the world with fervor and respect, and
asked the Lord to receive him when his time was come.

He thought about the reason for his existence, and obtained
no answer.

He thought about where he should go, and discovered that
he was surrounded.

The following day he would go back and hand himself over,
even if his fear of death returned.

He tried to find joy in the knowledge that he would go on
living for a few more hours. But it was futile; he had just discovered that, as in almost all the days of a life, man is powerless to
make a decision.

ELIJAH AWOKE THE NEXT DAY AND AGAIN LOOKED AT the Cherith.

Tomorrow, or a year from now, it would be only a bed of fine sand and smooth stones. The old inhabitants still referred to the site as Cherith, and perhaps they would give directions to those passing through by saying: "Such a place is on the bank of the river that runs near here." The travelers would make their way there, see the round stones and the fine sand, and reflect to themselves: "Here in this land there was once a river." But the only thing that mattered about a river, its flow of water, would no longer be there to quench their thirst.

Souls too, like rivulets and plants, needed a different kind of rain: hope, faith, a reason to live. When this did not come to pass, everything in that soul died, even if the body went on living;

and the people could say: "Here in this body there was once a man."

It was not the time to think about that. Again he remembered the conversation with the Levite just before they left the stable: what was gained from dying many deaths, if one alone sufficed? All he had to do was wait for Jezebel's soldiers. They would come, beyond any doubt, for there were few places to flee from Gilead; wrongdoers always fled to the desert—where they were found dead within a few days—or to the Cherith, where they were quickly captured.

The soldiers would therefore come soon. And he would rejoice at their sight.

◆

HE DRANK a bit of the crystalline water that ran beside him. He cleansed his face, then sought out shade where he could await his pursuers. A man cannot fight his destiny—he had already tried, and he had lost.

Despite the priests' belief that he was a prophet, he had decided to work as a carpenter; but the Lord had led him back to his path.

He was not the only one to abandon the life that the Lord had written for every person on earth. He had once had a friend with an excellent voice, whose father and mother had been unwilling to have him become a singer because it was a profession that brought dishonor to the family. A girl with whom he had been friends as a child could have been a dancer without equal; she too had been forbidden by her family, for the king might summon her, and no one knew how long his reign would last. Moreover, the atmosphere in the palace was considered sinful and hostile, ending permanently any possibility of a good marriage.

"Man was born to betray his destiny." God placed only impossible tasks in human hearts.

"Why?"

Perhaps because custom must be maintained.

But that was not a good answer. "The inhabitants of Lebanon are more advanced than are we, because they did not follow the customs of the navigators. When everyone else was using the same kind of ship, they decided to build something different. Many lost their lives at sea, but their ships continued to improve, and today they dominate the world's commerce. They paid a high price to adapt, but it proved to be worth the cost."

Perhaps mankind betrayed its destiny because God was not closer. He had placed in people's hearts a dream of an era when everything was possible—and then gone on to busy Himself with other things. The world had transformed itself, life had become more difficult, but the Lord had never returned to change men's dreams.

God was distant. But if He still sent His angels to speak to His prophets, it was because there was still something left to be done here. What could the answer be?

"Perhaps because our fathers fell into error, and they fear we will repeat their mistakes. Or perhaps they never erred, and thus will not know how to help us if we have some problem."

He felt he was drawing near. The rivulet was flowing at his side, a few crows were circling in the sky, the plants clinging insistently to life in the sandy, sterile terrain. Had they listened to the words of their forebears, what would they have heard?

"Rivulet, seek a better place for your limpid waters to reflect the brightness of the sun, for the desert will one day dry you up," the god of waters would have said, if perchance one existed. "Crows, there is more food in the forests than among rocks and sand," the god of the birds would have said. "Plants, spread your seeds far from here, because the world is full of humid, fertile ground, and you will grow more beautiful," the god of flowers would have said.

But the Cherith, like the plants and the crows, one of which had perched nearby, had the courage to do what other rivers, or birds, or flowers thought impossible.

Elijah fixed his gaze on the crow.

"I'm learning," he told the bird. "Though the lesson is a futile one, for I am condemned to death."

"You have discovered how everything is simple," the crow seemed to reply. "Having courage is enough."

Elijah laughed, for he was putting words into the mouth of a bird. It was an amusing game, one he had learned with a woman who made bread, and he decided to continue. He would ask the questions and offer himself an answer, as if he were a true sage.

The crow, however, took flight. Elijah went on waiting for Jezebel's soldiers to arrive, for dying a single time sufficed.

The day went by without anything happening. Could they have forgotten that the principal enemy of the god Baal still lived? Jezebel must know where he was; why did she not pursue him?

"Because I saw her eyes, and she is a wise woman," he told himself. "If I were to die, I would live on as a martyr of the Lord. If I'm thought of as just a fugitive, I'll be merely a coward who had no faith in his own words."

Yes, that was the princess's strategy.

◆

SHORTLY BEFORE NIGHTFALL, a crow—could it be the same one?—perched on the bough where he had seen it that morning. In its beak was a small piece of meat that it accidentally dropped.

To Elijah, it was a miracle. He ran to the spot beneath the tree, picked up the chunk of meat, and ate it. He didn't know from where it had come, nor did he wish to know; what was important was his being able to satisfy a small part of his hunger.

Even with his sudden movement, the crow did not fly away.

"This crow knows I'm going to starve to death here," he thought. "He's feeding his prey so he can have a better feast later."

Even as Jezebel fed the faith of Baal with news of Elijah's flight.

The two of them, man and crow, contemplated each other. Elijah recalled the game he had played that morning.

"I would like to talk to you, crow. This morning, I had the thought that souls need food. If my soul has not yet perished of hunger, it has something still to say."

The bird remained immobile.

"And, if it has something to say, I must listen. Because I have no one else with whom to speak," continued Elijah.

In his imagination Elijah was transformed into the crow.

"What it is that God expects of you?" he asked himself, as if he were the crow.

"He expects me to be a prophet."

"This is what the priests said. But it may not be what God desires."

"Yes, it is what He wants. An angel appeared to me in my shop and asked me to speak with Ahab. The voices I heard as a child—"

"Everyone hears voices as a child," interrupted the crow.

"But not everyone sees an angel," Elijah said.

This time the crow did not reply. After an interval, the bird—or rather, his own soul, delirious from the sun and loneliness of the desert—broke the silence.

"Do you remember the woman who used to make bread?" he asked himself.

◆

ELIJAH REMEMBERED. She had come to ask him to make some trays. While Elijah was doing as she asked, he heard her say that her work was a way of expressing the presence of God.

"From the way you make the trays, I can see that you have the same feeling," she had continued. "Because you smile as you work."

The woman divided human beings into two groups: those who took joy in, and those who complained about, what they did. The latter affirmed that the curse cast upon Adam by God was the only truth: *"Cursed is the ground for thy sake; in sorrow shalt thou eat of it all the days of thy life."* They took no pleasure in work and were annoyed on feast days, when they were obliged to rest. They used the Lord's words as an excuse for their futile lives, forgetting that He had also said to Moses: *"For the Lord shall greatly bless thee in the land which the Lord thy God giveth thee for an inheritance to possess it."*

"Yes, I remember the woman. She was right; I did enjoy my work in the carpentry shop. She taught me to talk to things."

"If you had not worked as a carpenter, you would not have been able to place your soul outside yourself, to pretend that it is a crow talking, and to understand that you are better and wiser than you believe," came the reply. "Because it was in the carpentry shop that you discovered the sacred that is in all things."

"I always took pleasure in pretending to talk to the tables

and chairs I built; wasn't that enough? And when I spoke to them, I usually found thoughts that had never entered my head. The woman had told me that it was because I had put the greater part of my soul into the work, and it was this part that answered me.

"But when I was beginning to understand that I could serve God in this way, the angel appeared, and—well, you know the rest."

"The angel appeared because you were ready," replied the crow.

"I was a good carpenter."

"It was part of your apprenticeship. When a man journeys toward his destiny, often he is obliged to change paths. At other times, the forces around him are too powerful and he is compelled to lay aside his courage and yield. All this is part of the apprenticeship."

Elijah listened attentively to what his soul was saying.

"But no one can lose sight of what he desires. Even if there are moments when he believes the world and the others are stronger. The secret is this: do not surrender."

"I never thought of being a prophet," Elijah said.

"You did, but you were convinced that it was impossible. Or that it was dangerous. Or that it was unthinkable."

Elijah rose.

"Why do you tell me what I have no wish to hear?"

Startled at the movement, the bird fled.

◆

THE BIRD RETURNED the next morning. Instead of resuming the conversation, Elijah began to observe it, for the animal always managed to feed itself and always brought him the food that remained.

A mysterious friendship developed between the pair, and Elijah began to learn from the bird. Observing it, he saw that it managed to find food in the desert, and he discovered that he could survive for a few more days if he learned to do the same. When the crow's flight turned into a circle, Elijah knew there was prey at hand; he would run to the spot and try to catch it. At first, many of the small animals living there escaped, but he gradually acquired the skill and agility to capture them. He used branches as spears and dug traps, which he disguised with a fine layer of twigs and sand. When the quarry fell, Elijah would divide his food with the crow, then set aside part to use as bait.

But the solitude in which he found himself was terrible and oppressive, which is why he decided again to pretend he was conversing with the crow.

"Who are you?" asked the crow.

"I'm a man who has found peace," replied Elijah. "I can live in the desert, provide for myself, and contemplate the endless beauty of God's creation. I have discovered that there resides in me a soul better than ever I thought."

They continued hunting together for another moon. Then

one night when his soul was possessed by sorrow, he asked himself again, "Who are you?"

"I don't know."

◆

ANOTHER MOON DIED and was reborn in the sky. Elijah felt that his body was stronger, his mind more clear. Tonight he turned to the crow, who was perched on the same branch as always, and answered the question he had asked some days before.

"I am a prophet. I saw an angel as I worked, and I cannot doubt what I am capable of doing, even if the entire world should tell me the opposite. I brought about a massacre in my country by challenging the one closest to the king's heart. I'm in the desert, as before I was in a carpentry shop, because my soul told me that a man must go through various stages before he can fulfill his destiny."

"Yes, and now you know who you are," commented the crow.

That night, when Elijah returned from the hunt, he went to drink and found that the Cherith had dried up. But he was so weary that he decided to sleep.

In his dream, his guardian angel, whom he had not seen for a long time, came to him.

"The angel of the Lord hath spoken to thy soul," said the guardian angel. "And hath ordered:

"*Get thee hence, and turn thee eastward, and hide thyself by the brook Cherith, that is before Jordan.*

"*Thou shalt drink of the brook; and I have commanded the ravens to feed thee there.*"

"My soul has heard," said Elijah in the dream.

"Then awake, for the angel of the Lord biddeth me hence and is desirous of speaking to thee."

Elijah leapt up, startled. What had happened?

Although it was night, the place was filled with light, and the angel of the Lord appeared.

"What hath brought thee here?" asked the angel.

"You brought me here."

"No. Jezebel and her soldiers caused thee to flee. This must thou never forget, for thy mission is to avenge the Lord thy God."

"I am a prophet, because you are in my presence and I hear your voice," Elijah said. "I have changed paths several times, as do all men. But I am ready to go to Samaria and destroy Jezebel."

"Thou hast found thy way, but thou mayest not destroy until thou learnest to build anew. I order thee:

"*Arise, get thee to Zarephath, which belongeth to Sidon, and dwell there; behold, I have commanded a widow woman there to sustain thee.*"

The next morning, Elijah looked for the crow, to bid him farewell. The bird, for the first time since he had arrived at the bank of the Cherith, did not appear.

ELIJAH JOURNEYED FOR DAYS BEFORE ARRIVING IN THE valley where lay the city of Zarephath, which its inhabitants knew as Akbar. When he was at the end of his strength, he saw a woman, dressed in black, gathering wood. The vegetation in the valley was sparse, and she had to be content with small, dry twigs.

"Who are you?" he asked.

The woman looked at the foreigner, not really understanding what he was saying.

"Bring me water to drink," Elijah said. "Bring me also a piece of bread."

The woman put aside the wood but still said nothing.

"Do not be afraid," Elijah insisted. "I am alone, hungry and thirsty, and haven't the strength to harm anyone."

"You're not from here," she said finally. "By the way you speak, you must be from the kingdom of Israel. If you knew me better, you'd be aware that I have nothing."

"You are a widow; this the Lord has told me. And I have even less than you. If you do not give me food and drink now, I will die."

The woman was taken aback; how could this foreigner know of her life?

"A man should feel shame at asking sustenance from a woman," she said, recovering.

"Do as I ask, please," Elijah insisted, knowing that his strength was beginning to fail. "When I am better, I will work for you."

The woman laughed.

"Moments ago, you told me something true; I am a widow, who lost her husband on one of my country's ships. I have never seen the ocean but I know it is like the desert: it slays those who challenge it . . . "

And she continued. "But now you tell me something false. As surely as Baal lives at the top of the Fifth Mountain, I have no food; there is nothing but a handful of flour in a barrel and a bit of oil in a flagon."

Elijah saw the horizon changing direction and knew he was about to faint. Gathering the last of his strength, he implored one final time, "I don't know if you believe in dreams; I don't know even if I believe in them. But the Lord told me that I would arrive here, and that I would find you. He has done things that caused me to doubt His wisdom, but never His existence. And thus the God of Israel asked that I tell the woman I met in Zarephath:

"The barrel of meal shall not waste, neither shall the cruse of oil fail, until the day the Lord sendeth rain upon the earth."

Without explaining how such a miracle could come about, Elijah fainted.

The woman stood gazing down at the man who lay at her feet. She knew that the God of Israel was a mere superstition; the Phoenician gods were more powerful, and they had made her country one of the most respected nations on earth. But she was happy; usually she had to ask others for alms, and now, as had not happened for a long time, a man needed her. This made her feel stronger, for it was manifest that there were those in worse circumstances than she.

"If someone asks a favor of me, it is because I still have some use on this earth," she reflected.

"I'll do as he asks, if only to relieve his suffering. I too have known hunger, and know its power to destroy the soul."

She went to her house and returned with a piece of bread and some water. She kneeled, placed the foreigner's head in her lap, and began to moisten his lips. Within a few minutes, he had regained his senses.

She held out the bread to him, and Elijah ate quietly, looking at the valley, the ravines, the mountains pointing silently heavenward. Elijah could see the reddish walls of the city of Zarephath dominating the passage through the valley.

"Give me lodging with you, for I am persecuted in my own country," Elijah said.

"What crime have you committed?" she asked.

"I'm a prophet of the Lord. Jezebel has ordered the death of all who refuse to worship the Phoenician gods."

"How old are you?"

"Twenty-three," Elijah replied.

She looked pityingly at the young man before her. He had long, dirty hair and a beard that was still sparse, as if he wished to appear older than his years. How could a poor fellow like this challenge the most powerful princess in the world?

"If you're Jezebel's enemy, you're my enemy too. She is a princess of Tyre, whose mission when she married your king was to convert your people to the true faith, or so say those who have met her."

She pointed toward one of the peaks that framed the valley.

"Our gods have lived on the Fifth Mountain for many generations, and they have kept peace in our country. But Israel lives in war and suffering. How can you go on believing in the One God? Give Jezebel time to carry out her work and you'll see that peace will reign in your cities too."

"I have heard the voice of the Lord," Elijah replied. "But your people have never climbed to the top of the Fifth Mountain to discover what exists there."

"Anyone who climbs the Fifth Mountain will die from the fire of the heavens. The gods don't like strangers."

She fell silent. She had remembered dreaming, the night before, of a very strong light. From the midst of that light came a voice saying: "Receive the stranger who comes seeking you."

"Give me lodging with you, for I have nowhere to sleep," Elijah insisted.

"I told you that I'm poor. I barely have enough for myself and my son."

"The Lord asked you to let me stay; He never abandons those He loves. Do what I ask of you. I will work for you. I'm a carpenter, I know how to work cedar; there will be no lack of something to do. This way, the Lord will use my hands to keep His promise: *The barrel of meal shall not waste, neither shall the cruse of oil fail, until the day the Lord sendeth rain upon the earth.*"

"Even if I wished to, I would have no way to pay you."

"There is no need. The Lord will provide."

Confused by the previous night's dream, and even with the knowledge that the stranger was an enemy of the princess of Tyre, the woman decided to obey.

ELIJAH'S PRESENCE WAS SOON NOTICED BY THE NEIGH-
bors. People commented that the widow had taken a foreigner into
her house, in disrespect of the memory of her husband—a hero
who had died attempting to expand his country's trade routes.

When she heard the rumors, the widow explained that he
was an Israelite prophet, weary from hunger and thirst. And
word spread that an Israelite prophet in flight from Jezebel was
hiding in the city. A delegation went to see the high priest.

"Bring the foreigner to my presence," he ordered.

And it was done. That afternoon, Elijah was led to the man
who, together with the governor and the leader of the military,
controlled all that took place in Akbar.

"What have you come here to do?" he asked. "Do you not
know that you are our country's enemy?"

"For years I have had commerce with Lebanon, and I respect your people and their customs. I am here because I am persecuted in Israel."

"I know the reason," said the high priest. "Was it a woman who made you flee?"

"In all my life, that woman was the most beautiful creature I have ever met, though I stood before her for only a brief moment. But her heart is like stone, and behind those green eyes hides the enemy who wishes to destroy my country. I did not flee; I await only the right moment to return."

The high priest laughed.

"If you're waiting for the right moment to return, prepare yourself to remain in Akbar for the rest of your life. We are not at war with your country; all we desire is to see the spread of the true faith, by peaceful means, throughout the world. We have no wish to repeat the atrocities committed by your people when you installed yourselves in Canaan."

"Is killing prophets a peaceful means?"

"If you cut off a monster's head, it ceases to exist. A few may die, but religious wars will be averted forever. And, from what the traders tell me, it was a prophet named Elijah who started all this, then fled."

The high priest stared at him, before continuing.

"A man who looked much like you."

"It is I," Elijah replied.

"Excellent. Welcome to the city of Akbar; when we need

something from Jezebel, we will pay for it with your head—the most important currency we have. Till then, seek out employment and learn to fend for yourself, because here there is no place for prophets."

Elijah was preparing to depart, when the high priest told him, "It seems that a young woman from Sidon is more powerful than your One God. She succeeded in erecting an altar to Baal, before which the old priests now kneel."

"Everything will happen as was written by the Lord," replied the prophet. "There are moments when tribulations occur in our lives, and we cannot avoid them. But they are there for some reason."

"What reason?"

"That is a question we cannot answer before, or even during, the trials. Only when we have overcome them do we understand why they were there."

◆

AS SOON AS ELIJAH had departed, the high priest called the delegation of citizens who had sought him out that morning.

"Do not concern yourselves about this," said the high priest. "Custom mandates that we offer hospitality to foreigners. Besides that, here he is under our control and we can observe his steps. The best way to know and destroy an enemy is to pretend to become his friend. When the time comes, he will be handed over to Jezebel, and our city will receive gold and other recompense. By then, we shall have learned how to destroy his ideas; for now, we know only how to destroy his body."

Although Elijah was a worshiper of the One God and a potential enemy of the princess, the high priest demanded that the right of asylum be honored. Everyone knew of the ancient custom: if a city were to deny shelter to a traveler, the sons of its inhabitants would later face the same difficulty. Since the greater part of Akbar had descendants scattered among the country's gigantic merchant fleet, no one dared challenge the law of hospitality.

Furthermore, it cost nothing to await the day when the Jewish prophet's head would be exchanged for large amounts of gold.

That night, Elijah supped with the widow and her son. As the Israelite prophet was now a valuable commodity to be bargained for in the future, several traders sent provisions enough to feed the three of them for a week.

"It appears the God of Israel is keeping His word," said the widow. "Not since my husband died has my table been as full as today."

LITTLE BY LITTLE ELIJAH BECAME PART OF THE LIFE OF Zarephath and, like all its inhabitants, came to call it Akbar. He met the governor, the commander of the garrison, the high priest, and the master glassmakers, who were admired throughout the region. When asked his reason for being there, he would tell the truth: Jezebel was slaying all the prophets in Israel.

"You're a traitor to your country, and an enemy of Phoenicia," they said. "But we are a nation of traders and know that the more dangerous a man is, the higher the price on his head."

And so passed several months.

At the entrance to the valley, a few Assyrian patrols had encamped, apparently intending to remain. The small group of soldiers represented no threat. But even so, the commander asked the governor to take steps.

"They have done nothing to us," said the governor. "They must be on a mission of trade, in search of a better route for their products. If they decide to make use of our roads, they will pay taxes—and we shall become even richer. Why provoke them?"

To complicate matters further, the widow's son fell ill for no apparent reason. Neighbors attributed the fact to the presence of the foreigner in her house, and the widow asked Elijah to leave. But he did not leave—the Lord had not yet called. Rumors began to spread that the foreigner had brought with him the wrath of the gods of the Fifth Mountain.

It was possible to control the army and calm the population about the foreign patrols. But, with the illness of the widow's son, the governor began having difficulty easing the people's minds about Elijah.

◆

A DELEGATION of the inhabitants of Akbar went to speak with the governor.

"We can build the Israelite a house outside the walls," they said. "In that way we will not violate the law of hospitality but will still be protected from divine wrath. The gods are displeased with this man's presence."

"Leave him where he is," replied the governor. "I do not wish political problems with Israel."

"What?" the townspeople asked. "Jezebel is pursuing all the prophets who worship the One God, and would slay them."

"Our princess is a courageous woman, and faithful to the gods of the Fifth Mountain. But, however much power she may have now, she is not an Israelite. Tomorrow she may fall into disfavor, and we shall have to face the anger of our neighbors; if we demonstrate that we have treated one of their prophets well, they will be kind to us."

The delegation left unsatisfied, for the high priest had said that one day Elijah would be traded for gold and other rewards. Nevertheless, even if the governor were in error, they could do nothing. Custom said that the ruling family must be respected.

IN THE DISTANCE, IN THE MIDDLE OF THE VALLEY, THE tents of the Assyrian warriors began to multiply.

The commander was concerned, but he had the support of neither the governor nor the high priest. He attempted to keep his warriors constantly trained, though he knew that none of them—nor even their grandfathers—had experience in combat. War was a thing of the past for Akbar, and all the strategies he had learned had been superseded by the new techniques and new weapons that other countries used.

"Akbar has always negotiated its peace," said the governor. "It will not be this time that we are invaded. Let the other countries fight among themselves: we have a weapon much more powerful than theirs—money. When they have finished destroying one another, we shall enter their cities—and sell our products."

The governor succeeded in calming the population about the Assyrians. But rumors were rife that the Israelite had brought the curse of the gods to Akbar. Elijah was becoming an ever greater problem.

◆

ONE AFTERNOON, the boy's condition worsened severely; he could no longer stand, nor could he recognize those who came to visit him. Before the sun descended to the horizon, Elijah and the widow kneeled at the child's bedside.

"Almighty Lord, who led the soldier's arrow astray and who brought me here, make this child whole again. He has done nothing, he is innocent of my sins and the sins of his fathers; save him, O Lord."

The boy barely moved; his lips were white, and his eyes were rapidly losing their glow.

"Pray to your One God," the woman asked. "For only a mother can know when her son's soul is departing."

Elijah felt the desire to take her hand, to tell her she was not alone and that Almighty God would attend him. He was a prophet; he had accepted that truth on the banks of the Cherith, and now the angels were at his side.

"I have no more tears," she continued. "If He has no compassion, if He needs a life, then ask Him to take me, and leave my son to walk through the valley and the streets of Akbar."

Elijah did all in his power to concentrate on his prayer; but that mother's suffering was so intense that it seemed to engulf the room, penetrating the walls, the door, everywhere.

He touched the boy's body; his temperature was not as high as in earlier days, and that was a bad sign.

◆

THE HIGH PRIEST had come by the house that morning and, as he had done for two weeks, applied herbal poultices to the boy's face and chest. In the preceding days, the women of Akbar had brought recipes for remedies that had been handed down for generations and whose curative powers had been proved on numerous occasions. Every afternoon, they gathered at the foot of the Fifth Mountain and made sacrifices so the boy's soul would not leave his body.

Moved by what was happening in the city, an Egyptian trader who was passing through Akbar gave, without charge, an extremely dear red powder to be mixed with the boy's food. According to legend, the technique of manufacturing the powder had been granted to Egyptian doctors by the gods themselves.

Elijah had prayed unceasingly for all this time.

But nothing, nothing whatsoever, had availed.

◆

"I KNOW WHY they have allowed you to remain here," the woman said, her voice softer each time she spoke, for she had gone many days without sleep. "I know there is a price on your head, and that one day you will be handed over to Israel in exchange for gold. If you save my son, I swear by Baal and the gods of the Fifth Mountain that you will never be captured. I know escape routes that have been forgotten for generations, and I will teach you how to leave Akbar without being seen."

Elijah did not reply.

"Pray to your One God," the woman asked again. "If He saves my son, I swear I will renounce Baal and believe in Him. Explain to your Lord that I gave you shelter when you were in need; I did exactly as He had ordered."

Elijah prayed again, imploring with all his strength. At that instant, the boy stirred.

"I want to leave here," the boy said in a weak voice.

His mother's eyes shone with happiness; tears rolled down her cheeks.

"Come, my son. We'll go wherever you like, do whatever you wish."

Elijah tried to pick him up, but the boy pushed his hand away.

"I want to do it by myself," he said.

He rose slowly and began to walk toward the outer room. After a few steps, he dropped to the floor, as if felled by a bolt of lightning.

Elijah and the widow ran to him; the boy was dead.

For an instant, neither spoke. Suddenly, the woman began to scream with all her strength.

"Cursed be the gods, cursed be they who have taken away my son! Cursed be the man who brought such misfortune to my home! My only child!" she screamed. "Because I respected the will of heaven, because I was generous with a foreigner, my son is dead!"

The neighbors heard the widow's lamentations and saw her son laid out on the floor of the house. The woman was still screaming, her fists pounding against the chest of the Israelite prophet beside her; he seemed to have lost any ability to react and did nothing to defend himself. While the women tried to comfort the widow, the men immediately seized Elijah by the arms and took him to the governor.

"This man has repaid generosity with hatred. He put a spell on the widow's house and her son died. We are sheltering someone who is cursed by the gods."

The Israelite wept, asking himself, "O my Lord and God, even this widow, who has been so generous to me, hast Thou chosen to afflict? If Thou hast slain her son, it can only be because I am failing the mission that has been entrusted to me, and it is I who deserve to die."

That evening, the council of the city of Akbar was convened, under the direction of the high priest and the governor. Elijah was brought to judgment.

"You chose to return hatred for love. For that reason, I condemn you to death," said the governor.

◆

"Even though your head is worth a satchel of gold, we cannot invite the wrath of the gods of the Fifth Mountain," the high priest said. "For later not all the gold in the world will bring peace back to this city."

Elijah lowered his head. He deserved all the suffering he could bear, for the Lord had abandoned him.

"You shall climb the Fifth Mountain," said the high priest. "You shall ask forgiveness from the gods you have offended. They will cause fire to descend from the heavens to slay you. If they do not, it is because they desire justice to be carried out at our hands; we shall be waiting for you at the descent from the mountain, and in accordance with ritual you will be executed the next morning."

Elijah knew all too well about sacred executions: they tore the heart from the breast and cut off the head. According to ancient beliefs, a man without a heart could not enter paradise.

"Why hast Thou chosen me for this, Lord?" he cried out, knowing that the men about him knew nothing of the choice the Lord had made for him. "Dost Thou not see that I am incapable of carrying out what Thou hast demanded of me?"

He heard no reply.

SHOUTING INSULTS AND HURLING STONES, THE MEN and women of Akbar followed in procession the group of guards conducting the Israelite to the face of the Fifth Mountain. Only with great effort were the soldiers able to contain the crowd's fury. After walking for half an hour, they came to the foot of the sacred mountain.

The group stopped before the stone altars, where people were wont to leave their offerings and sacrifices, their petitions and prayers. They all knew the stories of giants who lived in the area, and they remembered some who had challenged the prohibition only to be claimed by the fire from heaven. Travelers passing through the valley at night swore they could hear the laughter of the gods and goddesses amusing themselves from above.

Even if no one was certain of all this, none dared challenge the gods.

"Let's go," said a soldier, prodding Elijah with the tip of his spear. "Whoever kills a child deserves the worst punishment there is."

◆

ELIJAH STEPPED ONTO the forbidden terrain and began to climb the slope. After walking for some time, until he could no longer hear the shouts of the people of Akbar, he sat on a rock and wept; since that day in the carpentry shop when he saw the darkness dotted with brilliant points of light, he had succeeded only in bringing misfortune to others.

The Lord had lost His voices in Israel, and the worship of Phoenician gods must now be stronger than before. His first night beside the Cherith, Elijah had thought that God had chosen him to be a martyr, as He had done with so many others.

Instead, the Lord had sent a crow—a portentous bird— which had fed him until the Cherith ran dry. Why a crow and not a dove, or an angel? Could it all be merely the delirium of a man trying to hide his fear, or whose head has been too long exposed to the sun? Elijah was no longer certain of anything: perhaps Evil had found its instrument, and he was that instrument. Why had God sent him to Akbar, instead of returning him to put an end to the princess who had inflicted such evil on his people?

He had felt like a coward but had done as ordered. He had struggled to adapt to that strange, gracious people and their completely different way of life. Just when he thought he was fulfilling his destiny, the widow's son had died.

"Why me?"

◆

HE ROSE, walked a bit farther until he entered the mist covering the mountaintop. He could take advantage of the lack of visibility to flee from his persecutors, but what would it matter? He was weary of fleeing, and he knew that nowhere would he find his place in the world. Even if he succeeded in escaping now, he would bear the curse with him to another city, and other tragedies would come to pass. Wherever he went, he would take with him the shadow of those deaths. He preferred to have his heart ripped from his chest and his head cut off.

He sat down again, amid the fog. He had decided to wait a bit, so that those below would think he had climbed to the top of the mountain; then he would return to Akbar, surrendering to his captors.

"The fire of heaven." Many before had been killed by it, though Elijah doubted that it was sent by the Lord. On moonless nights its glow crossed the firmament, appearing suddenly and disappearing just as abruptly. Perhaps it burned. Perhaps it killed instantly, with no suffering.

◆

AS NIGHT FELL, the fog dissipated. He could see the valley below, the lights of Akbar, and the fires of the Assyrian encampment. He heard the barking of their dogs and the war chants of their soldiers.

"I am ready," he said to himself. "I accepted that I was a prophet, and did everything I did as best I could. But I failed, and now God needs someone else."

At that moment, a light descended upon him.

"The fire of heaven!"

The light, however, remained before him. And a voice said:

"I am an angel of the Lord."

Elijah kneeled and placed his face against the ground.

"I have seen you at other times, and have obeyed the angel of the Lord," replied Elijah, without raising his head. "And yet I have done nothing but sow misfortune wherever I go."

But the angel continued:

"When thou returnest to the city, ask three times for the boy to come back to life. The third time, the Lord will hearken unto thee."

"Why am I to do this?"

"For the grandeur of God."

"Even if it comes to pass, I have doubted myself. I am no longer worthy of my task," answered Elijah.

"Every man hath the right to doubt his task, and to forsake it from time to time; but what he must not do is forget it. Whoever doubteth not himself is unworthy—for in his unquestioning belief in his ability, he commiteth the sin of pride. Blessed are they who go through moments of indecision."

"Moments ago, you saw I was not even sure you were an emissary of God."

"Go, and obey what I have said."

AFTER MUCH TIME HAD PASSED, ELIJAH DESCENDED THE
mountain to the place of the altars of sacrifice. The guards were
awaiting him, but the multitude had returned to Akbar.

"I am ready for death," he said. "I have asked forgiveness
from the gods of the Fifth Mountain, and now they command
that, before my soul abandons my body, I go to the house of
the widow who took me in, and ask her to take pity on my
soul."

The soldiers led him back, to the presence of the high priest,
where they repeated what the Israelite had said.

"I shall do as you ask," the high priest told the prisoner.
"Since you have sought the forgiveness of the gods, you should
also seek it of the widow. So that you do not flee, you will go
accompanied by four armed soldiers. But harbor no illusion that

you will convince her to ask clemency; when morning comes, we shall execute you in the middle of the square."

The high priest wished to inquire what he had seen atop the mountain, but in the presence of the soldiers the answer might be awkward. He therefore decided to remain silent, but he approved of having Elijah ask for forgiveness in public; no one else could then doubt the power of the gods of the Fifth Mountain.

Elijah and the soldiers went to the poor, narrow street where he had dwelled for several months. The doors and windows of the widow's house were open so that, following custom, her son's soul could depart, to go to live with the gods. The body was in the center of the small room, with the entire neighborhood sitting in vigil.

When they noticed the presence of the Israelite, men and women alike were horrified.

"Out with him!" they screamed at the guards. "Isn't the evil he has caused enough? He is so perverse that the gods of the Fifth Mountain refused to dirty their hands with his blood!"

"Leave to us the task of killing him!" shouted a man. "We'll do it right now, without waiting for the ritual execution!"

Standing his ground against the shoves and blows, Elijah freed himself of the hands that grasped him and ran to the widow, who sat weeping in a corner.

"I can bring him back from the dead. Let me touch your son," he said. "For just an instant."

The widow did not even raise her head.

"Please," he insisted. "Even if it be the last thing you do for me in this life, give me the chance to try to repay your generosity."

Some men seized him to drag him away. But Elijah resisted, struggling with all his strength, imploring to be allowed to touch the dead child.

Although he was young and determined, he was finally pulled away to the door of the house. "Angel of the Lord, where are you?" he cried to the heavens.

At that moment, everyone stopped. The widow had risen and come toward him. Taking him by the hands, she led him to where the cadaver of her son lay, then removed the sheet that covered him.

"Behold the blood of my blood," she said. "May it descend upon the heads of your line if you do not achieve what you desire."

He drew near, to touch the boy.

"One moment," said the widow. "First, ask your God to fulfill my curse."

Elijah's heart was racing. But he believed what the angel had told him.

"May the blood of this boy descend upon the heads of my father and mother and upon my brothers, and upon the sons and daughters of my brothers, if I do not do that which I have said."

Then, despite all his doubts, his guilt, and his fears, "*He took him out of her bosom, and carried him up into a loft, where he abode, and laid him upon his own bed.*

"*And he cried unto the Lord, and said, O Lord, my God, hast Thou also brought evil upon the widow with whom I sojourn, by slaying her son?*

"*And he stretched himself upon the child three times, and cried unto the Lord, and said, O Lord, my God, I pray Thee, let this child's soul come into him again.*"

For long moments nothing happened. Elijah saw himself back in Gilead, standing before the soldier with an arrow pointing at his heart, aware that oftentimes a man's fate has nothing to do with what he believes or fears. He felt calm and confident as he had that day, knowing that, whatever the outcome might be, there was a reason that all of this had come to pass. Atop the Fifth Mountain, the angel had called this reason the "grandeur of God"; he hoped one day to understand why the Creator needed His creatures to demonstrate this glory.

It was then that the boy opened his eyes.

"Where's my mother?" he asked.

"Downstairs, waiting for you," replied Elijah, smiling.

"I had a strange dream. I was traveling through a dark hole, at a speed faster than the swiftest horse in Akbar. I saw a man— I am sure he was my father, though I never knew him. Then I came to a beautiful place where I wanted to stay; but another man—one I don't know but who seemed very good and brave— asked me kindly to turn away from there. I wanted to go on, but you awoke me."

The boy seemed sad; the place he had almost entered must be lovely.

"Don't leave me alone, for you made me come back from a place where I knew I'd be protected."

"Let us go downstairs," Elijah said. "Your mother wants to see you."

The boy tried to rise, but he was too weak to walk. Elijah took him in his arms and descended the stairs.

The people downstairs appeared overwhelmed by profound terror.

"Why are all these people here?" the boy asked.

Before Elijah could respond, the widow took the boy in her arms and began kissing him, weeping.

"What did they do to you, Mother? Why are you so sad?"

"I'm not sad, my son," she answered, drying her tears. "Never in my life have I been so happy."

Saying this, the widow threw herself on her knees and said in a loud voice:

"By this act I know that you are a man of God! The truth of the Lord comes from your words!"

Elijah embraced her, asking her to rise.

"Let this man go!" she told the soldiers. "He has overcome the evil that had descended upon my house!"

The people gathered there could not believe what they saw. A young woman of twenty, who worked as a painter, kneeled beside the widow. One by one, others imitated her gesture, including the soldiers charged with taking Elijah into captivity.

"Rise," he told them, "and worship the Lord. I am merely one of His servants, perhaps the least prepared."

But they all remained on their knees, their heads bowed.

"You spoke with the gods of the Fifth Mountain," he heard a voice say. "And now you can do miracles."

"There are no gods there. I saw an angel of the Lord, who commanded me to do this."

"You were with Baal and his brothers," said another person.

Elijah opened a path, pushing aside the kneeling people, and went out into the street. His heart was still racing, as if he had erred and failed to carry out the task that the angel had taught him. "To what avail is it to restore the dead to life if none believe the source of such power?" The angel had asked him to call out the name of the Lord three times but had told him nothing about how to explain the miracle to the multitude in the room below. "Can it be, as with the prophets of old, that all I desired was to show my own vanity?" he wondered.

He heard the voice of his guardian angel, with whom he had spoken since childhood.

"Thou hast been today with an angel of the Lord."

"Yes," replied Elijah. "But the angels of the Lord do not converse with men; they only transmit the orders that come from God."

"Use thy power," said the guardian angel.

Elijah did not understand what was meant by that. "I have no power but that which comes from the Lord," he said.

"Nor hath anyone. But all have the power of the Lord, and use it not."

And the angel said moreover:

"From this day forward, and until the moment thou returnest to the land thou hast abandoned, no other miracle will be granted thee."

"And when will that be?"

"The Lord needeth thee to rebuild Israel," said the angel. "Thou wilt tread thy land when thou hast learned to rebuild."

And he said nothing more.

PART II

THE HIGH PRIEST SAID THE PRAYERS TO THE RISING
sun and asked the god of the storm and the goddess of animals
to have mercy on the foolish. He had been told, that morning,
that Elijah had brought the widow's son back from the kingdom
of the dead.

The city was both frightened and excited. Everyone believed
the Israelite had received his powers from the gods of the Fifth
Mountain, and now it would be much more difficult to be rid of
him. "But the right moment will come," he told himself.

The gods would bring about an opportunity to do away
with him. But divine wrath had another purpose, and the
Assyrians' presence in the valley was a sign. Why were hundreds
of years of peace about to end? He had the answer: the invention
of Byblos. His country had developed a form of writing accessi-

ble to all, even to those who were unprepared to use it. Anyone could learn it in a short time, and that would mean the end of civilization.

The high priest knew that, of all the weapons of destruction that man could invent, the most terrible—and the most powerful—was the word. Daggers and spears left traces of blood; arrows could be seen at a distance. Poisons were detected in the end and avoided.

But the word managed to destroy without leaving clues. If the sacred rituals became widely known, many would be able to use them to attempt to change the Universe, and the gods would become confused. Till that moment, only the priestly caste knew the memory of the ancestors, which was transmitted orally, under oath that the information would be kept in secret. Or else years of study were needed to be able to decipher the characters that the Egyptians had spread throughout the world; thus only those who were highly trained—scribes and priests—could exchange written information.

Other peoples had their rudimentary forms of recording history, but these were so complicated that no one outside the regions where they were used would bother to learn them. The invention of Byblos, however, had one explosive aspect: it could be used in any country, independent of the language spoken. Even the Greeks, who generally rejected anything not born in their cities, had adopted the writing of Byblos as a common practice in their commercial transactions. As they were specialists in appropriating all that was novel, they had already baptized the invention of Byblos with a Greek name: *alphabet*.

Secrets guarded through centuries of civilization were at risk of being exposed to the light. Compared to this, Elijah's sacrilege in bringing someone back from the other bank of the river of death, as was the practice of the Egyptians, meant nothing.

"We are being punished because we are no longer able to safeguard that which is sacred," he thought. "The Assyrians are at our gates, they will cross the valley, and they will destroy the civilization of our ancestors."

And they would do away with writing. The high priest knew the enemy's presence was not mere happenstance.

It was the price to be paid. The gods had planned everything with great care so that none would perceive that they were responsible; they had placed in power a governor who was more concerned with trade than with the army, they had aroused the Assyrians' greed, had made rainfall ever more infrequent, and had brought an infidel to divide the city. Soon the final battle would be waged.

AKBAR WOULD GO ON EXISTING EVEN AFTER ALL THAT, but the threat from the characters of Byblos would be expunged from the face of the earth forever. The high priest carefully cleaned the stone that marked the spot where, many generations before, the foreign pilgrim had come upon the place appointed by heaven and had founded the city. "How beautiful it is," he thought. The stones were an image of the gods——hard, resistant, surviving under all conditions, and without the need to explain why they were there. The oral tradition held that the center of the world was marked by a stone, and in his childhood he had thought about searching out its location. He had nurtured the idea until this year. But when he saw the presence of the Assyrians in the depths of the valley, he understood he would never realize his dream.

"It's not important. It fell to my generation to be offered in sacrifice for having offended the gods. There are unavoidable things in the history of the world, and we must accept them."

He promised himself to obey the gods: he would make no attempt to forestall the war.

"Perhaps we have come to the end of days. There is no way around the crises that grow with each passing moment."

The high priest took up his staff and left the small temple; he had a meeting with the commander of Akbar's garrison.

◆

HE WAS NEARLY to the southern wall when he was approached by Elijah.

"The Lord has brought a boy back from the dead," the Israelite said. "The city believes in my power."

"The boy must not have been dead," replied the high priest. "It's happened before; the heart stops and then starts beating again. Today the entire city is talking about it; tomorrow, they will recall that the gods are close at hand and can hear what they say. Their mouths will fall silent once more. I must go; the Assyrians are preparing for battle."

"Hear what I have to say: after the miracle last night, I slept outside the walls because I needed a measure of calm. Then the same angel that I saw on the Fifth Mountain appeared to me again. And he told me: Akbar will be destroyed by the war."

"Cities cannot be destroyed," said the high priest. "They

will be rebuilt seventy times seven because the gods know where they have placed them, and they have need of them there."

◆

THE GOVERNOR APPROACHED, with a group of courtiers, and asked, "What are you saying?"

"That you should seek peace," Elijah repeated.

"If you are afraid, return to the place from which you came," the high priest replied coldly.

"Jezebel and her king are waiting for fugitive prophets, to slay them," said the governor. "But I should like you to tell me how you were able to climb the Fifth Mountain without being destroyed by the fire from heaven."

The high priest felt the need to interrupt that conversation. The governor was thinking about negotiating with the Assyrians and might want to use Elijah for his purposes.

"Do not listen to him," he said. "Yesterday, when he was brought into my presence to be judged, I saw him weep with fear."

"My tears were for the evil I felt I had caused you, for I fear but two things: the Lord, and myself. I did not flee from Israel, and I am ready to return as soon as the Lord permits. I will put an end to your beautiful princess, and the faith of Israel shall survive this threat too."

"One's heart must be very hard to resist the charms of Jezebel," the high priest said ironically. "However, even should that happen, we would send another woman even more beautiful, as we did long before Jezebel."

The high priest was telling the truth. Two hundred years before, a princess of Sidon had seduced the wisest of all Israel's rulers—King Solomon. She had bid him construct an altar to the goddess Astarte, and Solomon had obeyed. For that sacrilege, the Lord had raised up the neighboring armies and Solomon had nearly lost his throne.

"The same will happen with Ahab, Jezebel's husband," thought Elijah. The Lord would bring him to complete his task when the time came. But what did it avail him to try to convince these men who stood facing him? They were like those he had seen the night before, kneeling on the floor of the widow's house, praising the gods of the Fifth Mountain. Custom would never allow them to think in any other way.

◆

"A PITY that we must honor the law of hospitality," said the governor, apparently already having forgotten Elijah's words about peace. "If not for that, we could assist Jezebel in her labor of putting an end to the prophets."

"That is not the reason for sparing my life. You know that I am a valuable commodity, and you want to give Jezebel the pleasure of killing me with her own hands. However, since yesterday, the people attribute miraculous powers to me. They think I met the gods on the Fifth Mountain. For your part, it would not upset you to offend the gods, but you have no desire to vex the inhabitants of the city."

The governor and the high priest left Elijah talking to himself and walked toward the city walls. At that moment the high priest decided that he would kill the Israelite prophet at the first opportunity; what had till now been only merchandise had been transformed into a menace.

◆

WHEN HE SAW them walk away, Elijah lost hope; what could he do to serve the Lord? He then began to shout in the middle of the square, "People of Akbar! Last night, I climbed the Fifth Mountain and spoke with the gods who dwell there. When I returned, I was able to reclaim a boy from the kingdom of the dead!"

The people gathered about him; the story was already known throughout the city. The governor and the high priest stopped and retraced their steps to see what was happening. The Israelite prophet was saying that he had seen the gods of the Fifth Mountain worshiping a superior God.

"I'll have him slain," said the high priest.

"And the population will rise up against us," replied the governor, who had an interest in what the foreigner was saying. "It's better to wait for him to commit an error."

"Before I descended from the mountain," continued Elijah, "the gods charged me with helping the governor against the threat from the Assyrians! I know he is an honorable man and wishes to hear me; but there are those whose interests lie with war and will not allow me to come near him."

"The Israelite is a holy man," said an old man to the governor. "No one can climb the Fifth Mountain without being struck dead by the fire of heaven, but this man did so—and now he raises the dead."

"Sidon, Tyre, and all the cities of Phoenicia have a history of peace," said another old man. "We have been through other threats worse than this and overcome them."

Several sick and lame people began to approach, opening a path through the crowd, touching Elijah's garments and asking to be cured of their afflictions.

"Before advising the governor, heal the sick," said the high priest. "Then we shall believe the gods of the Fifth Mountain are with you."

Elijah recalled what the angel had said the night before: only those powers given to ordinary people would be permitted him.

"The sick are asking for help," insisted the high priest. "We are waiting."

"First we must attend to avoiding war. There will be more sick, and more infirm, if we fail."

The governor interrupted the conversation. "Elijah will come with us. He has been touched by divine inspiration."

Though he did not believe any gods existed on the Fifth Mountain, the governor had need of an ally to help him to convince the people that peace with the Assyrians was the only solution.

◆

AS THEY WALKED to their meeting with the commander, the high priest commented to Elijah, "You don't believe anything you just said."

"I believe that peace is the only way out. But I do not believe the top of the Fifth Mountain is inhabited by gods. I have been there."

"And what did you see?"

"An angel of the Lord. I had seen this angel before, in several places I have been," replied Elijah. "And there is but one God."

The high priest laughed.

"You mean that, in your opinion, the same god who sends the storm also made the wheat, even though they are completely different things?"

"Do you see the Fifth Mountain?" Elijah asked. "From whichever side you look, it appears different, though it is the same mountain. Thus it is with all of Creation: many faces of the same God."

◆

THEY CAME TO THE TOP of the wall, from which they could see the enemy encampment in the distance. In the desert valley, the white tents sprang into sight.

Some time earlier, when the sentinels had first noted the presence of the Assyrians at one end of the valley, spies had said that they were there on a mission of reconnaissance; the commander had suggested taking them prisoner and selling them as slaves. The governor had decided in favor of another strategy: doing nothing. He was gambling that by establishing good relations with them, he could open up a new market for the glass manufactured in Akbar. In addition, even if they were there to prepare for war, the Assyrians knew that small cities will always side with the victor. In this case, all the Assyrian generals desired was to pass through without resistance on their way to Sidon and Tyre, the cities that held the treasure and knowledge of his people.

The patrol had encamped at the entrance to the valley, and little by little reinforcements had arrived. The high priest claimed to know the reason: the city had a well, the only well in several days' travel in the desert. If the Assyrians planned to conquer Tyre or Sidon, they needed that water to supply their armies.

At the end of the first month, they could still be expelled. At the end of the second month, Akbar could still win easily and negotiate an honorable withdrawal of the Assyrian soldiers.

They waited for battle to break out, but there was no attack. At the end of the fifth month, they could still win the battle. "They're going to attack very soon, because they must be suffering from thirst," the governor told himself. He asked the commander to draw up defense strategies and to order his men into constant training to react to a surprise attack.

But he concentrated only on preparations for peace.

◆

HALF A YEAR HAD PASSED, and the Assyrian army had made no move. Tension in Akbar, which had grown during the first weeks of occupation, had now diminished almost entirely. People went about their lives: farmers once again returned to their fields; artisans made wine, glass, and soap; tradesmen continued to buy and sell their merchandise. Everyone believed that, as Akbar had not attacked the enemy, the crisis would soon be settled through negotiations. Everyone knew the governor was chosen by the gods and that he always made the wisest decision.

When Elijah arrived in the city, the governor had ordered rumors spread of the curse the foreigner brought with him; in this way, if the threat of war became insurmountable, he could blame the presence of the foreigner as the principal cause of the disaster. The inhabitants of Akbar would be convinced that with the death of the Israelite the Universe would return to normal. The governor would then explain that it was too late to demand that the Assyrians withdraw; he would order Elijah killed and explain to his people that peace was the best solution. In his view, the merchants—who desired peace—would force the others to agree to this idea.

During these months, he had fought the pressure from the high priest and the commander demanding that he attack at once. The gods of the Fifth Mountain had never abandoned him; now, with the miracle of the resurrection last night, Elijah's life was more important than his execution.

◆

"WHY IS THIS foreigner with you?" asked the commander.

"He has been enlightened by the gods," answered the governor. "And he will help us to find the best solution." He quickly changed the subject. "The number of tents appears to have increased today."

"And it will increase even more tomorrow," said the commander. "If we had attacked when they were nothing but a patrol, they probably wouldn't have returned."

"You're mistaken. Some of them would have escaped, and they would have returned to avenge themselves."

"When we delay the harvest, the fruit rots," insisted the commander. "But when we delay resolving problems, they continue to grow."

The governor explained that peace, the great pride of his people, had reigned in Phoenicia for almost three centuries. What would the generations yet unborn say if he were to interrupt this era of prosperity?

"Send an emissary to negotiate with them," said Elijah. "The best warrior is the one who succeeds in transforming an enemy into a friend."

"We don't know exactly what they want. We don't even know if they desire to conquer our city. How can we negotiate?"

"There are threatening signs. An army does not waste its time on military exercises far from its own country."

Each day saw the arrival of more soldiers, and the governor mused about the amount of water necessary for all those men. In a short time, the entire city would be defenseless before the enemy army.

"Can we attack now?" the high priest asked the commander.

"Yes, we can. We shall lose many men, but the city will be saved. But we must decide quickly."

"We must not do that, Governor. The gods of the Fifth Mountain told me that we still have time to find a pacific solution," Elijah said.

Even after hearing the conversation between the high priest and the Israelite, the governor feigned agreement. To him, it made little difference whether Sidon and Tyre were ruled by Phoenicians, by Canaanites, or by Assyrians; what mattered was that the city be able to go on trading its products.

"We must attack," insisted the high priest.

"One more day," said the governor. "It may be that things will resolve themselves."

He must decide forthwith the best way to face the Assyrian threat. He descended from the wall and headed for the palace, asking the Israelite to go with him.

On the way, he observed the people around him: the shepherds taking their flocks to the mountains; the farmers going to the fields, trying to wrest from the arid soil sustenance for themselves and their families. Soldiers were exercising with spears, and a few newly arrived merchants displayed their wares in the square. Incredibly, the Assyrians had not closed off the road that traversed the valley from end to end; tradesmen still moved about with their merchandise and paid the city its tax for transport.

"Now that they have amassed such a powerful force, why have they not closed the road?" Elijah asked.

"The Assyrian empire needs the products that arrive in the ports of Sidon and Tyre," replied the governor. "If the traders were threatened, they would interrupt the flow of supplies. The consequences would be more serious than a military defeat. There must be some way to avoid war."

"Yes," said Elijah. "If they want water, we can sell it to them."

The governor said nothing. But he understood that he could use the Israelite as a weapon against those who desired war; should the high priest persist with the idea of fighting the Assyrians, Elijah would be the only one who could face him. The governor suggested they take a walk together, to talk.

THE HIGH PRIEST REMAINED ATOP THE WALL, OBSERVING
the enemy.

"What can the gods do to deter the invaders?" asked the
commander.

"I have carried out sacrifices at the Fifth Mountain. I have
asked them to send us a more courageous leader."

"We should act as Jezebel has done: put an end to the
prophets. A simple Israelite, who yesterday was condemned to
die, is today used by the governor to entice the people to peace."

The commander looked at the mountain.

"We can have Elijah assassinated. And use my warriors to
remove the governor from his position."

"I shall order Elijah killed," replied the high priest. "As for
the governor, we can do nothing: his ancestors have been in

power for several generations. His grandfather was our chieftain, who handed power down to his son, who in turn handed it to him."

"Why does custom forbid our bringing to power someone more efficient?"

"Custom exists to maintain the world in order. If we meddle with it, the world itself will perish."

The high priest looked about him. The heavens and the earth, the mountains and the valley, everything fulfilling what had been written for it. Sometimes the ground shook; at other times—such as now—there were long periods without rain. But the stars continued undisturbed in their place, and the sun had not fallen onto the heads of men. All because, since the Flood, men had learned that it was impossible to change the order of Creation.

In the past, only the Fifth Mountain had existed. Men and gods had lived together, strolled through the gardens of paradise, talking and laughing with one another. But human beings had sinned, and the gods expelled them; having nowhere to send them, they created the earth surrounding the mountain, so they could cast them there, keep vigil over them, and ensure that they would forever remember that they abided on a plane far inferior to that of the dwellers of the Fifth Mountain.

The gods took care, however, to leave open a path of return; if humanity carefully followed the way, it would one day go back to the mountaintop. So that this idea would not be forgotten, they charged the priests and the rulers with keeping it alive in the minds of the people.

All peoples shared the same belief: if the families anointed by the gods were removed from power, the consequences would be grave. No one now remembered why these families had been chosen, but everyone knew they were related to the divine families. Akbar had existed for hundreds of years, and its affairs had always been administered by the ancestors of the present governor; it had been invaded many times, had been in the hands of oppressors and barbarians, but with the passing of time the invaders had left or been expelled. Afterward, the old order would be reestablished and the people would return to the life they had known before.

The priests' obligation was to preserve this order: the world had a destiny, and it was governed by laws. The era of attempting to fathom the gods was past; now was the time to respect them and do their will. They were capricious and easily vexed.

If not for the harvest rituals, the earth would bring forth no fruit. If certain sacrifices were neglected, the city would be infested with fatal diseases. If the god of weather were provoked anew, he could cause wheat and men to cease to grow.

"Behold the Fifth Mountain," the high priest told the commander. "From its peak, the gods rule over the valley and protect us. They have an eternal plan for Akbar. The foreigner will be killed, or return to his own land; the governor will one day be no more, and his son will be wiser than he. All that we experience today is fleeting."

"We have need of a new chieftain," said the commander. "If we continue in the hands of this governor, we shall be destroyed."

The high priest knew that this was what the gods desired, in order to put an end to the writing of Byblos. But he said nothing; he was pleased to have evidence once again that, unwittingly or not, the rulers always fulfilled the destiny of the Universe.

◆

WALKING THROUGH THE CITY with the governor, Elijah explained to him his plans for peace and was made his counselor. When they arrived at the square, more sick people approached, but he said that the gods of the Fifth Mountain had forbidden him to heal. At the end of the afternoon, he returned to the widow's house; the child was playing in the street, and Elijah gave thanks for having been the instrument of the Lord's miracle.

She was awaiting him for the evening meal. To his surprise, there was a bottle of wine on the table.

"People brought gifts to please you," she said. "And I want to ask your forgiveness for the injustice I did you."

"What injustice?" asked Elijah, surprised. "Don't you see that everything is part of God's design?"

The widow smiled, her eyes shone, and he saw for the first time that she was beautiful. She was at least ten years older than he, but at that moment he felt great tenderness for her. He was not accustomed to such sentiments, and he was filled with fear; he remembered Jezebel's eyes, and the wish he had made upon leaving Ahab's palace—to marry a woman from Lebanon.

"Though my life has been useless, at least I had my son. And his story will be remembered, because he returned from the kingdom of the dead," the woman said.

"Your life is not useless. I came to Akbar at the Lord's order, and you took me in. If someday your son's story is remembered, I am certain that yours will be also."

The woman filled two cups. They drank to the sun, which was setting, and to the stars of heaven.

"You have come from a distant country, following the signs of a God I did not know but who now has become my Lord. My son has also returned from a far-off land, and he will have a beautiful tale to tell his grandchildren. The priests will preserve and pass on his words to generations yet to come."

It was through the priests' memory that cities knew of their past, their conquests, the ancient gods, and the warriors who defended the land with their blood. Even though there were now new ways to record the past, the inhabitants of Akbar had confidence only in the memory of their priests: one could write anything he chose, but no one could remember things that never were.

"And what have I to tell?" the widow continued, filling the cup that Elijah had quickly drained. "I don't have the strength or the beauty of Jezebel. My life is like all the rest: a marriage arranged by my father and mother when I was a child, household tasks when I came of age, worship on holy days, my husband always busy with other things. When he was alive, we never spoke of anything important. He was preoccupied with his trade, I took care of the house, and that was how we spent the best of our years.

"After his death, nothing was left for me except poverty and raising my son. When he becomes a man, he will cross the seas and I shall no longer matter to anyone. I feel neither hate nor resentment, only a sense of my own uselessness."

Elijah refilled his cup. His heart was beginning to give signs of alarm; he was enjoying being at this woman's side. Love could be a more frightening experience than standing before Ahab's soldier with an arrow aimed at his heart; if the arrow had struck him, he would be dead—and the rest was up to God. But if love struck him, he alone would have to take responsibility for the consequences.

"I have so wished for love in my life," he thought. And yet, now that it was before him—and beyond doubt it was there; all he had to do was not run away from it—his sole thought was to forget it as quickly as possible.

His mind returned to the day he came to Akbar, after his exile on the Cherith. He was so weary and thirsty that he could remember nothing except the moment he recovered from fainting, and seeing her drip water onto his lips. His face was very close to hers, closer than he had ever been to any woman in his entire life. He had noticed that she had Jezebel's green eyes, but with a different glow, as if they could reflect the cedar trees, the ocean of which he had often dreamed but never known, and—how could it be?—her very soul.

"I should so like to tell her that," he thought. "But I don't know how. It's easier to speak of the love of God."

Elijah took another sip. She sensed that she had said something that displeased him, and she decided to change the subject.

"Did you climb the Fifth Mountain?" she asked.

He nodded.

She would have liked to ask what he had seen there in the heights and how he had escaped the fire of the heavens. But he seemed loath to discuss it.

"You are a prophet," she thought. "Read my heart."

Since the Israelite had come into her life, everything had changed. Even poverty was easier to bear, for that foreigner had awakened something she had never felt: love. When her son had fallen ill, she had fought the entire neighborhood so he could remain in her house.

She knew that to him the Lord was more important than anything that took place beneath the sky. She was aware that it was a dream impossible of fulfillment, for the man before her could go away at any moment, shed Jezebel's blood, and never return to tell of what had happened.

Even so, she would go on loving him, because for the first time in her life, she knew freedom. She could love him, even if he never knew; she did not need his permission to miss him, to think of him every moment of the day, to await him for the evening meal, and to worry about the plots that people could be weaving against the foreigner.

This was freedom: to feel what the heart desired, with no thought to the opinion of the rest. She had fought with her neighbors and her friends about the stranger's presence in her house; there was no need to fight against herself.

Elijah drank a bit of wine, excused himself, and went to his room. She went out, rejoiced at the sight of her son playing in front of the house, and decided to take a short walk.

She was free, for love liberates.

◆

ELIJAH STARED at the wall of his room for a long time. Finally, he decided to invoke his angel.

"My soul is in danger," he said.

The angel said nothing. Elijah was in doubt about continuing the conversation, but now it was too late: he could not call him forth for no reason.

"When I'm with that woman, I don't feel good."

"Just the opposite," answered the angel. "And that disturbs thee, because thou canst come to love her."

Elijah felt shame, for the angel knew his soul.

"Love is dangerous," he said.

"Very," replied the angel. "And so?"

He suddenly disappeared.

His angel had none of the doubts that tormented Elijah's soul. Yes, he knew what love was; he had seen the king of Israel abandon the Lord because Jezebel, a princess of Sidon, had conquered his heart. Tradition told that King Solomon had come close to losing his throne over a foreign woman. King David had sent one of his best friends to his death after falling in love with his friend's wife. Because of Delilah, Samson had been taken prisoner and had his eyes put out by the Philistines.

How could he not know what love was? History was filled with tragic examples. And even had he no knowledge of sacred Scripture, he had the example of his friends, and of the friends of friends, lost in long nights of waiting and suffering. If he'd had a wife in Israel, it would have been difficult for him to leave his city when the Lord commanded, and he would be dead now.

"I am waging combat in vain," he thought. "Love will win this battle, and I will love her all of my days. Lord, send me back to Israel so that I may never have to tell this woman what I feel. Because she does not love me and will say to me that her heart lies buried alongside the body of her heroic husband."

THE NEXT DAY, ELIJAH MET WITH THE COMMANDER AGAIN and learned that more tents had been erected.

"What is the present complement of warriors?" he asked.

"I give no information to an enemy of Jezebel."

"I am a counselor of the governor," replied Elijah. "He named me his assistant yesterday afternoon. You have been informed of this, and you owe me an answer."

The commander felt an urge to put an end to the foreigner's life.

"The Assyrians have two soldiers for each one of ours," he finally replied.

Elijah knew that, to succeed, the enemy needed a much larger force.

"We are approaching the ideal moment to begin peace negotiations," he said. "They will understand that we are being generous and we shall achieve better conditions. Any general knows that to conquer a city five invaders are needed for each defender."

"They'll have that number unless we attack now."

"Even with all their lines of supply, they will not have enough water for so many men. And the moment to send our envoys will have come."

"What moment is that?"

"We shall allow the number of Assyrian warriors to increase a bit more. When the situation becomes unbearable, they will be forced to attack. But, with the proportion of three or four to one of ours, they know they will end in defeat. That is when our envoys will offer peace, safe passage, and the sale of water. This is the governor's plan."

The commander said nothing and allowed the foreigner to leave. Even with Elijah dead, the governor could still insist on the idea. He swore to himself that if the situation came to that point he would kill the governor, then commit suicide, because he had no desire to witness the fury of the gods.

Nevertheless, under no circumstance would he let his people be betrayed by money.

◆

"TAKE ME BACK to the land of Israel, O Lord," cried Elijah every afternoon, as he walked through the valley. "Let not my heart continue imprisoned in Akbar."

Following a custom of the prophets he had known as a child, he began lashing himself with a whip whenever he thought of the widow. His back became raw flesh, and for two days he lay delirious with fever. When he awoke, the first thing he saw was the woman's face; she had tended to his wounds with ointment and olive oil. As he was too weak to descend the stairs, she brought food to his room.

◆

As soon as he was well, Elijah resumed walking through the valley.

"Take me back to the land of Israel, O Lord," he said. "My heart is trapped in Akbar, but my body can still continue the journey."

The angel appeared. It was not the angel of the Lord, whom he had seen on the mountain, but the one who watched over him, and to whose voice he was accustomed.

"The Lord heareth the prayers of those who ask to put aside hatred. But He is deaf to those who would flee from love."

◆

THE THREE OF THEM supped together every night. As the Lord had promised, meal had never been wanting in the barrel nor oil in the vessel.

They rarely spoke as they ate. One night, however, the boy asked, "What is a prophet?"

"Someone who goes on listening to the same voices he heard as a child. And still believes in them. In this way, he can know the angels' thoughts."

"Yes, I know what you are speaking of," said the boy. "I have friends no one else can see."

"Never forget them, even if adults call it foolishness. That way you will always know God's will."

"I'll see into the future, like the soothsayers of Babylon," said the boy.

"Prophets don't know the future. They only transmit the words that the Lord inspires in them at the present moment. That is why I am here, not knowing when I shall return to my own country; He will not tell me before it is necessary."

The woman's eyes became sad. Yes, one day he would depart.

◆

ELIJAH NO LONGER cried out to the Lord. He had decided that, when the moment arrived to leave Akbar, he would take the widow and her son. But he would say nothing until the time came.

Perhaps she would not want to leave. Perhaps she had not even divined his feelings for her, for he himself had been a long time in understanding them. If it should happen thus, it would be better; he could then dedicate himself wholly to the expulsion of Jezebel and the rebuilding of Israel. His mind would be too occupied to think about love.

"The Lord is my shepherd," he said, recalling an ancient

prayer of King David. "He restoreth my soul. He leadeth me beside still waters.

"And He will not let me forget the meaning of my life," he concluded in his own words.

◆

ONE AFTERNOON he returned home earlier than was his wont, to find the widow sitting in the doorway of the house.

"What are you doing?"

"I have nothing to do," she replied.

"Then learn something. At this moment, many people have stopped living. They do not become angry, nor cry out; they merely wait for time to pass. They did not accept the challenges of life, so life no longer challenges them. You are running that same risk; react, face life, but do not stop living."

"My life has begun to have meaning again," she said, casting her gaze downward. "Ever since you came here."

◆

FOR A FRACTION of a second, he felt he could open his heart to her. But he decided not to take the risk; she must surely be referring to something else.

"Start doing something," he said, changing the subject. "In that way, time will be an ally, not an enemy."

"But what can I learn?"

Elijah thought for a moment.

"The writing of Byblos. It will be useful if one day you have to travel."

The woman decided to dedicate herself body and spirit to that study. She had never thought of leaving Akbar, but from the way he spoke perhaps he was thinking of taking her with him.

Once more, she felt free. Once more, she awoke at morning and strode smiling through the streets of the city.

"ELIJAH STILL LIVES," THE COMMANDER TOLD THE HIGH priest two months later. "You have not succeeded in having him killed."

"In all of Akbar there is no man who will carry out that mission. The Israelite has comforted the sick, visited the imprisoned, fed the hungry. When anyone has a dispute to settle with his neighbor, he calls on him, and all accept his judgments, because they are just. The governor is using him to increase his own standing among the people, but no one sees this."

"The merchants have no wish for war. If the governor finds favor enough with the people to convince them that peace is better, we shall never be able to expel the Assyrians. Elijah must be killed immediately."

The high priest pointed to the Fifth Mountain, its peak cloud-covered as always.

"The gods will not allow their country to be humiliated by a foreign power. They will take action; something will come to pass, and we shall be able to grasp the opportunity."

"What kind of opportunity?"

"I do not know. But I shall remain vigilant for the signs. Do not provide any further truthful information about the Assyrian forces. When you are asked, say only that the proportion of the invading warriors is still four to one. And go on training your troops."

"Why should I do that? If they attain the proportion of five to one, we are lost."

"No. We shall be in a state of equality. When the battle begins, you will not be fighting an inferior enemy and therefore cannot be branded a coward who abuses the weak. Akbar's army will confront an adversary as powerful as itself, and it will win the battle—because its commander chose the right strategy."

Piqued by vanity, the commander accepted the proposal. And from that moment, he began to withhold information from the governor and from Elijah.

TWO MORE MONTHS PASSED, AND ONE MORNING THE
Assyrian army reached the proportion of five soldiers for each of
Akbar's defenders. They could attack at any moment.

For some time Elijah had suspected that the commander was
lying about the enemy forces, but this might yet turn to his
advantage: when the proportion reached the critical point, it
would be a simple matter to convince the populace that peace
was the only solution.

These were his thoughts as he headed toward the place in the
square where, once a week, he was wont to help the inhabitants
of the city to settle their disputes. In general, the issues were triv-
ial: quarrels between neighbors, old people reluctant to pay their
taxes, tradesmen who felt they had been cheated in their business
dealings.

The governor was there; it was his custom to appear now and again to see Elijah in action. The ill will the prophet had felt toward him had disappeared completely; he had discovered that he was a man of wisdom, concerned with solving problems before they arose—although he was not a spiritual man and greatly feared death. On several occasions he had conferred upon Elijah's decisions the force of law. At other times Elijah, having disagreed with a decision, had with the passage of time come to see that the governor was right.

Akbar was becoming a model of the modern Phoenician city. The governor had created a fairer system of taxation, had improved the streets of the city, and administered intelligently the profits from the imposts on merchandise. There was a time when Elijah had asked him to do away with the consumption of wine and beer, for most of the cases he was called upon to settle involved aggression by intoxicated persons. The governor had told him that a city could only be considered great if that type of thing took place. According to tradition, the gods were pleased when men enjoyed themselves after a day's work, and they protected drunkards.

In addition, the region enjoyed the reputation of producing one of the finest wines in the world, and foreigners would be suspicious if the inhabitants themselves did not consume the drink. Elijah respected the governor's decision, and he came to agree that happy people produce more.

"You need not put forth so much effort," the governor told

him before Elijah began his day's work. "A counselor helps the government with nothing more than his opinions."

"I miss my country and want to return. So long as I am involved in activity, I feel myself of use and forget that I am a foreigner," he replied.

"And better control my love for her," he thought to himself.

◆

THE POPULAR TRIBUNAL had come to attract an audience ever alert to what took place. The people were beginning to gather: some were the aged, no longer able to work in the fields, who came to applaud or jeer Elijah's decisions; others were directly involved in the matters to be discussed, either because they had been the victims or because they expected to profit from the outcome. There were also women and children who, lacking work, needed to fill their free time.

He began the morning's proceedings: the first case was that of a shepherd who had dreamed of a treasure buried near the pyramids of Egypt and needed money to journey there. Elijah had never been in Egypt, but he knew it was far away, and he said that he would be hard pressed to find the necessary means, but if the shepherd were to sell his sheep to pay for his dream, he would surely find what he sought.

Next came a woman who desired to learn the magical arts of Israel. Elijah said he was no teacher, merely a prophet.

As he was preparing to find an amicable solution to a case in which a farmer had cursed another man's wife, a soldier pushed his way through the crowd and addressed the governor.

"A patrol has captured a spy," the newcomer said, sweating profusely. "He's being brought here!"

A tremor ran through the crowd; it would be the first time they had witnessed a judgment of that kind.

"Death!" someone shouted. "Death to the enemy!"

Everyone present agreed, screaming. In the blink of an eye the news spread throughout the city, and the square was packed with people. The other cases were judged only with great difficulty, for at every instant someone would interrupt Elijah, asking that the foreigner be brought forth at once.

"I cannot judge such a case," he said. "It is a matter for the authorities of Akbar."

"For what reason have the Assyrians come here?" said one man. "Can they not see we have been at peace for many generations?"

"Why do they want our water?" shouted another. "Why are they threatening our city?"

For months none had dared speak in public about the presence of the enemy. Though all could see an ever-growing number of tents being erected on the horizon, though the merchants spoke of the need to begin negotiations for peace at once, the people of Akbar refused to believe that they were living under threat of invasion. Save for the quickly subdued incursion of some insignificant tribe, war existed only in the memory of priests. They spoke of a nation called Egypt, with horses and chariots of war and gods that looked like animals. But that had all happened long ago; Egypt was no longer a country of import, and the warriors, with their dark skin and strange language, had returned to their own land. Now the inhabitants of Sidon and Tyre dominated the seas and were spreading a new empire around the world, and though they were tried warriors, they had discovered a new way of fighting: trade.

"Why are they restless?" the governor asked Elijah.

"Because they sense that something has changed. We both know that, from this moment on, the Assyrians can attack at any time. Both you and I know that the commander has been lying about the number of the enemy's troops."

"But he wouldn't be mad enough to say that to anyone. He would be sowing panic."

"Every man can sense when he is in danger; he begins to react in strange ways, to have premonitions, to feel something in the air. And he tries to deceive himself, for he thinks himself incapable of confronting the situation. They have tried to deceive themselves till now; but there comes a moment when one must face the truth."

The high priest arrived.

"Let us go to the palace and convene the Council of Akbar. The commander is on his way."

"Do not do so," Elijah told the governor in a low voice. "They will force on you what you have no wish to do."

"We must go," insisted the high priest. "A spy has been captured, and urgent measures must be taken."

"Make the judgment in the midst of the people," murmured Elijah. "They will help you, for their desire is for peace, even as they ask for war."

"Bring the man here!" ordered the governor. The crowd shouted joyously; for the first time, they would witness a conclave of the Council.

"We cannot do that!" said the high priest. "It is a matter of great delicacy, one that requires calm in order to be resolved!"

A few jeers. Many protests.

"Bring him here," repeated the governor. "His judgment shall be in this square, amid the people. Together we have worked to transform Akbar into a prosperous city, and together we shall pass judgment on all that threatens us."

The decision was met with clapping of hands. A group of soldiers appeared dragging a blood-covered, half-naked man. He must have been severely beaten before being brought there.

All noise ceased. A heavy silence fell over the crowd; from another corner of the square could be heard the sound of pigs and children playing.

"Why have you done this to the prisoner?" shouted the governor.

"He resisted," answered one of the guards. "He claimed he wasn't a spy and said he had come here to talk to you."

The governor ordered that three chairs be brought from his

palace. His servants appeared, bearing the cloak of justice, which he always donned when a meeting of the Council of Akbar was convened.

◆

THE GOVERNOR and the high priest sat down. The third chair was reserved for the commander, who was yet to arrive.

"I solemnly declare in session the tribunal of the Council of Akbar. Let the elders draw near."

A group of old men approached, forming a semicircle around the chairs. This was the council of elders; in bygone times, their opinions were respected and obeyed. Today, however, the role of the group was merely ceremonial; they were present to accept whatever the ruler decided.

After a few formalities such as a prayer to the gods of the Fifth Mountain and the declaiming of the names of several ancient heroes, the governor addressed the prisoner.

"What is it you want?" he asked.

The man did not reply. He stared at him in a strange way, as if he were an equal.

"What is it you want?" the governor repeated.

The high priest touched his arm.

"We need an interpreter. He does not speak our language."

The order was given, and one of the guards left in search of a merchant who could serve as interpreter. Tradesmen never came to the sessions that Elijah held; they were constantly occupied with conducting their business and counting their profits.

While they waited, the high priest whispered, "They beat the prisoner because they are frightened. Allow me to carry out this judgment, and say nothing: panic makes everyone aggressive, and we must show authority, lest we lose control of the situation."

The governor did not answer. He too was frightened. He sought out Elijah with his eyes, but from where he sat could not see him.

A merchant arrived, forcibly brought by the guard. He complained that the tribunal was wasting his time and that he had many matters to resolve. But the high priest, looking sternly at him, bade him to be silent and to interpret the conversation.

"What do you want here?" the governor asked.

"I am no spy," the man replied. "I am a general of the army. I have come to speak with you."

The audience, completely silent till then, began to scream as soon as these words were translated. They called it a lie and demanded the immediate punishment of death.

The high priest asked for silence, then turned to the prisoner.

"About what do you wish to speak?"

"The governor has the reputation of being a wise man," said the Assyrian. "We have no desire to destroy this city: what interests us is Sidon and Tyre. But Akbar lies athwart the route, controlling this valley; if we are forced to fight, we shall lose time and men. I come to propose a treaty."

"The man speaks the truth," thought Elijah. He had noticed that he was surrounded by a group of soldiers who hid from view the spot where the governor was sitting. "He thinks as we do. The Lord has performed a miracle and will bring an end to this dangerous situation."

The high priest rose and shouted to the people, "Do you see? They want to destroy us without combat!"

"Go on," the governor told the prisoner.

The high priest, however, again intervened.

"Our governor is a good man who does not wish to shed a man's blood. But we are in a situation of war, and the prisoner before us is an enemy!"

"He's right!" shouted someone from the crowd.

Elijah realized his mistake. The high priest was playing on the crowd while the governor was merely trying to be just. He attempted to move closer, but he was shoved back. One of the soldiers held him by the arm.

"Stay here. After all, this was your idea."

He looked behind: it was the commander, and he was smiling.

"We must not listen to any proposal," the high priest continued, his passion flowing in his words and gestures. "If we show we are willing to negotiate, we shall also be showing that we are fearful. And the people of Akbar are courageous; they have the means to resist any invasion."

"This prisoner is a man seeking peace," said the governor, addressing the crowd.

Someone said, "Merchants seek peace. Priests desire peace. Governors administer peace. But an army wants only one thing: war!"

"Can't you see that we were able to face the religious threat from Israel without war?" bellowed the governor. "We sent neither armies nor navies, but Jezebel. Now they worship Baal, without our having to sacrifice even one man on the battlefield."

"They didn't send a beautiful woman, they sent their warriors!" shouted the high priest even more loudly.

The people were demanding the Assyrian's death. The governor took the high priest by the arm.

"Sit down," he said. "You go too far."

"The idea of public judgment was yours. Or rather it was the Israelite traitor's, who seems to command the acts of the ruler of Akbar."

"I shall settle accounts with him later. Now, we must discover what the Assyrian wants. For many generations, men tried to impose their will by force; they spoke of what they wanted but cared not what the people thought—and all those empires have been destroyed. Our people have grown because they learned how to listen; this is how we developed trade—by listening to what the other person desires and doing whatever was possible to satisfy him. The result is profit."

The high priest nodded.

"Your words seem wise, and that is the greatest danger of all. If you were speaking folly, it would be simple to prove you wrong. But what you have just said is leading us into a trap."

Those in the front row heard the argument. Until that moment, the governor had always sought out the Council's opinion, and Akbar had an excellent reputation. Sidon and Tyre had sent emissaries to see how the city was administered; its name had even reached the ears of the emperor, and with some small good fortune, the governor might end his days as a minister at the imperial court.

Today, his authority had been challenged publicly. If he did not make a decision, he would lose the respect of the people—and no longer be capable of making important decisions, for none would obey him.

"Continue," he told the prisoner, ignoring the high priest's furious gaze and demanding that the interpreter translate his question.

"I have come to propose an agreement," said the Assyrian. "Allow us to pass, and we shall march against Sidon and Tyre. When those cities have been overcome—as they surely will be, because a great many of their warriors are on ships, occupied with trade—we shall be generous with Akbar. And keep you as governor."

"Do you see?" asked the high priest, again rising to his feet. "They think our governor barters Akbar's honor for an office!"

The multitude began to roar in outrage. That half-naked,

wounded prisoner wanted to lay down rules! A defeated man was proposing the surrender of the city! Several people rushed forward to attack him; with much effort, the guards managed to keep control of the situation.

"Wait!" said the governor, trying to speak above the din. "We have before us a defenseless man, one who can arouse in us no fear. We know that our army is better prepared, that our warriors are braver. We need prove that to no one. Should we decide to fight, we will win the battle, but the losses will be enormous."

Elijah closed his eyes and prayed that the governor could convince his people.

"Our ancestors spoke to us of the Egyptian empire, but it is no more," he continued. "Now we are returning once again to the Golden Age. Our fathers and their fathers before them were able to live in peace; why should we be the ones to break this tradition? Modern warfare is carried out through commerce, not on the field of battle."

Little by little, the crowd fell silent. The governor was succeeding!

When the noise ceased, he turned to the Assyrian.

"What you are proposing is not enough. To cross our lands, you must also pay taxes, as do the merchants."

"Believe this, Governor: Akbar has no choice," replied the prisoner. "We have men enough to raze this city and kill its every inhabitant. You have long been at peace and have forgotten how to fight, while we have been conquering the world."

Murmurs began again in the crowd. Elijah thought, "He cannot betray indecisiveness now." But it was difficult to deal with the Assyrian prisoner, who even while captive imposed his conditions. Moment by moment, more people were arriving; Elijah noticed that the tradesmen, concerned about the unfolding of events, had deserted their places of work to join the audience. The judgment had taken on a dangerous significance; there was no longer any way to retreat from making a decision, whether for negotiation or for death.

◆

THE ONLOOKERS began to take sides; some defended peace while others demanded that Akbar resist. The governor whispered to the high priest, "This man has challenged me in public. But so have you."

The high priest turned to him. And, speaking so none could hear, told him to condemn the Assyrian to death immediately.

"I do not ask, I demand. It is I who keep you in power, and I can put an end to that whenever I wish, do you understand? I know sacrifices to appease the wrath of the gods, if we are forced to replace the ruling family. It will not be the first time; even in Egypt, an empire that lasted thousands of years, there have been many cases of dynasties being replaced. Yet the Universe continued in its order, and the heavens did not fall upon our heads."

The governor turned pale.

"The commander is in the middle of the crowd, with some of his soldiers. If you insist on negotiating with this man, I will tell everyone that the gods have abandoned you. And you will be deposed. Let us go on with the judgment. And you shall do exactly as I order."

If Elijah had been in sight, the governor would have had a way out: he could have asked the Israelite prophet to say he had seen an angel on the Fifth Mountain, as he had recounted. He would recall the story of the resurrection of the widow's son. And it would be the word of Elijah—who had already proved himself able to perform a miracle—against the word of a man who had never demonstrated any type of supernatural power.

But Elijah had deserted him, and he had no choice. In any case, it was only a prisoner, and no army in the world starts a war because it lost one soldier.

"You win, for now," he told the high priest. One day he would negotiate something in return.

The high priest nodded. The verdict was delivered at once.

"No one challenges Akbar," said the governor. "And no one enters our city without permission from its people. You have attempted to do so, and are condemned to death."

From where he stood, Elijah lowered his eyes. The commander smiled.

THE PRISONER, FOLLOWED BY AN EVER LARGER THRONG, was led to a place beside the walls. There his remaining clothing was torn away, leaving him naked. One of the soldiers shoved him toward the bottom of a hollow located nearby. The people gathered around the hole, jostling against one another for a better view.

"A soldier wears his uniform with pride, and makes himself visible to the enemy, because he has courage. A spy dresses as a woman, because he's a coward," shouted the governor, for all to hear. "Therefore I condemn you to depart this life shorn of the dignity of the brave."

The crowd jeered at the prisoner and applauded the governor.

The prisoner said something, but the interpreter was no longer at hand, and no one understood him. Elijah succeeded in making his way through the crowd to the governor—but it was too late. When he touched his cloak, he was pushed away violently.

"The fault lies with you. You wanted a public judgment."

"The fault is yours," replied Elijah. "Even if the Council of Akbar had met in secret, the commander and the high priest would have imposed their will. I was surrounded by soldiers during the entire process. They had everything planned."

Custom decreed that it was the high priest's task to select the duration of the torture. He knelt, picked up a stone, and handed it to the governor; it was not large enough to grant a swift death, nor so small as to extend the suffering for long.

"First, you."

"I am being forced to do this," said the governor in a low voice so that only the high priest could hear. "But I know it is the wrong path."

"For all these years, you have forced me to take the harshest positions while you enjoyed the fruits of decisions that pleased the people," the high priest answered, also in a low voice. "I have had to face doubt and guilt, and endure sleepless nights, pursued by the ghosts of errors I may have made. But because I did not lose my courage, today Akbar is a city envied by the entire world."

People began looking for stones of the chosen size. For a time, the only sound was that of pebbles and stones striking one another. The high priest continued. "It is possible I am mistaken in condemning this man to death. But as to the honor of our city, I am certain we are not traitors."

◆

THE GOVERNOR raised his hand and threw the first stone; the prisoner dodged it. Immediately, however, the multitude, shouting and jeering, began to stone him.

The man attempted to protect his face with his arms, and the stones struck his chest, his back, his stomach. The governor wanted to leave; he had seen this many times before and knew that death was slow and painful, that the man's face would become a pulp of bones, hair, and blood, that the people would continue throwing stones even after life had left his body.

Within minutes, the prisoner would abandon his defense and lower his arms; if he had been a good man in this life, the gods would guide one of the stones to strike the front of his skull, bringing unconsciousness. If not, if he had committed cruelties, he would remain conscious until the final moment.

The multitude shouted, hurling stones with growing ferocity, and the condemned man tried to defend himself as best he could. Suddenly, however, he dropped his arms and spoke in a language that all could understand. Dismayed, the crowd interrupted the stoning.

"Long live Assyria!" he shouted. "At this moment I look upon the image of my people and die joyfully, because I die as a general who tried to save the lives of his warriors. I go to join the gods and am content because I know we shall conquer this land!"

"You see?" the high priest said. "He heard and understood everything that was said during the judgment!"

The governor agreed. The man spoke their language, and now he knew of the divisions in the Council of Akbar.

"I am not in hell, because the vision of my country gives me dignity and strength! The vision of my country brings me joy! Long live Assyria!" he shouted once more.

Recovered from its surprise, the crowd again began throwing stones. The man kept his arms at his sides, not attempting to resist; he was a brave warrior. A few seconds later, the mercy of the gods manifested itself: a stone struck his forehead and he fell unconscious to the ground.

"We can go now," the high priest said. "The people of Akbar will see to finishing the task."

◆

ELIJAH DID NOT GO back to the widow's house. He began walking through the desert, not knowing exactly where he wanted to go.

"The Lord did nothing," he said to the plants and rocks. "And He could have done something."

He regretted his decision and blamed himself for the death of yet another man. If he had accepted the idea of the Council of Akbar meeting in secret, the governor could have taken Elijah with him; then it would have been the two of them against the high priest and the commander. Their chances, though still small, would have been better than in the public judgment.

Worse yet, he had been impressed by the high priest's way of addressing the crowd; even though he disagreed with what he said, he was obliged to recognize that here was someone with a profound understanding of leadership. He would try to remember every detail of what he had seen, for one day, in Israel, he would have to face the king and the princess from Sidon.

He wandered aimlessly, looking at the mountains, the city, and the Assyrian encampment in the distance. He was a mere dot in this valley, and there was an immense world around him, a world so large that even if he traveled his entire life he would never find where it ended. His friends, and his enemies, might perhaps better understand the earth where they lived, might travel to distant countries, navigate unknown seas, love a woman without guilt. None of them still heard the angels of their childhood, nor offered themselves in the Lord's struggle. They lived out their lives in the present moment, and they were happy.

He too was a person like all the others, and in this moment walking through the valley he wished above all else never to have heard the voice of the Lord, or of His angels.

But life is made not of desires but of the acts of each person. He recalled that several times in the past he had tried to renounce his mission, but he was still there, in the middle of that valley, because this the Lord had demanded.

"I could have been a mere carpenter, O Lord, and still be useful to Thy work."

But there Elijah stood, carrying out what had been demanded of him, bearing within him the weight of the war to come, the massacre of the prophets by Jezebel, the death by stoning of the Assyrian general, his fear of loving a woman of Akbar. The Lord had given him a gift, and he did not know what to do with it.

In the middle of the valley, a light appeared. It was not his guardian angel, the one he heard but seldom saw. It was an angel of the Lord, come to console him.

"I can do nothing further here," said Elijah. "When will I return to Israel?"

"When thou learnest to rebuild," answered the angel. "But remember that which God taught Moses before a battle. Make use of every moment so that later thou wilt not regret, nor lament having lost thy youth. To every age in the life of a man, the Lord bestoweth upon him its own misgivings."

I'm learning made me think about the Designer of the valleys, of the mountains, of the city of Akbar. Some merchants gave me inks of every color, because they want me to write for them. I thought of using them to describe the world I live in, but I know how difficult that is: although I have the colors, only the Lord can mix them with such harmony."

She kept her gaze on the Fifth Mountain. She was a completely different person from the woman he had met some months before gathering wood at the city gate. Her solitary presence in the midst of the desert inspired confidence and respect in him.

"Why do all the mountains have names except the Fifth Mountain, which is known by a number?" asked Elijah.

"So as not to create conflict among the gods," she replied. "According to tradition, if men had given that mountain the name of a specific god, the others would have become furious and destroyed the earth. Therefore it's called the Fifth Mountain, because it's the fifth mountain we see beyond the walls. In this way, we offend no one, and the Universe continues in its place."

They said nothing for a time. The woman broke the silence.

"Besides reflecting on colors, I also think about the danger in the writing of Byblos. It might offend the gods of Phoenicia and the Lord our God."

"Only the Lord exists," interrupted Elijah. "And every civilized country has its writing."

"But it's different. When I was a child, I used to go to the square to watch the word painter who worked for the merchants. His drawings were based on Egyptian script and demanded skill and knowledge. Now, ancient and powerful Egypt is in decadence, without money to buy anything, and no one uses its language anymore; sailors from Sidon and Tyre are spreading the writing of Byblos to the entire world. The sacred words and ceremonies can be placed on clay tablets and transmitted from one people to another. What will become of the world if unscrupulous people begin using the rituals to interfere with the Universe?"

Elijah understood what the woman was saying. The writing of Byblos was based on a very simple system: the Egyptian drawings first had to be transformed into sounds, and then a letter was designated for each sound. By placing these letters in order, it was possible to create all possible sounds and to describe everything there was in the Universe.

Some of these sounds were very difficult to pronounce. That difficulty had been solved by the Greeks, who had added five more letters, called *vowels*, to the twenty-odd characters of Byblos. They baptized this innovation *alphabet*, a name now used to define the new form of writing.

This had greatly facilitated commercial contact among differing peoples. The Egyptian system had required much space and a great deal of ability to draw the ideas, as well as profound understanding to interpret them; it had been imposed on conquered nations but had not survived the decline of the empire. The system of Byblos, however, was spreading rapidly through the world, and it no longer depended on the economic might of Phoenicia for its adoption.

The method of Byblos, with the Greek adaptation, had pleased the traders of the various nations; as had been the case since ancient times, it was they who decided what should remain in history and what would disappear with the death of a given king or a given person. Everything indicated that the Phoenician invention was destined to become the common language of business, surviving its navigators, its kings, its seductive princesses, its wine makers, its master glassmakers.

"Will God disappear from words?" the woman asked.

"He will continue in them," Elijah replied. "But each person will be responsible before Him for whatever he writes."

She took from the sleeve of her garment a clay tablet with something written on it.

"What does that mean?" Elijah asked.

"It's the word *love.*"

Elijah took the tablet in his hands, not daring to ask why she had given it to him. On that piece of clay, a few scratches summed up why the stars continued in the heavens and why men walked the earth.

He tried to return it to her, but she refused.

"I wrote it for you. I know your responsibility, I know that one day you will have to leave, and that you will become an enemy of my country because you wish to do away with Jezebel. On that day, it may come to pass that I shall be at your side, supporting you in your task. Or it may come to pass that I fight against you, for Jezebel's blood is the blood of my country; this word that you hold in your hands is filled with mystery. No one can know what it awakens in a woman's heart, not even prophets who speak with God."

"I know the word that you have written," said Elijah, storing the tablet in a fold of his cape. "I have struggled day and night against it, for, although I do not know what it awakens in a woman's heart, I know what it can do to a man. I have the courage to face the king of Israel, the princess of Sidon, the Council of Akbar, but that one word—*love*—inspires deep terror in me. Before you drew it on the tablet, your eyes had already seen it written in my heart."

They fell silent. Despite the Assyrian's death, the climate of tension in the city, the call from the Lord that could occur at any moment—none of this was as powerful as the word she had written.

Elijah held out his hand, and she took it. They remained thus until the sun hid itself behind the Fifth Mountain.

"Thank you," she said as they returned. "For a long time I had desired to spend the hours of sunset with you."

When they arrived home, an emissary from the governor was waiting for him. He asked Elijah to come with him immediately for a meeting.

◆

"YOU REPAID MY SUPPORT with cowardice," said the governor. "What should I do with your life?"

"I shall not live a second longer than the Lord desires," replied Elijah. "It is He who decides, not you."

The governor was surprised at Elijah's courage.

"I can have you decapitated at once. Or have you dragged through the streets of the city, saying that you brought a curse upon our people," he said. "And that would not be a decision of your One God."

"Whatever my fate, that is what will happen. But I want you to know I did not flee; the commander's soldiers kept me away. He wants war and will do everything to achieve it."

The governor decided to waste no more time on that pointless discussion. He had to explain his plan to the Israelite prophet.

"It's not the commander who wishes war; like a good military man he is aware that his army is smaller and inexperienced and that it will be decimated by the enemy. As a man of honor, he knows he risks causing shame to his descendants. But his heart has been turned into stone by pride and vanity.

"He thinks the enemy is afraid. He doesn't know that the Assyrian warriors are well trained: when they enter the army, they plant a tree, and every day they leap over the spot where the seed is buried. The seed becomes a shoot, and they leap over it. The shoot becomes a plant, and they go on jumping. They neither become annoyed nor find it a waste of time. Little by little, the tree grows, and the warriors leap higher. Patiently and with dedication, they're preparing to overcome obstacles.

"They're accustomed to recognizing a challenge when they see it. They've been observing us for months."

Elijah interrupted the governor.

"Then, in whose interest is war?"

"The high priest's. I saw that during the Assyrian prisoner's trial."

"For what reason?"

"I don't know. But he was shrewd enough to convince the commander and the people. Now the entire city is on his side, and I see only one way out of the difficult situation in which we find ourselves."

He paused for a long moment, then looked directly into the Israelite's eyes. "You."

The governor began pacing the chamber, his rapid speech betraying his nervousness.

"The merchants also desire peace, but they can do nothing. In any case, they are rich enough to install themselves in some other city or to wait until the conquerors begin buying their products. The rest of the populace have lost their senses and want us to attack an infinitely superior enemy. The only thing that can change their minds is a miracle."

Elijah became tense.

"A miracle?"

"You brought back a boy that death had already claimed. You've helped the people find their way, and though you are a foreigner you are loved by almost everyone."

"That was the situation until this morning," Elijah said. "But now it's changed; in the atmosphere you've just described, anyone who advocates peace will be considered a traitor."

"I don't want you to advocate anything. I want you to perform a miracle as great as the resurrection of that boy. Then you'll tell the people that peace is the only solution, and they'll listen to you. The high priest will lose completely whatever power he possesses."

There was a moment of silence. The governor continued.

"I am willing to make a pact: if you do what I'm asking, the religion of the One God will become obligatory in Akbar. You will please Him whom you serve, and I shall be able to negotiate terms of peace."

◆

ELIJAH CLIMBED THE STAIRS to his room in the upper story of the widow's house. At that moment he had in his hands an opportunity that no prophet had ever had before: to convert a Phoenician city. It would be the most painful way to show Jezebel that there was a price to pay for what she had done to his country.

He was excited by the governor's offer. He even thought of waking the woman who was sleeping downstairs but changed his mind; she must be dreaming about the beautiful afternoon they had spent together.

He called on his guardian angel. He appeared.

"You heard the governor's proposal," Elijah said. "This is a unique chance."

"Nothing is a unique chance," the angel replied. "The Lord giveth men many opportunities. And do not forget what was said: no further miracle will be permitted thee until thou returnest to the bosom of thy country."

Elijah lowered his head. At that moment the angel of the Lord appeared and hushed his guardian angel. And he said:

"Behold the next of thy miracles:

"Thou wilt gather the people together before the mountain. On one side, thou shalt order built an altar to Baal, and that a bullock be placed on it. On the other side, thou shalt raise an altar to the Lord thy God, and on it also place a bullock.

"And thou shalt say to the worshipers of Baal: invoke the name of your god, and I shall invoke the name of the Lord. Let them be first, and let them spend from morning until noon praying and calling on Baal to come forth and receive what is offered him.

"They will cry out aloud, and cut themselves with knives, asking that the bullock be received by their god, but nothing will happen.

"When they weary, thou shalt fill four barrels with water and pour it over thy bullock. Thou shalt do this a second time. And thou shalt do this still a third time. Then call upon the Lord of Abraham, Isaac, and Israel, asking Him to show His power to all.

"At that moment, the Lord will send the fire from heaven and consume thy sacrifice."

Elijah knelt and gave thanks.

"However," continued the angel, "this miracle can be wrought but once in thy lifetime. Choose whether thou desirest to do it here, to avoid a battle, or in thy homeland, to free thy people from Jezebel."

And the angel of the Lord departed.

◆

THE WOMAN AWOKE EARLY and saw Elijah sitting in the doorway of the house. His eyes were deep in their sockets, like those of one who has not slept.

She would have liked to ask what had happened the night before, but she feared his response. It was possible that the sleepless night had been provoked by his talk with the governor and by the threat of war; but there might be another reason—the clay tablet she had given him. If so, and she raised the subject, she risked hearing that the love of a woman was not in accord with God's design.

She said only the words, "Come and eat something."

Her son awakened also. The three sat down at the table and ate.

"I should have liked to stay with you yesterday," Elijah said, "but the governor needed me."

"Do not concern yourself with him," she said, a calm feeling reentering her heart. "His family has ruled Akbar for generations, and he will know what to do in the face of the threat."

"I also spoke with an angel. And he demanded of me a very difficult decision."

"Nor should you be disturbed because of angels; perhaps it's better to believe that the gods change with the times. My ancestors worshiped the Egyptian gods, who had the forms of animals. Those gods went away, and until you arrived, I was brought up to make sacrifices to Asherat, El, Baal, and all the dwellers on the Fifth Mountain. Now I have known the Lord, but He too may leave us one day, and the next gods may be less demanding."

The boy asked for water. There was none.

"I'll go and fetch it," said Elijah.

"I want to go with you," the boy said.

They walked toward the well. On the way they passed the spot where the commander had since the early hours been training his soldiers.

"Let's watch for a while," said the boy. "I'll be a soldier when I grow up."

Elijah did as he asked.

"Which of us is best at using a sword?" asked one warrior.

"Go to the place where the spy was stoned yesterday," said the commander. "Pick up a stone and insult it."

"Why should I do that? The stone would not answer me back."

"Then attack it with your sword."

"My sword will break," said the soldier. "And that wasn't what I asked; I want to know who's the best at using a sword."

"The best is the one who's most like a rock," answered the commander. "Without drawing its blade, it proves that no one can defeat it."

"The governor is right: the commander is a wise man," thought Elijah. "But the greatest wisdom is blinded by the glare of vanity."

◆

THEY CONTINUED on their way. The boy asked why the soldiers were training so much.

"It's not just the soldiers, but your mother too, and I, and those who follow their heart. Everything in life demands training."

"Even being a prophet?"

"Even to understand angels. We so want to talk with them that we don't listen to what they're saying. It's not easy to listen: in our prayers we always try to say where we have erred, and what we should like to happen to us. But the Lord already knows all of this, and sometimes asks us only to hear what the Universe is telling us. And to be patient."

The boy looked at him in surprise. He probably understood nothing, but even so Elijah felt the need to continue the conversation. Perhaps when he came to manhood one of these words might assist him in a difficult situation.

"All life's battles teach us something, even those we lose. When you grow up, you'll discover that you have defended lies, deceived yourself, or suffered for foolishness. If you're a good warrior, you will not blame yourself for this, but neither will you allow your mistakes to repeat themselves."

He decided to speak no further; a boy of that age could not understand what he was saying. They walked slowly, and Elijah looked at the streets of the city that had sheltered him and was about to disappear. Everything depended on the decision he must make.

Akbar was more silent than usual. In the central square, people talked in hushed tones, as if fearful that the wind might carry their words to the Assyrian camp. The more elderly among them swore that nothing would happen, while the young were excited at the prospect of battle, and the merchants and artisans made plans to go to Sidon and Tyre until calm was restored.

"It is easy for them to leave," he thought. Merchants can transport their goods anywhere in the world. Artisans too can work, even in places where a strange language is spoken. "But I must have the Lord's permission."

◆

THEY CAME to the well, where they filled two vessels with water. Usually the place was crowded with people; women meeting to wash clothes, dye fabrics, and comment on everything that happened in the city. Nothing could be kept secret close to the well;

news about business, family betrayals, problems between neighbors, the intimate lives of the rulers—every matter, serious or superficial, was discussed, commented upon, criticized, or applauded there. Even during the months in which the enemy forces had grown unceasingly, Jezebel, the princess who had conquered the king of Israel, remained the favorite topic. People praised her boldness, her courage, and were certain that, should anything happen to the city, she would come back to her country to avenge it.

That morning, however, almost no one was there. The few women present said that it was necessary to go to the fields and harvest the largest possible amount of grain, for the Assyrians would soon close off the entrance and exit to the city. Two of them were making plans to go to the Fifth Mountain and offer sacrifices to the gods; they had no wish to see their sons die in combat.

"The high priest said that we can resist for many months," one woman commented to Elijah. "We need only to have the necessary courage to defend Akbar's honor and the gods will come to our aid."

The boy was frightened.

"Is the enemy going to attack?" he asked.

Elijah did not reply; it depended on the choice that the angel had offered him the night before.

"I'm afraid," the boy said insistently.

"That proves that you find joy in living. It's normal to feel fear at certain moments."

◆

ELIJAH AND THE BOY returned home before the morning was over. They found the woman ringed by small vessels with inks of various colors.

"I have to work," she said, looking at the unfinished letters and phrases. "Because of the drought, the city is full of dust. The brushes are always dirty, the ink mixes with dust, and everything becomes more difficult."

Elijah remained silent; he did not want to share his concerns with anyone. He sat in a corner of the downstairs room, absorbed in his thoughts. The boy went out to play with his friends.

"He needs silence," the woman said to herself and tried to concentrate on her work.

She took the rest of the morning to complete a few words that could have been written in half the time, and she felt guilt for not doing what was expected of her; after all, for the first time in her life she had the chance to support her family.

She returned to her work. She was using papyrus, a material that a trader on his way from Egypt had recently brought, asking her to write some commercial letters that he had to send to Damascus. The sheet was not of the best quality, and the ink blurred frequently. "Even with all these difficulties, it's better than drawing on clay."

Neighboring countries had the custom of sending their messages on clay tablets or on animal skins. Although their country was in decadence, with an obsolete script, the Egyptians had discovered a light, practical way of recording their commerce and their history; they cut into strips a plant that grew on the banks of the Nile and through a simple process glued the strips side by side, forming a yellowish sheet. Akbar had to import papyrus because it could not be grown in the valley. Though it was expensive, merchants preferred using it, for they could carry the written sheets in their pockets, which was impossible to do with clay tablets and animal skins.

"Everything is becoming simpler," she thought. A pity that the government's authorization was needed to use the Byblos alphabet on papyrus. Some outmoded law still obliged written texts to pass inspection by the Council of Akbar.

As soon as her work was done, she showed it to Elijah, who had been watching her the entire time without comment.

"Do you like the result?" she asked.

He seemed to come out of a trance.

"Yes, it's pretty," he replied, giving no mind to what he was saying.

He must be talking with the Lord. And she did not want to interrupt him. She left, to call the high priest.

When she returned with the high priest, Elijah was still in the same spot. The two men stared at each other. For a long time, neither spoke.

The high priest was the first to break the silence.

"You are a prophet, and speak with angels. I merely interpret the ancient laws, carry out rituals, and seek to defend my people from the errors they commit. Therefore I know this is not a struggle between men; it is a battle of gods—and I must not absent myself from it."

"I admire your faith, though you worship gods that do not exist," answered Elijah. "If the present situation is, as you say, worthy of a celestial battle, the Lord will use me as an instrument to defeat Baal and his companions on the Fifth Mountain. It would have been better for you to order my assassination."

"I thought of it. But it wasn't necessary; at the proper moment the gods acted in my favor."

Elijah did not reply. The high priest turned and picked up the papyrus on which the woman had just written her text.

"Well done," he commented. After reading it carefully, he took the ring from his finger, dipped it in one of the small vessels of ink, and applied his seal in the left corner. If anyone were found carrying a papyrus without the high priest's seal, he could be condemned to death.

"Why do you always have to do that?" she asked.

"Because these papyri transport ideas," he replied. "And ideas have power."

"They're just commercial transactions."

"But they could be battle plans. Or our secret prayers. Nowadays, with letters and papyrus, it has become a simple matter to steal the inspiration of a people. It is difficult to hide clay tablets, or animal skins, but the combination of papyrus and the alphabet of Byblos can bring an end to the civilization of any nation, and destroy the world."

A woman came running.

"Priest! Priest! Come see what's happening!"

Elijah and the widow followed him. People were coming from every corner, heading for the same place; the air was close to unbreathable from the dust they raised. Children ran ahead, laughing and shouting. The adults walked slowly, in silence.

When they arrived at the southern gate to the city, a small multitude was already gathered there. The high priest pushed his way through the crowd and came upon the reason for the confusion.

A sentinel of Akbar was kneeling, his arms spread, his hands tied to a large piece of wood on his shoulders. His clothes were in tatters, and his left eye had been gouged out by a small tree branch.

On his chest, written with slashes of a knife, were some Assyrian characters. The high priest understood Egyptian, but the Assyrian language was not important enough to be learned and memorized; it was necessary to ask the help of a trader who was at the scene.

"'*We declare war*,'" the man translated.

The onlookers spoke not a word. Elijah could see panic written on their faces.

"Give me your sword," the high priest said to one of the soldiers.

The soldier obeyed. The high priest asked that the governor and the commander be notified of what had happened. Then, with a swift blow, he plunged the blade into the kneeling sentinel's heart.

The man moaned and fell to the ground. He was dead, free of the pain and shame of having allowed himself to be captured.

"Tomorrow I shall go to the Fifth Mountain to offer sacrifices," he told the frightened people. "And the gods will once again remember us."

Before leaving, he turned to Elijah.

"You see it with your own eyes. The heavens are still helping."

"One question, nothing more," said Elijah. "Why do you wish to see your people sacrificed?"

"Because it is what must be done to kill an idea."

After seeing him talk with the woman that morning, Elijah had understood what that idea was: the alphabet.

"It is too late. Already it spreads throughout the world, and the Assyrians cannot conquer the whole of the earth."

"And who says they cannot? After all, the gods of the Fifth Mountain are on the side of their armies."

◆

FOR HOURS HE WALKED the valley, as he had done the afternoon before. He knew there would be at least one more afternoon and night of peace: no war was fought in darkness, because the soldiers could not distinguish the enemy. That night, he knew, the Lord was giving him the chance to change the destiny of the city that had taken him into its bosom.

"Solomon would know what to do," he told his angel. "And David, and Moses, and Isaac. They were men the Lord trusted, but I am merely an indecisive servant. The Lord has given me a choice that should be His."

"The history of our ancestors seemeth to be full of the right men in the right places," answered the angel. "Do not believe it: the Lord demandeth of people only that which is within the possibilities of each of them."

"Then He has made a mistake with me."

"Whatever affliction that cometh, finally goeth away. Such are the glories and tragedies of the world."

"I shall not forget that," Elijah said. "But when they go away, the tragedies leave behind eternal marks, while the glories leave useless memories."

The angel made no reply.

"Why, during all this time I have been in Akbar, could I not find allies to work toward peace? What importance has a solitary prophet?"

"What importance hath the sun, in its solitary travel through the heavens? What importance hath a mountain rising in the middle of a valley? What importance hath an isolated well? Yet it is they that indicate the road the caravan is to follow."

"My heart drowns in sorrow," said Elijah, kneeling and extending his arms to heaven. "Would that I could die here and now, and never have my hands stained with the blood of my people, or a foreign people. Look behind you. What do you see?"

"Thou knowest that I am blind," said the angel. "Because mine eyes still retain the light of the Lord's glory, I can perceive nothing else. I can see only what thy heart telleth me. I can see only the vibrations of the dangers that threaten thee. I cannot know what lieth behind thee . . . "

"Then I'll tell you: there lies Akbar. Seen at this time of day, with the afternoon sun lighting its profile, it's lovely. I have grown accustomed to its streets and walls, to its generous and hospitable folk. Though the city's inhabitants are still prisoners of commerce and superstition, their hearts are as pure as any nation on earth. With them I have learned much that I did not know; in return, I have listened to their laments and—inspired by God—have been able to resolve their internal conflicts. Many times have I been at risk, and someone has always come to my aid. Why must I choose between saving this city and redeeming my people?"

"Because a man must choose," answered the angel. "Therein lieth his strength: the power of his decisions."

"It is a difficult choice; it demands that I accept the death of one people to save another."

"Even more difficult is defining a path for oneself. He who maketh no choice is dead in the eyes of the Lord, though he go on breathing and walking in the streets.

"Moreover," the angel continued, "no one dieth. The arms

of eternity open for every soul, and each one will carry on his task. There is a reason for everything under the sun."

Elijah again raised his arms to the heavens.

"My people fell away from the Lord because of a woman's beauty. Phoenicia may be destroyed because a priest thinks that writing is a threat to the gods. Why does He who made the world prefer to use tragedy to write the book of fate?"

Elijah's cries echoed through the valley to return to his ears.

"Thou knowest not whereof thou speakest," the angel replied. "There is no tragedy, only the unavoidable. Everything hath its reason for being: thou needest only distinguish what is temporary from what is lasting."

"What is temporary?" asked Elijah.

"The unavoidable."

"And what is lasting?"

"The lessons of the unavoidable."

Saying this, the angel disappeared.

That night, at the evening meal, Elijah told the woman and the boy, "Prepare your things. We may depart at any moment."

"You haven't slept for two days," said the woman. "An emissary from the governor was here this afternoon, asking for you to go to the palace. I said you were in the valley and would spend the night there."

"You did well," he replied, going straightway to his room and falling into a deep sleep.

He was awakened the next morning by the sound of musical instruments. When he went downstairs to see what was happening, the boy was already at the door.

"Look!" he said, his eyes gleaming with excitement. "It's war!"

A battalion of soldiers, imposing in their battle gear and armaments, was marching toward the southern gate of Akbar. A group of musicians followed them, marking the battalion's pace to the beat of drums.

"Yesterday you were afraid," Elijah told the boy.

"I didn't know we had so many soldiers. Our warriors are the best!"

He left the boy and went into the street; he must find the governor at any cost. The other inhabitants of the city had been awakened by the sound of the war anthems and were enthralled;

for the first time in their lives they were seeing the march of an organized battalion in its military uniforms, its lances and shields reflecting the first rays of dawn. The commander had achieved an enviable feat; he had prepared his army without anyone becoming aware of it, and now—or so Elijah feared—he could make everyone believe that victory over the Assyrians was possible.

He pushed his way through the soldiers and came to the front of the column. There, mounted on horses, the commander and the governor were leading the march.

"We have an agreement!" said Elijah, running to the governor's side. "I can perform a miracle!"

The governor made no reply. The garrison marched past the city wall and into the valley.

"You know this army is an illusion!" Elijah insisted. "The Assyrians have a five-to-one advantage, and they are experienced warriors! Don't allow Akbar to be destroyed!"

"What do you desire of me?" the governor asked, without halting his steed. "Last night I sent an emissary so we could talk, and they said you were out of the city. What else could I do?"

"Facing the Assyrians in the open field is suicide! You know that!"

The commander was listening to the conversation, making no comment. He had already discussed his strategy with the governor; the Israelite prophet would have a surprise.

Elijah ran alongside the horses, not knowing exactly what he should do. The column of soldiers left the city, heading toward the middle of the valley.

"Help me, Lord," he thought. "Just as Thou stopped the sun to help Joshua in combat, stop time and let me convince the governor of his error."

As soon as he thought this, the commander shouted, "Halt!"

"Perhaps it's a sign," Elijah told himself. "I must take advantage of it."

The soldiers formed two lines of engagement, like human walls. Their shields were firmly anchored in the earth, their swords pointing outward.

"You believe you are looking at Akbar's warriors," the governor said to Elijah.

"I'm looking at young men who laugh in the face of death," was the reply.

"Know then that what we have here is only a battalion. The greater part of our men are in the city, on top of the walls. We have placed there caldrons of boiling oil ready to be poured on the heads of anyone trying to scale them.

"We have stores divided among several locations, so that flaming arrows cannot do away with our food supply. According to the commander's calculations, we can hold out for almost two months against a siege. While the Assyrians were making ready, so too were we."

"I was never told this," Elijah said.

"Remember this: even having helped the people of Akbar, you are still a foreigner, and some in the military could mistake you for a spy."

"But you wished for peace!"

"Peace is still possible, even after combat begins. But now we shall negotiate under conditions of equality."

The governor related that messengers had been dispatched to Sidon and Tyre advising of the gravity of their position. It had been difficult for him to ask for help; others might think him incapable of controlling the situation. But he had concluded that this was the only solution.

The commander had developed an ingenious plan; as soon as combat began, he would return to the city to organize the resistance. The troops in the field were to kill as many of the enemy as possible, then withdraw to the mountains. They knew the valley better than anyone and could attack the Assyrians in small skirmishes, thus reducing the pressure of the siege.

Relief would come soon, and the Assyrian army would be decimated. "We can resist for sixty days, but that will not be necessary," the governor told Elijah.

"But many will die."

"We are all in the presence of death. And no one is afraid, not even I."

The governor was surprised at his own courage. He had never before been in a battle, and as the moment of combat drew nearer, he had made plans to flee the city. That morning he had agreed with some of his most faithful friends on the best means of retreat. He could not go to Sidon or Tyre, where he would be considered a traitor, but Jezebel would receive him because she needed men she could trust.

But when he stepped onto the field of battle, he had seen in the soldiers' eyes an immense joy, as if they had trained their entire lives for an objective and the great moment had finally come.

"Fear exists until the moment when the unavoidable happens," he told Elijah. "After that, we must waste none of our energy on it."

Elijah was confused. He felt the same way, though he was ashamed to recognize it; he recalled the boy's excitement when the troops had marched past.

"Away with you," the governor said. "You're a foreigner, unarmed, and have no need to fight for something you do not believe in."

Elijah did not move.

"They will come," said the commander. "You were caught by surprise, but we are prepared."

Even so, Elijah remained where he stood.

They scanned the horizon: no dust. The Assyrian army was not on the move.

The soldiers in the first rank held their spears firmly, pointed forward; the bowmen had their strings half-drawn, ready to loose their arrows at the commander's order. A few men slashed at the air with their swords to keep their muscles warm.

"Everything is ready," the commander repeated. "They are going to attack."

Elijah noticed the euphoria in his voice. He must be eager for the battle to begin, eager to demonstrate his bravery. Beyond a doubt he was imagining the Assyrian warriors, the sword blows, the shouting and confusion, and picturing himself being remembered by the Phoenician priests as an example of efficiency and courage.

The governor interrupted his thoughts.

"They're not moving."

Elijah remembered what he had asked of the Lord, for the sun to stand still in the heavens as He had done for Joshua. He tried to talk with his angel but did not hear his voice.

Little by little the spearmen lowered their weapons, the archers relaxed the tension on their bowstrings, the swordsmen replaced their weapons in their scabbards. The burning sun of midday arrived; several warriors fainted from the heat. Even so, for the rest of the day the detachment remained at readiness.

When the sun set, the warriors returned to Akbar; they appeared disappointed at having survived another day.

Elijah alone stayed behind in the valley. He had been wandering about for some time when the light appeared. The angel of the Lord was before him.

"God hath heard thy prayers," the angel said. "And hath seen the torment in thy soul."

Elijah turned to the heavens and gave thanks for the blessing.

"The Lord is the source of all glory and all power. He stopped the Assyrian army."

"No," the angel replied. "Thou hast said that the choice must be His. And He hath made the choice for thee."

"Let's go," the woman told her son.

"I don't want to go," the boy replied. "I'm proud of Akbar's soldiers."

His mother bade him gather his belongings. "Take only what you can carry," she said.

"You forget we're poor, and I don't have much."

Elijah went up to his room. He looked about him, as if for the first and last time; he quickly descended and stood watching the widow store her inks.

"Thank you for taking me with you," she said. "I was only fifteen when I married, and I had no idea what life was. Our families had arranged everything; I had been raised since childhood for that moment and carefully prepared to help my husband in all circumstances."

"Did you love him?"

"I taught my heart to do so. Because there was no choice, I convinced myself that it was the best way. When I lost my husband, I resigned myself to the sameness of day and night; I asked the gods of the Fifth Mountain—in those times I still believed in them—to take me as soon as my son could live on his own.

"That was when you appeared. I've told you this once before, and I want to repeat it now: from that day on, I began to notice the beauty of the valley, the dark outline of the mountains projected against the sky, the moon ever-changing shape so the wheat could grow. Many nights while you slept I walked about Akbar, listening to the cries of newborn infants, the songs of men who had been drinking after work, the firm steps of the sentinels on the city walls. How many times had I seen that landscape without noticing how beautiful it was? How many times had I looked at the sky without seeing how deep it is? How many times had I heard the sounds of Akbar around me without understanding that they were part of my life?

"I once again felt an immense will to live. You told me to study the characters of Byblos, and I did. I thought only of pleasing you, but I came to care deeply about what I was doing, and I discovered something: *the meaning of my life was whatever I wanted it to be.*"

Elijah stroked her hair. It was the first time he had done so.

"Why haven't you always been like this?" she asked.

"Because I was afraid. But today, waiting for the battle to start, I heard the governor's words, and I thought of you. Fear reaches only to the point where the unavoidable begins; from there on, it loses its meaning. And all we have left is the hope that we are making the right decision."

"I'm ready," she said.

"We shall return to Israel. The Lord has told me what I must do, and so I shall. Jezebel will be removed from power."

She said nothing. Like all Phoenician women, she was proud of her princess. When they arrived there, she would try to convince the man at her side to change his mind.

"It will be a long journey, and we shall find no rest until I have done what He has asked of me," said Elijah, as if guessing her thoughts. "Still, your love will be my mainstay, and in the moments I grow weary in the battles in His name, I can find repose in your arms."

The boy appeared, carrying a small bag on his shoulder. Elijah took it and told the woman, "The hour has come. As you traverse the streets of Akbar, remember each house, each sound. For you will never again see them."

"I was born in Akbar," she said. "The city will forever remain in my heart."

Hearing this, the boy vowed to himself never to forget his mother's words. If someday he could return, he would look upon the city as if seeing her face.

◆

IT WAS ALREADY DARK when the high priest arrived at the foot of the Fifth Mountain. In his right hand he held a staff; in his left he carried a large sack.

From the sack he took the sacred oil and anointed his forehead and wrists. Then, using the staff, he drew in the sand a bull and a panther, the symbols of the God of the Storm and of the Great Goddess. He said the ritual prayers; finally he opened his arms to heaven to receive the divine revelation.

The gods spoke no more. They had said all they wished to say and now demanded only the carrying out of the rites. The prophets had disappeared everywhere in the world, save in Israel, a backward, superstitious country that still believed men could communicate with the creators of the Universe.

He recalled that generations before, Sidon and Tyre had traded with a king of Jerusalem called Solomon. He was building a great temple and desired to adorn it with the best the world offered; he had commanded that cedars be bought from Phoenicia, which they called Lebanon. The king of Tyre had provided the necessary materials and had received in exchange twenty cities in Galilee, but was not pleased with them. Solomon had then helped him to construct his first ships, and now Phoenicia had the largest merchant fleet in the world.

At that time, Israel was still a great nation, despite worshiping a single god whose name was not even known and who was usually called just "the Lord." A princess of Sidon had succeeded in returning Solomon to the true faith, and he had erected an altar to the gods of the Fifth Mountain. The Israelites insisted that "the Lord" had punished the wisest of their kings, bringing about the wars that had threatened his reign.

His son Rehoboam, however, carried on the worship that his father had initiated. He ordered two golden calves to be made, and the people of Israel worshiped them. It was then that the prophets appeared and began a ceaseless struggle against the rulers.

Jezebel was right: the only way to keep the true faith alive was by doing away with the prophets. Although she was a gentle woman, brought up in the way of tolerance and of horror at the thought of war, she knew that there comes a moment when violence is the only answer. The blood that now stained her hands would be forgiven by the gods she served.

"Soon, my hands too will be stained with blood," the high priest told the silent mountain before him. "Just as the prophets are the curse of Israel, writing is the curse of Phoenicia. Both bring about an evil beyond redress, and both must be stopped while it is still possible. The god of weather must not desert us now."

He was concerned about what had happened that morning; the enemy army had not attacked. The god of weather had abandoned Phoenicia in the past because he had become irritated at its inhabitants. As a consequence, the light of the lamps had stilled, the lambs and cows had abandoned their young, the wheat and barley had failed to ripen. The Sun god commanded that important beings be sent to search for him—the eagle and the God of the Storm—but no one succeeded in finding him. Finally, the Great Goddess sent a bee, which found him asleep in a forest and stung him. He awoke furious and began to destroy everything around him. It was necessary to bind him and remove the wrath from his soul, but from that time onward, all returned to normal.

If he decided to leave again, the battle would not take place. The Assyrians would remain permanently in the entrance to the valley, and Akbar would continue to exist.

"Courage is fear that prays," he said. "That is why I am here, because I cannot vacillate at the moment of combat. I must show the warriors of Akbar that there is a reason to defend the city. It is neither the well, nor the marketplace, nor the governor's palace. We shall confront the Assyrian army because we must set the example."

The Assyrian triumph would end the threat of the alphabet for all time to come. The conquerors would impose their language and their customs, but they would go on worshiping the same gods on the Fifth Mountain; that was what truly mattered.

"In the future, our navigators will take to other lands the feats of our warriors. The priests will recall the names and the date when Akbar attempted to resist the Assyrian invasion. Painters will draw Egyptian characters on papyrus; the scribes of Byblos will be dead. The sacred texts will continue only in the hands of those born to study them. Then the later generations will try to imitate what we have done, and we shall build a better world.

"But now," he continued, "we must first lose this battle. We shall fight bravely, but our situation is inferior, and we shall die with glory."

At that moment the high priest listened to the night and saw that he was right. The silence anticipated the moment of an important battle, but the inhabitants of Akbar were misinterpreting it; they had laid down their weapons and were amusing themselves at precisely the moment when they had need of vigilance. They paid no heed to nature's example: the animals fell silent when danger was at hand.

"Let the gods' designs be fulfilled. May the heavens not fall upon the earth, for we have acted rightly; we have obeyed tradition," he concluded.

ELIJAH, THE WOMAN, AND THE BOY WENT IN A WESTERLY direction, toward Israel; they did not need to pass near the Assyrian encampment because it was located to the south. The full moon made the walk easier but also cast strange shadows and sinister forms on the rocks and stones of the valley.

In the midst of the darkness, the angel of the Lord appeared. He bore a sword of fire in his right hand.

"Whither goest thou?" he asked.

"To Israel," Elijah answered.

"Hath the Lord summoned thee?"

"I know the miracle that God expects me to perform. And now I know where I am to execute it."

"Hath the Lord summoned thee?" repeated the angel.

Elijah remained silent.

"Hath the Lord summoned thee?" asked the angel for the third time.

"No."

"Then return to the place whence thou comest, for thou hast yet to fulfill thy destiny. The Lord hath still to summon thee."

"If nothing else, permit them to leave, for they have no reason to remain," implored Elijah.

But the angel was no longer there. Elijah dropped the bag he was carrying, sat in the middle of the road, and wept bitterly.

"What happened?" asked the woman and the boy, who had seen nothing.

"We're going back," he said. "Such is the Lord's desire."

◆

HE WAS NOT ABLE to sleep well. He awoke in the night and sensed the tension in the air around him; an evil wind blew through the streets, sowing fear and distrust.

"In the love of a woman, I have discovered the love for all creatures," he prayed silently. "I need her. I know that the Lord will not forget that I am one of His instruments, perhaps the weakest of those He has chosen. Help me, O Lord, because I must repose calmly amidst the battles."

He recalled the governor's comment about the uselessness of fear. Despite that, sleep eluded him. "I need energy and tranquillity; give me rest while it is still possible."

He thought of summoning his angel and talking with him for

a while, but knowing he might be told things he had no wish to hear, he changed his mind. To relax, he went downstairs; the bags that the woman had prepared for their flight had not been undone.

He considered returning to his room. He remembered what the Lord had told Moses: *"And what man is there that hath betrothed a wife, and hath not taken her? Let him go and return unto his house, lest he die in the battle, and another man take her."*

They had not yet known each other. But it had been a wearying night, and this was not the moment to do so.

He decided to unpack the bags and return everything to its place. He discovered that, besides the few clothes she possessed, she was carrying the instruments for drawing the characters of Byblos.

He picked up a stylus, moistened a small clay tablet, and began to sketch a few letters; he had learned to write by watching the woman as she worked.

"What a simple and ingenious thing," he thought, in an effort to turn his mind to other concerns. Often, on his way to the well for water, he had heard the women commenting, "The Greeks stole our most important invention," but Elijah knew it was not that way: the adaptation they had made by including vowels had transformed the alphabet into something that the peoples of all nations could use. Furthermore, they called their collections of parchments *biblia*, in honor of the city where the invention had occurred.

The Greek *biblia* were written on animal hides. Elijah felt this was a very fragile way of storing words; hides were less resistant than clay tablets and could be easily stolen. Papyrus came apart after some handling and was destroyed by water. "*Biblia* and papyrus will not last; only clay tablets are destined to remain forever," he reflected.

If Akbar survived for a time longer, he would recommend that the governor order his country's entire history written on clay tablets and stored in a special room, so that generations yet to come might consult them. In this way, if one day the priests of Phoenicia, who kept in their memory the history of their people, were decimated, the feats of warriors and poets would not be forgotten.

He amused himself for some time by writing the same letters but by ordering them differently, forming several words. He was enchanted with the result. The task relaxed him, and he returned to his bed.

◆

HE AWOKE some time later at the sound of the door to his room crashing to the floor.

"It's not a dream. It's not the armies of the Lord in combat."

Shadows came from all sides, screaming like madmen in a language he did not understand.

"The Assyrians."

Other doors fell, walls were leveled by powerful hammer blows, the shouts of the invaders mixed with cries for help rising from the square. He attempted to stand, but one of the shadows knocked him to the ground. A muffled sound shook the floor below.

"Fire," Elijah thought. "They've set the house on fire."

"It's you," he heard someone saying in Phoenician. "You're the leader. Hiding like a coward in a woman's house."

He looked at the face of the person who had just spoken; flames lit the room, and he could see a man with a long beard, in a military uniform. Yes, the Assyrians had come.

"You invaded at night?" he asked, disoriented.

The man did not respond. Elijah saw the flash of swords drawn from their scabbards, and one of the warriors slashed his right arm.

Elijah closed his eyes; the scenes of an entire lifetime passed before him in a fraction of a second. He was once again playing in the street of the city of his birth, traveling to Jerusalem for the first time, smelling the odor of cut wood in the carpenter's shop, marveling at the vastness of the sea and at the garments people wore in the great cities of the coast. He saw himself walking the valleys and mountains of the Promised Land, remembered when he first saw Jezebel, who seemed like a young girl and charmed all who came near. He witnessed a second time the massacre of the prophets, heard anew the voice of the Lord ordering him into the desert. He saw again the eyes of the woman who awaited him at the gates of Zarephath, which its inhabitants called Akbar, and understood that he had loved her from the first moment. Once more he climbed the Fifth Mountain, brought a child back to life, and was welcomed by the people as a sage and a judge. He looked at the heavens, where the constellations were rapidly changing position, was dazzled by the moon that displayed its four phases in a single instant, felt heat, cold, fall and spring, experienced the rain and the lightning's flash.

Clouds swept past in millions of different shapes, and the water of rivers again ran in their beds. He relived the day that he had seen the first Assyrian tent being erected, then the second, then several, many, the angels that came and went, the fiery sword on the road to Israel, sleepless nights, drawings on clay tablets, and—

He was back in the present. He thought about what was happening on the floor below; he had to save the widow and her son at any cost.

"Fire!" he told one of the enemy soldiers. "The house is on fire!"

He was not afraid; his only concern was for the widow and her child. Someone pushed his head against the floor, and he felt the taste of earth in his mouth. He kissed it, told it how much he loved it, and explained that he had done everything possible to avoid what was happening. He tried to wrest free of his captors, but someone had his foot on his chest.

"She must have fled," he thought. "They wouldn't harm a defenseless woman."

A deep calm took hold of his heart. Perhaps the Lord had come to realize that he was the wrong man and had found another prophet to rescue Israel from sin. Death had finally come, in the way he had hoped, through martyrdom. He accepted his fate and waited for the fatal blow.

Seconds went by; the voices were still shouting, blood still ran from his wound, but the fatal blow had not come.

"Ask them to kill me at once!" he shouted, knowing that at least one of them spoke his language.

No one heeded his words. They were arguing heatedly, as if something had gone wrong. Some of the soldiers began kicking him, and for the first time Elijah noticed the instinct for survival reasserting itself. This created in him a sensation of panic.

"I can't wish for life any longer," he thought desperately. "Because I'm not leaving this room alive."

But nothing happened. The world seemed to be suspended endlessly in that confusion of shouts, noises, and dust. Perhaps the Lord had done as He had with Joshua and time had stood still amid the combat.

That was when he heard the woman's screams from below. With an effort surpassing human strength, Elijah pushed aside two of the guards and struggled to his feet, but he was quickly struck down; a soldier kicked him in the head, and he fainted.

◆

A FEW MINUTES LATER he recovered consciousness. The Assyrians had dragged him into the street.

Still dizzy, he raised his head; every house in the neighborhood was in flames.

"An innocent, helpless woman is caught in there! Save her!"

Cries, people running in every direction, confusion everywhere. He tried to rise but was struck down again.

"Lord, Thou canst do with me as Thou wilt, for I have dedicated my life and my death to Thy cause," Elijah prayed. "But save the woman who took me in!"

Someone raised him by his arms.

"Come and see," said the Assyrian officer who knew his language. "You deserve it."

Two guards seized him and pushed him toward the door. The house was rapidly being devoured by flames, and the light from the fire illuminated everything around it. He heard cries coming from all sides: children sobbing, old men begging for forgiveness, desperate women searching for their children. But he had ears only for the pleas for help of the woman who had afforded him shelter.

"What is happening? A woman and child are inside! Why have you done this to them?"

"Because she tried to hide the governor of Akbar."

"I'm not the governor! You're making a terrible mistake!"

The Assyrian officer pushed him toward the door. The ceiling had collapsed in the fire, and the woman was half-buried in the debris. Elijah could see only her arm, moving desperately from side to side. She was asking for help, begging them not to let her be burned alive.

"Why spare me," he implored, "and do this to her?"

"We're not going to spare you, but we want you to suffer as much as possible. Our general died without honor, stoned to death, in front of the city walls. He came in search of life and was condemned to death. Now you will have the same fate."

Elijah struggled desperately to free himself, but the guards carried him away. They passed through the streets of Akbar, in infernal heat; the soldiers were sweating heavily, and some of them appeared shocked at the scene they had just witnessed. Elijah thrashed about, clamoring against the heavens, but the Assyrians were as silent as the Lord Himself.

They arrived at the square. Most of the buildings in the city were ablaze, and the sound of flames mingled with the cries of Akbar's inhabitants.

"How good that death still exists."

Since that day in the stable, how often Elijah had thought this!

The corpses of Akbar's warriors, most of them without uniforms, were spread out on the ground. He saw people running in every direction, not knowing where they were going, not knowing what they sought, guided by nothing more than the necessity of pretending they were doing something, fighting against death and destruction.

"Why do they do that?" he thought. "Don't they see the city is in the hands of the enemy and there is nowhere to flee?" Everything had happened very quickly. The Assyrians had taken advantage of their large superiority in numbers and had been able to spare their warriors from combat. Akbar's soldiers had been exterminated almost without a struggle.

They stopped in the middle of the square. Elijah was made to kneel on the ground and his hands were tied. He no longer heard the woman's screams; perhaps she had died quickly, without going through the slow torture of being burned alive. The Lord had her in His hands. And she was carrying her son at her bosom.

Another group of Assyrian soldiers brought a prisoner whose face was disfigured by numerous blows. Even so, Elijah recognized the commander.

"Long live Akbar!" he shouted. "Long life to Phoenicia and its warriors, who engage the enemy by day! Death to the cowards who attack in darkness!"

He barely had time to finish the phrase. An Assyrian general's sword descended, and the commander's head rolled along the ground.

"Now it is my turn," Elijah told himself. "I'll meet her again in paradise, where we shall stroll hand in hand."

At that moment, a man approached and began to argue with the officers. He was an inhabitant of Akbar who was wont to attend the meetings in the square. Elijah recalled having helped him resolve a serious dispute with a neighbor.

The Assyrians were arguing among themselves, their words growing louder and louder, and pointing at him. The man kneeled, kissed the feet of one of them, extended his hand toward the Fifth Mountain, and wept like a child. The invaders' fury appeared to subside.

The discussion seemed to go on endlessly. The man implored and wept the entire time, pointing to Elijah and to the house where the governor lived. The soldiers appeared dissatisfied with the conversation.

Finally, the officer who spoke his language approached.

"Our spy," he said, indicating the man, "says that we are mistaken. It was he who gave us the plans to the city, and we have confidence in what he says. It's not you we wish to kill."

He pushed him with his foot. Elijah fell to the ground.

"He says you would go to Israel and remove the princess who usurped the throne. Is that true?"

Elijah did not answer.

"Tell me if it's true," the officer insisted. "And you can leave here and return to your dwelling in time to save that woman and her son."

"Yes, it's true," he said. Perhaps the Lord had listened to him and would help him to save them.

"We could take you captive to Sidon and Tyre," the officer continued. "But we still have many battles before us, and you'd be a weight on our backs. We could demand a ransom for you, but from whom? You're a foreigner even in your own country."

The officer put his foot on Elijah's face.

"You're useless. You're no good to the enemy and no good to friends. Just like your city; it's not worth leaving part of our army here, to keep it under our rule. After we conquer the coastal cities Akbar will be ours in any case."

"I have one question," Elijah said. "Just one question."

The officer looked at him warily.

"Why did you attack at night? Don't you know that wars are fought by day?"

"We did not break the law; there is no custom that forbids it," answered the officer. "And we had a long time to become familiar with the terrain. All of you were so preoccupied with custom that you forgot that times change."

Without a further word, the group left him. The spy approached and untied his hands.

"I promised myself that I would one day repay your generosity; I have kept my word. When the Assyrians entered the palace, one of the servants told them that the man they were looking for had taken refuge in the widow's house. While they went there, the real governor was able to flee."

Elijah was not listening. Fire crackled everywhere, and the screams continued.

In the midst of the confusion, it was evident that one group still maintained discipline; obeying an invisible order, the Assyrians were silently withdrawing.

The battle of Akbar was over.

◆

"SHE'S DEAD," he told himself. "I don't want to go there, for she is dead. Or she was saved by a miracle and will come looking for me."

His heart nevertheless bade him rise to his feet and go to the house where they lived. Elijah struggled with himself; at that moment, more than a woman's love was at stake—his entire life, his faith in the Lord's designs, the departure from the city of his birth, the idea that he had a mission and was capable of completing it.

He looked about him, searching for a sword with which to take his own life, but with the Assyrians had gone every weapon in Akbar. He thought of throwing himself onto the flames of the burning houses, but he feared the pain.

For some moments he stood paralyzed. Little by little, he began recovering his awareness of the situation in which he found himself. The woman and her child must have already left this world, but he must bury them in accord with custom. At that moment the Lord's work—whether or not He existed—was his only succor. After finishing his religious duty, he would yield to pain and doubt.

Moreover, there was a possibility that they still lived. He could not remain there, doing nothing.

"I don't want to see their burned faces, the skin falling from their flesh. Their souls are already running free in heaven."

◆

NEVERTHELESS, HE BEGAN walking toward the house, choking and blinded by the smoke that prevented his finding his way. He gradually began to comprehend the situation in the city. Although the enemy had withdrawn, panic was mounting in an alarming manner. People continued to wander aimlessly, weeping, petitioning the gods on behalf of their dead.

He looked for someone to help him. A lone man was in sight, in a total state of shock; his mind seemed distant.

"It's best to go straightway and not ask for help." He knew Akbar as if it were his native city and was able to orient himself, even without recognizing many of the places that he was accustomed to passing. In the street the cries he heard were now more coherent. The people were beginning to understand that a tragedy had taken place and that it was necessary to react.

"There's a wounded man here!" said one.

"We need more water! We're not going to be able to control the fire!" said another.

"Help me! My husband is trapped!"

He came to the place where, many months before, he had been received and given lodging as a friend. An old woman was sitting in the middle of the street, almost in front of the house, completely naked. Elijah tried to help her but was pushed away.

"She's dying!" the old woman cried. "Do something! Take that wall off her!"

And she began screaming hysterically. Elijah took her by the arms and shoved her aside, for the noise she was making prevented his hearing the widow's moans. Everything around him was total destruction—the roof and walls had collapsed, and it was difficult to recognize where he had last seen her. The flames had died down but the heat was still unbearable; he stepped over the rubble covering the floor and went toward the place where the woman's bedroom had been.

Despite the confusion outside, he was able to make out a moan. It was her voice.

He instinctively shook the dust from his garments, as if trying to improve his appearance. He remained silent, trying to concentrate. He heard the crackling of the fire, the cries for help from people buried in the neighboring houses, and felt the urge to tell them to be silent because he must discover where the woman and her son were. After a long time, he heard the sound again; someone was scratching on the wood beneath his feet.

He fell to his knees and began digging like one possessed. He removed the dirt, stones, and wood. Finally, his hand touched something warm: it was blood.

"Please, don't die," he said.

"Leave the rubble over me," he heard her voice say. "I don't want you to see my face. Go and help my son."

He continued to dig, and she repeated, "Go and find the body of my son. Please, do as I ask."

Elijah's head fell against his chest, and he began weeping softly.

"I don't know where he's buried," he said. "Please, don't go; how I long to have you remain with me. I need you to teach me how to love; my heart is ready now."

"Before you arrived, for so many years I called out to death. It must have heard and come looking for me."

She moaned. Elijah bit his lips but said nothing. Someone touched his shoulder.

Startled, he turned and saw the boy. He was covered with dust and soot but appeared unhurt.

"Where is my mother?" he asked.

"I'm here, my son," answered the voice from beneath the ruins. "Are you injured?"

The boy began to cry. Elijah took him in his arms.

"You're crying, my son," said the voice, ever weaker. "Don't do that. Your mother took a long time to learn that life has meaning; I hope I have been able to teach it to you. In what condition is the city where you were born?"

Elijah and the boy remained silent, each clinging to the other.

"It's fine," Elijah lied. "A few warriors died, but the Assyrians have withdrawn. They were after the governor, to avenge the death of one of their generals."

Again, silence. And again her voice, still weaker than before.

"Tell me that my city is safe."

He knew that she would be gone at any moment.

"The city is whole. And your son is well."

"What about you?"

"I have survived."

He knew that with these words he was liberating her soul and allowing her to die in peace.

"Ask my son to kneel," the woman said after a time. "And I want you to swear to me, in the name of the Lord thy God."

"Whatever you want. Anything that you want."

"You once told me that the Lord is everywhere, and I believed you. You said that souls don't go to the top of the Fifth Mountain, and I also believed what you said. But you didn't explain where they go.

"This is the oath: you two will not weep for me, and each

will take care of the other until the Lord allows each of you to follow his path. From this moment on, my soul will become one with all I have known on this earth: I am the valley, the mountains that surround it, the city, the people walking in its streets. I am its wounded and its beggars, its soldiers, its priests, its merchants, its nobles. I am the ground that they tread, and the well that slakes each one's thirst.

"Don't weep for me, for there is no reason to be sad. From this moment on, I am Akbar, and the city is beautiful."

The silence of death descended, and the wind ceased to blow. Elijah no longer heard the cries outside or the flames crackling in neighboring houses; he heard only the silence and could almost touch it in its intensity.

Then Elijah led the boy away, rent his own garments, turned to the heavens, and bellowed with all the strength of his lungs, "O Lord my God! For Thy cause have I left Israel and cannot offer Thee my blood as did the prophets who remained there. I have been called a coward by my friends and a traitor by my enemies.

"For Thy cause have I eaten only what crows brought me and have crossed the desert to Zarephath, which its inhabitants call Akbar. Guided by Thy hand, I met a woman; guided by Thee, my heart learned to love her. But at no time did I forget my true mission; during all the days I spent here I was always ready to depart.

"Beautiful Akbar is in ruins, and the woman who trusted me lies beneath them. Where have I sinned, O Lord? At what moment have I strayed from what Thou desirest of me? If Thou art discontent with me, why hast Thou not taken me from this world? Instead, Thou hast afflicted yet again those who succored me and loved me.

"I do not understand Thy designs. I see no justice in Thy acts. In bearing the suffering Thou hast imposed on me, I am sorely wanting. Remove Thyself from my life, for I too am reduced to ruins, fire, and dust."

Amidst the fire and desolation, the light appeared to Elijah. And the angel of the Lord was before him.

"Why are you here?" asked Elijah. "Don't you see that it is too late?"

"I have come to say that once again the Lord hath heard thy prayer and thy petition will be granted thee. No more shalt thou hear thy angel, nor shall I meet again with thee till thou hast undergone thy days of trial."

Elijah took the boy by the hand and they began to walk aimlessly. The smoke, till then dispersed by the winds, was now concentrated in the streets, making the air impossible to breathe. "Perhaps it's a dream," he thought. "Perhaps it's a nightmare."

"You lied to my mother," the boy said. "The city is destroyed."

"What does that matter? If she did not see what was happening around her, why not allow her to die in peace?"

"Because she trusted you, and said that she was Akbar."

Elijah cut his foot on one of the broken pieces of glass and pottery strewn on the ground. The pain proved to him that he was not dreaming; everything around him was terribly real. They arrived at the square where—how long ago?—he had met with the people and helped them to resolve their disputes; the sky was gilded by flames from the fires.

"I don't want my mother to be this that I'm looking at," the boy insisted. "You lied to her."

The boy was managing to keep his oath; Elijah had not seen a single tear on his face. "What can I do?" he thought. His foot was bleeding, and he decided to concentrate on the pain, to ward off despair.

He looked at the sword cut the Assyrian had made in his body; it was not as deep as he had imagined. He sat down with the boy at the same spot where he had been bound by his enemies, and saved by a traitor. He noticed that people were no longer running; they were walking slowly from place to place, amidst the smoky, dusty ruins, as if they were the living dead. They seemed like souls abandoned by the heavens and condemned to walk the earth eternally. Nothing made sense.

Some of the people reacted; they still heeded the women's voices and the confused orders from the soldiers who had survived the massacre. But they were few and were not achieving any result.

The high priest had once said that the world was the collective dream of the gods. What if, fundamentally, he was right? Could he now help the gods to awaken from this nightmare and then make them sleep again to dream a gentler dream? When Elijah had nocturnal visions, he always awoke and then slept anew; why should the same not occur with the creators of the Universe?

He stumbled over the dead. None of them was now concerned with having to pay taxes, Assyrian encampments in the valley, religious rituals, or the existence of a wandering prophet who perhaps one day had spoken to them.

"I can't remain here permanently. The legacy that she left me is this boy, and I shall be worthy of it, even if it be the last thing I do on the face of the earth."

With a great effort, he rose, took the boy by the hand, and they began to walk. Some of the people were sacking the shops and tents that had been smashed. For the first time, he attempted to react to what had happened, by asking them not to do that.

But the people pushed him aside, saying, "We're eating the remains of what the governor devoured by himself. Get out of the way."

Elijah did not have the strength to argue; he led the boy out of the city, where they began to walk through the valley. The angels, with their swords of fire, would come no more.

"A full moon."

Far from the dust and smoke, he could see the night illuminated by moonlight. Hours before, when he was attempting to leave the city for Jerusalem, he had been able to find his way without difficulty; the Assyrians had had the same advantage.

The boy stumbled over a body and screamed. It was the high priest; his arms and legs had been cut off, but he was still alive. His eyes were fixed on the heights of the Fifth Mountain.

"As you see," he said in a labored but calm voice, "the Phoenician gods have won the celestial battle." Blood was spurting from his mouth.

"Let me end your suffering," Elijah replied.

"Pain means nothing, compared to the joy of having done my duty."

"Your duty was to destroy a city of righteous men?"

"A city does not die, only its inhabitants and the ideas they bore within themselves. One day, others will come to Akbar, drink its water, and the stone that its founder left behind will be polished and cared for by new priests. Leave me now; my pain will soon be over, while your despair will endure for the rest of your life."

The mutilated body was breathing with difficulty, and Elijah left him. At that moment, a group of people—men, women, and children—came running toward him and encircled him.

"It was you!" they shouted. "You dishonored your homeland and brought a curse upon our city!"

"May the gods bear witness to this! May they know who is to blame!"

The men pushed him and shook him by the shoulders. The boy pulled loose from his hands and disappeared. The others struck him in the face, the chest, the back, but his only thoughts were for the boy; he had not even been able to keep him at his side.

The beating did not last long; perhaps his assailants were themselves weary of so much violence. Elijah fell to the ground.

"Leave this place!" someone said. "You have repaid our love with your hatred!"

The group withdrew. Elijah did not have the strength to rise to his feet. When he recovered from the shame, he had ceased to be the same man. He desired neither to die nor to go on living. He desired nothing: he possessed no love, no hate, no faith.

◆

HE AWOKE to someone touching his face. It was still night, but the moon was no longer in the sky.

"I promised my mother that I'd take care of you," the boy said. "But I don't know what to do."

"Go back to the city. The people there are good, and someone will take you in."

"You're hurt. I need to attend to your arm. Maybe an angel will come and tell me what to do."

"You're ignorant, you know nothing about what's happening!" Elijah shouted. "The angels will come no more because we're common folk, and everyone is weak when faced with suffering. When tragedy occurs, let people fend for themselves!"

He took a deep breath, trying to calm himself; there was no point in arguing further.

"How did you find your way here?"

"I never left."

"Then you saw my shame. You saw that there is nothing left for me to do in Akbar."

"You told me that all life's battles teach us something, even those we lose."

He remembered the walk to the well the morning before. But it seemed as if years had passed since then, and he felt the urge to tell him that those beautiful words meant nothing when one faces suffering; but he decided not to upset the boy.

"How did you escape the fire?"

The boy lowered his head. "I hadn't gone to sleep. I decided to spend the night awake, to see if you and my mother were going to meet in her room. I saw the first soldiers come in."

Elijah rose and began to walk. He was looking for the stone in front of the Fifth Mountain where one afternoon he had watched the sunset with the woman.

"I mustn't go," he thought. "I'll become even more desperate."

But some force drew him in that direction. When he arrived there, he wept bitterly; like the city of Akbar, the spot was marked by a stone, but he alone in that entire valley understood its significance; it would neither be praised by new inhabitants, nor polished by couples discovering the meaning of love.

He took the boy in his arms and once again slept.

"I'M HUNGRY AND THIRSTY," THE BOY TOLD ELIJAH AS soon as he awoke.

"We can go to the home of one of the shepherds who live nearby. It's likely nothing happened to them because they didn't live in Akbar."

"We need to repair the city. My mother said that she was Akbar."

What city? No longer was there a palace, a market, or walls. The city's good people had turned into robbers, and its young soldiers had been massacred. Nor would the angels return, though this was the least among his problems.

"Do you think that last night's destruction, suffering, and deaths have a meaning? Do you think that it's necessary to destroy thousands of lives to teach someone something?"

The boy looked at him in alarm.

"Put from your mind what I just said," Elijah told him. "We're going to look for the shepherd."

"And we're going to rebuild the city," the boy insisted.

Elijah did not reply. He knew he would no longer be able to use his authority with the people, who accused him of having brought misfortune. The governor had taken flight, the commander was dead; soon Sidon and Tyre might fall under foreign domination. Perhaps the woman was right: the gods were always changing, and this time it was the Lord who had gone away.

"When will we go back there?" the boy asked again.

Elijah took him by the shoulders and began shaking him forcefully.

"Look behind you! You're not some blind angel but a boy who intended to spy on his mother's acts. What do you see? Have you noticed the columns of rising smoke? Do you know what that means?"

"You're hurting me! I want to leave here, I want to go away!"

Elijah stopped, disconcerted at himself: he had never acted in such a way. The boy broke loose and began running toward the city. Elijah overtook him and kneeled at his feet.

"Forgive me. I don't know what I'm doing."

The boy sobbed, but not a single tear ran down his cheeks. Elijah sat beside him, waiting for him to regain his calm.

"Don't leave," he asked. "When your mother went away, I promised her I'd stay with you until you could follow your own path."

"You also promised that the city was whole. And she said—"

"There's no need to repeat it. I'm confused, lost in my own guilt. Give me time to find myself. I didn't mean to hurt you."

The boy embraced him. But his eyes shed no tears.

◆

THEY CAME TO THE HOUSE in the middle of the valley; a woman was at the door, and two children were playing in front. The flock was in the enclosure, which meant that the shepherd had not yet left for the mountains that morning.

Startled, the woman looked at the man and boy walking toward her. Her instinct was to send them away at once, but custom—and the gods—demanded that she honor the universal law of hospitality. If she did not receive them now, her own children might in the future suffer the same fate.

"I have no money," she said. "But I can give you a little water and something to eat."

They sat on a small porch with a straw roof, and she brought dried fruit and a jar of water. They ate in silence, experiencing, for the first time since the events of the night before, something of the normal routine that marked their every day. The children, frightened by the newcomers' appearance, had taken refuge inside the house.

When they finished their meal, Elijah asked about the shepherd.

"He'll be here soon," she said. "We heard a lot of noise, and somebody came by this morning saying that Akbar had been destroyed. He went to see what happened."

The children called her, and she went inside.

"It will avail me nothing to try to convince the boy," Elijah thought. "He'll not leave me in peace until I do what he asks. I must show him that it is impossible; only then will he be persuaded."

The food and water achieved a miracle: he again felt himself a part of the world.

His thoughts flowed with incredible speed, seeking solutions rather than answers.

◆

SOME TIME LATER, the aged shepherd arrived. He looked at the man and boy with fear, concerned for the safety of his family. But he quickly understood what was happening.

"You must be refugees from Akbar," he said. "I've just returned from there."

"And what's happening?" asked the boy.

"The city was destroyed, and the governor ran away. The gods have disorganized the world."

"We lost everything we had," said Elijah. "We ask that you receive us."

"I think my wife has already received you, and fed you. Now you must leave and face the unavoidable."

"I don't know what to do with the boy. I'm in need of help."

"Of course you know. He's young, he seems intelligent, and he has energy. And you have the experience of someone who's known many victories and defeats in life. The combination is perfect, because it can help you to find wisdom."

The man looked at the wound on Elijah's arm. He said it was not serious; he entered the house and returned with some herbs and a piece of cloth. The boy helped him apply the poultice. When the shepherd said that he could do it alone, the boy told him that he had promised his mother to take care of this man.

The shepherd laughed.

"Your son is a man of his word."

"I'm not his son. And he's a man of his word too. He'll rebuild the city because he has to bring my mother back, the way he did with me."

Suddenly, Elijah understood the boy's concern, but before he could do anything, the shepherd shouted to his wife, who was coming out of the house at that moment. "It's better to start rebuilding life right away," he said. "It will take a long time for everything to return to what it was."

"It will never return."

"You look like a wise young man, and you can understand many things that I cannot. But nature has taught me something that I shall never forget: a man who depends on the weather and the seasons, as only a shepherd does, manages to survive the unavoidable. He cares for his flock, treats each animal as if it were the only one, tries to help the mothers with their young, is never too far from a place where the animals can drink. Still, now and again one of the lambs to which he gave so much of himself dies in an accident. It might be a snake, some wild animal, or even a fall over a cliff. But the unavoidable always happens."

Elijah looked in the direction of Akbar and recalled his conversation with the angel. The unavoidable always happens.

"You need discipline and patience to overcome it," the shepherd said.

"And hope. When that no longer exists, one can't waste his energy fighting against the impossible."

"It's not a question of hope in the future. It's a question of re-creating your own past."

The shepherd was no longer in a hurry; his heart was filled with pity for the refugees who stood facing him. As he and his family had been spared the tragedy, it cost nothing to help them, and thus to thank the gods. Moreover, he had heard talk of the Israelite prophet who had climbed the Fifth Mountain without being slain by the fire from heaven; everything indicated that it was the man before him.

"You can stay another day if you wish."

"I didn't understand what you said before," commented Elijah. "About re-creating your own past."

"I have long seen people passing through here on their way to Sidon and Tyre. Some of them complained that they had not achieved anything in Akbar and were setting out for a new destiny.

"One day these people would return. They had not found what they were seeking, for they carried with them, along with their bags, the weight of their earlier failure. A few returned with a government position, or with the joy of having given their children a better life, but nothing more. Their past in Akbar had left them fearful, and they lacked the confidence in themselves to take risks.

"On the other hand, there also passed my door people full of ardor. They had profited from every moment of life in Akbar and through great effort had accumulated the money for their journey. To these people, life was a constant triumph and would go on being one.

"These people also returned, but with wonderful tales to tell. They had achieved everything they desired because they were not limited by the frustrations of the past."

◆

THE SHEPHERD'S WORDS touched Elijah's heart.

"It is not difficult to rebuild a life, just as it is not impossible to raise Akbar from its ruins," the shepherd continued. "It is enough to be aware that we go on with the same strength that we had before. And to use that in our favor."

The man gazed into Elijah's eyes.

"If you have a past that dissatisfies you, forget it now," he went on. "Imagine a new story of your life, and believe in it. Concentrate only on those moments in which you achieved what you desired, and this strength will help you to accomplish what you want."

"There was a moment when I desired to be a carpenter, and later I wanted to be a prophet sent to save Israel," Elijah thought. "Angels descended from the heavens, the Lord spoke to me. Until I understood that He is not just and that His motives are always beyond my understanding."

The shepherd called to his wife, saying that he was not leaving; he had already been to Akbar on foot, and he was too weary to walk farther.

"Thank you for receiving us," Elijah said.

"It is no burden to shelter you for one night."

The boy interrupted the conversation. "We want to go back to Akbar."

"Wait till morning. The city is being sacked by its own inhabitants, and there is nowhere to sleep."

The boy looked at the ground, bit his lip, and once again held back tears. The shepherd led them into the house, calmed his wife and children, and, to distract them, spent the rest of the day talking about the weather.

THE NEXT DAY THEY AWOKE EARLY, ATE THE MEAL PRE-
pared by the shepherd's wife, and went to the door of the house.

"May your life be long and your flock grow ever larger," said
Elijah. "I have eaten what my body had need of, and my soul has
learned what it did not know. May God never forget what you
did for us, and may your sons not be strangers in a strange
land."

"I don't know to which God you refer; there are many who
dwell on the Fifth Mountain," the shepherd said brusquely, then
quickly changed his tone. "Remember the good things you have
done. They will give you courage."

"I have done very few such things, and none of them was
because of my abilities."

"Then it's time to do more."

"Perhaps I could have prevented the invasion."

The shepherd laughed.

"Even if you were governor of Akbar, you would not be able to stop the unavoidable."

"Perhaps the governor of Akbar should have attacked the Assyrians when they first arrived in the valley with few troops. Or negotiated peace, before war broke out."

"Everything that could have happened but did not is carried away with the wind and leaves no trace," said the shepherd. "Life is made of our attitudes. *And there are certain things that the gods oblige us to live through.* Their reason for this does not matter, and there is no action we can take to make them pass us by."

"Why?"

"Ask a certain Israelite prophet who lived in Akbar. He seems to have the answer to everything."

The man went to the fence. "I must take my flock to pasture," he said. "Yesterday they didn't go out, and they're impatient."

He took his leave with a wave of his hand, departing with his sheep.

THE BOY AND THE MAN WALKED THROUGH THE VALLEY.

"You're walking slowly," the boy said. "You're afraid of what might happen to you."

"I'm afraid only of myself," Elijah replied. "They can do me no harm because my heart has ceased to be."

"The God that brought me back from death is alive. He can bring back my mother, if you do the same thing to the city."

"Forget that God. He's far away and no longer does the miracles we hope for from Him."

The old shepherd was right. From this moment on, it was necessary to reconstruct his own past, forget that he had once thought himself to be a prophet who would free Israel but had failed in his mission of saving even one city.

The thought gave him a strange sense of euphoria. For the

first time in his life he felt free, ready to do whatever he desired whenever he wished. True, he would hear no more angels, but as compensation he was free to return to Israel, to go back to work as a carpenter, to travel to Greece to learn the thoughts of wise men, or to journey with Phoenician navigators to the lands across the sea.

First, however, he must avenge himself. He had dedicated the best years of his youth to an unheeding God who was constantly giving commands and always did things in His own fashion. Elijah had learned to accept His decisions and to respect His designs.

But his loyalty had been rewarded by abandonment, his dedication had been ignored, his efforts to comply with the Supreme Being's will had led to the death of the only woman he had ever loved.

"Thou hast the strength of the world and the stars," said Elijah in his native tongue, so that the boy beside him would not understand the words. "Thou canst destroy a city, a country, as we destroy insects. Send, then, Thy fire from heaven and end my life, for if Thou dost not, I shall go against Thy handiwork."

Akbar loomed in the distance. He took the boy's hand and grasped it tightly.

"From this moment until we go through the city gates, I am going to walk with my eyes closed, and you must guide me," he told the boy. "If I die on the way, do what you have asked me to do: rebuild Akbar, even if to do so you must first grow to manhood and learn to cut wood or work stone."

The boy did not reply. Elijah closed his eyes and allowed himself to be led. He heard the blowing of the wind and the sound of his own steps in the sand.

He remembered Moses, who, after liberating the Chosen People and leading them through the desert, surmounting enormous difficulties, had been forbidden by God to enter Canaan. At the time, Moses had said:

"*I pray Thee, let me go over, and see the good land that is beyond Jordan.*"

The Lord, however, had been offended by his entreaty. And He had answered, "*Let it suffice thee; speak no more unto Me of this matter. Lift up thine eyes westward, and northward, and southward, and eastward, and behold it with thine eyes; for thou shalt not go over this Jordan.*"

Thus had the Lord rewarded the long and arduous task of Moses: He had not permitted him to set foot in the Promised Land. What would have happened if he had disobeyed?

Elijah again turned his thoughts to the heavens.

"O Lord, this battle was not between Assyrians and Phoenicians but between Thee and me. Thou didst not foretell to me our singular war, and as ever, Thou hast triumphed and seen Thy will made manifest. Thou hast destroyed the woman I loved and the city that took me in when I was far from my homeland."

The sound of the wind was louder in his ears. Elijah was afraid, but he continued.

"I cannot bring the woman back, but I can change the fate of Thy work of destruction. Moses accepted Thy will and did not cross the river. But I shall go forward: slay me now, because if Thou allowest me to arrive at the gates of the city, I shall rebuild that which Thou wouldst sweep from the face of the earth. And I shall go against Thy judgment."

He fell silent. He emptied his mind and waited for death. For a long time he concentrated on nothing beyond the sound of his footsteps in the sand; he did not want to hear the voices of angels or threats from heaven. His heart was free, and no longer did he fear what might befall him. Yet in the depths of his soul was the beginning of disquiet, as if he had forgotten a thing of importance.

After much time had passed, the boy stopped, then tugged on Elijah's arm.

"We've arrived," he said.

Elijah opened his eyes. The fire from heaven had not descended on him, and before him were the ruined walls of Akbar.

He looked at the boy, who now clutched Elijah's hand as if fearing that he might escape. Did he love him? He had no idea. But such reflections could wait till later; for now, he had a task to carry out—the first in many years not imposed upon him by God.

From where they stood, he could smell the odor of burning. Scavenger birds circled overhead, awaiting the right moment to devour the corpses of the sentinels that lay rotting in the sun. Elijah approached one of the fallen soldiers and took the sword from his belt. In the confusion of the previous night, the Assyrians had forgotten to gather up the weapons outside the city walls.

"Why do you want that?" the boy asked.

"To defend myself."

"The Assyrians aren't here anymore."

"Even so, it's good to have it with me. We have to be prepared."

His voice shook. It was impossible to know what might happen from the moment they crossed the half-destroyed wall, but he was ready to kill whoever tried to humiliate him.

"Like this city, I too was destroyed," he told the boy. "But also like this city, I have not yet completed my mission."

The boy smiled.

"You're talking the way you used to," he said.

"Don't be fooled by words. Before, I had the objective of removing Jezebel from the throne and turning Israel back to the Lord; now that He has forgotten us, we must forget Him. My mission is to do what you have asked of me."

The boy looked at him warily.

"Without God, my mother will not come back from the dead."

Elijah ran his hand over the boy's hair.

"Only your mother's body has gone away. She is still among us, and as she told us, she is Akbar. We must help her recover her beauty."

◆

THE CITY was almost deserted. Old people, women, and children were walking aimlessly through its streets, in a repetition of the scene he had witnessed the night of the invasion. They seemed uncertain of what to do next.

Each time Elijah's path crossed that of someone else, the boy saw him grip the handle of his sword. But the people displayed indifference; most recognized the prophet from Israel, some nodded at him, but none directed a single word to him, not even one of hatred.

"They've lost even the sense of rage," he thought, looking toward the top of the Fifth Mountain, the summit of which was covered as always by its eternal clouds. Then he recalled the Lord's words:

"I will cast your carcasses upon the carcasses of your idols, and my soul shall abhor you. And I will make your cities waste, and bring the land into desolation.

"And upon them that are left alive of you I will send a faintness into their hearts; and the sound of a shaken leaf shall chase them; and they shall fall when none pursueth."

"BEHOLD, O LORD, WHAT THOU HAST WROUGHT: THOU hast kept Thy promise, and the living dead still walk the earth. And Akbar is the city chosen to shelter them."

Elijah and the boy continued to the main square, where they sat and rested on pieces of rubble while they surveyed their surroundings. The destruction seemed more severe and unrelenting than he had thought; the roofs of most of the houses had collapsed; filth and insects had taken over everything.

"The dead must be removed," he said. "Or plague will enter the city through the main gate."

The boy kept his eyes downward.

"Raise your head," Elijah said. "We have much work to do, so your mother can be content."

But the boy did not obey; he was beginning to understand: somewhere among the ruins was the body that had brought him into life, and that body was in a condition similar to all the others scattered on every side.

Elijah did not insist. He rose, lifted a corpse to his shoulders, and carried it to the middle of the square. He could not remember the Lord's recommendations about burying the dead; what he must do was prevent the coming of plague, and the only solution was to burn them.

He worked the entire morning. The boy did not stir from his place, nor did he raise his eyes for an instant, but he kept his promise to his mother: no tear dropped to Akbar's soil.

A woman stopped and stood for a time observing Elijah's efforts.

"The man who solved the problems of the living now puts in order the bodies of the dead," she commented.

"Where are the men of Akbar?" Elijah asked.

"They left, and they took with them the little that remained. There is nothing left worth staying for. The only ones who haven't deserted the city are those incapable of leaving: the old, widows, and orphans."

"But they were here for generations. They can't give up so easily."

"Try to explain that to someone who has lost everything."

"Help me," said Elijah, taking another corpse onto his shoulders and placing it on the pile. "We're going to burn them, so that the plague god will not come to visit us. He is horrified by the smell of burning flesh."

"Let the plague god come," said the woman. "And may he take us all, as soon as possible."

Elijah went on with his task. The woman sat down beside the boy and watched what he was doing. After a time, she approached him again.

"Why do you want to save this wretched city?"

"If I stop to reflect on it, I'll conclude I'm incapable of accomplishing what I desire," he answered.

The old shepherd was right: the only solution was to forget a past of uncertainty and create a new history for oneself. The former prophet had died together with a woman in the flames of her house; now he was a man without faith in God and beset by doubts. But he was still alive, even after challenging divine retribution. If he wished to continue on this path, he must do what he had proposed.

The woman chose one of the lighter bodies and dragged it by the heels, taking it to the pile that Elijah had started.

"It's not from fear of the plague god," she said. "Or for Akbar, since the Assyrians will soon return. It's for that boy sitting there with his head hanging; he has to learn that he still has his life ahead of him."

"Thank you," said Elijah.

"Don't thank me. Somewhere in these ruins we'll find the body of my son. He was about the same age as the boy."

She lifted her hand to her face and wept copiously. Elijah took her gently by the arm.

"The pain you and I feel will never go away, but work will help us to bear it. Suffering has no strength to wound a weary body."

They spent the entire day at the macabre task of collecting and piling up the dead; most of them were youths, whom the Assyrians had identified as part of Akbar's army. More than once he recognized friends, and wept—but he did not interrupt his task.

◆

AT THE END of the afternoon, they were exhausted. Even so, the work done was far from sufficient, and no other inhabitant of Akbar had assisted.

The pair approached the boy, who lifted his head for the first time.

"I'm hungry," he said.

"I'm going to go look for something," the woman answered. "There's plenty of food hidden in the various houses in Akbar; people were preparing for a long siege."

"Bring food for me and for yourself, for we are ministering to the city with the sweat of our brows," said Elijah. "But if the boy wants to eat, he will have to take care of himself."

The woman understood; she would have done the same with her son. She went to the place where her house had stood; almost everything had been ransacked by looters in search of objects of value, and her collection of vases, created by the great master glassmakers of Akbar, lay in pieces on the floor. But she found the dried fruits and grain that she had cached.

She returned to the square, where she divided part of the food with Elijah. The boy said nothing.

An old man approached them.

"I saw that you spent all day gathering the bodies," he said. "You're wasting your time; don't you know the Assyrians will be back, after they conquer Sidon and Tyre? Let the plague god come here and destroy them."

"We're not doing this for them, or for ourselves," Elijah answered. "She is working to teach a child that there is still a future. And I am working to show him there is no longer a past."

"So the prophet is no more a threat to the great princess of Sidon: what a surprise! Jezebel will rule Israel till the end of her days, and we shall always have a refuge if the Assyrians are not generous to the conquered."

Elijah did not reply. The name that had once awakened in him such hatred now sounded strangely distant.

"Akbar will be rebuilt, in any case," the old man insisted. "The gods choose where cities are erected, and they will not abandon it; but we can leave that labor for the generations to come."

"We can, but we will not."

Elijah turned his back on the old man, ending the conversation.

The three of them slept in the open air. The woman embraced the boy, noting that his stomach was growling from hunger. She considered giving him food but quickly dismissed the idea: fatigue truly did diminish pain, and the boy, who seemed to be suffering greatly, needed to busy himself with something. Perhaps hunger would persuade him to work.

THE NEXT DAY, ELIJAH AND THE WOMAN RESUMED their labors. The old man who had approached them the night before came to them again.

"I don't have anything to do and I could help you," he said. "But I'm too weak to carry bodies."

"Then gather bricks and small pieces of wood. Sweep away the ashes."

The old man began doing as they asked.

◆

WHEN THE SUN reached its zenith, Elijah sat on the ground, exhausted. He knew that his angel was at his side, but he could not hear him. "To what avail? He was unable to help me when I needed him, and now I don't want his counsel; all I desire is to put this city in order, to show God I can face Him, and then leave for wherever I want to go."

Jerusalem was not far away, just seven days' travel on foot, with no really difficult places to pass through, but there he was hunted as a traitor. Perhaps it would be better to go to Damascus, or find work as a scribe in some Greek city.

He felt something touch him. He turned and saw the boy holding a small jar.

"I found it in one of the houses," the boy said.

It was full of water. Elijah drank it to the final drop.

"Eat something," he said. "You're working and deserve your reward."

For the first time since the night of the invasion, a smile appeared on the boy's lips, and he ran to the spot where the woman had left the fruits and grain.

Elijah returned to his work, entering destroyed homes, pushing aside the rubble, picking up the bodies, and carrying them to the pile in the middle of the square. The bandage that the shepherd had put on his arm had fallen off, but that mattered little; he had to prove to himself that he was strong enough to regain his dignity.

The old man, who now was amassing the refuse scattered throughout the square, was right: soon the enemy would be back, to harvest fruits they had not sown. Elijah was laboring for the invaders—the assassins of the only woman he had ever loved in his life. The Assyrians were superstitious and would rebuild

Akbar in any case. According to ancient beliefs, the gods had spaced the cities in an organized manner, in harmony with the valleys, the animals, the rivers, the seas. In each of these they had set aside a sacred place to rest during their long voyages about the world. When a city was destroyed, there was always a great risk that the skies would tumble to the earth.

Legend said that the founder of Akbar had passed through there, hundreds of years before, journeying from the north. He decided to sleep at the spot and, to mark where he had left his things, planted a wooden staff upright in the ground. The next day, he was unable to withdraw it, and he quickly understood the will of the Universe; he marked with a stone the place where the miracle had occurred, and he discovered a spring nearby. Little by little, tribes began settling around the stone and the well; Akbar was born.

The governor had once explained to Elijah that, following Phoenician custom, every city was the *third point*, the element linking the will of heaven to the will of the earth. The Universe made the seed transform itself into a plant, the soil allowed it to grow, man harvested it and took it to the city, where the offerings to the gods were consecrated before they were left at the sacred mountains. Even though he had not traveled widely, Elijah was aware that a similar vision was shared by many nations of the world.

The Assyrians feared leaving the gods of the Fifth Mountain without food; they had no desire to disturb the equilibrium of the Universe.

"Why am I thinking such thoughts, if this is a struggle between my will and that of the Lord, who has left me alone in the midst of tribulations?"

The sensation he had felt the day before, when he challenged God, returned: he was forgetting something of importance, and however much he forced his memory, he could not recall it.

ANOTHER DAY WENT BY. MOST OF THE BODIES HAD
been collected when a second woman approached.

"I have nothing to eat," she said.

"Nor have we," answered Elijah. "Yesterday and today we
divided among three what had been intended for one. Discover
where you can obtain food, then inform me."

"Where can I learn that?"

"Ask the children. They know everything."

Ever since he had offered Elijah water, the boy had seemed
to recover some part of his taste for life. Elijah had told him to
help the old man gather up the trash and debris but had not succeeded in keeping him working for long; he was now playing
with the other boys in a corner of the square.

"It's better this way. He'll have his time to sweat when he's a man." But Elijah did not regret having made him spend an entire night hungry, under the pretext that he must work; if he had treated him as a poor orphan, the victim of the evil of murderous warriors, he would never have emerged from the depression into which he had been plunged when they entered the city. Now Elijah planned to leave him by himself for a few days to find his own answers to what had taken place.

"How can children know anything?" said the woman who had asked him for food.

"See for yourself."

The woman and the old man who were helping Elijah saw her talking to the young boys playing in the street. They said something, and she turned, smiled, and disappeared around one corner of the square.

"How did you find out that the children knew?" the old man asked.

"Because I was once a boy, and I know that children have no past," he said, remembering once again his conversation with the shepherd. "They were horrified the night of the invasion, but they're no longer concerned about it; the city has been transformed into an immense park where they can come and go without being bothered. Naturally they would come across the food that people had put aside to withstand the siege of Akbar.

"A child can always teach an adult three things: to be happy for no reason, to always be busy with something, and to know how to demand with all his might that which he desires. It was because of that boy that I returned to Akbar."

◆

THAT AFTERNOON, more old men and women added their numbers to the labor of collecting the dead. The children put to flight the scavenger birds and brought pieces of wood and cloth. When night fell, Elijah set fire to the immense pile of corpses. The survivors of Akbar contemplated silently the smoke rising to the heavens.

As soon as the task was completed, Elijah was felled by exhaustion. Before sleeping, however, the sensation he had felt that morning came again: something of importance was struggling desperately to enter his memory. It was nothing that he had learned during his time in Akbar but an ancient story, one that seemed to make sense of everything that was happening.

◆

THAT NIGHT, a man entered Jacob's tent and wrestled with him until the break of day. And when he saw that he prevailed not against him, he said, "Let me go."

Jacob answered, "I will not let thee go, except thou bless me."

Then the man said to him: "As a prince, hast thou power with God and with men, and hast prevailed. What is thy name?" And he said, Jacob.

And the man answered: "Thy name shall be called no more Jacob, but Israel."

ELIJAH AWOKE WITH A START AND LOOKED AT THE FIRMA-
ment. That was the story that was missing!

Long ago, the patriarch Jacob had encamped, and during the
night, someone had entered his tent and wrestled with him until
daybreak. Jacob accepted the combat, even knowing that his
adversary was the Lord. At morning, he had still not been
defeated; and the combat ceased only when God agreed to bless
him.

The story had been transmitted from generation to generation so that no one would ever forget: *sometimes it was necessary to
struggle with God.* Every human being at some time had tragedy
enter his life; it might be the destruction of a city, the death of a
son, an unproved accusation, a sickness that left one lame forever.
At that moment, God challenged one to confront Him and to

answer His question: "Why dost thou cling fast to an existence so short and so filled with suffering? What is the meaning of thy struggle?"

The man who did not know how to answer this question would resign himself, while another, one who sought a meaning to existence, feeling that God had been unjust, would challenge his own destiny. It was at this moment that fire of a different type descended from the heavens—not the fire that kills but the kind that tears down ancient walls and imparts to each human being his true possibilities. Cowards never allow their hearts to blaze with this fire; all they desire is for the changed situation to quickly return to what it was before, so they can go on living their lives and thinking in their customary way. The brave, however, set afire that which was old and, even at the cost of great internal suffering, abandon everything, including God, and continue onward.

"The brave are always stubborn."

From heaven, God smiles contentedly, for it was this that He desired, that each person take into his hands the responsibility for his own life. For, in the final analysis, He had given His children the greatest of all gifts: the capacity to choose and determine their acts.

Only those men and women with the sacred flame in their hearts had the courage to confront Him. And they alone knew the path back to His love, for they understood that tragedy was not punishment but challenge.

Elijah retraced in his mind each of his steps. Upon leaving the carpentry shop, he had accepted his mission without dispute. Even though it was real—and he felt it was—he had never had the opportunity to see what was happening in the paths that he had chosen not to follow because he feared losing his faith, his dedication, his will. He thought it very dangerous to experience the path of common folk—he might become accustomed to it and find pleasure in what he saw. He did not understand that he was a person like any other, even if he heard angels and now and again received orders from God; in his certainty that he knew what he wanted, he had acted in the selfsame way as those who at no time in their lives had ever made an important decision.

He had fled from doubt. From defeat. From moments of indecision. But the Lord was generous and had led him to the abyss of the unavoidable, to show him that man must *choose*—and not *accept*—his fate.

Many, many years before, on a night like this, Jacob had not allowed God to leave without blessing him. It was then that the Lord had asked: "*What is thy name?*"

The essential point was this: to have a name. When Jacob had answered, God had baptized him *Israel.* Each one has a name from birth but must learn to baptize his life with the word he has chosen to give meaning to that life.

"I am *Akbar,*" she had said.

The destruction of the city and the death of the woman he

loved had been necessary for Elijah to understand that he too must have a name. And at that moment he named his life *Liberation*.

◆

HE STOOD and looked at the square before him: smoke still rose from the ashes of those who had lost their lives. By setting fire to the bodies he had challenged an ancient custom of the country, which demanded that the dead be buried in accord with ritual. He had struggled with God and with custom by choosing incineration, but he felt no sense of sin when a new solution was needed to a new problem. God was infinite in His mercy, and implacable in His severity with those who lacked the courage to dare.

He looked around the square again: some of the survivors still had not slept and kept their gaze fixed on the flames, as if the fire were also consuming their memories, their pasts, Akbar's two hundred years of peace and torpor. The time for fear and hope had ended: now there remained only rebuilding or defeat.

Like Elijah, they too could choose a name for themselves. *Reconciliation, Wisdom, Lover, Pilgrim*—there were as many choices as stars in the sky, but each one had need to give a name to his life.

Elijah rose and prayed, "I fought Thee, Lord, and I am not ashamed. And because of it I discovered that I am on my path because such is my wish, not because it was imposed on me by my father and mother, by the customs of my country, or even by Thee.

"It is to Thee, O Lord, that I would return at this moment. I wish to praise Thee with the strength of my will and not with the cowardice of one who has not known how to choose another path. But for Thee to confide to me Thy important mission, I must continue this battle against Thee, until Thou bless me."

To rebuild Akbar. What Elijah thought was a challenge to God was, in truth, his reencounter with Him.

THE WOMAN WHO HAD ASKED ABOUT FOOD REAP-
peared the next morning. She was accompanied by several other
women.

"We found some deposits," she said. "Because so many died,
and so many fled with the governor, we have enough food for a
year."

"Seek older people to oversee the distribution of food,"
Elijah said. "They have experience at organization."

"The old ones have lost the will to live."

"Ask them to come anyway."

The woman was making ready to leave when Elijah stopped
her.

"Do you know how to write, using letters?"

"No."

"I have learned, and I can teach you. You'll need this skill to help me administer the city."

"But the Assyrians will return."

"When they arrive, they'll need our help to manage the affairs of the city."

"Why should we do this for the enemy?"

"So that each of us can give a name to his life. The enemy is only a pretext to test our strength."

◆

AS ELIJAH HAD FORESEEN, the old people came.

"Akbar needs your help," he told them. "Because of that, you don't have the luxury of being old; we need the youth that you once had and have lost."

"We do not know where to find it," one of them replied. "It vanished among the wrinkles and the disillusion."

"That's not true. You never had illusions, and it is that which caused your youth to hide itself away. Now is the moment to find it again, for we have a dream in common: to rebuild Akbar."

"How can we do the impossible?"

"With ardor."

Eyes veiled behind sorrow and discouragement made an effort to shine again. They were no longer the useless citizens who attended judgments searching for something to talk about later in the day; now they had an important mission before them. They were needed.

The stronger among them separated the usable materials from the damaged houses and utilized them to repair those that were still standing. The older ones helped spread in the fields the ashes of the incinerated bodies, so that the city's dead might be remembered at the next harvest; others took on the task of separating the grains stocked haphazardly throughout the city, making bread, and raising water from the well.

TWO NIGHTS LATER, ELIJAH GATHERED ALL THE INHAB-
itants in the square, now cleared of most of the debris. Torches
were lit, and he began to speak.

"We have no choice," he said. "We can leave this work for
the foreigner to do; but that means giving away the only chance
that a tragedy offers us: that of rebuilding our lives.

"The ashes of the dead that we burned some days ago will
become the plants that are reborn in the spring. The son who was
lost the night of the invasion will become the many children running freely through the ruined streets and amusing themselves by
invading forbidden places and houses they had never known.
Until now only the children have been able to overcome what took
place, because they have no past—for them, everything that matters is the present moment. So we shall try to act as they do."

"Can a man cast from his heart the pain of a loss?" asked a woman.

"No. But he can find joy in something won."

Elijah turned, pointed to the top of the Fifth Mountain, forever covered in clouds. The destruction of the walls had made it visible from the middle of the square.

"I believe in One God, though you think that the gods dwell in those clouds on the Fifth Mountain. I don't want to argue whether my God is stronger or more powerful; I would speak not of our differences but of our similarities. Tragedy has united us in a single sentiment: despair. Why has that come to pass? Because we thought that everything was answered and decided in our souls, and we could accept no changes.

"Both you and I belong to trading nations, but we also know how to act as warriors," he continued. "And a warrior is always aware of what is worth fighting for. He does not go into combat over things that do not concern him, and he never wastes his time over provocations.

"A warrior accepts defeat. He does not treat it as a matter of indifference, nor does he attempt to transform it into a victory. The pain of defeat is bitter to him; he suffers at indifference and becomes desperate with loneliness. After all this has passed, he licks his wounds and begins everything anew. A warrior knows that war is made of many battles; he goes on.

"Tragedies do happen. We can discover the reason, blame others, imagine how different our lives would be had they not occurred. But none of that is important: they did occur, and so be it. From there onward we must put aside the fear that they awoke in us and begin to rebuild.

"Each of you will give yourselves a new name, beginning at this very moment. This will be the sacred name that brings together in a single word all that you have dreamed of fighting for. For my name, I have chosen *Liberation*."

The square was silent for some time. Then the woman who had been the first to help Elijah rose to her feet.

"My name is *Reencounter*," she said.

"My name is *Wisdom*," said an old man.

The son of the widow whom Elijah had loved shouted, "My name is *Alphabet*."

The people in the square burst into laughter. The boy, embarrassed, sat down again.

"How can anybody call himself *Alphabet*?" shouted another boy.

Elijah could have interfered, but it was good for the boy to learn to defend himself.

"Because that was what my mother did," the boy said. "Whenever I look at drawn letters, I'll remember her."

This time no one laughed. One by one, the orphans, widows, and old people of Akbar spoke their names, and their new identities. When the ceremony was over, Elijah asked everyone to go to sleep early: they had to resume their labors the next morning.

He took the boy by the hand, and the two went to the place in the square where a few pieces of cloth had been extended to form a tent.

Starting that night, he began teaching him the writing of Byblos.

THE DAYS BECAME WEEKS, AND THE FACE OF AKBAR was changing. The boy quickly learned to draw the letters and had already begun creating words that made sense; Elijah charged him with writing on clay tablets the history of the rebuilding of the city.

The clay tablets were baked in an improvised oven, transformed into ceramics, and carefully stored away by an aged couple. At the meetings at the end of each afternoon, Elijah asked the old folk to tell of what they had seen in their childhood, and he wrote down the greatest possible number of stories.

"We shall keep Akbar's memory on a material that fire cannot destroy," he explained. "One day our children and the children of their children will know that defeat was not accepted, and that the unavoidable was overcome. This can serve as an example for them."

Each night, after his lessons with the boy, Elijah would walk through the deserted city until he came to the beginning of the road leading to Jerusalem; he would think about departing, then turn around.

The heavy work demanded that he concentrate on the present moment. He knew that the inhabitants of Akbar were relying on him for the rebuilding; he had already disappointed them once, when he had been unable to prevent the death of the enemy general—and thus avoid war. But God always gives His children a second chance, and he must take advantage of this new opportunity. In addition, he was becoming ever fonder of the boy and desired to teach him not only the characters of Byblos but also faith in the Lord and the wisdom of his ancestors.

Even so, he did not forget that in his own land reigned a foreign princess and a foreign god. There were no more angels bearing flaming swords; he was free to leave whenever he desired, and to do whatever he wished.

Each night, he thought of departing. And each night he would lift his hands to the heavens and pray.

"Jacob fought the whole night through and was blessed at daybreak. I have fought Thee for days, for months, and Thou refusest me Thy ear. But if Thou lookest about Thee, Thou wilt know that I am winning: Akbar is rising from its ruins, and I am rebuilding what Thou, using the Assyrian sword, made ashes and dust.

"I shall struggle with Thee until Thou bless me, and bless the fruits of my labor. One day Thou shalt have to answer me."

◆

WOMEN AND CHILDREN carried water to the fields, struggling against the drought that seemed to have no end. One day, when the inclement sun shone down in all its force, Elijah heard someone say, "We work without ceasing, we no longer recall the pains of that night, and we even forget that the Assyrians will return as soon as they have sacked Tyre, Sidon, Byblos, and all of Phoenicia. This is a good thing for us.

"But because we concentrate so much on rebuilding the city, it seems that everything remains the same; we do not see the result of our effort."

Elijah reflected for some time on what he had heard. And he ordered that, at the end of each day of work, the people gather at the foot of the Fifth Mountain to contemplate together the sunset.

Most were so weary that they exchanged not a word, but they discovered that it is important to allow thought to wander as aimlessly as the clouds in the sky. In this way, anxiety fled from each person's heart and they found inspiration and strength for the day to come.

ELIJAH AWOKE SAYING THAT TODAY HE WOULD NOT LABOR.

"In my land, this is the Day of Atonement."

"There is no sin in your soul," a woman told him. "You have done the best that you can."

"But custom must be maintained. And I shall keep it."

The women left, bearing water for the fields, the old men went back to their task of erecting walls and shaping the wood for doors and windows. The children helped to mold the small clay bricks that would later be baked in fire. Elijah watched them with immense joy in his heart. Then he went out from Akbar and walked toward the valley.

He wandered about aimlessly, praying the prayers that he had learned in childhood. The sun was not yet completely risen, and from the place where he stood he could see the enormous shadow of the Fifth Mountain covering part of the valley. He felt a horrible premonition: the struggle between the God of Israel and the gods of the Phoenicians would go on for many generations, and for many thousands of years.

◆

HE RECALLED that one night he had climbed to the top of the mountain and spoken with an angel. But since Akbar's destruction he had never again heard the voices from heaven.

"O Lord, today is the Day of Atonement, and my list of sins against Thee is long," he said, turning toward Jerusalem. "I have been weak, for I have forgotten my strength. I have been compassionate when I should have been firm. I have failed to choose, for fear of making the wrong decision. I have yielded before the time to do so, and I have blasphemed when I should have given thanks.

"Still, Lord, I have also a long list of Thy sins against me. Thou hast made me suffer more than was just, by taking from this world one that I loved. Thou hast destroyed the city that received me, Thou hast confounded my search, Thy harshness almost made me forget the love I have for Thee. For all that time I have struggled with Thee, yet Thou dost not accept the worthiness of my combat.

"If we compare the list of my sins with the list of Thy sins, Thou shalt see that Thou art in my debt. But, as today is the Day of Atonement, give me Thy forgiveness and I shall forgive Thee, so that we may go on walking at each other's side."

At that moment, a wind blew, and he heard his angel say to

him, "Thou hast done well, Elijah. God hath accepted thy combat."

Tears streamed from his eyes. He knelt and kissed the valley's arid soil.

"Thanks unto you for having come, for I still have one doubt: is it not a sin to do this?"

The angel said, "If a warrior fight with his instructor, doth he offend him?"

"No. It is the only way to teach the technique that he must learn."

"Then continue, until the Lord call thee back to Israel," said the angel. "Rise and go on proving that thy struggle hath meaning, because thou hast known how to cross the current of the unavoidable. Many navigate it and founder; others are swept to places for which they were not fated. But thou confrontest the crossing with dignity; thou hast guided the path of thy vessel well and transformed pain into action."

"How sad that you are blind," said Elijah. "Otherwise you would see how orphans, widows, old people have been able to rebuild a city. Soon, all will be as it was."

"Would that it not be so," said the angel. "Remember that they have paid a high price so that their lives could be changed."

Elijah smiled. The angel was right.

"Would that thou mightest act as do men who are given a second chance: do not twice commit the same error. Never forget the reason for thy life."

"I shall not forget," he replied, happy that the angel had returned.

CARAVANS NO LONGER CAME THROUGH THE VALLEY; the Assyrians must have destroyed the roads and changed the trade routes. Day after day, children scaled the only turret in the wall that had escaped destruction; they were charged with watching the horizon and alerting the city to the return of enemy warriors. Elijah planned to receive them with dignity and hand over command.

Then he could depart.

But with each passing day the feeling grew that Akbar had become part of his life. Perhaps his mission was not to remove Jezebel from the throne but to be there with these people for the rest of his life, carrying out the humble role of servant for the Assyrian conqueror. He would help to reestablish trade routes, learn the language of the enemy, and during his moments of repose, oversee the library, which was daily more complete.

Whereas on a night already lost in time the city had appeared to be at its end, it now seemed possible to make it even more beautiful than it had been. The work of rebuilding encompassed widening streets, erecting sturdier roofs, and creating an ingenious system for bringing water from the well to the most distant places. And his soul too was being restored; each day he learned something new from the old people, from the children, from the women. That group, which had not abandoned Akbar only because of the absolute impossibility of doing so, was now a competent, disciplined company.

"If the governor had known that they were of such help, he would have created another type of defense, and Akbar would not have been destroyed."

Elijah thought a moment, then saw that he was mistaken. Akbar needed to be destroyed so that all could awaken the forces that lay dormant inside their own being.

Months went by without the Assyrians showing any sign of life. By now Akbar was almost complete, and Elijah could think of the future. The women had repaired pieces of cloth and made new garments from them. The old folk were reorganizing the dwellings and attending to the city's sanitation. The children were helping when asked, but they usually spent the day at play: that is a child's foremost obligation.

Elijah lived with the boy in a small stone house rebuilt on

the site that had once been a storage place for merchandise. Each night the inhabitants of Akbar would sit around a fire in the main square, telling stories that they had heard earlier in their lives, alongside the boy, who noted everything on clay tablets that were baked the next day. The library was growing before their very eyes.

The woman who had lost her son was also learning the characters of Byblos. When Elijah saw that she could create words and phrases, he charged her with teaching the alphabet to the rest of the population; in this way, when the Assyrians returned, they could be used as interpreters or teachers.

"This was just what the high priest wanted to prevent," an old man, who had taken the name *Ocean* because he desired to have a soul as great as the sea, said one afternoon. "That the writing of Byblos survive to threaten the gods of the Fifth Mountain."

"Who can prevent the unavoidable?" Elijah replied.

The people of Akbar would toil by day, watch the sunset together, and recount stories during the night.

Elijah was proud of his work. And with each day that passed he grew more impassioned with it.

One of the children charged with keeping the vigil descended in a run.

"I saw dust on the horizon!" he said excitedly. "The enemy is returning!"

Elijah climbed to the turret and saw that the news was correct.

He reckoned that they would be at the gates of Akbar the next day.

That afternoon he told the inhabitants that they should not attend the sunset but gather in the square. When the day's work was over, he stood before the assembled group and saw that they were afraid.

"Today we shall tell no stories of the past, nor speak of Akbar's future," he said. "We shall talk about ourselves."

No one said a word.

"Some time ago, a full moon shone in the sky. That night, what all of us had foreseen, but did not want to accept, came to pass: Akbar was destroyed. When the Assyrian army departed, the best among our men were dead. Those who had escaped saw that it was futile to remain here, and they determined to go. Only the old, the widows, and the orphans were left—that is, the useless.

"Look about you; the square is more beautiful than ever, the buildings are more solid, the food is divided among us, and everyone is learning the writing invented in Byblos. Somewhere in this city is a collection of tablets on which we have written our stories, and generations yet to be born will remember what we did.

"Today we know that the old, the widows, the orphans, also departed. They left in their place a band of youths of every age, filled with enthusiasm, who have given name and meaning to their lives.

"At each moment of rebuilding, we knew that the Assyrians

would return. We knew that one day we would be obliged to hand our city over to them and, together with the city, our efforts, our sweat, our joy at seeing it more beautiful than before."

The light from the fire illuminated tears coursing down the faces of some of the people. Even the children, who customarily played during the evening meetings, were listening attentively to his words. Elijah continued.

"This does not matter. We have carried out our duty to the Lord because we accepted His challenge and the honor of His struggle. Before that night, He had urged us, saying, *Walk!* But we heeded Him not. Why?

"Because each of us had already decided his own future: I thought only of removing Jezebel from the throne, the woman who is now called *Reencounter* wanted her son to become a navigator, the man who today bears the name *Wisdom* wished merely to spend the rest of his days drinking wine in the square. We were accustomed to the sacred mystery of life and gave little importance to it.

"Then the Lord thought to Himself: *They would not walk? Then let them be idle for a long time!*

"And only then did we understand His message. The steel of Assyrian blades swept away our youth, and cowardice swept away our adults. Wherever they are at this moment, they are still idle; they have accepted God's curse.

"We, however, struggle with the Lord, just as we struggle

with the men and women we love in our lifetimes. For it is that struggle with the divine that blesses us and makes us grow. We grasp the opportunity in the tragedy and do our duty by Him, by proving we were able to obey the order to *walk*. Even in the worst of circumstances, we have forged ahead.

"There are moments when God demands obedience. But there are moments in which He wishes to test our will and challenges us to understand His love. We understood that will when Akbar's walls tumbled to the ground: they opened our horizon and allowed each of us to see his capabilities. We stopped thinking about life and chose to live it.

"The result is good."

Elijah saw that the people's eyes were shining again. They had understood.

"Tomorrow I shall deliver Akbar without a struggle; I am free to leave whenever I choose, for I have done what the Lord expected of me. But my blood, my sweat, and the only love I have known are in the soil of this city, and I have decided to remain here the rest of my days, to prevent its being destroyed again. Make whatever decision you wish but never forget one thing: all of you are much better than you believed.

"Take advantage of the chance that tragedy has given you; not everyone is capable of doing so."

Elijah rose, ending the meeting. He told the boy that he would return late and said he should go to bed without waiting for his arrival.

◆

HE WENT TO THE TEMPLE, the only place that had escaped the destruction and had not needed rebuilding, though the statues of the gods had been taken away by the Assyrians. With all respect, he touched the stone that, according to tradition, marked the spot where an ancestor had embedded a staff in the ground and been unable to wrest it free.

He thought how, in his country, places such as this were being erected by Jezebel, and a part of his people bowed down before Baal and his deities. Once again the premonition ran through his soul that the war between the Lord of Israel and the gods of Phoenicia would go on for a long time, beyond anything his imagination could encompass. As in a vision, he saw stars crossing the sun and raining death and destruction on both countries. Men who spoke strange languages rode animals of steel and dueled in the middle of the clouds.

"It is not this that thou shouldst now see, for the time hath not yet come," he heard his angel say. "Look out the window."

Elijah did as he was ordered. Outside, the full moon illuminated the streets and houses of Akbar, and despite the late hour he could hear conversations and laughter from the city's inhabitants. Even facing the Assyrians' return, the people kept the will to live, ready to confront a new stage in their lives.

He saw a form and knew that it was the woman he had

loved, who now returned to walk with pride through her city. He smiled, feeling her touch his face.

"I am proud," she seemed to be saying. "Akbar truly is still beautiful."

He felt the urge to weep, then remembered the boy, who had never shed a tear for his mother. He checked his sobs and thought anew of the most beautiful parts of the story that together they had lived, from the meeting at the city gates, till the moment she had written the word *love* on a clay tablet. Once again he could see her garment, her chair, the fine sculpting of her nose.

"You told me you were Akbar. Well, I have taken care of you, healed your wounds, and now I return you to life. May you be happy among your new companions.

"And I want to tell you something: I too was Akbar and did not know."

He knew that she was smiling.

"Long since, the desert wind wiped away our footprints in the sand. But at every second of my existence, I remember what happened, and you still walk in my dreams and in my reality. Thank you for having crossed my path."

He slept there, in the temple, feeling the woman caressing his hair.

THE CHIEF TRADER SAW A RAGGED GROUP OF PEOPLE IN
the middle of the road. Thinking they were robbers, he ordered
the caravan to take up arms.

"Who are you?" he asked.

"We are the people of Akbar," replied a bearded man with
shining eyes. The leader of the caravan noticed that he spoke
with a foreign accent.

"Akbar was destroyed. We have been charged by the governments of Sidon and Tyre to find a well so caravans can cross the
valley again. Communication with the rest of the land cannot be
interrupted forever."

"Akbar still exists," the man said. "Where are the Assyrians?"

"The entire world knows where they are," laughed the caravan leader. "Making the soil more fertile. And feeding the birds and wild animals for a long time now."

"But they were a powerful army."

"There's no such thing as power or an army, if we find out where they're going to attack. Akbar sent word that they were approaching, and Sidon and Tyre set an ambuscade for them at the end of the valley. Whoever didn't die in battle was sold as slaves by our navigators."

The ragged people cheered and embraced one another, crying and laughing at the same time.

"Who are you people?" insisted the trader. "And who are you?" he asked, pointing to their leader.

"We are the young warriors of Akbar" was the reply.

◆

THE THIRD HARVEST had begun, and Elijah was the governor of Akbar. There had been great resistance at first; the old governor had attempted to return and reoccupy his position, for such did custom dictate. The inhabitants of the city, however, refused to admit him and for days threatened to poison the water in the well. The Phoenician authorities finally yielded to their demands; after all, Akbar's only importance was the water it supplied to travelers, and the government of Israel was in the hands of a princess of Tyre. By conceding the position of governor to an Israelite, the Phoenician rulers could begin to consolidate a stronger commercial alliance.

The news spread throughout the region, carried by the merchant caravans that had begun circulating again. A minority in Israel considered Elijah the worst of traitors, but at the proper moment Jezebel would take on the task of eliminating this resistance, and peace would return to the region. The princess was content, for one of her worst foes had in the end become her greatest ally.

◆

RUMORS OF A NEW Assyrian invasion began to arise, and the walls of Akbar were rebuilt. A new system of defense was developed, with sentinels and outposts spread between Tyre and Akbar; in this way, if one of the cities was besieged, the other could send troops overland while assuring the delivery of food by sea.

The city prospered before one's very eyes: the new Israelite governor had created a rigorous system, based on writing, to control taxes and merchandise. The old folk of Akbar attended to it all, using new techniques for supervision, and patiently resolved the problems that arose.

The women divided their time between tending to the crops and weaving. During the period of isolation, to recover the small amount of cloth that had remained, they had been obliged to create new patterns of embroidery; when the first merchants arrived in the city, they were enchanted by the designs and placed several orders.

The children too had learned the writing of Byblos; Elijah was certain that one day this would be of help to them.

As was always his wont before the harvest, he strolled through the fields that afternoon, giving thanks to the Lord for the countless blessings bestowed upon him for all these years. He saw people with their baskets filled with grain, and around them children at play. He waved to them, and they returned his greeting.

Smiling, he walked toward the stone where, long ago, he had been given a clay tablet with the word *love*. It was his custom to visit that spot every day to watch the sunset and recall each instant that they had spent together.

"*AND IT CAME TO PASS AFTER MANY DAYS, THAT THE WORD OF
the Lord came to Elijah in the third year, saying, Go, shew thyself unto Ahab;
and I will send rain upon the earth.*"

FROM THE STONE WHERE HE SAT, ELIJAH SAW THE world shudder about him. The sky turned black for an instant, but the sun quickly shone again.

He saw the light. An angel of the Lord was before him.

"What has happened?" asked Elijah, startled. "Has the Lord pardoned Israel?"

"No," answered the angel. "He desireth that thou return to liberate thy people. Thy struggle with Him is ended, and—at this moment—he hath blessed thee. He hath given thee leave to continue His work in that land."

Elijah was astonished.

"But, now, just when my heart has again found peace?"

"Recall the lesson once taught thee," said the angel. "And recall the words the Lord spake unto Moses:

233

"*And thou shalt remember all the way which the Lord thy God led thee to humble thee, and to prove thee. To know what was in thine heart.*

"*Lest when thou hast eaten and art full, and hast built goodly houses, and dwelt therein, and when thy herds and thy flocks multiply, then thine heart be lifted up, and thou forget the Lord thy God.*"

Elijah turned to the angel. "What about Akbar?" he asked.

"It can live without thee, for thou hast left an heir. It will survive for many years."

The angel of the Lord disappeared.

ELIJAH AND THE BOY ARRIVED AT THE FOOT OF THE
Fifth Mountain. Weeds had grown between the stones of the
altars; since the high priest's death no one had gone there.

"Let's climb it," he said.

"It's forbidden."

"Yes, it's forbidden. But that doesn't mean it's dangerous."

He took him by both hands, and they began climbing
toward the top. They stopped from time to time to gaze at the
valley below; the absence of rain had left its mark throughout the
countryside, and with the exception of the cultivated fields
around Akbar, everything seemed a desert as harsh as those of
Egypt.

"I've heard my friends say the Assyrians are coming back,"
the boy said.

"That could be, but what we have done was worthwhile; it was the way that God chose to teach us."

"I don't know if He bothers much with us," the boy said. "He didn't have to be so severe."

"He must have tried other means before discovering that we were not listening to Him. We were too accustomed to our lives and no longer read His words."

"Where are they written?"

"In the world around us. Merely be attentive to what happens in your life, and you will discover where, every moment of the day, He hides His words and His will. Seek to do as He asks: this alone is the reason you are in the world."

"If I discover it, I'll write it on clay tablets."

"Do so. But write them, above all, in your heart; there they can be neither burned nor destroyed, and you will take them wherever you go."

They walked for some time more. The clouds were now very close.

"I don't want to go there," the boy said, pointing to them.

"They will do you no harm: they're just clouds. Come with me."

He took him by the hands, and they climbed. Little by little, they found themselves entering the fog. The boy clung to him, and although Elijah tried to talk to him now and again, he said not a word. They walked among the naked rocks of the summit.

"Let's go back," asked the boy.

Elijah decided not to insist; the boy had already experienced great difficulties and much fear in his short life. He did as he was asked; they came out from the fog and could once again discern the valley below.

"Someday, look in Akbar's library for what I wrote for you. It's called *The Manual of the Warrior of Light.*"

"Am I a warrior of light?" replied the boy.

"Do you know what my name is?" asked Elijah.

"*Liberation.*"

"Sit here beside me," said Elijah, pointing to a rock. "I cannot forget my name. I must continue with my task, even if at this moment all I desire is to be at your side. That was why Akbar was rebuilt, to teach us that it is necessary to go onward, however difficult it may appear."

"You're going away."

"How do you know?" he asked, surprised.

"I wrote it on a tablet, last night. Something told me; it may have been my mother, or an angel. But I already felt it in my heart."

Elijah caressed the boy's head.

"You have learned to read God's will," he said contentedly. "So there's nothing that I need to explain to you."

"What I read was the sadness in your eyes. It wasn't difficult. Other friends of mine noticed it too."

"This sadness you read in my eyes is part of my story. Only a small part that will last but a few days. Tomorrow, when I depart for Jerusalem, it will not have the strength it had before, and little by little it will disappear. Sadness does not last forever when we walk in the direction of that which we always desired."

"Is it always necessary to leave?"

"It's always necessary to know when a stage of one's life has ended. If you stubbornly cling to it after the need has passed, you lose the joy and meaning of the rest. And you risk being shaken to your senses by God."

"The Lord is stern."

"Only with those He has chosen."

◆

ELIJAH LOOKED AT AKBAR below. Yes, God sometimes could be very stern, but never beyond a person's capacity: the boy was unaware that they were sitting where Elijah had received an angel of the Lord and learned how to bring him back from the dead.

"Are you going to miss me?" Elijah asked.

"You told me that sadness disappears if we press ahead. There's still much to do to leave Akbar as beautiful as my mother deserves. She walks in its streets."

"Come back to this place when you have need of me. And look toward Jerusalem: I shall be there, seeking to give meaning to my name, *Liberation*. Our hearts are linked forever."

"Was that why you brought me to the top of the Fifth Mountain? So I could see Israel?"

"So you could see the valley, the city, the other mountains, the rocks and clouds. The Lord often has his prophets climb mountains to converse with Him. I always wondered why He did that, and now I know the answer: when we are on high, we can see everything else as small.

"Our glory and our sadness lose their importance. Whatever we conquered or lost remains there below. From the heights of the mountain, you see how large the world is, and how wide its horizons."

The boy looked about him. From the top of the Fifth Mountain, he could smell the sea that bathed the beaches of Tyre. And he could hear the desert wind that blew from Egypt.

"Someday I'll govern Akbar," he told Elijah. "I know what's big. But I also know every corner of the city. I know what needs to be changed."

"Then change it. Don't let things remain idle."

"Couldn't God have chosen a better way of showing us all this? There was a time when I thought He was evil."

Elijah said nothing. He recalled a conversation, many years before, with a Levite prophet while the two awaited death at the hands of Jezebel's soldiers.

"Can God be evil?" the boy insisted.

"God is all-powerful," answered Elijah. "He can do anything, and nothing is forbidden to Him, for if it were, there would exist someone more powerful than He, to prevent His doing certain things. In that case, I should prefer to worship and revere that more powerful someone."

He paused for several instants to allow the boy to fathom the meaning of his words. Then he continued.

"Still, because of His infinite power, He chose to do only Good. If we reach the end of our story, we shall see that often Good is disguised as Evil, but it goes on being the Good, and is part of the plan that He created for humanity."

He took the boy by the hand, and together they descended the mountain in silence.

◆

THAT NIGHT, the boy went to sleep in his arms. As soon as day began to break, Elijah carefully removed him from his bosom so he would not awaken him.

He quickly donned the only garment he possessed and departed. On the road, he picked up a piece of wood from the ground and used it as a staff. He planned never to be without it: it was the remembrance of his struggle with God, of the destruction and rebuilding of Akbar.

Without looking back, he continued toward Israel.

FIVE YEARS LATER, ASSYRIA AGAIN INVADED THE COUNTRY,
this time with a more professional army and more competent generals. All
Phoenicia fell under the domination of the foreign conqueror except Tyre and
Zarephath, which its inhabitants called Akbar.

The boy became a man, governed the city, and was judged a sage by his
contemporaries. He died in the fullness of his years, surrounded by loved
ones and saying always that "it was necessary to keep the city beautiful and
strong, for his mother still strolled its streets." Because of their joint system
of defense, Tyre and Zarephath were not occupied by the Assyrian king
Sennacherib until 701 B.C., almost 160 years after the events related in this
book.

From that time on, Phoenician cities never recovered their importance
and began to suffer a series of invasion——by the Neo-Babylonians, the

Persians, the Macedonians, the Seleucids, and, finally, by Rome. Even so, they continue to exist in our own time because, according to ancient tradition, the Lord never selected at random the places He wished to see inhabited. Tyre, Sidon, and Byblos are still part of Lebanon, which even today remains a battlefield.

ELIJAH RETURNED TO ISRAEL AND CALLED THE PROPHETS together at Mount Carmel. There he asked them to divide into two groups: those who worshiped Baal, and those who believed in the Lord. Following the angel's instructions, he offered a bullock to the first group and asked them to call out to the heavens for their gods to receive it. The Bible says:

"And it came to pass at noon, that Elijah mocked them, and said, Cry aloud: for he is a god; either he is talking, or he is pursuing, or he is in a journey, or peradventure he sleepeth, and must be awaked.

"And they cried aloud, and cut themselves after their manner with knives and lancets, till the blood gushed out upon them.

"And there was neither voice, nor any to answer, nor any that regarded."

Then Elijah took his animal and offered it, following the angel's instructions. At that moment the fire of heaven descended and "consumed the burnt sacrifice, and the wood, and the stones." Minutes later, a heavy rain fell, ending four years of drought.

From that moment, civil war broke out. Elijah ordered the execution of the prophets who had betrayed the Lord, and Jezebel sought him everywhere, to kill him. He fled, however, to the eastern part of the Fifth Mountain, which faced Israel.

The Syrians invaded the country and killed King Ahab, husband of the princess of Tyre, with an accidentally shot arrow that entered an opening in his armor. Jezebel took refuge in her palace and, following several popular revolts and the rise and fall of various governments, was captured. She preferred leaping from a window to giving herself up to the men sent to arrest her.

Elijah remained on the mountain until the end of his days. The Bible says that one afternoon, when he was conversing with Elisha, the prophet he had named as his successor, "there appeared a chariot of fire, and horses of fire, and parted them both asunder; and Elijah went up by a whirlwind into heaven."

Almost eight hundred years later, Jesus bade Peter, James, and John to climb a mountain. The Gospel according to Matthew relates that Jesus "was transfigured before them; and his face did shine as the sun, and his raiment was white as the light. And, behold, there appeared unto them Moses and Elias talking with him."

Jesus asks the apostles not to speak of this vision until the Son of Man be risen from the dead, but they reply that this will happen only when Elijah returns.

Matthew 17:10–13 tells the rest of the story:

Zd his disciples asked him, saying, Why then say the scribes that Elias must first come?

"And Jesus answered and said unto them, Elias truly shall first come, and restore all things. But I say unto you, That Elias is come already, and they knew him not, but have done unto him whatsoever they listed.

"Then the disciples understood that he spake unto them of John the Baptist."

MARIA CONCEIVED WITHOUT SIN, PRAY FOR US WHO
call on Thee. Amen.

About the Translator

CLIFFORD E. LANDERS is professor of political science at Jersey City State College and a premier translator of Latin American fiction. He has translated into English many of Brazil's top writers, including Jorge Amado, Rubem Fonseca, and Chico Buarque. He lives in Montclair, New Jersey.

Veronika Decides to Die

Translated from the Portuguese
by Margaret Jull Costa

For S. T. de L., who began to help me without my realizing it

Behold I give unto you power to tread
on serpents . . . and nothing shall
by any means hurt you.

Luke 10:19

On November 11, 1997, Veronika decided that the moment to kill herself had—at last!—arrived. She carefully cleaned the room that she rented in a convent, turned off the heat, brushed her teeth, and lay down.

S HE PICKED up the four packs of sleeping pills from her bedside table. Instead of crushing them and mixing them with water, she decided to take them one by one, because there is always a gap between intention and action, and she wanted to feel free to turn back halfway. With each pill she swallowed, however, she felt more convinced: After five minutes the packs were empty.

Since she didn't know exactly how long it would take her to lose consciousness, she had placed on the bed that month's issue of a French magazine, *Homme*, which had just arrived in the library where she worked. She had no particular interest in computer science, but, as she leafed through the magazine, she came across an article about a computer game (one of those CD-ROMS) created by Paulo Coelho, a Brazilian writer she had happened to meet at a lecture in the café at the Grand Union Hotel. They had exchanged a few words, and she had ended up being invited by his publisher to join them for supper. There were a lot of people there, though, and they hadn't had a chance to talk in depth about anything.

The fact that she had met the author led her to think that he was part of her world, and that reading an article about his work could help pass the time. While she was waiting for death, Veronika started reading about computer science, a subject in which she was not the least bit interested, but then that was in keeping with what she had done all her life, always looking for the easy option, for whatever was nearest at hand. Like that magazine, for example.

To her surprise, though, the first line of text shook her out of her natural passivity (the tranquilizers had not yet dissolved in her stomach, but Veronika was by nature passive), and, for the first time in her life, it made her ponder the truth of a saying that was very fashionable among her friends: "Nothing in this world happens by chance."

Why that first line, at precisely the moment when she had begun to die? What was the hidden message she saw before her, assuming there are such things as hidden messages rather than mere coincidences?

Underneath an illustration of the computer game, the journalist began his article by asking: "Where is Slovenia?"

Honestly, she thought, *no one ever knows where Slovenia is.*

But Slovenia existed nonetheless, and it was outside, inside, in the mountains around her and in the square she was looking out at: Slovenia was her country.

She put the magazine to one side; there was no point now in getting indignant with a world that knew absolutely nothing about the

Slovenes; her nation's honor no longer concerned her. It was time to feel proud of herself, to recognize that she had been able to do this, that she had finally had the courage and was leaving this life: What joy! Also she was doing it as she had always dreamed she would—by taking sleeping pills, which leave no mark.

Veronika had been trying to get hold of the pills for nearly six months. Thinking that she would never manage it, she had even considered slashing her wrists. It didn't matter that the room would end up awash in blood, and the nuns would be left feeling confused and troubled, for suicide demands that people think of themselves first and of others later. She was prepared to do all she could so that her death would cause as little upset as possible, but if slashing her wrists was the only way, then she had no option—and the nuns could clean up the room and quickly forget the whole story, otherwise they would find it hard to rent out the room again. We may live at the end of the twentieth century, but people still believe in ghosts.

Obviously she could have thrown herself off one of the few tall buildings in Ljubljana, but what about the further suffering a fall from such a height would cause her parents? Apart from the shock of learning that their daughter had died, they would also have to identify a disfigured corpse; no, that was a worse solution than bleeding to death, because it would leave indelible marks on two people who only wanted the best for her.

They would get used to their daughter's death eventually. But it must be impossible to forget a shattered skull.

Shooting, jumping off a high building, hanging, none of these options suited her feminine nature. Women, when they kill themselves, choose far more romantic methods—like slashing their wrists or taking an overdose of sleeping pills. Abandoned princesses and Hollywood actresses have provided numerous examples of this.

Veronika knew that life was always a matter of waiting for the right moment to act. And so it proved to be the case. In response to her complaints that she could no longer sleep at night, two friends of hers managed to get hold of two packs each of a powerful drug, used by musicians at a local nightclub. Veronika left the four packs on her bedside table for a week, courting approaching death and saying good-bye—entirely unsentimentally—to what people called life.

Now she was there, glad she had gone all the way, and bored because she didn't know what to do with the little time that was left to her.

She thought again about the absurd question she had just read. How could an article about computers begin with such an idiotic opening line: "Where is Slovenia?"

Having nothing more interesting to do, she decided to read the whole article, and she learned that the said computer game had been made in Slovenia—that strange country that no one seemed quite able to place, except the people who lived there—because it was a cheap source of labor. A few months before, when the product was launched, the French manufacturer had given a party for journalists from all over the world in a castle in Vled.

Veronika remembered reading something about the party, which had been quite an event in the city, not just because the castle had been redecorated in order to match as closely as possible the medieval atmosphere of the CD-ROM, but because of the controversy in the local press: Jour-

4

nalists from Germany, France, Britain, Italy and Spain had been invited, but not a single Slovene.

Homme's correspondent—who was visiting Slovenia for the first time, doubtless with all expenses paid, and determined to spend his visit talking to other journalists, making supposedly interesting comments and enjoying the free food and drink at the castle—had decided to begin his article with a joke that must have appealed to the sophisticated intellectuals of his country. He had probably told his fellow journalists on the magazine various untrue stories about local customs, too, and said how badly Slovene women dress.

That was *his* problem. Veronika was dying, and she had other concerns, such as wondering if there was life after death, or when her body would be found. Nevertheless—or perhaps precisely because of the important decision she had taken—the article bothered her.

She looked out of the convent window that gave on to the small square in Ljubljana. *If they don't know where Slovenia is, then Ljubljana must be a myth*, she thought. Like Atlantis or Lemuria, or the other lost continents that fill men's imaginations. No one, anywhere in the world, would begin an article asking where Mount Everest was, even if they had never been there. Yet, in the middle of Europe, a journalist on an important magazine felt no shame at asking such a question, because he knew that most of his readers would not know where Slovenia was, still less its capital, Ljubljana.

It was then that Veronika found a way of passing the time, now that ten minutes had gone by and she had still not noticed any physical changes. The final act of her life would be to write a letter to the magazine, explaining that Slovenia was one of the five republics into which the former Yugoslavia had been divided.

The letter would be her suicide note. She would give no explanation of the real reasons for her death.

When they find her body, they will conclude that she had killed herself because a magazine did not know where her country was. She laughed to think of the controversy in the newspapers, with some for and some against her suicide, committed in honor of her country's cause. And she was shocked by how quickly she could change her mind, since only moments before she had thought exactly the opposite—that the world and other geographical problems were no longer her concern.

She wrote the letter. That moment of good humor almost made her have second thoughts about the need to die, but she had already taken the pills; it was too late to turn back.

Anyway, she had had such moments before, and besides, she was not killing herself because she was a sad, embittered woman, constantly depressed. She had spent many afternoons walking joyfully along the streets of Ljubljana or gazing—from the window in her convent room—at the snow falling on the small square with its statue of the poet. Once, for almost a month, she had felt as if she were walking on air, all because a complete stranger, in the middle of that very square, had given her a flower.

She believed herself to be completely normal. Two very simple reasons lay behind her decision to die, and she was sure that, were she to leave a note explaining, many people would agree with her.

The first reason: Everything in her life was the same and, once her youth was gone, it would be downhill all the way, with old age beginning to leave irreversible marks, the onset of illness, the departure of friends. She would gain nothing by continuing to live; indeed, the likelihood of suffering would only increase.

The second reason was more philosophical: Veronika read the newspapers, watched TV, and she was aware of what was going on in the world. Everything was wrong, and she had no way of putting things right—that gave her a sense of complete powerlessness.

In a short while, though, she would have the final experience of her life, which promised to be very different: death. She wrote the letter to the magazine, then abandoned the topic and concentrated on more pressing matters, more appropriate to what she was living, or rather, dying, through at that moment.

She tried to imagine what it would be like to die but failed to reach any conclusion.

Besides, there was no point worrying about that, for in a few moments she would find out.

How many minutes?

She had no idea. But she relished the thought that she was about to find out the answer to the question that everyone asked themselves: Does God exist?

Unlike many people, this had not been the great inner debate of her life. Under the old Communist regime, the official line in schools had been that life ended with death, and she had gotten used to the idea. On the other hand, her parents' generation and her grandparents' generation still went to church, said prayers, and went on pilgrimages, and were utterly convinced that God listened to what they said.

At twenty-four, having experienced everything she could experience—and that was no small achievement—Veronika was almost certain that everything ended with death. That is why she had chosen suicide: freedom at last. Eternal oblivion.

In her heart of hearts, though, there was still a doubt: What if God did exist? Thousands of years of civilization had made of suicide a taboo, an affront to all religious codes: Man struggles to survive, not to succumb. The human race must procreate. Society needs workers. A couple has to have a reason to stay together, even when love has ceased to exist, and a country needs soldiers, politicians and artists.

If God exists, and I truly don't believe he does, he will know that there are limits to human understanding. He was the one who created this confusion in which there is poverty, injustice, greed, and loneliness. He doubtless had the best of intentions, but the results have proved disastrous; if God exists, he will be generous with those creatures who chose to leave this Earth early, and he might even apologize for having made us spend time here.

To hell with taboos and superstitions. Her devout mother would say: "God knows the past, the present, and the future." In that case, he had placed her in this world in the full knowledge that she would end up killing herself, and he would not be shocked by her actions.

Veronika began to feel a slight nausea, which became rapidly more intense.

In a few moments, she would no longer be able to concentrate on the square outside her window. She knew it was winter; it must have been about four o'clock in the afternoon, and the sun was setting fast. She knew that other people would go on living. At that moment a young man passed her window and saw her, utterly unaware that she was about to die. A group of Bolivian musicians (where is Bolivia? why don't magazine articles ask that?) was playing in front of the statue of France Prešeren, the great Slovenian poet, who had made such a profound impact on the soul of his people.

Would she live to hear the end of that music drifting up from the square? It would be a beautiful memory of this life: the late afternoon, a melody recounting the dreams of a country on the other side of the world, the warm cozy room, the handsome young man passing by, full of life, who had decided to stop and was now standing looking up at her. She realized that the pills were beginning to take effect and that he was the last person who would see her.

He smiled. She returned his smile—she had nothing to lose. He waved; she decided to pretend she was looking at something else; the young man was going too far. Disconcerted, he continued on his way, forgetting that face at the window forever.

But Veronika was glad to have felt desired by somebody one last time. She wasn't killing herself because of a lack of love. It wasn't because she felt unloved by her family or had money problems or an incurable disease.

Veronika had decided to die on that lovely Ljubljana afternoon, with Bolivian musicians playing in the square, with a young man passing by her window, and she was happy with what her eyes could see and her ears could hear. She was even happier that she would not have to go on seeing those same things for another thirty, forty, or fifty years, because they would lose all their originality and be transformed into the tragedy of a life in which everything repeats itself and where one day is exactly like another.

Her stomach was beginning to churn now, and she was feeling very ill indeed. *It's odd,* she thought. *I thought an overdose of tranquilizers should have sent me straight to sleep.* What she was experiencing, though, was a strange buzzing in her ears and a desire to vomit.

If I throw up, I won't die.

She decided not to think about the stabbing pains in her stomach and tried to concentrate on the rapidly falling night, on the Bolivians, on the people who were starting to shut up their shops and go home. The noise in her ears was becoming more and more strident, and, for the first time since she had taken the pills, Veronika felt fear, a terrible fear of the unknown.

It did not last long. Soon afterward, she lost consciousness.

When she opened her eyes, Veronika did not think, This must be heaven. *Heaven would never use a fluorescent tube to light a room, and the pain—which started a fraction of a second later—was typical of the Earth. Ah, that Earth pain—unique, unmistakable.*

S HE TRIED to move, and the pain increased. A series of bright dots appeared, but, even so, Veronika knew that those dots were not the stars of paradise but the consequences of the intense pain she was feeling.

"She's coming to," she heard a woman say. "You've landed slap bang in hell, so you'd better make the most of it."

No, it couldn't be true; that voice was deceiving her. It wasn't hell, because she felt really cold and she was aware of plastic tubes coming out of her nose and mouth. One of the tubes—the one stuck down her throat—made her feel as if she were choking.

She made an attempt to remove it, but her arms were strapped down.

"I'm joking, it's not really hell," the voice went on. "It's worse than hell, not that I've ever actually been there. You're in Villete."

Despite the pain and the choking feeling, Veronika realized at once what had happened. She had tried to kill herself, and someone had arrived in time to save her. It could have been one of the nuns, a friend who had decided to drop by unannounced, someone delivering something she had forgotten she had ordered. The fact is she had survived, and she was in Villete.

Villete, the famous and much-feared lunatic asylum, which had been in existence since 1991, the year of the country's independence. At that time, believing that the partitioning of the former Yugoslavia would be achieved through peaceful means (after all, Slovenia had only experienced eleven days of war), a group of European businessmen had obtained permission to set up a hospital for mental patients in the old barracks, abandoned because of high maintenance costs.

Shortly afterward, however, the wars commenced: first in Croatia, then in Bosnia. The businessmen were worried. The money for the investment came from capitalists scattered all round the globe, from people whose names they didn't even know, so there was no possibility of sitting down in front of them, offering a few excuses, and asking them to be patient. They resolved the problem by adopting practices that were far from commendable in a psychiatric hospital, and for the young nation that had just emerged from a benign communism, Villete came to symbolize all the worst aspects of capitalism: To be admitted to the hospital, all you needed was money.

There was no shortage of people who, in their desire to get rid of some family member because of arguments over an inheritance (or over that person's embarrassing behavior), were willing to pay large sums of money to obtain a medical report that would allow the internment of their problem children or parents. Others, fleeing from debts or trying to justify certain attitudes that could otherwise result in long prison sentences, spent a brief time in the asylum and then simply left without paying any penalty or undergoing any judicial process.

Villete was the place from which no one had ever escaped, where genuine lunatics—sent there by the courts or by other hospitals—mingled with those merely accused of insanity or those pretending to be insane. The result was utter confusion, and the press was constantly publishing tales of ill treatment and abuse, although they had never been given permission to visit Villete and see what was actually happening. The government was investigating the complaints but could get no proof; the shareholders threatened to spread the word that foreign investment was difficult in Slovenia, and so the institution managed to remain afloat; indeed, it went from strength to strength.

"My aunt killed herself a few months ago," the female voice continued. "For almost eight years she was too afraid even to leave her room, eating, getting fat, smoking, taking tranquilizers and sleeping most of the time. She had two daughters and a husband who loved her."

Veronika tried but failed to move her head in the direction of the voice.

"I only saw her fight back once, when her husband took a lover. Then she kicked up a fuss, lost a few pounds, smashed some glasses and—for weeks on end—kept the rest of the whole neighborhood awake with her shouting. Absurd though it may seem, I think that was the happiest time of her life. She was fighting for something; she felt alive and capable of responding to the challenges facing her."

What's all that got to do with me? thought Veronika, unable to say anything. *I'm not your aunt and I haven't got a husband.*

"In the end, her husband got rid of his lover," said the woman, "and gradually, my aunt returned to her former passivity. One day she phoned to say that she wanted to change her life: She'd given up smoking. That same week, after increasing the number of tranquilizers she was taking because she'd stopped smoking, she told everyone that she wanted to kill herself.

"No one believed her. Then, one morning she left a message on my machine, saying good-bye, and she gassed herself. I listened to that message several times: I had never heard her sound so calm, so resigned to her fate. She said she was neither happy nor unhappy, and that was why she couldn't go on."

Veronika felt sorry for the woman telling the story, for she seemed to be doing so in an attempt to understand her aunt's death. In a world where everyone struggles to survive whatever the cost, how could one judge those people who decide to die?

No one can judge. Each person knows the extent of their own suffering or the total absence of meaning in their lives. Veronika wanted to explain that, but instead she choked on the tube in her mouth, and the woman hurried to her aid.

She saw the woman bending over her bound body, which was full of tubes and protected against her will. She openly expressed desire to destroy it. She moved her head from side to side, pleading with her eyes for them to remove the tubes and let her die in peace.

"You're upset," said the woman. "I don't know if you're sorry about what you did or if you still want to die; that doesn't interest me. What interests me is doing my job. If the patient gets agitated, the regulations say I must give them a sedative."

Veronika stopped struggling, but the nurse was already injecting something into her arm. Soon afterward, she was back in a strange dreamless world, where the only thing she could remember was the face of the woman she had just seen: green eyes, brown hair, and a very distant air, the air of someone doing things because she has to do them, never questioning why the rules say this or that.

Paulo Coelho heard about Veronika's story three months later, when he was having supper in an Algerian restaurant in Paris with a Slovenian friend, also called Veronika, who happened to be the daughter of the doctor in charge at Villete.

LATER, WHEN he decided to write a book about the subject, he considered changing his friend's name in order not to confuse the reader. He thought of calling her Blaska or Edwina or Marietzja, or some other Slovenian name, but he ended up keeping the real names. When he referred to his friend Veronika, he would call her his friend Veronika. When he referred to the other Veronika, there would be no need to describe her at all, because she would be the central character in the book, and people would get irritated if they were always having to read "Veronika the lunatic," or "Veronika the one who tried to commit suicide." Besides, both he and his friend Veronika would only take up a very brief part of the book, this one.

His friend Veronika was horrified at what her father had done, especially bearing in mind that he was the director of an institution seeking respectability and was himself working on a thesis that would be judged by the conventional academic community.

"Do you know where the word 'asylum' comes from?" she was saying. "It dates back to the Middle Ages, from a person's right to seek refuge in churches and other holy places. The right to asylum is something any civilized person can understand. So how could my father, the director of an asylum, treat someone like that?"

Paulo Coelho wanted to know all the details of what had happened, because he had a genuine reason for finding out about Veronika's story.

The reason was the following: He himself had been committed to an asylum or, rather, mental hospital, as they were better known. And this had happened not once but three times, in 1965, 1966, and 1967. The place where he had been interned was the Dr. Eiras Sanatorium in Rio de Janeiro.

Precisely why he had been committed to the hospital was something that, even today, he found odd. Perhaps his parents were confused by his unusual behavior. Half shy, half extrovert, he had the desire to be an "artist," something that everyone in the family considered a perfect recipe for ending up a social outcast and dying in poverty.

When Paulo Coelho thought about it—and, it must be said, he rarely did—he considered the real madman to have been the doctor who had agreed to commit him for the flimsiest of reasons (as in any family, the tendency is always to place the blame on others, and to state adamantly that the parents didn't know what they were doing when they made that drastic decision).

Paulo laughed when he learned of the strange letter to the newspapers that Veronika had left behind, complaining that an important French magazine didn't even know where Slovenia was.

"No one would kill themselves over something like that."

"That's why the letter had no effect," said his friend Veronika, embarrassed. "Yesterday, when I checked in at the hotel, the receptionist thought Slovenia was a town in Germany."

He knew the feeling, for many foreigners believed the Argentine city of Buenos Aires to be the capital of Brazil.

But apart from having foreigners blithely compliment him on the beauty of his country's capital city (which was to be found in the neighboring country of Argentina), Paulo Coelho shared with Veronika the fact just mentioned but which is worth restating: He too had been committed to a mental hospital and, as his first wife had once remarked, "should never have been let out."

But he *was* let out. And when he left the sanatorium for the last time, determined never to go back, he had made two promises: (*a*) that he would one day write about the subject, and (*b*) that he would wait until both his parents were dead before touching publicly on the issue, because he didn't want to hurt them, since both had spent many years of their lives blaming themselves for what they had done.

His mother had died in 1993, but his father, who had turned eighty-four in 1997, was still alive and in full possession of his mental faculties and his health, despite having emphysema (even though he'd never smoked) and despite living entirely off frozen food because he couldn't get a housekeeper who would put up with his eccentricities.

So, when Paulo Coelho heard Veronika's story, he discovered a way of talking about the issue without breaking his promises. Even though he had never considered suicide, he had an intimate knowledge of the world of the mental hospital—the treatments, the relationships between doctors and patients, the comforts and anxieties of living in a place like that.

So let us allow Paulo Coelho and his friend Veronika to leave this book for good, and let us get on with the story.

Veronika didn't know how long she had slept. She remembered waking up at one point—still with the life-preserving tubes in her mouth and nose—and hearing a voice say:

Do YOU want me to masturbate you?"

But now, looking round the room with her eyes wide open, she didn't know if that had been real or a hallucination. Apart from that one memory, she could remember nothing, absolutely nothing.

The tubes had been taken out, but she still had needles stuck all over her body, wires connected to the areas around her heart and her head, and her arms were still strapped down. She was naked, covered only by a sheet, and she felt cold, but she was determined not to complain. The small area surrounded by green curtains was filled by the bed she was lying on, the machinery of the Intensive Care Unit, and a white chair on which a nurse was sitting reading a book.

This time the woman had dark eyes and brown hair. Even so Veronika was not sure if it was the same person she had talked to hours—or was it days?—ago.

"Can you unstrap my arms?"

The nurse looked up, said a brusque no, and went back to her book.

I'm alive, thought Veronika. *Everything's going to start all over again. I'll have to stay in here for a while, until they realize that I'm perfectly normal. Then they'll let me out, and I'll see the streets of Ljubljana again, its main square, the bridges, the people going to and from work.*

Since people always tend to help others——just so that they can feel they are better than they really are——they'll give me my job back at the library. In time I'll start frequenting the same bars and nightclubs, I'll talk to my friends about the injustices and problems of the world, I'll go to the movies, take walks around the lake.

Since I only took sleeping pills, I'm not disfigured in any way: I'm still young, pretty, intelligent, I won't have any difficulty getting boyfriends, I never did. I'll make love with them in their houses or in the woods, I'll feel a certain degree of pleasure, but the moment I reach orgasm, the feeling of emptiness will return. We won't have much to talk about, and both he and I will know it. The time will come to make our excuses—— "It's late," or "I have to get up early tomorrow"——and we'll part as quickly as possible, avoiding looking each other in the eye.

I'll go back to my rented room in the convent. I'll try to read a book, turn on the TV to see the same old programs, set the alarm clock to wake up at exactly the same time I woke up the day before, and mechanically repeat my tasks at the library. I'll eat a sandwich in the park opposite the theater, sitting on the same bench, along with other people who also choose the same benches on which to sit and have their lunch, people who all have the same vacant look but pretend to be pondering extremely important matters.

Then I'll go back to work; I'll listen to the gossip about who's going out with whom, who's suffering from what, how such and such a person was in tears about her husband,

and I'll be left with the feeling that I'm privileged: I'm pretty, I have a job, I can have any boyfriend I choose. So I'll go back to the bars at the end of the day, and the whole thing will start again.

My mother, who must be out of her mind with worry over my suicide attempt, will recover from the shock and will keep asking me what I'm going to do with my life, why I'm not the same as everyone else, things really aren't as complicated as I think they are. "Look at me, for example, I've been married to your father for years, and I've tried to give you the best possible upbringing and set you the best possible example."

One day I'll get tired of hearing her constantly repeating the same things, and to please her I'll marry a man whom I oblige myself to love. He and I will end up finding a way of dreaming of a future together: a house in the country, children, our children's future. We'll make love often in the first year, less in the second, and after the third year, people perhaps think about sex only once every two weeks and transform that thought into action only once a month. Even worse, we'll barely talk. I'll force myself to accept the situation, and I'll wonder what's wrong with me, because he no longer takes any interest in me, ignores me, and does nothing but talk about his friends as if they were his real world.

When the marriage is just about to fall apart, I'll get pregnant. We'll have a child, feel closer to each other for a while, and then the situation will go back to what it was before.

I'll begin to put on weight like the aunt that nurse was talking about yesterday— or was it days ago? I don't really know. And I'll start to go on diets, systematically defeated each day, each week, by the weight that keeps creeping up regardless of the controls

I put on it. At that point I'll take those magic pills that stop you from feeling depressed; then I'll have a few more children, conceived during nights of love that pass all too quickly. I'll tell everyone that the children are my reason for living, when in reality my life is their reason for living.

People will always consider us a happy couple, and no one will know how much solitude, bitterness, and resignation lies beneath the surface happiness.

Until one day, when my husband takes a lover for the first time, and I will perhaps kick up a fuss like the nurse's aunt or think again of killing myself. By then, though, I'll be too old and cowardly, with two or three children who need my help, and I'll have to bring them up and help them find a place in the world before I can just abandon everything. I won't commit suicide: I'll make a scene; I'll threaten to leave and take the children with me. Like all men, my husband will back down; he'll tell me he loves me and that it won't happen again. It won't even occur to him that, if I really did decide to leave, my only option would be to go back to my parents' house and stay there for the rest of my life, forced to listen to my mother going on and on all day about how I lost my one opportunity for being happy, that he was a wonderful husband despite his peccadilloes, that my children will be traumatized by the separation.

Two or three years later, another woman will appear in his life. I'll find out——because I saw them or because someone told me——but this time I'll pretend I don't know. I used up all my energy fighting against that other lover; I've no energy left; it's best to accept life as it really is and not as I imagined it to be. My mother was right.

He will continue being a considerate husband; I will continue working at the library, eating my sandwiches in the square opposite the theater, reading books I never quite manage to finish, watching television programs that are the same as they were ten, twenty, fifty years ago.

Except that I'll eat my sandwiches with a sense of guilt because I'm getting fatter; and I won't go to bars anymore because I have a husband expecting me to come home and look after the children.

After that it's a matter of waiting for the children to grow up and of spending all day thinking about suicide, without the courage to do anything about it. One fine day I'll reach the conclusion that that's what life is like: There's no point worrying about it; nothing will change. And I'll accept it.

Veronika brought her interior monologue to a close and made a promise to herself: She would not leave Villete alive. It was best to put an end to everything now, while she was still brave and healthy enough to die.

She fell asleep and woke up several times, noticing that the number of machines around her was diminishing, the warmth of her body was growing, and the nurses' faces kept changing; but there was always someone beside her. Through the green curtain she heard the sound of someone crying, groans, or voices whispering in calm, technical tones. From time to time, a distant machine would buzz and she would hear hurried footsteps along the corridor. Then the voices would lose their calm, technical tone and become tense, issuing rapid orders.

In one of her lucid moments, a nurse asked her: "Don't you want to know how you are?"

"I already know," replied Veronika. "And it has nothing to do with what you can see happening in my body; it's what's happening in my soul."

The nurse tried to continue the conversation, but Veronika pretended to be asleep.

When Veronika opened her eyes again for the first time, she realized that she had been moved; she was in what looked like a large ward. She still had an IV drip in her arm, but all the other wires and needles had been removed.

A TALL DOCTOR, wearing the traditional white coat, in sharp contrast to the artificial black of his dyed hair and beard, was standing at the foot of her bed. Beside him a young junior doctor holding a clipboard was taking notes.

"How long have I been here?" she asked, noticing that she spoke with some difficulty, slurring her words slightly.

"You've been in this ward for two weeks, after five days spent in the Intensive Care Unit," replied the older man. "And just be grateful that you're still here."

The younger man seemed surprised, as if that final remark did not quite fit the facts. Veronika noticed his reaction at once, which alerted her instincts. Had she been here longer than she had thought? Was she still in some danger? She began to pay attention to each gesture, each movement the two men made; she knew it was pointless asking questions; they would never tell her the truth, but if she was clever, she could find out what was going on.

"Tell me your name, address, marital status, and date of birth," the older man said. Veronika knew her name, her marital status, and her date of birth, but she realized that there were blanks in her memory: She couldn't quite remember her address.

The doctor shone a light in her eyes and examined them for a long time, in silence. The young man did the same thing. They exchanged glances that meant absolutely nothing.

"Did you say to the night nurse that we couldn't see into your soul?" asked the younger man.

Veronika couldn't remember. She was having difficulty knowing who she was and what she was doing there.

"You have been kept in an artificially induced sleep with tranquilizers, and that might affect your memory a bit, but please try to answer all our questions."

And the doctors began an absurd questionnaire, wanting to know the names of the principal Ljubljana newspapers, the name of the poet whose statue was in the main square (ah, that she would never forget, every Slovene has the image of Prešeren engraved on his or her soul), the color of her mother's hair, the names of her colleagues at work, the titles of the most popular books at the library.

To begin with Veronika considered not replying—her memory was still confused—but as the questionnaire continued, she began reconstructing what she'd forgotten. At one point she remembered that she was now in a mental hospital, and that the mad were not obliged to be coherent; but for her own good, and to keep the doctors by her side, at least so she can find out something more about her state, she began making a mental effort to respond. As she recited the names and facts, she was recovering not only her memory but also her personality, her desires, her way of seeing life. The idea of suicide, which that morning seemed to be buried beneath several layers of sedatives, resurfaced.

"Fine," said the older man at the end of the questionnaire.

"How much longer must I stay here?"

The younger man lowered his eyes, and she felt as if everything were hanging in the air, as if, once that question was answered, a new chapter of her life would be written, and no one would be able to change it.

"You can tell her," said the older man. "A lot of other patients have already heard the rumors, and she'll find out in the end anyway; it's impossible to keep secrets around here."

"Well, you decided your own fate," sighed the young man, weighing each word. "So you had better know the consequence of your actions. During the coma brought on by the pills you took, your heart was irreversibly damaged. There was a necrosis of the ventricle—"

"Put it in layman's terms," said the older man. "Get straight to the point."

"Your heart was irreversibly damaged, and soon it will stop beating altogether."

"What does that mean?" she asked, frightened.

"If your heart stops beating, that means only one thing, death. I don't know what your religious beliefs are, but—"

"When will my heart stop beating?" asked Veronika, interrupting him.

"Within five days, a week at most."

Veronika realized that behind his professional appearance and behavior, behind the concerned manner, the young man was taking immense pleasure in what he was saying, as if she deserved the punishment and would serve as an example to all the others.

During her life Veronika had noticed that a lot of people she knew would talk about the horrors in other people's lives as if they were genuinely trying to help them, but the truth was that they took pleasure in the suffering of others, because that made them believe they were happy and that life had been generous with them. She hated that kind of person, and she wasn't going to give the young man an opportunity to take advantage of her state in order to mask his own frustrations.

She kept her eyes fixed on his and, smiling, said: "So I succeeded, then."

"Yes," came the reply. But any pleasure he had taken in giving her the tragic news had vanished.

During the night, however, she began to feel afraid. It was one thing to die quickly after taking some pills; it was quite another to wait five days or a week for death to come, when she had already been through so much.

S HE HAD always spent her life waiting for something: for her father to come back from work, for the letter from a lover that never arrived, for her end-of-year exams, for the train, the bus, the phone call, the holiday, the end of the holidays. Now she was going to have to wait for death, which had made an appointment with her.

This could only happen to me. Normally, people die on precisely the day they least expect.

She had to get out of there and get some more pills. If she couldn't, and the only solution was to jump from a high building in Ljubljana, that's what she'd do. She had tried to save her parents any unnecessary suffering, but now she had no option.

She looked around her. All the beds were occupied by sleeping people, some of whom were snoring loudly. There were bars on the windows.

At the end of the ward there was a small bright light that filled the place with strange shadows and meant that the ward could be kept under constant vigilance. Near the light a woman was reading a book.

These nurses must be very cultivated, they spend their whole lives reading.

Veronika's bed was the farthest from the door; between her and the woman there were nearly twenty other beds. She got up with difficulty because, if she was to believe what the doctor had said, she hadn't walked for nearly three weeks. The nurse looked up and saw the girl approaching, dragging her IV drip with her.

"I want to go to the toilet," she whispered, afraid of waking the madwomen.

The woman gestured vaguely toward the door. Veronika's mind was working fast, looking everywhere for an escape route, a crack, a way out. *It has to be quick, while they think I'm still too frail, incapable of acting.*

She peered about her. The toilet was a cubicle with no door. If she wanted to get out of there, she would have to grab the nurse and overpower her in order to get the key , but she was too weak for that.

"Is this a prison?" she asked the nurse, who had stopped reading and was now watching her every movement.

"No, it's a mental hospital."

"But I'm not crazy."

The woman laughed.

"That's what they all say."

"All right then, I am crazy, but what does that mean?"

The woman told Veronika not to stay too long on her feet, and sent her back to her bed.

"What does it mean to be crazy?" insisted Veronika.

"Ask the doctor tomorrow. But go to sleep now, otherwise I'll have to give you a sedative, whether you want it or not."

Veronika obeyed. On her way back she heard someone whispering from one of the beds:

"Don't you know what it means to be crazy?"

For a moment she considered ignoring the voice: She didn't want to make friends, to develop a social circle, to create allies for a great mass revolt. She had only one fixed idea: death. If she really couldn't escape, she would find some way to kill herself right there, as soon as possible.

But the woman asked her the same question she had asked the nurse.

"Don't you know what it means to be crazy?"

"Who are you?"

"My name is Zedka. Go to your bed. Then, when the nurse thinks you're asleep, crawl back over here."

Veronika returned to her bed and waited for the nurse to resume her reading. What did it mean to be crazy? She hadn't the slightest idea, because the word was used in a completely anarchic way. People would say, for example, that certain sportsmen were crazy because they wanted to break records, or that artists were crazy because they led such strange, insecure lives, different from the lives of normal people. Then there were the thinly clad people walking the streets of Ljubljana in winter, whom Veronika had often seen pushing supermarket trolleys full of plastic bags and rags and proclaiming the end of the world.

She didn't feel sleepy. According to the doctor, she had slept for almost a week, too long for someone who was used to living without great emotions but with rigid timetables for rest.

What did it mean to be crazy? Perhaps she should ask one of the lunatics.

Veronika crouched down, pulled the needle out of her arm and went over to Zedka's bed, trying to ignore her churning stomach. She didn't know if the feeling of nausea came from her weakened heart or the effort she was making to move.

"I don't know what it means to be crazy," whispered Veronika. "But I'm not. I'm just a failed suicide."

"Anyone who lives in her own world is crazy. Like schizophrenics, psychopaths, maniacs. I mean people who are different from others."

"Like you?"

"On the other hand," Zedka continued, pretending not to have heard the remark, "you have Einstein, saying that there was no time or space, just a combination of the two. Or Columbus, insisting that on the other side of the world lay not an abyss but a continent. Or Edmund Hillary, convinced that a man could reach the top of Everest. Or the Beatles, who created an entirely different sort of music and dressed like people from another time. Those people—and thousands of others—all lived in their own world."

This madwoman talks a lot of sense, thought Veronika, remembering stories her mother used to tell her about saints who swore they had spoken to Jesus or the Virgin Mary. Did *they* live in a world apart?

"I once saw a woman wearing a low-cut dress; she had a glazed look in her eyes, and she was walking the streets of Ljubljana when it was five degrees below zero. I thought she must be drunk, and I went to help her, but she refused my offer to lend her my jacket. Perhaps in her world it was summer and her body was warmed by the desire of the person waiting for her. Even if that person only existed in her delirium, she had the right to live and die as she wanted, don't you think?"

Veronika didn't know what to say, but the madwoman's words made sense to her. Who knows; perhaps she was the woman who had been seen half-naked walking the streets of Ljubljana?

"I'm going to tell you a story," said Zedka. "A powerful wizard, who wanted to destroy an entire kingdom, placed a magic potion in the well from which all the inhabitants drank. Whoever drank that water would go mad.

"The following morning, the whole population drank from the well and they all went mad, apart from the king and his family, who had a well set aside for them alone, which the magician had not managed to poison. The king was worried and tried to control the population by issuing a series of edicts governing security and public health. The policemen and the inspectors, however, had also drunk the poisoned water, and they thought the king's decisions were absurd and resolved to take no notice of them.

"When the inhabitants of the kingdom heard these decrees, they became convinced that the king had gone mad and was now giving nonsensical orders. They marched on the castle and called for his abdication.

"In despair the king prepared to step down from the throne, but the queen stopped him, saying: 'Let us go and drink from the communal well. Then we will be the same as them.'

"And that was what they did: The king and the queen drank the water of madness and immediately began talking nonsense. Their subjects repented at once; now that the king was displaying such wisdom, why not allow him to continue ruling the country?

"The country continued to live in peace, although its inhabitants behaved very differently from those of its neighbors. And the king was able to govern until the end of his days."

Veronika laughed.

"You don't seem crazy at all," she said.

"But I am, although I'm undergoing treatment since my problem is that I lack a particular chemical. While I hope that the chemical gets rid of my chronic depression, I want to continue being crazy, living my life the way I dream it, and not the way other people want it to be. Do you know what exists out there, beyond the walls of Villete?"

"People who have all drunk from the same well."

"Exactly," said Zedka. "They think they're normal, because they all do the same thing. Well, I'm going to pretend that I have drunk from the same well as them."

"I already did that, and that's precisely my problem. I've never been depressed, never felt great joy or sadness, at least none that lasted. I have the same problems as everyone else."

For a while Zedka said nothing; then: "They told us you're going to die."

Veronika hesitated for a moment. Could she trust this woman? She needed to take the risk.

"Yes, within about five or six days. I keep wondering if there's a way of dying sooner. If you, or someone else, could get me some more pills, I'm sure my heart wouldn't survive this time. You must understand how awful it is to have to wait for death; you must help me."

Before Zedka could reply, the nurse appeared with an injection.

"I can give you the injection myself," she said, "or, depending on how you feel about it, I can ask the guards outside to help me."

"Don't waste your energy," said Zedka to Veronika. "Save your strength, if you want to get what you asked me for."

Veronika got up, went back to her bed, and allowed the nurse to do her work.

It was her first normal day in the mental hospital. She left the ward, had some breakfast in the large refectory where men and women were eating together. She noticed how different it was from the way these places were usually depicted in films—hysterical scenes, shouting, people making demented gestures—everything seemed wrapped in an aura of oppressive silence; it seemed that no one wanted to share their inner world with strangers.

AFTER BREAKFAST (which wasn't bad at all; no one could blame Villete's terrible reputation on the meals) they all went out to take the sun. In fact there wasn't any sun—the temperature was below zero, and the garden was covered with snow.

"I'm not here to preserve my life, but to lose it," said Veronika to one of the nurses.

"You must still go out and take the sun."

"You're the ones who are crazy; there isn't any sun."

"But there is light, and that helps to calm the patients. Unfortunately our winter lasts a long time; if it didn't, we'd have a lot less work."

It was useless arguing; she went out and walked a little, looking around her and surreptitiously seeking some way of escaping. The wall was high, as required by the builders of the old type of barracks, but the watchtowers for the sentries were empty. The garden was surrounded by military-looking buildings, which now housed the male and female wards, the administrative offices, and the employees' rooms. After a first, rapid inspection, she noticed that the only place that was really guarded was the main gate, where everyone who entered and left had their papers checked by two guards.

Everything seemed to be falling into place in her mind again. In order to exercise her memory, she began trying to remember small things, like the place where she used to leave the key to her room, the record she'd just bought, the last book she was asked for at the library.

"I'm Zedka," said a woman, approaching.

The previous night Veronika hadn't been able to see her face as fully; she had crouched down beside the bed all the time they were talking. Zedka must have been about thirty-five and seemed absolutely normal.

"I hope the injection didn't bother you too much. After a while the body gets habituated, and the sedatives lose their effect."

"I'm fine."

"About our conversation last night, do you remember what you asked me?"

"Of course I do."

Zedka took her by the arm, and they began to walk along together, among the many leafless trees in the courtyard. Beyond the walls you could see the mountains disappearing into the clouds.

"It's cold, but a lovely morning all the same," said Zedka. "Oddly enough I never used to suffer from depression on cold, gray, cloudy days like this. I felt as if nature was in harmony with me, that it reflected my soul. On the other hand, when the sun appeared, the children would come out to play in the streets, and everyone was happy that it was such a lovely day, and then I would feel terrible, as if that display of exuberance in which I could not participate was somehow unfair."

Delicately Veronika detached herself from the woman. She didn't like physical contact.

"You didn't finish what you were saying. You were saying something about what I asked you last night."

"There's a group of people here, men and women who could have left, who could be back home, but who don't want to leave. There are many reasons for this: Villete isn't as bad as people say, although it's far from being a five-star hotel. Here inside, everyone can say what they like, do what they want, without being criticized. After all, they're in a mental hospital. Then, when there are government inspections, these men and women behave like dangerous maniacs, because some are here at the state's expense. The doctors know this, but there must be some order from the owners that allows the situation to continue, because there are more vacancies than there are patients."

"Could they get hold of some pills for me?"

"Try to contact them; they call their group the Fraternity."

Zedka pointed to a woman with white hair, who was talking animatedly with some younger women.

"Her name is Mari, she belongs to the Fraternity. Ask her."

Veronika started walking toward Mari, but Zedka stopped her: "No, not now, she's having fun. She's not going to stop something that gives her pleasure just to be nice to a complete stranger. If she should react badly, you'll never have another chance to approach her. The 'insane' always believe in first impressions."

Veronika laughed at the way Zedka said the word "insane," but she was worried too, because everything here seemed so normal, so nice. After so many years of going straight from work to a bar, from that bar to the bed of some lover, from his bed to her room, from her room to her mother's house, she was now experiencing something she had never dreamed of: a mental hospital, insanity, an insane asylum, where people were not ashamed to say that they were crazy, where no one stopped doing something they were enjoying just to be nice to others.

She began to doubt that Zedka was serious, or if it wasn't just a way by which mental patients could pretend that the world they lived in was better than that of others. But what did it matter? She was experiencing something interesting, different, totally unexpected. Imagine a place where people pretend to be crazy in order to do exactly what they want.

At that precise moment Veronika's heart turned over. She suddenly remembered what the doctor had said, and she felt frightened.

"I want to walk alone a little," she said to Zedka. She was, after all, "crazy" too, and she no longer had to worry about pleasing anyone.

The woman moved off, and Veronika stood looking at the mountains beyond the walls of Villete. A faint desire to live seemed about to surface, but Veronika determinedly pushed it away.

I must get hold of those pills as soon as possible.

She reflected on her situation there; it was far from ideal. Even if they allowed her to do all the crazy things she wanted to do, she wouldn't know where to start.

She had never done anything crazy.

(> (> (>

After some time in the garden, everyone went back to the refectory and had lunch. Immediately afterward, the nurses led both men and women to a huge living room divided into lots of different areas; there were tables, chairs, sofas, a piano, a television, and large windows through which you could see the gray sky and the low clouds. None of the windows had bars on them, because the room opened onto the garden. The doors were closed because of the cold, but all you had to do was turn the handle, and you could go outside again and walk once more among the trees.

Most people went and sat down in front of the television. Others stared into space, others talked in low voices to themselves, but who has not done the same at some moment in their lives? Veronika noticed that the older woman, Mari, was now with a larger group in one of the corners of the vast room. Some other patients were walking nearby, and Veronika tried to join them in order to eavesdrop on what the group members were saying.

She tried to disguise her intentions as best she could, but whenever she came close, they all fell silent and turned as one to look at her.

"What do you want?" said an elderly man, who seemed to be the leader of the Fraternity (if such a group really existed and Zedka was not actually crazier than she seemed).

"Nothing, I was just passing."

They exchanged glances and made a few jerky gestures with their heads. One said to the other: "She was just passing." The other repeated the remark more loudly this time, and soon they were all shouting the same words.

Veronika didn't know what to do and stood there paralyzed with fear. A burly, shifty-looking male nurse came over, wanting to know what was going on.

"Nothing," said one member of the group. "She was just passing. She's standing right there, but she's still just passing."

The whole group burst into laughter. Veronika assumed an ironic air, smiled, turned and moved off, so that no one would notice that her eyes were filling with tears. She went straight out into the garden without bothering to put on a coat or jacket. A nurse tried to persuade her to come back inside, but another appeared soon after and whispered something in his ear. The two of them left her in peace, in the cold. There was no point taking care of someone who was condemned to die.

She was confused, tense, irritated with herself. She had never allowed herself to be provoked; she had learned early that whenever a new situation presented itself, you had to remain cool and distant. Those crazy people, however, had managed to make her feel shame, fear, rage, a desire to murder them all, to wound them with words she hadn't dared to utter.

Perhaps the pills or the treatment they had administered to get her out of her coma had transformed her into a frail woman, incapable of fending for herself. She had confronted far worse situations in her adolescence, and yet for the first time, she had been unable to hold back her tears. She needed to get back to the person she used to be, someone able to respond with irony, to pretend that the insults didn't bother her because she was better than all of them. Who in that group had had the courage to desire death? Who among them could teach her about life when they were all huddled behind the walls of Villete? She would never want to depend on their help for anything, even if she had to wait five or six days to die.

"One day's already gone. There are only another four or five left."

She walked a little, letting the freezing cold enter her body and calm her blood that was flowing too fast. Her heart that was beating too hard.

Honestly, here I am, with my days literally numbered, giving importance to remarks made by people I've never even seen before, people who soon I'll never see again. And yet I suffer and get upset; I want to attack and defend. Why waste my time?

But she *was* wasting the little time left to her, fighting for her tiny bit of space in that strange community where you had to put up a fight if you didn't want others imposing their rules on you.

I can't believe it, I never used to be like this. I never used to fight over stupid things.

She stopped in the middle of the icy garden. It was precisely because she had found everything so stupid that she had ended up accepting what life had naturally imposed on her. In adolescence she thought it was too early to choose; now, in young adulthood, she was convinced it was too late to change.

And what had she spent all her energies on until then? On trying to ensure that her life continued exactly as it always had. She had given up many of her desires so that her parents would continue to love her as they had when she was a child, even though she knew that real love changes and grows with time and discovers new ways of expressing itself. One day, when she had listened to her mother telling her, in tears, that her marriage was over, Veronika had sought out her father; she had cried, threatened, and finally extracted a promise from him that he would not leave home, never imagining the high price her parents would have to pay for this.

When she decided to get a job, she rejected a tempting offer from a company that had just been set up in her recently created country in favor of a job at the public library, where you didn't earn much money but where you were secure. She went to work every day, always keeping to the same timetable, always making sure she wasn't perceived as a threat by her superiors; she was content; she didn't struggle, and so she didn't grow: All she wanted was her salary at the end of the month.

She rented the room in the convent because the nuns required all tenants to be back at a certain hour, and then they locked the door: Anyone still outside after that had to sleep on the street. She always had a genuine excuse to give boyfriends, so as not to have to spend the night in hotel rooms or strange beds.

When she used to dream of getting married, she imagined herself in a little house outside Ljubljana, with a man quite different from her father—a man who earned enough to support his family, one who would be content just to be with her in a house with an open fire and to look out at the snow-covered mountains.

She had taught herself to give men a precise amount of pleasure; never more, never less, only what was necessary. She didn't get angry with anyone, because that would mean having to react, having to do battle with the enemy and then having to face unforeseen consequences, such as vengeance.

When she had achieved almost everything she wanted in life, she had reached the conclusion that her existence had no meaning, because every day was the same. And she had decided to die.

Veronika went back in and walked over to the group gathered in one corner of the room. The people were talking animatedly but fell silent as soon as she approached.

She went straight over to the oldest man, who seemed to be the leader. Before anyone could stop her, she gave him a resounding slap in the face.

"Aren't you going to react?" she asked out loud, so that everyone in the room could hear her. "Aren't you going to do something?"

"No," the man said and passed a hand over his face. A little thread of blood ran from his nose. "You won't be troubling us for very long."

She left the living room and went triumphantly back to her ward. She had done something that she had never done in her entire life.

Three days had passed since the incident with the group that Zedka called the Fraternity. Veronika regretted that slap, not because she was afraid of the man's reaction but because she had done something different. If she wasn't careful, she might end up convinced that life was worth living, and that would cause her pointless pain, since she would soon have to leave this world anyway.

45

Her only option was to keep away from everything and everyone, to try to be in every way as she had been before, to obey Villete's rules and regulations. She adapted herself to the routine imposed by the hospital: rising early, eating breakfast, going for a walk in the garden, having lunch, going to the living room, for another walk in the garden, then supper, television, and bed.

Before Veronika went to sleep, a nurse always appeared with medication. All the other women took pills; Veronika was the only one who was given an injection. She never complained; she just wanted to know why she was given so many sedatives, since she had never had any problems sleeping. They explained that the injection was not a sedative but medication for her heart.

And so, by falling in with that routine, her days in the hospital all began to seem the same. When the days are all the same, they pass more quickly; in another two or three days she would no longer have to brush her teeth or comb her hair. Veronika noticed her heart growing rapidly weaker: She easily ran out of breath, she got pains in her chest, she had no appetite, and the slightest effort made her dizzy.

After the incident with the Fraternity, she had sometimes thought: *If I had a choice, if I had understood earlier that the reason my days were all the same was because I wanted them like that, perhaps . . .*

But the reply was always the same: *There is no perhaps, because there is no choice.* And her inner peace returned, because everything had already been decided.

During this period she formed a relationship with Zedka (not a friendship, because friendship requires a lot of time spent together, and that wouldn't be possible). They used to play cards—which helps the time pass more rapidly—and sometimes they would walk together in silence in the garden.

On one particular morning, immediately after breakfast, they all went out to take the sun, as the regulations demanded. A nurse, however, asked Zedka to go back to the ward, because it was her treatment day.

Veronika, who was having breakfast with her, heard the request.

"What treatment's that?"

"It's an old treatment, from the sixties, but the doctors think it might hasten my recovery. Do you want to come and watch?"

"You said you were depressed. Isn't taking the medication enough to replace the chemical you're lacking?"

"Do you want to watch?" insisted Zedka.

She was going to step outside the routine, thought Veronika. *She was going to discover new things, when she didn't need to learn anything more—all she needed was patience.* But her curiosity got the better of her and she nodded.

"This isn't a show, you know," said the nurse. "She's going to die. She's hardly seen anything. Let her come with us."

Veronika watched the woman, still smiling, being strapped to the bed.

Tell her what's going on," said Zedka to the male nurse. "Otherwise she'll be frightened."

He turned and showed Veronika the syringe. He seemed pleased to be treated like a doctor explaining to a younger doctor the correct procedures and the proper treatments.

"This syringe contains a dose of insulin," he said, speaking in a grave, technical tone of voice. "It's used by diabetics to combat high blood glucose. However, when the dose is much larger than normal, the consequent drop in blood glucose provokes a state of coma."

He tapped the needle lightly, to get rid of any air, and then stuck it in a vein in Zedka's foot.

"That's what's going to happen now. She's going to enter a state of induced coma. Don't be frightened if her eyes glaze, and don't expect her to recognize you when she's under the effects of the medication."

"That's awful, inhuman," Veronika said. " People struggle to get out of a coma, not to go into one."

"People struggle to live, not to commit suicide," replied the nurse, but Veronika ignored the remark. "And a state of coma allows the organism to rest; its functions are all drastically reduced, and any existing tension disappears."

He continued to inject the liquid while he was talking, and Zedka's eyes were growing dull.

"Don't worry," Veronika was saying to her. "You're absolutely normal; the story you told me about the king . . ."

"Don't waste your time. She can't hear you anymore."

The woman on the bed, who a few minutes before had seemed so lucid and full of life, now had her eyes fixed on some point in the distance, and liquid was bubbling from one corner of her mouth.

"What did you do?!" she shouted at the nurse.

"Just my job."

Veronika started calling to Zedka, shouting, threatening that she would go to the police, the press, the human rights organizations.

"Calm down. You may be in a mental hospital, but you still have to abide by certain rules."

She saw that the man was utterly serious, and she was afraid. But since she had nothing to lose, she went on shouting.

From where she was, Zedka could see the ward and the beds, all empty except for one, to which her body was strapped, and beside which a girl was standing, staring in horror. The girl didn't know that the person in the bed was still alive with all her biological functions working perfectly, but that her soul was flying, almost touching the ceiling, experiencing a sense of profound peace.

Z EDKA WAS making an astral journey, something that had been a surprise during her first experience of insulin shock. She hadn't mentioned it to anyone; she was only there to be cured of depression and, as soon as she was in a fit state, she hoped to leave that place forever. If she started telling them that she had left her body, they would think she was crazier than when she had entered Villete. However, as soon as she had returned to her body, she began reading up on both subjects: insulin shock and that strange feeling of floating in space.

There wasn't much written about the treatment. It had been used for the first time around 1930 but had been completely banned in psychiatric hospitals because of the possibility of irreversible damage to the patient. During one such session she had visited Dr. Igor's office in her astral form, at precisely the moment when he was discussing the subject with one of the owners of the hospital. "It's a crime," Dr. Igor was saying. "Yes, but it's cheap and it's quick!" replied the other man. "Anyway, who's interested in the rights of the insane? No one's going to complain."

Even so, some doctors still considered it a quick way of treating depression. Zedka had sought out and borrowed everything that had been written about insulin shock, especially firsthand reports by patients who had experienced it. The story was always the same: horrors and more horrors; not one of them had experienced anything resembling what she was living through at that moment.

She concluded—quite rightly—that there was no relationship between insulin and the feeling that her consciousness was leaving her body. On the contrary, the tendency with that kind of treatment was to diminish the patient's mental capacity.

She started researching the existence of the soul, read a few books on occultism, and then one day she stumbled on a vast literature that described exactly what she was experiencing: It was called "astral travel," and many people had already had the same experience. Some had merely set out to describe what they had felt, while others had developed techniques to provoke it. Zedka now knew those techniques by heart, and she used them every night to go wherever she wished.

The descriptions of those experiences and visions varied, but they all had certain points in common: the strange, irritating noise that preceded the separation of the body from the spirit, followed by a shock, a rapid loss of consciousness, and then the peace and joy of floating in the air, attached to the body by a silvery cord, a cord that could be stretched indefinitely, although there were legends (in books, of course) that said the person would die if they allowed that silver thread to break.

Her experience, however, showed that she could go as far as she wanted and the cord never broke. But generally speaking the books had been very useful in teaching her how to get more and more out of her astral traveling. She had learned, for example, that when she wanted to move from one place to another, she had to concentrate on projecting herself into space, imagining exactly where she wanted to go. Unlike the routes followed by planes—which leave from one place and fly the necessary distance to reach another—an astral journey was made through mysterious tunnels. You imagined yourself in a place, you entered the appropriate tunnel at a terrifying speed, and the other place would appear.

It was through books too that she had lost her fear of the creatures inhabiting space. Today there was no one else in the ward. The first time she had left her body, however, she had found a lot of people watching her, amused by her look of surprise.

Her first reaction was to assume that these were dead people, ghosts haunting the hospital. Then, with the help of books and of her own experience, she realized that, although there were a few disembodied spirits wandering about there, among them were people as alive as she was, who had either developed the technique of leaving their bodies or who were not even aware of what was happening to them because, in some other part of the world, they were sleeping deeply while their spirits roamed freely abroad.

Today—knowing that this was her last astral journey on insulin, because she had just been to visit Dr. Igor's office and overheard him saying he was ready to release her—she decided to remain inside Villete. From the moment she went out through the main gate, she would never again return, not even in spirit, and she wanted to say good-bye.

To say good-bye. That was the really difficult part. Once in a mental hospital, a person grows used to the freedom that exists in the world of insanity and becomes addicted to it. You no longer have to take on responsibilities, to struggle to earn your daily bread, to be bothered with repetitive, mundane tasks. You could spend hours looking at a picture or making absurd doodles. Everything is tolerated because, after all, the person is mentally ill. As she herself had the occasion to observe, most of the inmates showed a marked improvement once they entered the hospital. They no longer had to hide their symptoms, and the "family" atmosphere helped them to accept their own neuroses and psychoses.

At the beginning Zedka had been fascinated by Villete and had even considered joining the Fraternity once she was cured. But she realized that if she was sensible, she could continue doing everything she enjoyed doing outside, as long as she dealt with the challenges of daily life. As someone had said, all you had to do was to keep your insanity under control. You could cry, get worried or angry like any other normal human being, as long as you remembered that, up above, your spirit was laughing out loud at all those thorny situations.

She would soon be back home with her children and her husband, and that part of her life also had its charms. Of course it would be difficult to find work; after all, in a small town like Ljubljana news travels fast, and her internment in Villete was already common knowledge to many people. But her husband earned enough to keep the family, and she could use her free time to continue making her astral journeys, though not under the dangerous influence of insulin.

There was only one thing she did not want to experience again: the reason that had brought her to Villete.

Depression.

The doctors said that a recently discovered substance, serotonin, was one of the compounds responsible for how human beings felt. A lack of serotonin impaired one's capacity to concentrate at work, to sleep, to eat, and to enjoy life's pleasures. When this substance was completely absent, the person experienced despair, pessimism, a sense of futility, terrible tiredness, anxiety, difficulties in making decisions, and would end up sinking into permanent gloom, which would lead either to complete apathy or to suicide.

Other more conservative doctors said that any drastic change in life could trigger depression—moving to another country, losing a loved one, divorce, an increase in the demands of work or family. Some modern studies, based on the number of internments in winter and summer, pointed to the lack of sunlight as one of the causes of depression.

In Zedka's case, however, the reasons were simpler than anyone suspected: there was man hidden in her past, or rather, the fantasy she had built up about a man she had known a long time ago.

It was so stupid. Plunging into depression and insanity all because of a man whose current whereabouts she didn't even know, but with whom she had fallen hopelessly in love in her youth, since, like every normal young girl, Zedka had needed to experience the Impossible Love.

However, unlike her friends, who only dreamed of the Impossible Love, Zedka had decided to go further; she had actually tried to realize that dream. He lived on the other side of the ocean, and she sold everything to go and join him. He was married, but she accepted her role as mistress, plotting secretly to make him her husband. He barely had enough time for himself, but she resigned herself to spending days and nights in a cheap hotel room, waiting for his rare telephone calls.

Despite her determination to put up with everything in the name of love, the relationship did not work out. He never said anything directly, but one day Zedka realized that she was no longer welcome, and she returned to Slovenia.

She spent a few months barely eating and remembering every second they had spent together, reviewing again and again their moments of joy and pleasure in bed, trying to fix on something that would allow her to believe in the future of that relationship. Her friends were worried about the state she was in, but something in Zedka's heart told her it was just a passing phase; personal growth has its price, and she was paying it without complaint. And so it was: One morning she woke up with an immense will to live; for the first time in ages, she ate heartily and then went out and found a job. She found not only a job, but also the attentions of a handsome, intelligent young man, much sought after by other women. A year later she was married to him.

She aroused both the envy and the applause of her girlfriends. The two of them went to live in a comfortable house, with a garden that looked over the river that flows through Ljubljana. They had children and took trips to Austria or Italy during the summer.

When Slovenia decided to separate from Yugoslavia, he was drafted into the army. Zedka was a Serb—that is, the enemy—and her life seemed on the point of collapse. In the ten tense days that followed, with the troops prepared for confrontation, and no one knowing quite what the result of the declaration of independence would be and how much blood would have to be spilled because of it, Zedka realized how much she loved him. She spent the whole time praying to a God who, until then, had seemed remote, but who now seemed her only hope. She promised the saints and angels anything as long as she could have her husband back.

And so it was. He came back, the children were able to go to the school where they taught the Slovene language, and the threat of war shifted to the neighboring republic of Croatia.

Three years had passed. Yugoslavia's war with Croatia moved to Bosnia, and reports began to circulate of massacres committed by the Serbs. Zedka thought it unjust to label a whole nation as criminals because of the folly of a few madmen. Her life took on a meaning she had never expected. She defended her people with pride and courage, writing in newspapers, appearing on television, organizing conferences. None of this bore any fruit, and even today foreigners still believe all the Serbs were responsible for those atrocities, but Zedka knew she had done her duty, and that she could not abandon her brothers and sisters at such a difficult time. She could count on the support of her Slovene husband, of her children, and of people who were not manipulated by the propaganda machines of either side.

One evening, she walked past the statue of Prešeren, the great Slovene poet, and she began to think about his life. When he was thirty-four, he went into a church and saw an adolescent girl, Julia Primic, with whom he fell passionately in love. Like the ancient minstrels, he began to write her poems, in the hope of one day marrying her.

It turned out that Julia was the daughter of an upper middle-class family, and, apart from that chance sighting inside the church, Prešeren never again managed to get near her. But that encounter inspired his finest poetry and created a whole legend around his name. In the small central square of Ljubljana, the statue of the poet stares fixedly at something. If you follow his gaze, you will see, on the other side of the square, the face of a woman carved into the stone of one of the houses. That was where Julia had lived. Even after death Prešeren gazes for all eternity on his Impossible Love.

And what if he had fought a little harder?

Zedka's heart started beating fast. Perhaps it was a presentiment of something bad, an accident involving one of her children. She raced back home only to find them watching television and eating popcorn.

The sadness, however, did not pass. Zedka lay down and slept for nearly twelve hours, and when she woke she didn't feel like getting up. Prešeren's story had brought back to her the image of her lost lover, who had never again contacted her.

And Zedka asked herself: Did I fight hard enough? Should I have accepted my role as mistress, rather than wanting things to go as I expected them to? Did I fight for my first love with the same energy with which I fought for my people?

Zedka persuaded herself that she had, but the sadness would not go away. What once had seemed to her a paradise—the house near the river, the husband whom she loved, the children eating popcorn in front of the television—was gradually transformed into a hell.

Today, after many astral journeys and many encounters with highly evolved beings, Zedka knew that this was all nonsense. She had used her Impossible Love as an excuse, a pretext for breaking the ties with the life she led, which was far from being the life she really expected for herself.

But twelve months earlier, the situation had been quite different: She began frantically looking for that distant lover, she spent a fortune on international phone calls, but he no longer lived in the same city, and it was impossible to find him. She sent letters by express mail, which were always returned. She phoned all his friends, but no one had any idea what had happened to him.

Her husband was completely unaware of what was going on, and that infuriated her, because he should at least have suspected something, made a scene, complained, threatened to put her out in the street. She became convinced that the international telephone operators, the post-man, and all her girlfriends had been bribed by him to pretend indifference. She sold the jewelry that had been given to her when she married and bought a plane ticket to the other side of the ocean, until someone managed to convince her that America was a very large place and there was no point going there if you didn't know quite what you were looking for.

One evening she lay down, suffering for love as she had never suffered before, not even when she had come back to the awful day-to-day life of Ljubljana. She spent that night and the following two days in her room. On the third day her husband—so kind, so concerned about her—called a doctor. Did he really not know that Zedka was trying to get in touch with the other man, to commit adultery, to exchange her life as a respected wife for life as someone's secret mistress, to leave Ljubljana, her home, her children forever?

The doctor arrived. She became hysterical and locked the door, only opening it again when the doctor had left. A week later, she no longer had sufficient strength of will to get out of bed and began to use the bed as a toilet. She did not think anymore; her head was completely taken up by fragmentary memories of the man, who, she was convinced, was also unsuccessfully looking for her.

Her infuriatingly generous husband changed the sheets, smoothed her hair, said that it would all be all right in the end. The children no longer came into her bedroom, not since she had slapped one of them for no reason, and then knelt down, kissed his feet, begging forgiveness, tearing her nightgown into shreds in order to show her despair and repentance.

After another week, in which she spat out the food offered to her, drifted in and out of reality several times, spent whole nights awake and whole days asleep, two men came into her room without knocking. One of them held her down while the other gave her an injection, and she woke up in Villete.

"Depression," she heard the doctor say to her husband. "Sometimes it's provoked by the most banal things, for example, the lack of a chemical substance, serotonin, in the organism."

From the ceiling in the ward, Zedka watched the nurse approaching, syringe in hand. The girl was still standing there, trying to talk to her body, terrified by her vacant gaze. For some moments Zedka considered the possibility of telling her about everything that was happening, but then she changed her mind; people never learn anything by being told; they have to find out for themselves.

T HE NURSE placed the needle in Zedka's arm and injected her with glucose. As if grabbed by an enormous arm, her spirit left the ceiling, sped through a dark tunnel and returned to her body.

"Hello, Veronika."

The girl looked frightened.

"Are you all right?"

"Yes, I'm fine. Fortunately, I've managed to survive this dangerous treatment, but it won't be repeated."

"How do you know? Here no one respects the patient's wishes."

Zedka knew because, during her astral journey, she had gone to Dr. Igor's office.

"I can't explain why, I just know. Do you remember the first question I ever asked you?"

"Yes, you asked me if I knew what being crazy meant."

"Exactly. This time I'm not going to tell you a story. I'll just say that insanity is the inability to communicate your ideas. It's as if you were in a foreign country, able to see and understand everything that's going on around you but incapable of explaining what you need to know or of being helped, because you don't understand the language they speak there."

"We've all felt that."

"And all of us, one way or another, are insane."

Outside the barred window, the sky was thick with stars, and the moon, in its first quarter, was rising behind the mountains. Poets loved the full moon; they wrote thousands of poems about it, but it was the new moon that Veronika loved best because there was still room for it to grow, to expand, to fill the whole of its surface with light before its inevitable decline.

T HAT NIGHT she felt like going over to the piano in the living room, and celebrating that night with a lovely sonata she had learned at school. Looking up at the sky, she had an indescribable sense of well-being, as if the infinite nature of the universe had revealed her own eternity to her. She was separated, however, from her desire by a steel door and a woman who was always, endlessly reading a book. Besides, no one played the piano at that hour of night; she would wake up the whole neighborhood.

Veronika laughed. The "neighborhood" were the wards full of crazy people, and those crazy people were, in turn, full of drugs to make them sleep.

Her sense of well-being continued, though. She got up and went over to Zedka's bed, but she was sound asleep too, perhaps recovering from the horrible experience she had been through.

"Go back to bed," said the nurse. "Good girls should be dreaming of angels or lovers."

"Don't treat me like a child. I'm not some tame madwoman who's afraid of everything; I'm raving, hysterical, I don't even respect my own life, or the lives of others. Anyway, today I feel more vigilant. I've looked at the moon, and I need to talk to someone."

The nurse looked at her, surprised by her reaction.

"Are you afraid of me?" asked Veronika. "In a couple of days' time I'll be dead; what have I got to lose?"

"Why don't you go for a walk, dear, and let me finish my book?"

"Because this is a prison, and there's a prison warden pretending to read a book, just to make others think she's an intelligent woman. The fact is, though, that she's watching every movement in the ward, and she guards the keys to the door as if they were a treasure. It's all in the regulations, and so she must obey them. That way she can pretend to have an authority she doesn't have in her everyday life, with her husband and children."

Veronika was trembling without quite knowing why.

"Keys?" said the nurse. "The door is always open. You don't think I'd stay locked up in here with a load of mental patients, do you?"

What does she mean the door's open? A few days ago I wanted to get out of here, and this woman even went with me to the toilet. What is she talking about?

"Don't take me too seriously," said the nurse. "The fact is we don't need a lot of security here, because of the sedatives we dole out. You're shivering, are you cold?"

"I don't know. I think it must have something to do with my heart."

"If you like, you can go for a walk."

"What I'd really like is to play the piano."

"The living room is quite separate, so your piano playing won't disturb anyone. Do what you like."

Veronika's trembling changed into low, timid, suppressed sobs. She knelt down, laid her head on the woman's lap, and cried and cried.

The nurse put down the book and stroked Veronika's hair, allowing that wave of sadness and tears its natural expression. There they sat for almost half an hour, one crying, the other consoling, though neither knew why or what.

The sobbing finally ceased. The nurse helped her up, took her by the arm, and led her to the door.

"I've got a daughter your age. When you were first admitted, full of drips and tubes, I kept wondering why a pretty young girl, with her whole life ahead of her, should want to kill herself. Then all kinds of rumors started flying around: about the letter that you left behind, which I never believed could be the real motive, and how you didn't have long to live because of some incurable heart problem. I couldn't get the image of my own daughter out of my head: What if she decided to do something like that? Why do certain people try to go against the natural order of things, which is to fight for survival whatever happens?"

"That's why I was crying," said Veronika. "When I took the pills, I wanted to kill someone I hated. I didn't know that other Veronikas existed inside me, Veronikas that I could love."

"What makes a person hate themselves?"

"Cowardice, perhaps. Or the eternal fear of being wrong, of not doing what others expect. A few moments ago I was happy, I forgot I was under sentence of death; then, when I remembered the situation I'm in, I felt frightened."

The nurse opened the door, and Veronika went out.

How could she ask me that? What does she want, to understand why I was crying? Doesn't she realize I'm a perfectly normal person, with the same desires and fears as everyone else, and that a question like that, now that it's all too late, could throw me into panic?

As she was walking down the corridors, lit by the same faint light as in the ward, Veronika realized that it *was* too late: She could no longer control her fear.

I must get a grip on myself. I'm the kind of person who sticks to any decision she makes, who always sees things through.

It's true that in her life she had seen many things through to their ultimate consequences, but only unimportant things, like prolonging a quarrel that could easily have been resolved with an apology, or not phoning a man she was in love with simply because she thought the relationship would lead nowhere. She was intransigent about the easy things, as if trying to prove to herself how strong and indifferent she was, when in fact she was just a fragile woman who had never been an outstanding student, never excelled at school sports, and had never succeeded in keeping the peace at home.

She had overcome her minor defects only to be defeated by matters of fundamental importance. She had managed to appear utterly independent when she was, in fact, desperately in need of company. When she entered a room everyone would turn to look at her, but she almost always ended the night alone, in the convent, watching a TV that she hadn't even bothered to have properly tuned. She gave all her friends the impression that she was a woman to be envied, and she expended most of her energy in trying to behave in accordance with the image she had created of herself.

Because of that she had never had enough energy to be herself, a person who, like everyone else in the world, needed other people in order to be happy. But other people were so difficult. They reacted in unpredictable ways, they surrounded themselves with defensive walls, they behaved just as she did, pretending they didn't care about anything. When someone more open to life appeared, they either rejected them outright or made them suffer, consigning them to being inferior, ingenuous.

She might have impressed a lot of people with her strength and determination, but where had it left her? In the void. Utterly alone. In Villete. In the anteroom of death.

Veronika's remorse over her attempted suicide resurfaced, and she firmly pushed it away again. Now she was feeling something she had never allowed herself to feel: hatred.

Hatred. Something almost as physical as walls, pianos, or nurses. She could almost touch the destructive energy leaking out of her body. She allowed the feeling to emerge, regardless of whether it was good or bad; she was sick of self-control, of masks, of appropriate behavior. Veronika wanted to spend her remaining two or three days of life behaving as inappropriately as she could.

She had begun by slapping an old man in the face, she had burst into tears in front of a nurse; she had refused to be nice and to talk to the others when what she really wanted was to be alone; and now she was free enough to feel hatred, although intelligent enough not to smash everything around her and risk spending what remained of her life under sedation and in a bed in a ward.

At that moment she hated everything: herself, the world, the chair in front of her, the broken radiator in one of the corridors, people who were perfect, criminals. She was in a mental hospital, and so, she could allow herself to feel things that people usually hide. We are all brought up only to love, to accept, to look for ways around things, to avoid conflict. Veronika hated everything, but mainly she hated the way she had lived her life, never bothering to discover the hundreds of other Veronikas who lived inside her and who were interesting, crazy, curious, brave, bold.

Then she started to feel hatred for the person she loved most in the world: her mother. A wonderful wife who worked all day and washed the dishes at night, sacrificing her own life so that her daughter would have a good education, know how to play the piano and the violin, dress like a princess, have the latest sneakers and jeans, while she mended the same old dress she had worn for years.

How can I hate someone who only ever gave me love? thought Veronika, confused, trying to check her feelings. But it was too late; her hatred had been unleashed; she had opened the door to her personal hell.

She hated the love she had been given because it had asked for nothing in return, which was absurd, unreal, against the laws of nature.

That love asking for nothing in return had managed to fill her with guilt, with a desire to fulfill another's expectations, even if that meant giving up everything she had dreamed of for herself. It was a love that for years had tried to hide from her the difficulties and the corruption that existed in the world, ignoring the fact that one day she would have to find this out, and would then be defenseless against them.

And her father? She hated her father too, because, unlike her mother, who worked all the time, he knew how to live; he took her to bars and to the theater, they had fun together; and when he was still young, she had loved him secretly, not the way one loves a father, but as a man. She hated him because he had always been so charming and so open with everyone except her mother, the only person who really deserved such treatment.

She hated everything. The library with its pile of books full of explanations about life; the school that had forced her to spend whole evenings learning algebra, even though she didn't know a single person, apart from teachers and mathematicians, who needed algebra in order to be happy. Why did they make them learn so much algebra or geometry or any of that mountain of other useless things?

Veronika pushed open the door to the living room, went over to the piano, opened the lid, and, summoning up all her strength, pounded on the keys. A mad, cacophonous, jangled chord echoed around the empty room, bounced off the walls, and returned to her in the guise of a shrill sound that seemed to tear at her soul. Yet it was an accurate portrait of her soul at that moment.

She pounded on the keys again, and again the dissonant notes reverberated around her.

"I'm crazy. I'm allowed to do this. I can hate, I can pound away at the piano. Since when have mental patients known how to play notes in the right order?"

She pounded the piano again, once, twice, ten, twenty times, and each time she did it, her hatred seemed to diminish, until it vanished completely.

Then, once more, a deep peace flooded through her and Veronika again looked out at the starry sky and at the new moon, her favorite, filling the room she was in with gentle light. The impression returned of Infinity and Eternity walking hand in hand; you only had to look for one of them—for example, the limitless universe—to feel the presence of the other, Time that never ends, that never passes, that remains in the Present, where all of life's secrets lie. As she had been walking from the ward to that room, she had felt such pure hatred that now she had no more rancor left in her heart. She had finally allowed her negative feelings to surface, feelings that had been repressed for years in her soul. She had actually *felt* them, and they were no longer necessary, they could leave.

(/ (/ (/

She sat on in silence, enjoying the present moment, letting love fill up the empty space left behind by hatred. When she felt the moment had come, she turned to the moon and played a sonata in homage to it, knowing that the moon was listening and would feel proud, and that this would provoke the jealousy of the stars. Then she played music for the stars, for the garden, for the mountains she could not see in the darkness but which she knew were there.

While she was playing that music for the garden, another crazy person appeared: Eduard, a schizophrenic who was beyond all cure. She was not frightened by his presence; on the contrary, she smiled, and to her surprise, he smiled back.

The music could penetrate even his remote world, more distant than the moon itself; it could even perform miracles.

"I must buy a new key ring," thought Dr. Igor, as he opened the door to his small consulting room in Villete. The old one was falling to pieces, and a small decorative metal shield had just fallen to the floor.

D R. IGOR bent down and picked it up. What should he do with that shield bearing the Ljubljana coat of arms? He might as well throw it away, although he could have it mended and ask them to make a new leather strap, or else he could give it to his nephew to play with. Both alternatives seemed equally absurd. A key ring doesn't cost very much, and his nephew had no interest in shields; he spent all his time watching television or playing with electronic toys imported from Italy. Dr. Igor could still not bring himself to throw it out, however, so he put it back in his pocket; he would decide what to do with it later on.

That was why he was the director of the hospital and not a patient, because he thought a lot before making any decisions.

He turned on the light; as winter advanced, dawn came ever later. Dislocation, divorce, and the absence of light were the main reasons for the increase in the number of cases of depression. Dr. Igor was hoping that spring would arrive early and solve half his problems.

He looked at his diary for the day. He needed to find some way to prevent Eduard from dying of hunger; his schizophrenia made him unpredictable, and now he had stopped eating. Dr. Igor had already prescribed intravenous feeding, but he couldn't keep that up for ever. Eduard was a strong young man of twenty-eight, but even with an IV drip, he would eventually waste away, becoming more and more skeletal.

What would Eduard's father think? He was one of the young Slovene republic's best-known ambassadors. He had been one of the people behind the delicate negotiations with Yugoslavia in the early 1990s. He, after all, had managed to work for years for the Belgrade government, surviving his detractors, who accused him of working for the enemy, and he was still in the diplomatic corps, except this time he represented a different country. He was a powerful and influential man, feared by everyone.

Dr. Igor felt momentarily worried, just as before he had been worried about the shield on his key ring, but he immediately dismissed the thought. As far as the ambassador was concerned, it didn't matter whether his son looked well or not; he had no intention of taking him to official functions or having Eduard accompany him to the various places in the world where he was sent as a government representative. Eduard was in Villete, and there he would stay forever, or at least as long as his father continued earning his nice fat salary.

Dr. Igor decided to stop the intravenous feeding and allow Eduard to waste away a little more, until he felt like eating again. If the situation got worse, he would write a report and pass responsibility on to the council of doctors who administered Villete. "The best way to avoid trouble is to share responsibility," his father had taught him. He had been a doctor too, and although he had had various deaths on his hands, he had never had any problem with the authorities.

Once Dr. Igor had ordered Eduard's treatment to stop, he moved on to the next case. According to the report Zedka Mendel had completed her course of treatment and could be allowed to leave. Dr. Igor wanted to see for himself. There was nothing a doctor dreaded more than getting complaints from the families of patients who had been in Villete, which was what nearly always happened, for it was rare for a patient to readjust successfully to normal life after a period spent in a mental hospital.

It wasn't the fault of the hospital, or of any of the hospitals scattered around the world; the problem of readjustment was exactly the same everywhere. Just as prison never corrects the prisoner—it only teaches him to commit more crimes—so hospitals merely got patients used to a completely unreal world, where everything was allowed and where no one had to take responsibility for their actions.

There was only one way out: to discover a cure for insanity. And Dr. Igor has engaged his heart and soul in just that, developing a thesis that would revolutionize the psychiatric world. In mental hospitals, temporary patients who lived alongside incurable patients began a process of social degeneration that, once started, was impossible to stop. Zedka Mendel would come back to the hospital eventually, this time of her own volition, complaining of nonexistent ailments simply in order to be close to people who seemed to understand her better than those in the outside world.

If, however, he could find a way of combatting vitriol, the poison which Dr. Igor believed to be the cause of insanity, his name would go down in history and people would finally know where Slovenia was. That week, he had been given a heaven-sent opportunity in the shape of a would-be suicide; he was not going to lose this opportunity for all the money in the world.

Dr. Igor felt happy. Although he was obliged for economic reasons to accept treatments, like insulin shock for example, that had long ago been condemned by the medical profession, the same economic reasons lay behind Villete's instigation of a new psychiatric treatment. As well as having the time and the staff to carry out his researches into vitriol, he also had the owners' permission to allow the group calling itself the Fraternity to remain in the hospital. The shareholders in the institution tolerated—note that word well, not "encouraged," but "tolerated"—a longer period of internment than was strictly necessary. They argued that, for humanitarian reasons, they should give the recently cured the option of deciding for themselves when would be the best moment for them to rejoin the world, and that had led to a group of people deciding to stay in Villete, as if at a select hotel or a club for those with similar interests and views. Thus Dr. Igor managed to keep the insane and the sane in the same place, allowing the latter to have a positive influence on the former. To prevent things from degenerating and to stop the insane having a negative effect on those who had been cured, every member of the Fraternity had to leave the hospital at least once a day.

Dr. Igor knew that the reasons given by the shareholders for allowing the presence of healthy people in the hospital—"humanitarian reasons" they said—were just an excuse. They were afraid that Ljubljana, Slovenia's small but charming capital, did not have a sufficient number of wealthy crazy people to sustain this expensive, modern building. Besides, the public health system ran a number of first-class mental hospitals of its own, and that left Villete at a disadvantage in the mental health market.

When the shareholders had converted the old barracks into a hospital, their target market had been the men and women likely to be affected by the war with Yugoslavia. The war, however, had been brief. The shareholders had felt certain that war would return, but it didn't.

Moreover, recent research had shown that while wars did have their psychological victims, they were far fewer than, say, the victims of stress, tedium, congenital illness, loneliness, and rejection. When a community had a major problem to face—for example, war, hyperinflation, or plague—there was a slight increase in the number of suicides but a marked decline in cases of depression, paranoia, and psychosis. These returned to their normal levels as soon as that problem had been overcome, indicating, or so Dr. Igor thought, that people only allow themselves the luxury of being insane when they are in a position to do so.

He had before him another recent survey, this time from Canada, the country an American newspaper had recently voted to have the highest standard of living. Dr. Igor read:

According to *Statistics Canada*, 40% of people between 15 and 34, 33% of people between 35 and 54 and 20% of people between 55 and 64 have already had some kind of mental illness. It is thought that one in every five individuals suffers some form of psychiatric disorder and one in every eight Canadians will be hospitalised at least once in their lifetime because of mental disturbances.

They've got a bigger market there than we have, he thought. The happier people can be, the unhappier they are.

Dr. Igor analyzed a few more cases, thinking carefully about those he should share with the council and those he should resolve alone. By the time he had finished, day had broken, and he turned off the light.

He immediately ordered his first appointment to be shown in: the mother of the patient who had tried to commit suicide.

"I'm Veronika's mother. How is my daughter?"

Dr. Igor wondered if he should tell her the truth and save her any unpleasant surprises—after all, he had a daughter with the same name—but he decided it was best to say nothing.

"We don't know yet," he lied. "We need another week."

"I've no idea why Veronika did it," said the woman tearfully. "We've always been loving parents, we sacrificed everything to give her the best possible upbringing. Although my husband and I have had our ups and downs, we've kept the family together, as an example of perseverance in adversity. She's got a good job, she's nice-looking, and yet . . ."

". . . and yet she tried to kill herself," said Dr. Igor. "There's no reason to be surprised; that's the way it is. People just can't cope with happiness. If you like, I could show you the statistics for Canada."

"Canada?"

The woman seemed startled. Dr. Igor saw that he had managed to distract her and went on.

"Look, you haven't come here to find out how your daughter is, but to apologize for the fact that she tried to commit suicide. How old is she?"

"Twenty-four."

"So she's a mature, experienced woman who knows what she wants and is perfectly capable of making her own choices. What has that got to do with your marriage or with the sacrifices that you and your husband made? How long has she lived on her own?"

"Six years."

"You see? She's fundamentally independent. But, because of what a certain Austrian doctor—Dr. Sigmund Freud, I'm sure you've heard of him—wrote about unhealthy relationships between parents and children, people today still blame themselves for everything. Do you imagine that Indians believe that the son-turned-murderer is a victim of his parents' upbringing? Tell me."

"I haven't the faintest idea," replied the woman, who couldn't get over her bewilderment at the doctor's behavior. Perhaps he was influenced by his patients.

"Well, I'll tell you," said Dr. Igor. "The Indians believe the murderer to be guilty, not society, not his parents, not his ancestors. Do the Japanese commit suicide because a son of theirs decides to take drugs and go out and shoot people? The reply is the same: no! And, as we all know, the Japanese will commit suicide at the drop of a hat. The other day I read that a young Japanese man killed himself because he had failed his university entrance exams."

"Do you think I could talk to my daughter?" asked the woman, who was not interested in the Japanese, the Indians, or the Canadians.

"Yes, yes, in a moment," said Dr. Igor, slightly annoyed by the interruption. "But first, I want you to understand one thing: apart from certain grave pathological cases, people only go insane when they try to escape from routine. Do you understand?"

"I do," she replied. "And if you think that I won't be capable of looking after her, you can rest assured, I've *never* tried to change my life."

"Good." Dr. Igor seemed relieved. "Can you imagine a world in which, for example, we were not obliged to repeat the same thing every day of our lives? If, for example, we all decided to eat only when we were hungry, what would housewives and restaurants do?"

It would be more normal to eat only when we were hungry, thought the woman, but she said nothing, afraid that he might not let her speak to Veronika.

"Well, it would cause tremendous confusion," she said at last. "I'm a housewife myself, and I know what I'm talking about."

"So we have breakfast, lunch, and supper. We have to wake up at a certain hour every day and rest once a week. Christmas exists so that we can give each other presents, Easter so that we can spend a few days at the lake. How would you like it if your husband were gripped by a sudden, passionate impulse and decided he wanted to make love in the living room?"

The woman thought: *What is the man talking about? I came here to see my daughter.*

"I would find it very sad," she said, carefully, hoping she was giving the right answer.

"Excellent," roared Dr. Igor. "The bedroom is the correct place for making love. To make love anywhere else would set a bad example and promote the spread of anarchy."

"Can I see my daughter?" said the woman.

Dr. Igor gave up. This peasant would never understand what he was talking about; she wasn't interested in discussing insanity from a philosophical point of view, even though she knew her daughter had made a serious suicide attempt and had been in a coma.

He rang the bell and his secretary appeared.

"Call the young woman who tried to commit suicide," he said. "The one who wrote the letter to the newspapers, saying that she was killing herself in order to put Slovenia on the map."

"I don't want to see her. I've cut all my links with the outside world."

I T H A D been hard to say that in the lounge, with everyone else there. But the nurse hadn't been exactly discreet either, and had announced in a loud voice that her mother was waiting to see her, as if it were a matter of general interest.

She didn't want to see her mother; it would only upset both of them. It was best that her mother should think of her as dead. Veronika had always hated good-byes.

The man disappeared whence he had come, and she went back to looking at the mountains. After a week the sun had finally returned, something she had known would happen the previous night, because the moon had told her while she was playing the piano.

No, that's crazy, I'm losing my grip. Planets don't talk, or only to self-styled astrologers. If the moon spoke to anyone, it was to that schizophrenic.

The very moment she thought this, she noticed a sharp pain in her chest, and her arm went numb. Veronika felt her head spinning. A heart attack!

She entered a kind of euphoric state, as if death had freed her from the fear of dying. So it was all over. She might still experience some pain, but what were five minutes of agony in exchange for an eternity of peace? The only possible response was to close her eyes: In films the thing she most hated to see were dead people with staring eyes.

But the heart attack was different from what she had imagined; her breathing became laboured, and Veronika was horrified to realize that she was about to experience the worst of her fears: suffocation. She was going to die as if she were being buried alive or had suddenly been plunged into the depths of the sea.

She stumbled, fell, felt a sharp blow on her face, continued making heroic efforts to breathe, but the air wouldn't go in. Worst of all, death did not come. She was entirely conscious of what was going on around her, she could still see colors and shapes, although she had difficulty hearing what others were saying; the cries and exclamations seemed distant, as if coming from another world. Apart from this, everything else was real; the air wouldn't enter her lungs, it would simply not obey the commands of her lungs and her muscles, and still she did not lose consciousness.

She felt someone touch her and turn her over, but now she had lost control of her eye movements, and her eyes were flickering wildly, sending hundreds of different images to her brain, combining the feeling of suffocation with a sense of complete visual confusion.

After a while the images became distant too, and just when the agony reached its peak, the air finally rushed into her lungs, making a tremendous noise that left everyone in the room paralyzed with fear.

Veronika began to vomit copiously. Once the near-tragedy had passed, some of the crazy people there began to laugh, and she felt humiliated, lost, paralyzed.

A nurse came running in and gave her an injection in the arm.

"It's all right, calm down, it's over now."

"I didn't die!" she started shouting, crawling toward the other patients, smearing the floor and the furniture with her vomit. "I'm still in this damn hospital, forced to live with you people, living a thousand deaths every day, every night, and not one of you feels an ounce of pity for me."

She turned on the nurse, grabbed the syringe from his hand, and threw it out into the garden.

"And what do you want? Why don't you just inject me with poison, since I'm already condemned to die? How can you be so heartless?"

Unable to control herself any longer, she sat down on the floor again and started crying uncontrollably, shouting, sobbing loudly, while some of the patients laughed and made remarks about her filthy clothes.

"Give her a sedative," said a doctor, hurrying in. "Get this situation under control."

The nurse, however, was frozen to the spot. The doctor went out again and returned with two more male nurses and another syringe. The men grabbed the hysterical girl struggling in the middle of the room, while the doctor injected the last drop of sedative into a vein in her vomit-smeared arm.

She was in Dr. Igor's consulting room, lying on an immaculate white bed with clean sheets on it.

H E WAS listening to her heart. She was pretending that she was still asleep, but something inside her must have changed, judging by the doctor's muttered words:

"Don't you worry. In your state of health, you could live to be a hundred."

Veronika opened her eyes. Someone had taken her clothes off. Who? Dr. Igor? Did that mean he had seen her naked? Her brain wasn't working properly.

"What did you say?"

"I said not to worry."

"No, you said I could live to be a hundred."

The doctor went over to his desk.

"You said I could live to be a hundred," Veronika repeated.

"Nothing is certain in medicine," said Dr. Igor, trying to cover up. "Everything's possible."

"How's my heart?"

"The same."

She didn't need to hear any more. When faced with a serious case, doctors always say: "You'll live to be a hundred," or "There's nothing seriously wrong with you," or "You have the heart and blood pressure of a young girl," or even "We need to redo the tests." They're probably afraid the patient will go berserk in the consulting room.

She tried to get up, but couldn't; the whole room started to spin.

"Just lie down a bit longer, until you feel better. You're not bothering me."

Oh good, thought Veronika. *But what if I were?*

Being an experienced physician, Dr. Igor remained silent for some time, pretending to read the papers on his desk. When we're with other people and they say nothing, the situation becomes irritating, tense, unbearable. Dr. Igor was hoping that the girl would start talking so that he could collect more data for his thesis on insanity and the cure he was developing.

But Veronika didn't say a word. *She may still be suffering from a high level of Vitriol poisoning*, thought Dr. Igor, and decided to break the silence, which was becoming tense, irritating, unbearable.

"So you like to play the piano," he said, trying to sound as nonchalant as possible.

"And the lunatics enjoy it too. Yesterday there was a guy listening who was utterly transfixed."

"Yes, Eduard. He mentioned to someone how much he'd enjoyed it. Who knows, he might start eating normally again."

"A schizophrenic liking music? And he mentioned it to someone else?"

"Yes. And I imagine you have no idea what you're talking about."

That doctor—who looked more like a patient, with his dyed black hair—was right. Veronika had often heard the word "schizophrenic," but she had no idea what it meant.

"Is there a cure, then?" she asked, hoping to find out more about schizophrenics.

"It can be controlled. We still don't really know what goes on in the world of insanity. Everything's still so new, and the treatments change every decade or so. A schizophrenic is a person who already has a natural tendency to absent himself from this world, until some factor, sometimes serious, sometimes superficial, depending on the individual circumstances, forces him to create his own reality. It can develop into a state of complete alienation, what we call catatonia, but people do occasionally recover, at least enough to allow the patient to work and lead a near-normal life. It all depends on one thing: environment."

"You say they create their own reality," said Veronika, "but what is reality?"

"It's whatever the majority deems it to be. It's not necessarily the best or the most logical, but it's the one that supports the desires of society as a whole. You see this thing I've got around my neck?"

"You mean your tie?"

"Exactly. Your answer is the logical, coherent answer an absolutely normal person would give: It's a tie! A lunatic, however, would say that what I have round my neck is a ridiculous, useless bit of colored cloth tied in a very complicated way, which makes it harder to get air into your lungs and difficult to turn your neck. I have to be careful when I'm anywhere near a fan, or I could be strangled by this bit of cloth.

"If a lunatic were to ask me what this tie is for, I would have to say, absolutely nothing. It's not even purely decorative, since nowadays it's become a symbol of slavery, power, aloofness. The only really useful function a tie serves is the sense of relief when you get home and take it off; you feel as if you've freed yourself from something, though quite what you don't know.

"But does that sense of relief justify the existence of ties? No. Nevertheless, if I were to ask a madman and a normal person what this is, the sane person would say: 'A tie.' It doesn't matter who's correct, what matters is who's right."

"So just because I gave the right name to a bit of colored cloth you conclude that I'm not mad."

No, you're not mad, thought Dr. Igor, who was an authority on the subject, with various diplomas hanging on the walls of his consulting room. Attempting to take your own life was something proper to a human being; he knew a lot of people who were doing just that, and yet they lived outside the hospital, feigning innocence and normality, merely because they had not chosen the scandalous route of suicide. They were killing themselves gradually, poisoning themselves with what Dr. Igor called Vitriol.

Vitriol was a toxic substance whose symptoms he had identified in his conversations with the men and women he had met. Now he was writing a thesis on the subject, which he would submit to the Slovenian Academy of Sciences for its scrutiny. It was the most important step in the field of insanity since Dr. Pinel had ordered that patients should be unshackled, astonishing the medical world with the idea that some of them might even be cured.

As with the libido—the chemical reaction responsible for sexual desire, which Dr. Freud had identified, but which no laboratory had ever managed to isolate—Vitriol was released by the human organism whenever a person found him- or herself in a frightening situation, although it had yet to be picked up in any spectrographic tests. It was easily recognized, though, by its taste, which was neither sweet nor savory—a bitter taste. Dr. Igor, the as-yet-unrecognized discoverer of this fatal substance, had given it the name of a poison much favored in the past by emperors, kings, and lovers of all kinds whenever they needed to rid themselves of some obstructive person.

A golden age, the age of kings and emperors, when you could live and die romantically. The murderer would invite his or her victim to partake of a magnificent supper, the servant would pour them drinks served in two exquisite glasses, and one of the drinks would be laced with Vitriol. Imagine the excitement aroused by each gesture the victim made, picking up the glass, saying a few tender or aggressive words, drinking as if the glass contained some delicious beverage, giving his host one last startled look, then falling to the floor.

But this poison, which was now very expensive and difficult to obtain, had been replaced by more reliable methods of extermination—revolvers, bacteria, and so on. Dr. Igor, a natural romantic, had rescued this name from obscurity and given it to the disease of the soul he had managed to diagnose, and whose discovery would soon astonish the world.

It was odd that no one had ever described Vitriol as a mortal poison, although most of the people affected could identify its taste, and they referred to the process of poisoning as bitterness. To a greater or lesser degree, everyone had some bitterness in their organism, just as we are all carriers of the tuberculosis bacillus. But these two illnesses only attack when the patient is debilitated; in the case of bitterness, the right conditions for the disease occur when the person becomes afraid of so-called reality.

Certain people, in their eagerness to construct a world no external threat can penetrate, build exaggeratedly high defenses against the outside world, against new people, new places, different experiences, and leave their inner world stripped bare. It is there that bitterness begins its irrevocable work.

The will was the main target of bitterness (or Vitriol, as Dr. Igor preferred to call it). The people attacked by this malaise began to lose all desire, and, within a few years, they became unable to leave their world, where they had spent enormous reserves of energy constructing high walls in order to make reality what they wanted it to be.

In order to avoid external attack, they had also deliberately limited internal growth. They continued going to work, watching television, having children, complaining about the traffic, but these things happened automatically, unaccompanied by any particular emotion, because, after all, everything was under control.

The great problem with poisoning by bitterness was that the passions—hatred, love, despair, enthusiasm, curiosity—also ceased to manifest themselves. After a while the embittered person felt no desire at all. He or she lacked the will either to live or to die, that was the problem.

That is why embittered people find heroes and madmen a perennial source of fascination, for they have no fear of life or death. Both heroes and madmen are indifferent to danger and will forge ahead regardless of what other people say. The madman committed suicide, the hero offered himself up to martyrdom in the name of a cause, but both would die, and the embittered would spend many nights and days remarking on the absurdity and the glory of both. It was the only moment when the embittered person had the energy to clamber up his defensive walls and peer over at the world outside, but then his hands and feet would grow tired, and he would return to daily life.

The chronically embittered person only noticed his illness once a week, on Sunday afternoons. Then, with no work or routine to relieve the symptoms, he would feel that something was very wrong, since he found the peace of those endless afternoons infernal and felt only a keen sense of constant irritation.

Monday would arrive, however, and the embittered man would immediately forget his symptoms, although he would curse the fact that he never had time to rest and would complain that the weekends always passed far too quickly.

From the social point of view, the only advantage of the disease was that it had become the norm, and internment was no longer necessary except in cases where the poisoning was so severe that the patient's behavior began to affect others. Most embittered people, though, could continue to live outside, constituting no threat to society or to others, since, because of the high walls with which they had surrounded themselves, totally isolated them from the world, even though they appeared to participate in it.

Dr. Sigmund Freud had discovered the libido and a cure for the problems it caused, in the form of psychoanalysis. Apart from discovering the existence of Vitriol, Dr. Igor needed to prove that a cure for it was also possible. He wanted to leave his mark on the history of medicine, although he had no illusions about the difficulties he would face when it came to publishing his ideas, for "normal" people were content with their lives and would never admit to the existence of such an illness, while the "sick" fed a gigantic industry of mental hospitals, laboratories, conferences, and so on.

I know the world will not recognize my efforts, he said to himself, proud of being misunderstood. After all, that was the price every genius had to pay.

"Is anything wrong, doctor?" asked the girl. "You seem to have drifted off into the world of your patients."

Dr. Igor ignored the disrespectful comment.

"You can go now," he said.

Veronika didn't know if it was day or night. Dr. Igor had the light on, but then he did every morning. It was only when she reached the corridor and saw the moon that she realized she had slept far longer than she had thought.

O N T H E way to the ward, she noticed a framed photograph on the wall: It was of the main square in Ljubljana, before the statue of the poet Prešeren had been put up; it showed couples strolling, probably on a Sunday.

She looked at the date on the photograph: the summer of 1910.

The summer of 1910. There were all those people, whose children and grandchildren had already died, frozen in one particular moment of their lives. The women wore voluminous dresses, and the men were all wearing a hat, jacket, gaiters, tie (or "that colored piece of cloth," as the insane call it), and carrying an umbrella under one arm.

And how hot would it have been then? The temperature must have been what it would be today in summer, ninety-five degrees in the shade. If an Englishman turned up in clothing more suited to the heat—in Bermuda shorts and shirtsleeves—what would those people have thought?

"He must be crazy."

She had understood perfectly what Dr. Igor meant, just as she understood that, although she had always felt loved and protected, there had been one missing element that would have transformed that love into a blessing: She should have allowed herself to be a little crazier.

Her parents would still have loved her, but, afraid of hurting them, she had not dared to pay the price of her dream. That dream was now buried in the depths of her memory, although sometimes it was awoken by a concert or by a beautiful record she happened to hear. Whenever that happened, though, the feeling of frustration was so intense that she immediately sent it back to sleep again.

Veronika had known since childhood that her true vocation was to be a pianist.

This was something she had felt ever since her first lesson, at twelve. Her teacher had recognized her talent too and had encouraged her to become a professional. But, whenever she had felt pleased about a competition she had just won and said to her mother that she intended to give up everything and dedicate herself to the piano, her mother would look at her fondly and say: "No one makes a living playing the piano, my love."

"But you were the one who wanted me to have lessons."

"To develop your artistic gifts, that's all. A husband likes that kind of thing in a wife; he can show you off at parties. Forget about being a pianist, and go and study law, that's the profession of the future."

Veronika did as her mother asked, sure that her mother had enough experience of life to understand reality. She finished her studies, went to university, got a good degree, but ended up working as a librarian.

"I should have been crazier." But, as it undoubtedly happens with most people, she had found this out too late.

She was about to continue on her way when someone took her by the arm. The powerful sedative was still flowing in her veins; that's why she didn't react when Eduard, the schizophrenic, delicately began to lead her in a different direction—toward the living room.

The moon was still new, and Veronika had already sat down at the piano—in response to Eduard's silent request—when she heard a voice coming from the refectory, someone speaking with a foreign accent. Veronika could not remember having heard it in Villete before.

"I don't want to play the piano just now, Eduard. I want to know what's going on in the world, what they're talking about over there, who that man is."

Eduard smiled, perhaps not understanding a word she was saying, but she remembered what Dr. Igor had said: Schizophrenics could move in and out of their separate realities.

"I'm going to die," she went on, hoping that her words were making sense to him. "Today death brushed my face with its wing and will probably be knocking at my door if not tomorrow, then soon afterward. It's not a good idea for you to get used to listening to the piano every night.

"No one should let themselves get used to anything, Eduard. Look at me; I was beginning to enjoy the sun again, the mountains, even life's problems, I was beginning to accept that the meaninglessness of life was no one's fault but mine. I wanted to see the main square in Ljubljana again, to feel hatred and love, despair and tedium—all those simple, foolish things that make up everyday life, but that give pleasure to your existence. If one day I could get out of here, I would allow myself to be crazy. Everyone is indeed crazy, but the craziest are the ones who don't know they're crazy; they just keep repeating what others tell them to.

"But none of that's possible, do you see? In the same way, you can't spend the whole day waiting for night to come. Or for one of the patients to play the piano, because soon that will end. My world and yours are about to come to an end."

She got up, tenderly touched the boy's face, and then went to the refectory.

When she opened the door, she came upon an unusual scene; the tables and chairs had been pushed back against the walls, forming a large central space. There, sitting on the floor, were the members of the Fraternity, listening to a man in a suit and tie.

" . . . then they invited Nasrudin, the great master of the Sufi tradition, to give a lecture," he was saying.

When the door opened, everyone in the room looked at Veronika. The man in the suit turned to her.

"Sit down."

She sat down on the floor next to Mari, the white-haired woman who had been so aggressive on their first encounter. To Veronika's surprise, Mari gave her a welcoming smile.

The man in the suit went on: "Nasrudin arranged to give a lecture at two o'clock in the afternoon, and it looked set to be a great success: The thousand seats were completely sold out and more than seven hundred people were left outside, watching the lecture on closed-circuit television.

"At two o'clock precisely an assistant of Nasrudin's came in, saying that, for unavoidable reasons, the lecture would begin late. Some got up indignantly, asked for their money back, and left. Even so a lot of people remained both inside and outside the lecture hall.

"By four in the afternoon, the Sufi master had still not appeared, and people gradually began to leave the place, picking up their money at the box office. The working day was coming to an end; it was time to go home. By six o'clock, the original seventeen hundred spectators had dwindled to less than a hundred.

"At that moment Nasrudin came in. He appeared to be extremely drunk and began to flirt with a beautiful young woman sitting in the front row.

"Astonished, the people who had remained began to feel indignant. How could the man behave like that after making them wait four solid hours? There were some disapproving murmurs, but the Sufi master ignored them. He went on, in a loud voice, to say how sexy the young woman was, and invited her to go with him to France."

Some teacher! thought Veronika. *Just as well I've never believed in such things.*

"After cursing the people who were complaining, Nasrudin tried to get up but fell heavily to the floor. Disgusted, more people decided to leave, saying it was pure charlatanism, that they would denounce the degrading spectacle to the press.

Only nine people remained. As soon as the final group of outraged spectators had left, Nasrudin got up; he was completely sober, his eyes glowed, and he had about him an air of great authority and wisdom. "Those of you who stayed are the ones who will hear me," he said. "You have passed through the two hardest tests on the spiritual road: the patience to wait for the right moment and the courage not to be disappointed with what you encounter. It is you I will teach."

"And Nasrudin shared with them some of the Sufi techniques."

The man paused and took a strange flute out of his pocket.

"Let's take a short break now, and then we'll do our meditation."

The members of the group stood up. Veronika didn't know what to do.

"You get up too," said Mari, grabbing her hand. "We've got a five-minute break."

"I'll leave, I don't want to be in the way."

Mari led her to one corner.

"Haven't you learned anything, not even with the approach of death? Stop thinking all the time that you're in the way, that you're bothering the person next to you. If people don't like it, they can complain. And if they don't have the courage to complain, that's their problem."

"That day, when I came over to you, I was doing something I'd never dared to do before."

"And you allowed yourself to be cowed by a joke made by a lunatic. Why didn't you just stick to your guns? What did you have to lose?"

"My dignity, by being where I wasn't welcome."

"What's dignity? It's wanting everyone to think you're good, well-behaved, full of love for your fellow man. Have some respect for nature, watch a few films about animals, and see how they fight for their own space. We all heartily approved of that slap of yours."

Veronika did not have any more time to spend fighting for space, and so she changed the subject and asked who the man in the suit was.

"You're improving." Mari laughed. "You now ask questions without worrying about whether you're being indiscreet or not. He's a Sufi master."

"What does 'Sufi' mean?"

"Wool."

Veronika didn't understand. Wool?

"Sufism is the spiritual tradition of the dervishes. Its teachers never strive to show how wise they are, and their disciples go into a trance by performing a kind of whirling dance."

"What's the point of that?"

"I'm not quite sure, but our group has resolved to investigate all prohibited experiences. All my life, the government taught us that the only purpose of searching for a spiritual meaning to life was to make people forget about their real problems. Now tell me this: Wouldn't you say that trying to understand life was a real problem?"

Yes, it was, although Veronika wasn't sure any more what the word "real" meant.

The man in the suit—a Sufi master, according to Mari—asked them all to sit in a circle. From a vase he removed all the flowers but one, a single red rose, and this he placed in the center of the group.

"You see how far we've come?" said Veronika to Mari. "Some madman decided it was possible to grow flowers in winter, and nowadays, throughout Europe, we have roses all year round. Do you think even a Sufi master, with all his knowledge, could do that?"

Mari seemed to guess her thoughts.

"Save your criticisms for later."

"I'll try to, although all I have is the present, and a very brief one too, it seems."

"That's all anyone has, and it's always very brief, although, of course, some people believe they have a past where they can accumulate things and a future where they will accumulate still more. By the way, speaking of the present moment, do you masturbate a lot?"

Although still under the effects of the sedative she had been given, Veronika was immediately reminded of the first words she had heard in Villete.

"When I was first brought here and was still full of tubes from the artificial respirator, I clearly heard someone asking me if I wanted to be masturbated. What *is* all that about? Why do you people spend your time thinking about such things?"

"It's the same outside; it's just that here we don't need to hide the fact."

"Was it you who asked me?"

"No, but I think that, as far as pleasure is concerned, you do need to discover how far you can go. Next time, with a little patience, you might be able to take your partner there too, instead of waiting to be guided by him. Even if you have only two days to live, I don't think you should leave this life without knowing how far you can go."

"Only if my partner is the schizophrenic who's right now waiting to hear me play the piano again."

"He's certainly nice looking."

The man in the suit interrupted their conversation with a call for silence. He told everyone to concentrate on the rose and to empty their minds.

"The thoughts will come back, but try to push them to one side. You have two choices: to control your mind or to let your mind control you. You're already familiar with the latter experience, allowing yourself to be swept along by fears, neuroses, insecurity, for we all have self-destructive tendencies.

"Don't confuse insanity with a loss of control. Remember that in the Sufi tradition, the master—Nasrudin—is the one everyone calls the madman. And it is precisely because his fellow citizens consider him insane that Nasrudin can say whatever he thinks and do whatever he wants. So it was with court jesters in the Middle Ages; they could alert the king to dangers that the ministers would not dare to comment on because they were afraid of losing their positions.

"That's how it should be with you; stay insane, but behave like normal people. Run the risk of being different, but learn to do so without attracting attention. Concentrate on this flower and allow the real "I" to reveal itself."

"What is the real "I"?" asked Veronika. Perhaps everyone else there knew, but what did it matter: She must learn to care less about annoying others.

The man seemed surprised by the interruption, but he answered her question.

"It's what you are, not what others make of you."

Veronika decided to do the exercise, concentrating as hard as she could on discovering who she was. During those days in Villete, she had felt things she had never before felt with such intensity—hatred, love, fear, curiosity, a desire to live. Perhaps Mari was right: Did she really know what it meant to have an orgasm? Or had she only gone as far as men had wanted to take her?

The man started playing the flute. Gradually the music calmed her soul, and she managed to concentrate on the rose. It might have been the effect of the sedative, but the fact was that since she had left Dr. Igor's consulting room, she had felt extremely well.

She knew she was going to die soon, why be afraid? It wouldn't help at all, it wouldn't prevent the fatal heart attack; the best plan would be to enjoy the days and hours that remained, doing things she had never done before.

The music was soft, and the dim light in the refectory created an almost religious atmosphere. Religion: Why didn't she try going deep inside herself and see what remained of her beliefs and her faith?

The music, however, was leading her elsewhere: Empty your mind, stop thinking about anything, simply *be*. Veronika gave herself up to the experience; she stared at the rose, saw who she was, liked what she saw, and felt only regret that she had been so hasty.

When the meditation was over and the Sufi master had left, Mari stayed on for a while in the refectory, talking to the other members of the Fraternity. Veronika said she was tired and left at once; after all, the sedative she had been given that morning had been strong enough to knock out a horse, and yet she had still had strength enough to remain awake all that time.

T HAT'S YOUTH for you; it sets its own limits without even asking if the body can take it. Yet the body always does."

Mari wasn't tired; she had slept late, then decided to go for a walk in Ljubljana—Dr. Igor required the members of the Fraternity to leave Villete every day. She had gone to the movies and fallen asleep again in her seat, watching a profoundly boring film about marital conflict. Was there no other subject? Why always repeat the same stories—husband with lover, husband with wife and sick child, husband with wife, lover, and sick child? There were more important things in the world to talk about.

The conversation in the refectory did not last long; the meditation had left the group members feeling relaxed and they were all ready to go back to their wards, except Mari, who instead went out into the garden.

On the way she passed the living room and saw that the young woman had not yet managed to get to bed. She was playing for Eduard the schizophrenic, who had perhaps been waiting all that time by the piano. Like children, the insane will not budge until their desires have been satisfied.

The air was icy. Mari came back in, grabbed a coat and went out again. Outside, far from everyone's eyes, she lit a cigarette. She smoked slowly and guiltlessly, thinking about the young woman, the piano music she could hear, and life outside the walls of Villete, which was becoming unbearably difficult for everyone.

In Mari's view this difficulty was due not to chaos or disorganization or anarchy, but to an excess of order. Society had more and more rules, and laws that contradicted the rules, and new rules that contradicted the laws. People felt too frightened to take even a step outside the invisible regulations that guided everyone's lives.

Mari knew what she was talking about; until her illness had brought her to Villete, she had spent forty years of her life working as a lawyer. She had lost her innocent vision of justice early in her career, and had come to understand that the laws had not been created to resolve problems but in order to prolong quarrels indefinitely.

It was a shame that Allah, Jehovah, God—it didn't matter what name you gave him—did not live in the world today, because if he did, we would still be in paradise, while he would be mired in appeals, requests, demands, injunctions, preliminary verdicts, and would have to justify to innumerable tribunals his decision to expel Adam and

Eve from paradise for breaking an arbitrary rule with no foundation in law: Of the tree of the knowledge of good and evil thou shalt not eat.

If he had not wanted that to happen, why did he put the tree in the middle of the garden and not outside the walls of paradise? If she were called upon to defend the couple, Mari would undoubtedly accuse God of administrative negligence, because, in addition to planting the tree in the wrong place, he had failed to surround it with warnings and barriers, had failed to adopt even minimal security arrangements, and had thus exposed everyone to danger.

Mari could also accuse him of inducement to criminal activity, for he had pointed out to Adam and Eve the exact place where the tree was to be found. If he had said nothing, generation upon generation would have passed on this earth without anyone taking the slightest interest in the forbidden fruit, since the tree was presumably in a forest full of similar trees, and therefore of no particular value.

But God had proceeded quite differently. He had devised a rule and then found a way of persuading someone to break it, merely in order to invent punishment. He knew that Adam and Eve would become bored with perfection and would, sooner or later, test his patience. He set a trap, perhaps because he, Almighty God, was also bored with everything going so smoothly: If Eve had not eaten the apple, nothing of any interest would have happened in the last few billion years.

When the law was broken, God—the omnipotent judge—even pretended to pursue them, as if he did not already know every possible hiding place. With the angels looking on, amused by the game (life must have been very dreary for them since Lucifer left heaven), he began to walk about the garden. Mari thought what a wonderful scene in a suspense movie that episode from the Bible would make: God's footsteps, the couple exchanging frightened glances, the feet suddenly stopping in their hiding place.

"Where art thou?" asked God.

"I heard thy voice in the garden, and I was afraid, because I was naked; and I hid myself," Adam replied, without knowing that by making this statement, he had confessed himself guilty of a crime.

So, by means of a simple trick, pretending not to know where Adam was or why he had run away, God got what he wanted. Even so, in order to leave no doubts among the audience of angels who were intently watching the episode, he decided to go further.

"Who told thee that thou was naked?" said God, knowing that this question could have only one possible response: "Because I ate of the tree of the knowledge of good and evil."

With that question, God demonstrated to his angels that he was a just God, and that his condemnation of the couple was based on solid evidence. From then on, it wasn't a matter of whether it was the woman's fault or of their asking for forgiveness: God needed an example, so that no other being, earthly or heavenly, would ever again dare to go against his decisions.

God expelled the couple, and their children paid for the crime too (as still happens with the children of criminals) and thus the judiciary system was invented: the law, the transgression of the law (no matter how illogical or absurd), judgment (in which the more experienced triumphs over the ingenuous), and punishment.

Since all of humanity was condemned with no right of appeal, humankind decided to create a defense mechanism against the eventuality of God deciding to wield his arbitrary power again. However, millennia of study resulted in so many legal measures that, ultimately, we went too far, and justice became a tangle of clauses, jurisprudence, and contradictory texts that no one could quite understand.

So much so that, when God had a change of heart and sent his Son to save the world, what happened? He fell into the hands of the very justice he had invented.

The tangle of laws created such confusion that the Son ended up nailed to a cross. It was no simple trial; he was passed from Ananias to Caiphas, from the priest to Pilate, who alleged that there were insufficient laws in the Roman code. From Pilate to Herod, who, in turn, alleged that the Jewish code did not permit the death sentence. From Herod back to Pilate again, who, looking for a way out, offered the people a juridical deal: He had the Son beaten and then displayed to the people with his wounds, but it didn't work.

Like prosecutors nowadays Pilate decided to save himself at the expense of the condemned man: he offered to exchange Jesus for Barabbas, knowing that, by then, justice had become a grand spectacle requiring a denouement: the death of the prisoner.

Finally Pilate used the article of law that gave the judge, and not the person being judged, the benefit of the doubt. He washed his hands, which means: "I'm not quite sure either way." It was just another ruse to preserve the Roman juridical system without injuring relations with local magistrates, and even transferring the weight of the decision onto the people, just in case the sentence should cause any problems, and some inspector from the imperial capital came to see for himself what was going on.

Justice. Law. Although both were vital in order to protect the innocent, they did not always work to everyone's liking. Mari was glad to be far from all that confusion, although tonight, listening to the piano, she was not quite so sure that Villete was the right place for her.

"If I were to decide once and for all to leave here, I wouldn't go back to the law. I'm not going to spend my time with crazy people who think they're normal and important, but whose sole function in life is to make everything more difficult for others. I'll be a seamstress, an embroiderer, I'll sell fruit outside the municipal theater. I've already made my contribution to the futile insanity of the law."

In Villete you were allowed to smoke, but not to stub your cigarette out on the lawn. With great pleasure she did what was forbidden, because the great advantage of being there was not having to respect the rules and not even having to put up with any major consequences if you broke them.

She went over to the front gate. The guard—there was always a guard there, after all, that was the law—nodded to her and opened the door.

"I'm not going out," she said.

"Lovely piano music," said the guard. "I've listened to it nearly every night."

"It won't last much longer," she said and walked rapidly away so as not to have to explain.

Mari remembered what she had read in the young girl's eyes the moment she had come into the refectory: fear.

Fear. Veronika might feel insecurity, shyness, shame, constraint, but why fear? That was only justifiable when confronted by a real threat: ferocious animals, armed attackers, earthquakes, but not a group of people gathered together in a refectory.

But human beings are like that, she thought. *We've replaced nearly all our emotions with fear.*

And Mari knew what she was talking about, because that was what had brought her to Villete: panic attacks.

In her room Mari had a veritable library of articles on the subject. Now people talked about it openly, and she had recently seen a German television program in which people discussed their experiences. In that same program, a survey revealed that a significant percentage of the population suffers from panic attacks, although most of those affected tried to hide the symptoms, for fear of being considered insane.

But at the time when Mari had her first attack, none of this was known. *It was absolute hell,* she thought, lighting another cigarette.

The piano was still playing; the girl seemed to have enough energy to play all night.

A lot of the inmates had been affected by the young woman's arrival in the hospital, Mari among them. At first she had tried to avoid her, afraid to awaken the young woman's desire to live; since there was no escape, it was better that she should keep on wanting to die. Dr. Igor had let it be known that, even though she would continue to be given daily injections, her physical condition would visibly deteriorate and there would be no way of saving her.

The inmates had understood the message and kept their distance from the condemned woman. However, without anyone knowing quite why, Veronika had begun fighting for her life, and the only two people who approached her were Zedka, who would be leaving tomorrow and didn't talk that much anyway, and Eduard.

Mari needed to have a word with Eduard; he always respected her opinions. Did he not realize he was drawing Veronika back into the world, and that that was the worst thing he could do to someone with no hope of salvation?

She considered a thousand ways of explaining the situation to him, but all of them would only make him feel guilty, and that she would never do. Mari thought a little and decided to let things run their normal course. She was no longer a lawyer, and she did not want to set a bad example by creating new laws of behavior in a place where anarchy should reign.

But the presence of the young woman had touched a lot of people there, and some were ready to rethink their lives. At one of the meetings with the Fraternity, someone had tried to explain what was happening. Deaths in Villete tended to happen suddenly, without giving anyone time to think about it, or after a long illness, when death is always a blessing.

The young woman's case, though, was dramatic because she was so young and because she now wanted to live again—something they all knew to be impossible. Some people asked themselves, *What if that happened to me? I do have a chance to live. Am I making good use of it?*

Some were not bothered with finding an answer; they had long ago given up and now formed part of a world in which neither life nor death, space or time, existed. Others, however, were being forced to think hard, and Mari was one of them.

Veronika stopped playing for a moment and looked out at Mari in the garden. She was wearing only a light jacket against the cold night air? Did she want to die?

N O, I WAS *the one who wanted to die.*

She turned back to the piano. In the last days of her life, she had finally realized her grand dream: to play with heart and soul, for as long as she wanted and whenever the mood took her. It didn't matter to her that her only audience was a young schizophrenic; he seemed to understand the music, and that was what mattered.

Mari had never wanted to kill herself. On the contrary, five years before, in the same movie theater she had visited today, she had watched, horrified, a film about poverty in El Salvador and thought how important her life was. At that time—with her children grown up and making their way in their own professions—she had decided to give up the tedious, unending job of being a lawyer in order to dedicate the rest of her days to working for some humanitarian organization. The rumors of civil war in the country were growing all the time, but Mari didn't believe them. It was impossible that, at the end of the twentieth century, the European Community would allow a new war at its gates.

O N THE other side of the world, however, there was no shortage of tragedies, and one of those tragedies was El Salvador's, where starving children were forced to live on the streets and turn to prostitution.

"It's terrible," she said to her husband, who was sitting in the seat next to her.

He nodded.

Mari had been putting off the decision for a long time, but perhaps now was the moment to talk to him. They had been given all the good things that life could possibly offer them: a home, work, good children, modest comforts, interests, and culture. Why not do something for others for a change? Mari had contacts in the Red Cross, and she knew that volunteers were desperately needed in many parts of the world.

She was tired of struggling with bureaucracy and law suits, unable to help people who had spent years of their lives trying to resolve problems not of their own making. Working with the Red Cross, though, she would see immediate results.

She decided that, when they left the movie theater, she would invite her husband for a coffee so that they could discuss the idea.

Just as a Salvadoran government official appeared on screen to offer a bored excuse for some new injustice, Mari suddenly noticed her heart beating faster.

She told herself it was nothing. Perhaps the stuffy atmosphere in the movie was getting to her; if the symptoms persisted she would go out to the foyer to get a breath of fresh air.

But events took on their own momentum; her heart began beating faster and faster, and she broke out in a cold sweat.

She felt afraid and tried hard to concentrate on the film, in an attempt to dispel any negative thoughts, but realized she could no longer follow what was happening on the screen. Mari could see the images and the subtitles, but she seemed to have entered a completely different reality, where everything going on around her seemed strange and out of kilter, as if taking place in a world she did not know.

"I don't feel well," she said to her husband.

She had put off making that remark as long as possible, because it meant admitting that there was something wrong, but she could not hold out any longer.

"Let's go outside," he said.

When he took his wife's hand to help her to her feet, he noticed it was ice cold.

"I don't think I can get that far. Please tell me what's happening to me."

Her husband felt afraid too. Sweat was pouring down Mari's face, and there was a strange light in her eyes.

"Keep calm. I'll go out and call a doctor."

She was gripped by despair. What he said made absolute sense, but everything—the theater, the semidarkness, the people sitting side by side staring up at the brilliant screen—all of it seemed so threatening. She was certain she was alive, she could even touch the life around her as if it were something solid. And that had never happened to her before.

"On no account leave me here alone. I'll get up and go out with you, but take it slowly."

They both made their apologies to the people in the same row and began walking to the exit at the back of the cinema. Mari's heart was now beating furiously, and she was certain, absolutely certain, that she would never get out of that place. Everything she did, every gesture she made—placing one foot in front of the other, saying "Excuse me," holding on to her husband's arm, breathing in and out—seemed terrifyingly conscious and deliberate.

She had never felt so frightened in her life. "I'm going to die right here in this movie theater."

And she was convinced that she knew what was happening because, many years before, a friend of hers had died in a movie theater of a cerebral aneurism.

Cerebral aneurisms are like time bombs. They are tiny varicose veins that form along the arteries—like the ballooning you get on worn tires—and they can remain there undetected during a whole lifetime. No one knows they've got an aneurism, unless it's discovered accidentally—for example, after a brain scan carried out for other reasons—or at the moment when it actually ruptures, flooding everything with blood, leaving the person in an immediate state of coma, usually followed by death.

While she was walking down the aisle of the dark theater, Mari remembered the friend she had lost. The strangest thing, though, was the effect this ruptured aneurism was having on her perception. She seemed to have been transported to a different planet, seeing each familiar thing as if for the first time.

And then there was the terrifying, inexplicable fear, the sheer panic of being alone on that other planet: Death.

I must stop thinking. I'll pretend that everything's all right and then everything will be.

She tried to act naturally, and for a few seconds the sense of oddness diminished. The two minutes that elapsed between first feeling the palpitations and reaching the exit with her husband were the most terrifying two minutes of her life.

When they reached the brightly lighted foyer, everything seemed to start up again. The colors were so garish, the noises from the street seemed to rush in on her from all sides, and everything seemed utterly unreal. She started to notice certain details for the first time; for example, the clarity of vision that covers only the small area on which we fix our gaze, while the rest remains completely unfocused.

There was more. She knew that everything she could see around her was just a scene created by electrical impulses inside her brain, using light impulses that passed through a gelatinous organ called the eye.

No, she must stop thinking. That's how she could be brought to sanity.

By then her fear of an aneurism had passed; she had managed to get out of the theater and was still alive. The friend who had died, on the other hand, never even had time to leave her seat.

"I'll call an ambulance," said her husband, when he saw his wife's ashen face and bloodless lips.

"Call a taxi," she said, hearing the sounds leaving her mouth, conscious of the vibration of each vocal cord.

Going to a hospital would mean accepting that she really was seriously ill, and Mari was determined to do her utmost to restore everything to normality.

They left the foyer, and the icy cold air seemed to have a positive effect; Mari recovered some control over herself, although the inexplicable feelings of panic and terror persisted. While her husband was desperately trying to find a taxi, which were scarce at that time of day, she sat down on the curb and tried not to look at her surroundings: the children playing, the buses passing, the music coming from a nearby street fair—all seemed absolutely surreal, frightening, alien.

Finally a taxi appeared.

"To the hospital," said her husband, helping his wife in.

"Please, let's just go home," she said. She didn't want to be in any more strange places; she was desperately in need of familiar, ordinary things that might diminish the fear she was feeling.

While the taxi was driving them home, her heart rate gradually slowed, and her temperature began to return to normal.

"I'm beginning to feel better," she said to her husband. "It must have been something I ate."

When they reached their house, the world again seemed exactly as it had been since her childhood. When she saw her husband go over to the phone, she asked him what he was doing.

"I'm going to call a doctor."

"There's no need. Look at me—I'm fine."

The color had returned to her cheeks, her heart was beating normally, and the uncontrollable fear had vanished.

Mari slept heavily that night and awoke convinced that someone must have put some drug in the coffee they had drunk before they went into the theater. It was a dangerous prank, and she was fully prepared, at the end of the afternoon, to call the prosecutor and go to the bar to try and find the person responsible.

She went to work, read through several pending lawsuits, and tried to occupy herself with various other tasks, for the experience of the previous day had left a residue of fear, and she wanted to prove to herself that it would never happen again.

She discussed the film on El Salvador with one of her colleagues and mentioned in passing that she was fed up with doing the same thing every day: "Perhaps it's time I retired."

"You're one of the best lawyers we've got," said the colleague. "Besides, law is one of the few professions where age is in your favor. Why not take a long vacation instead? I'm sure you'd come back to work with renewed energy."

"I want to do something completely different with my life. I want to have an adventure, help other people, do something I've never done before."

The conversation ended there. She went down to the square, had lunch in a more expensive restaurant than the one she normally went to, and returned to the office early. That moment marked the beginning of her withdrawal.

The rest of the employees had still not come back, and Mari took the opportunity to look over the work still on her desk. She opened the drawer to take out the pencil she always kept in the same place, and she couldn't find it. For a fraction of a second, it occurred to her that her failure to put the pencil back in its proper place was an indication that she was perhaps behaving oddly.

That was enough to make her heart start pounding again, and the terror of the previous night returned in full force.

Mari was frozen to the spot. The sun was coming in through the shutters, lending a brighter, more aggressive tone to everything around her, but she again had the feeling that she was about to die at any minute. It was all so strange; what was she doing in that office?

I don't believe in you, God, but please, help me.

Again she broke out in a cold sweat and realized that she was unable to control her fear. If someone came in at that moment, they would notice her frightened eyes, and she would be lost.

Cold air.

The cold air had made her feel better the previous night, but how could she get as far as the street? Once more she was noticing each detail of what was happening to her—her breathing rate (there were moments when she felt that if she did not make a special effort to inhale and exhale, her body would be incapable of doing so itself), the movement of her head (the images succeeded one another as if there were television cameras whirring inside it), her heart beating faster and faster, her body bathed in a cold, sticky sweat.

And then the terror, an awful, inexplicable fear of doing anything, of taking a single step, of leaving the chair she was sitting in.

It will pass.

It had passed last time, but now she was at work; what could she do? She looked at the clock, and it seemed to her an absurd mechanism, two needles turning on the same axis, indicating a measurement of time that no one had ever explained. Why twelve and not ten, like all our other measurements?

I mustn't think about these things, they make me crazy.

Crazy. Perhaps that was the right word to describe what was wrong with her. Summoning all her willpower, she got to her feet and made her way to the toilets. Fortunately the office was still empty, and, in a minute that seemed to last an eternity, she managed to reach them. She splashed her face with water, and the feeling of strangeness diminished, although the fear remained.

It will pass, she said to herself. *Yesterday it did.*

She remembered that, the day before, the whole thing had lasted about thirty minutes. She locked herself in one of the toilets, sat on the toilet seat, and put her head between her knees. That position, however, seemed only to amplify the sound of her heart beating, and Mari immediately sat up again.

It will pass.

She stayed there, thinking that she no longer knew who she was; that she was hopelessly lost. She heard the sound of people coming in and out of the toilets, faucets being turned on and off, pointless conversations about banal subjects. More than once someone tried to open the door of the cubicle where she was sitting, but she said something in a murmur, and no one insisted. The noise of toilets flushing was like some horrendous force of nature, capable of demolishing an entire building and sweeping everyone down into hell.

But, as she had foreseen, the fear passed, and her heartbeat returned to normal. It was just as well that her secretary was incompetent enough not even to notice her absence, otherwise the whole office would have been in the toilets asking if she was all right.

When she knew that she had regained control of herself, Mari opened the cubicle door, again splashed her face with water for a long time, and went back to the office.

"You haven't got any makeup on," said a trainee. "Do you want to borrow some of mine?"

Mari didn't even bother to reply. She went into the office, picked up her handbag and her personal belongings, and told her secretary that she would be spending the rest of the day at home.

"But you've got loads of appointments," protested her secretary.

"You don't give orders, you receive them. Do exactly as I say, and cancel the appointments."

The secretary stared at this woman with whom she had been working for nearly three years, and who had never once been rude to her before. Something must be seriously wrong with her, perhaps someone had told her that her husband was at home with his lover, and she wanted to catch them *in flagrante*.

She's a good lawyer, she knows what she's doing, said the girl to herself. Doubtless tomorrow she would come and apologize to her.

There was no tomorrow. That night Mari had a long conversation with her husband and described all the symptoms she had experienced. Together they reached the conclusion that the palpitations, the cold sweats, the feelings of displacement, impotence, lack of control, could all be summed up in one word: fear. Together husband and wife pondered what was happening. He thought it might be a brain tumor, but he didn't say anything. She thought she was having premonitions of some terrible event, but she didn't say anything either. They tried to find some common ground for discussion, like logical, reasonable, mature people.

"Perhaps you'd better have some tests done."

Mari agreed, on one condition, that no one, not even their children, should know anything about it.

The next day she applied for and was given thirty days' unpaid leave from the office. Her husband thought of taking her to Austria, where there were many eminent specialists in disorders of the brain, but she refused to leave the house; the attacks were becoming more frequent and lasted longer.

With Mari dosed up on tranquilizers, the two of them managed, with great difficulty, to get as far as a hospital in Ljubljana, where Mari underwent a vast range of tests. Nothing unusual was found, not even an aneurism—a source of consolation to Mari for the rest of her life.

But the panic attacks continued. While her husband did the shopping and the cooking, Mari obsessively cleaned the house every day, just to keep her mind fixed on other things. She started reading all the psychiatry books she could find, only immediately to put them down again because she seemed to recognize her own malaise in each of the illnesses they described.

The worst of it was that, although the attacks were no longer a novelty, she still felt the same intense fear and sense of alienation from reality, the same loss of self-control. In addition, she started to feel guilty about her husband, obliged to do his own job as well as all the housework, cleaning apart.

As time passed, and the situation remained unresolved, Mari began to feel and express a deep irritation. The slightest thing made her lose her temper and start shouting, then sob hysterically.

After her thirty days' leave was over, one of Mari's colleagues turned up at the house. He had phoned every day, but Mari either didn't answer the phone or else asked her husband to say she was busy. That afternoon he simply stood there ringing the bell until she opened the front door.

Mari had had a quiet morning. She made some tea, and they talked about the office, and he asked her when she would be coming back to work.

"Never."

He remembered their conversation about El Salvador.

"You've always worked hard, and you have the right to choose what you want to do," he said, with no rancor in his voice. "But I think that, in cases such as these, work is the best therapy. Do some traveling, see the world, go wherever you think you might be useful, but the doors of the office are always open, awaiting your return."

When she heard this, Mari burst into tears, which she often did now, with great ease.

Her colleague waited for her to calm down. Like a good lawyer, he didn't ask anything; he knew he had a greater chance of getting a reply to his silence than to any question.

And so it was. Mari told him the whole story, from what had happened in the movie theater to her recent hysterical attacks on her husband, who had given her so much support.

"I'm crazy," she said.

"Possibly," he replied, with an all-knowing air, but with real tenderness in his voice. "In that case, you have two options: Either get some treatment or continue being ill."

"There isn't any treatment for what I'm feeling. I'm still in full possession of all my mental faculties, and I'm worried because this situation has gone on now for such a long time. I don't haven't any of the classic symptoms of insanity, like withdrawal from reality, apathy, or uncontrolled aggression—just fear."

"That's what all crazy people say, that they're perfectly normal."

The two of them laughed, and she made more tea. They talked

about the weather, the success of Slovenian independence, the growing tensions between Croatia and Yugoslavia. Mari watched TV all day and was very well informed.

Before saying good-bye, her colleague touched on the subject again.

"They've just opened a new hospital in the city," he said, "backed by foreign money and offering first-class treatment."

"Treatment for what?"

"Imbalances, shall we say. And excessive fear is definitely an imbalance."

Mari promised to think about it, but she still took no real decision. She continued to have panic attacks for another month, until she realized that not only her personal life but her marriage was on the point of collapse. Again she asked for some tranquilizers and again she managed to set foot outside the house, for only the second time in sixty days.

She took a taxi and went to the new hospital. On the way, the driver asked if she was going to visit someone.

"They say it's very comfortable, but apparently they've got some real nutters in there too, and part of the treatment includes electric shocks."

"I'm going to visit someone," said Mari.

It took only an hour of conversation for Mari's two months of suffering to come to an end. The director of the hospital—a tall man with dyed hair, who answered to the name of Dr. Igor—explained that it was merely a panic disorder, a recently recognized illness in the annals of world psychiatry.

"That doesn't mean it's a new illness," he explained, taking care to make himself clear.

"What happens is that the people affected by it tend to hide, afraid they'll be mistaken for lunatics. It's just a chemical imbalance in the body, as is depression."

Dr. Igor wrote her a prescription and told her to go back home.

"I don't want to go back now," said Mari. "Even after all you've told me, I won't have the courage to go out on the street. My marriage has become a hell, and my husband needs time to recover from these months he's spent looking after me."

As always happened in such cases—because the shareholders wanted to keep the hospital working at full capacity—Dr. Igor accepted her as a patient, although making it absolutely clear that it wasn't necessary.

Mari received the necessary medication, along with the appropriate psychiatric treatment, and the symptoms diminished and finally disappeared altogether.

During that time, however, the story of her internment in the hospital went the rounds of the small city of Ljubljana. Her colleague, the same friend who had a cup of tea with her only weeks ago, the companion who shared with her God knows how many moments of joy and trepidation, came to visit her in Villete. He complimented her on her courage in following his advice and getting help, but he then went on to explain the real reason for his visit: "Perhaps it really is time you retired."

Mari knew what lay behind those words; no one was going to entrust their affairs to a lawyer who had been a mental patient.

"You said that work was the best therapy. I need to come back, even if only for a short time."

She waited for a response, but he said nothing. Mari went on: "You were the one who suggested I get treatment. When I was considering retirement, my idea was to leave on a high note, fulfilled, having made a free, spontaneous decision. I don't want to leave my job just like that, defeated. At least give me a chance to win back my self-esteem, and then I'll ask to retire."

The lawyer cleared his throat. "I suggested you get treatment, I didn't say anything about going into hospital."

"But it was a question of survival. I was too afraid to go out into the street; my marriage was falling apart."

Mari knew she was wasting her words. Nothing she could say would persuade him; after all, it was the prestige of the office that was at risk. Even so, she tried once more.

"Inside here, I've lived with two sorts of people: those who have no chance of ever going back into society and those who are completely cured, but who prefer to pretend to be mad rather than face up to life's responsibilities. I want and need to learn to like myself again, I have to convince myself that I'm capable of taking my own decisions. I can't be pushed into decisions not of my own making."

"We're allowed to make a lot of mistakes in our lives," said her colleague, "except the mistake that destroys us."

There was no point in continuing the conversation; in his opinion Mari had committed the fatal error.

Two days later she received a visit from another lawyer, this time from a different practice, her now ex-colleagues' greatest rival. Mari cheered up; perhaps he knew she was free to take up a new post, and there was a chance she could regain her place in the world.

The lawyer came into the visiting room, sat down opposite her, smiled, asked if she was feeling better and then took various papers out of his briefcase.

"I'm here at your husband's request," he said.

"This is an application for divorce. Obviously he'll continue to pay all your hospital bills for as long as you remain in here."

This time Mari did not attempt to argue. She signed everything, even though she knew that, in accordance with the law she had studied and practiced, she could prolong the quarrel indefinitely. She then went straight to see Dr. Igor and told him that her symptoms had returned.

Dr. Igor knew she was lying, but he nevertheless extended her internment for an indefinite period.

Veronika decided she would have to go to bed, but Eduard was still standing by the piano.

I'M TIRED, Eduard. I need to sleep." She would have liked to continue playing for him, dredging up from her anesthetized memory all the sonatas, requiems, and adagios she used to know, because he knew how to admire without appearing to demand anything of her. But her body could take no more.

He was so good-looking. If only he would take one step outside his world and see her as a woman, then her last nights on this earth might be the most beautiful of her entire life: Eduard was the only one capable of understanding that Veronika was an artist. Through the pure emotion of a sonata or a minuet she had forged a bond with this man such as she had never known with anyone else.

Eduard was the ideal man, sensitive, educated; a man who had destroyed an indifferent world in order to recreate it again in his head, this time with new colours, new characters, new stories. And this new world included a woman, a piano and a moon that was continuing to grow.

"I could fall in love right now and give everything I have to you," she said, knowing that he couldn't understand her. "All you ask from me is a little music, but I am much more than I ever thought I was, and I would like to share other things with you that I have only just begun to understand."

Eduard smiled. Had he understood? Veronika felt afraid—all the manuals of good behavior say that you should never speak of love so directly, and never to a man you barely know. But she decided to continue, because she had nothing to lose.

"You're the only man on the face of the earth with whom I could fall in love, Eduard, for the simple reason that, when I die, you will not miss me. I don't know what schizophrenics feel, but I'm sure they never miss anyone.

"Perhaps, to begin with, you'll miss the fact that there's no more night music, but the moon will still rise, there'll be someone willing to play sonatas for you, especially in a hospital, where each and every one of us is a 'lunatic.'"

She didn't quite know what the relationship was between lunatics and the moon, but it must be a strong one, if they used a word like that to describe the insane.

"And I won't miss you either, Eduard, because I will be dead, far from here. And since I'm not afraid of losing you, I don't care what you think or don't think about me. Tonight I played for you like a woman in love. It was wonderful. It was the best moment of my entire life."

She looked at Mari outside in the garden. She remembered her words. And again she looked at the man standing in front of her.

Veronika took off her sweater and moved closer to Eduard. If she was going to do something, let it be now. Mari would put up with the cold out there for a long time, and only then would she come back in.

He stepped back. The question in his eyes was this: When was she going to play the piano again? When would she play a new piece of music to fill his soul with the same color, pain, suffering, and joy of those insane composers who had leapt the generations with their work?

The woman outside told me to masturbate and to find out how far I can go. Can I really go farther than I've ever been before?

She took his hand and tried to pull him toward the sofa, but Eduard politely declined. He preferred to remain standing where he was, beside the piano, waiting patiently for her to play again.

Veronika was disconcerted at first and then realized that she had nothing to lose. She was dead; what was the point of continuing to feed the fears or preconceptions that had always limited her life? She took off her blouse, her trousers, her bra, her panties, and stood before him naked.

Eduard laughed. She didn't know why, she merely noted that he had laughed. Delicately she took his hand and placed it on her genitals; his hand remained there, immobile. Veronika gave up the idea and removed his hand.

Something was exciting her far more than any physical contact with this man: the fact that she could do whatever she wanted, that there were no limits. Apart from the woman outside, who might come back in at any moment, nobody else would be awake.

Her blood began to race, and the cold—which she had felt when she took off her clothes—was fading. Veronika and Eduard were both standing up, face to face, she naked, he fully clothed. Veronika slid her own hand down to her genitals and started to masturbate; she had done it before, either alone or with certain partners, but never in a situation like this, where the man showed no apparent interest in what was happening.

And this was exciting, very exciting. Standing up, legs apart, Veronika was touching her genitals, her breasts, her hair, surrendering herself as she had never done before, not because she wanted to see Eduard leave his distant world, but because this was something she had never experienced before.

She started talking, saying unthinkable things, things that her parents, her friends, her ancestors would have considered absolute filth. Her first orgasm came, and she bit her lips so as not to cry out with pleasure.

Eduard was looking at her. There was a different light in his eyes, as if he understood, even if it was only the energy, heat, sweat, and smell that her body gave off. Veronika was still not satisfied. She knelt down and started masturbating again.

She wanted to die of orgasmic pleasure, thinking about and realizing everything that had always been forbidden to her: she begged him to touch her, to force her, to use her in any way he wanted. She wished Zedka were there too, because a woman knows how to touch another woman's body better than any man, because she already knows all its secrets.

On her knees before Eduard, who remained standing, she felt possessed, touched, and she used coarse words to describe what she wanted him to do to her. Another orgasm came, stronger than ever, as if everything around her were about to explode. She remembered the heart attack she had had that morning, but what did that matter, she would die in one great explosion of pleasure. She was tempted to touch Eduard—he was there before her—but she did not want to risk spoiling the moment. She was going far, very far, just as Mari had said.

She imagined herself both queen and slave, dominatrix and victim. In her imagination she was making love with men of all skin colors—white, black, yellow—with homosexuals and beggars. She was anyone's, and anyone could do anything to her. She had one, two, three orgasms, one after another. She imagined everything she had never imagined before, and she gave herself to all that was most base and most pure. At last, unable to contain herself any longer, she cried out with pleasure, with the pain of all those orgasms, all those men and women who had entered and left her body through the doors of her mind.

She lay down on the ground and stayed there, drenched in sweat, her soul full of peace. She had concealed her hidden desires even from herself, unable to say why, but she needed no answer. It was enough that she had done what she had done. She had surrendered herself.

Gradually the universe returned to its proper place and Veronika stood up. Eduard had not moved in all that time, but there seemed to be something different about him: There was a tenderness in his eyes, a very human tenderness.

It was so good that I can see love in everything, even in the eyes of a schizophrenic.

She was beginning to put her clothes back on when she felt a third presence in the room.

Mari was there. Veronika didn't know when she had come in or what she had heard or seen, but even so she felt no shame or fear. She merely looked at her distantly, as one does at someone who has come too close.

"I did as you suggested," she said. "And I went a long, long way."

Mari said nothing; she had just been reliving certain vital moments of her past life, and she was feeling slightly uneasy. Perhaps it was time to return to the world, to face up to things out there, to say that everyone could be a member of a great Fraternity, even if they had never been in a mental hospital.

Like this young girl, for example, whose only reason for being in Villete was because she had made an attempt on her own life. She had never known panic, depression, mystical visions, psychoses—the limits to which the mind can take us. Although she had known many men, she had never experienced the most hidden part of her own desires, and the result was that half of her life had been unknown to her. If only everyone could know and live with their inner craziness. Would the world be a worse place for it? No, people would be fairer and happier.

"Why did I never do that before?"

"He wants you to play more music," said Mari, looking at Eduard. "I think he deserves it."

"I will, but answer my question first: Why did I never do that before? If I'm free, if I can think whatever I choose to think, why have I always avoided imagining forbidden situations?"

"Forbidden? Listen, I was a lawyer, and I know the law. I was also a Catholic, and I used to know whole sections of the Bible by heart. What do you mean by 'forbidden'?"

Mari went over to her and helped her on with her sweater.

"Look me in the eye, and never forget what I'm about to tell you. There are only two prohibitions, one according to man's law, the other according to God's. Never force a sexual relationship on anyone, because that is considered to be rape. And never have sexual relations with children, because that is the worst of all sins. Apart from that, you're free. There's always someone who wants exactly what you want."

Mari didn't have the patience to teach important things to someone who was about to die. With a smile, she said good night and left the room.

Eduard didn't move; he was waiting for the music. Veronika needed to reward him for the immense pleasure he had given her, merely by staying with her and witnessing her insanity without horror or repulsion. She sat down at the piano and started to play again.

Her soul was light, and not even the fear of death tormented her now. She had experienced what she had always kept hidden from herself. She had experienced the pleasures of virgin and prostitute, of slave and queen, albeit more slave than queen.

That night, as if by a miracle, all the songs she had known returned to her memory, and she played in order to give Eduard as much pleasure as she herself had experienced.

When he turned on the light, Dr. Igor was surprised to see the young woman sitting in the waiting room outside his office.

I T'S STILL very early. And I'm completely booked all day."

"I know it's early," she said. "And the day hasn't yet begun. I just need to talk for a while, only a short while. I need your help."

She had dark shadows under her eyes and her hair was dull, the typical symptoms of someone who has spent the whole night awake.

Dr. Igor decided to show her into his room.

He asked her to sit down while he turned on the light and opened the curtains. It would be dawn in less than an hour, and then he would be able to save on electricity; the shareholders were very tough on expenses, however insignificant.

He glanced rapidly through his diary: Zedka had had her last insulin shock and had reacted positively, that is, she had managed to survive that inhuman treatment. It's just as well, in this particular case, that Dr.

Igor had demanded that the hospital council sign a declaration taking full responsibility for the consequences.

He started reading some reports. Two or three patients had behaved aggressively during the night. Among them, according to the nurses' report, was Eduard. He had gone back to his ward at about four in the morning and had refused to take his sleeping tablets. Dr. Igor would have to act. However liberal Villete might be inside, it was necessary to preserve its image as a harsh, conservative institution.

"I've got something very important to ask you," said Veronika.

But Dr. Igor ignored her. Picking up his stethoscope, he began to listen to her heart and lungs. He tested her reflexes and examined the back of her retina with a small flashlight. He saw that there were now almost no signs of Vitriol poisoning.

He immediately went to the phone and asked the nurse to bring in some medication with a complicated name.

"It seems you didn't have your injection last night," he said.

"But I'm feeling much better."

"I just have to look at your face: dark shadows under the eyes, tiredness, the lack of immediate reflexes. If you want to make the most of the little time left to you, please do as I say."

"That's exactly why I'm here. I want to make the most of that little time, but in my own way. How much time have I actually got?"

Dr. Igor peered at her over the top of his glasses.

"You can tell me," she said. "I'm not afraid or indifferent or anything. I want to live, but I know that's not enough, and I'm resigned to my fate."

"What is it you want, then?"

The nurse came in with the injection. Dr. Igor nodded and the nurse gently rolled up the sleeve of Veronika's sweater.

"How much time have I got left?" said Veronika again, while the nurse gave her the injection.

"Twenty-four hours, perhaps less."

She looked down and bit her lip but managed to maintain her composure.

"I want to ask two favors. First, that you give me some medication, an injection or whatever, so that I can stay awake and enjoy every moment that remains of my life. I'm very tired, but I don't want to sleep. I've got a lot to do, things that I always postponed for some future date, in the days when I thought life would last forever. Things I'd lost interest in, when I started to believe that life wasn't worth living."

"And what's the second favor?"

"I want to leave here so that I can die outside. I need to visit Ljubljana castle. It's always been there, and I've never even had the curiosity to go and see it at close range. I need to talk to the woman who sells chestnuts in winter and flowers in the spring. We passed each other so often, and I never once asked her how she was. And I want to go out without a jacket and walk in the snow, I want to find out what extreme cold feels like, I, who was always so well wrapped up, so afraid of catching a cold.

"In short, Dr. Igor, I want to feel the rain on my face, to smile at any man I feel attracted to, to accept all the coffees men might buy for me. I want to kiss my mother, tell her I love her, weep in her lap, unashamed of showing my feelings, because they were always there even though I hid them.

"I might go into a church and look at those images that never meant anything to me and see if they say something to me now. If an interesting man invites me out to a club, I'll accept, and I'll dance all night until I drop. Then I'll go to bed with him, but not the way I used to go to bed with other men, trying to stay in control, pretending things I didn't feel. I want to give myself to one man, to the city, to life and, finally, to death."

When Veronika had finished speaking, there was a heavy silence. Doctor and patient looked each other in the eye, absorbed, perhaps distracted by all the many possibilities that a mere twenty-four hours could offer.

"I'm going to give you some stimulants, but I don't recommend you take them," Dr. Igor said at last. "They'll keep you awake, but they'll also take away the peace you need in order to experience everything you want to experience."

Veronika was starting to feel ill; whenever she was given that injection, something bad always happened inside her body.

"You're looking very pale. Perhaps you'd better go to bed, and we'll talk again tomorrow."

Once more she felt like crying, but she remained in control.

"There won't be a tomorrow, as you well know. I'm tired, Dr. Igor, very tired. That's why I asked for the tablets. I spent all night awake, half desperate, half resigned. I could succumb to another hysterical attack of fear, as happened yesterday, but what's the point? If I've still got twenty-four hours of life left, and there are so many experiences waiting for me, I decided it would be better to put aside despair.

"Please, Dr. Igor, let me live a little of the time remaining to me, because we both know that tomorrow will be too late."

"Go and sleep," said the doctor, "and come back here at midday. Then we'll speak again."

Veronika saw there was no way out.

"I'll go and sleep and then I'll come back, but could I just talk to you for a few more minutes?"

"It'll have to be a few. I'm very busy today."

"I'll come straight to the point. Last night, for the first time, I masturbated in a completely uninhibited way. I thought all the things I'd never dared to think, I took pleasure in things that before frightened or repelled me."

Dr. Igor assumed his most professional air. He didn't know where this conversation might lead, and he didn't want any problems with his superiors.

"I discovered that I'm a pervert, doctor. I want to know if that played some part in my attempted suicide. There are so many things I didn't know about myself."

I just have to give her an answer, he thought. *There's no need to call in the nurse to witness the conversation, to avoid any future lawsuits for sexual abuse.*

"We all want different things," he replied. "And our partners do too. What's wrong with that?"

"You tell me."

"There's everything wrong with it. Because when everyone dreams, but only a few realize their dreams, that makes cowards of us all."

"Even if those few are right?"

"The person who's right is just the person who's strongest. In this case, paradoxically, it's the cowards who are the brave ones, and they manage to impose their ideas on everyone else."

Dr. Igor didn't want to go any further.

"Now, please, go and rest a little; I have other patients to see. If you do as I say, I'll see what can be done about your second request."

Veronika left the room. The doctor's next patient was Zedka, who was due to be discharged, but Dr. Igor asked her to wait a little; he needed to take a few notes on the conversation he had just had.

In his dissertation about Vitriol, he would have to include a long chapter on sex. After all, so many neuroses and psychoses had their origins in sex. He believed that fantasies were electrical impulses from the brain, which, if not realized, released their energy into other areas.

During his medical studies, Dr. Igor had read an interesting treatise on sexual deviance, sadism, masochism, homosexuality, coprophagy, coprolalia, voyeurism—the list was endless.

At first, he considered these things examples of deviant behavior in a few maladjusted people incapable of having a healthy relationship with their partners. As he advanced in his profession as psychiatrist, however, and talked to his patients, he realized that everyone has an unusual story to tell. His patients would sit down in the comfortable armchair in his office, stare hard at the floor, and begin a long dissertation on what they called "illnesses" (as if he were not the doctor) or perversions (as if he were not the psychiatrist charged with deciding what was and wasn't perverse).

And one by one, these normal people would describe fantasies that were all to be found in that famous treatise on erotic minorities: a book, in fact, that defended the right of everyone to have the orgasm they chose, as long as it did not violate the rights of their partner.

Women who had studied in convent schools dreamed of being sexually humiliated; men in suits and ties, high-ranking civil servants, told him of the fortunes they spent on Rumanian prostitutes just so that they could lick their feet. Boys in love with boys, girls in love with their fellow schoolgirls. Husbands who wanted to watch their wives having sex with strangers, women who masturbated every time they found some hint that their men had committed adultery. Mothers who had to suppress an impulse to give themselves to the first delivery man who rang the doorbell, fathers who recounted secret adventures with the bizarre transvestites who managed to slip through the strict border controls.

And orgies. It seemed that everyone, at least once in their life, wanted to take part in an orgy.

Dr. Igor put down his pen for a moment and thought about himself: What about him? Yes, he would like it too. An orgy, as he imagined it, must be something completely anarchic and joyful, in which the feeling of possession no longer existed, just pleasure and confusion.

Was that one of the main reasons why there were so many people poisoned by bitterness? Marriages restricted to an enforced monogamy, within which, according to studies that Dr. Igor kept safely in his medical library, sexual desire disappeared in the third or fourth year of living together. After that, the wife felt rejected and the man felt trapped, and Vitriol, or bitterness, began to eat away at everything.

People talked more openly to a psychiatrist than they did to a priest because a doctor couldn't threaten them with Hell. During his long career as a psychiatrist, Dr. Igor had heard almost everything they had to tell him.

To *tell* him, for they rarely *did* anything. Even after many years in the profession, he still asked himself why they were so afraid of being different.

When he tried to find out the reason, the most common responses were: "My husband would think I was behaving like a prostitute," or, when it was a man: "My wife deserves my respect."

The conversation usually stopped there. There was no point saying that everyone has a different sexual profile, as individual as their fingerprints; no one wanted to believe that. It was very dangerous being uninhibited in bed; there was always the fear that the other person might still be a slave to their preconceived ideas.

I'm not going to change the world, Dr. Igor thought resignedly, asking the nurse to send in the ex-depressive, Zedka, *but at least I can say what I think in my thesis.*

Eduard saw Veronika leaving Dr. Igor's consulting room and making her way to the ward. He felt like telling her his secrets, opening his heart to her, with the same honesty and freedom with which, the previous night, she had opened her body to him.

It had been one of the severest tests he had been through since he was admitted to Villete as a schizophrenic. But he had managed to resist, and he was pleased, although his desire to return to the world was beginning to unsettle him.

"Everyone knows this young girl isn't going to last until the end of the week. There'd be no point."

Or perhaps, precisely because of that, it would be good to share his story with her. For three years he had spoken only to Mari, and even then he wasn't sure she had entirely understood him; as a mother, she was bound to think his parents were right, that they had just wanted the best for him, that his visions of paradise were the foolish dreams of an adolescent completely out of touch with the real world.

Visions of paradise. That was exactly what had led him down into hell, into endless arguments with his family, into such a powerful feeling of guilt that he had felt incapable of doing anything and had finally sought refuge in another world. If it hadn't been for Mari, he would still be living in that separate reality.

Then Mari had appeared; she had taken care of him and made him feel loved again. Thanks to her, Eduard was still capable of knowing what was going on around him.

A few days ago a young woman the same age as him had sat down at the piano to play the *Moonlight Sonata*. Eduard had once more felt troubled by his visions of paradise and he couldn't have said if it was the fault of the music or the young woman or the moon or the long time he had spent in Villete.

He followed her as far as the women's ward, to find his way barred by a nurse.

"You can't come in here, Eduard. Go into the garden, it's nearly dawn, and it's going to be a lovely day."

Veronika looked back.

"I'm going to sleep for a bit," she said gently. "We'll talk when I wake up."

Veronika didn't know why, but that young man had become part of her world, or the little that remained of it. She was certain that Eduard was capable of understanding her music, of admiring her talent; even if he couldn't utter a word, his eyes said everything, as they did at that moment, at the door of the ward, speaking of things she didn't want to hear about.

Tenderness. Love.

Living with mental patients is fast making me insane. Schizophrenics don't feel things like that, not for other human beings.

Veronika felt like turning back and giving him a kiss, but she didn't; the nurse would see and tell Dr. Igor, and the doctor would certainly not allow a woman who kissed schizophrenics to leave Villete.

Eduard looked at the nurse. His attraction for the young girl was stronger than he had thought, but he had to control himself. He would go and ask Mari's advice, she was the only person with whom he shared his secrets. She would doubtless tell him what he wanted to hear, that in such a case, love was both dangerous and pointless. Mari would ask Eduard to stop being so foolish and to go back to being a normal schizophrenic (and then she would giggle gleefully at her own nonsensical words).

He joined the other inmates in the refectory, ate what he was given, and went outside for the obligatory walk in the garden. While "taking the sun" (on that day the temperature was below zero), he tried to approach Mari, but she looked as if she wanted to be left alone. She didn't need to say anything, Eduard knew enough about solitude to respect other people's needs.

A new inmate came over to Eduard. He obviously didn't know anyone yet.

"God punished humanity," he said. "He punished it with the plague. However, I saw him in my dreams and he asked me to come and save Slovenia."

Eduard started to move away, while the man continued shouting: "Do you think I'm crazy? Then read the Gospels. God sent his only Son and his Son has risen again."

But Eduard couldn't hear him anymore. He was looking at the mountains beyond and wondering what was happening to him. Why did he feel like leaving there if he had finally found the peace he had so longed for? Why risk shaming his parents again, just when all the family problems were resolved? He began to feel agitated, pacing up and down, waiting for Mari to emerge from her silence so that they could talk, but she seemed as remote as ever.

He knew how to escape from Villete. However strict the security might seem, it was actually full of holes, simply because, once people entered Villete, they felt little desire to leave. On the west side there was a wall that could quite easily be scaled since it was full of footholds; anyone who wanted to climb it would soon find himself out in the countryside and, five minutes later, on a road heading north to Croatia. The war was over, brothers were once more brothers, the frontiers were no longer guarded as they had been before; with a little luck he could be in Belgrade in six hours.

Eduard had already been on that road several times, but he had always decided to go back because he had still not received the signal to go forward. Now things were different: The signal had finally come in the form of a young woman with green eyes, brown hair, and the startled look of someone who thinks she knows what she wants.

Eduard thought of climbing the wall there and then, of leaving and never being seen in Slovenia again. But the girl was sleeping and he needed at least to say good-bye to her.

When everyone had finished "taking the sun" and the Fraternity had gathered in the lounge, Eduard joined them.

"What's that lunatic doing here?" asked the oldest member of the group.

"Leave him alone," said Mari. "Anyway, we're crazy too."

They all laughed and started talking about the previous day's lecture. The question was this: Could Sufi meditation really change the world? Theories were put forward, as were suggestions, methodologies, contrary ideas, criticisms of the lecturer, ways of improving what had been tested over many centuries.

Eduard was sick of this kind of discussion. These people locked themselves up in a mental hospital and set about saving the world without actually taking any risks because they knew that, outside, they would be thought ridiculous, even if some of their ideas were very practical. Everyone had their own theory about everything, and they believed that their truth was the only one that mattered. They spent days, nights, weeks, and years talking, never accepting the fact that, good or bad, an idea only exists when someone tries to put it into practice.

What was Sufi meditation? What was God? What was salvation if, that is, the world needed saving? Nothing. If everyone there—and outside Villete too—just lived their lives and let others do the same, God would be in every moment, in every grain of mustard, in the fragment of cloud that is there one moment and gone the next. God was there, and yet people believed they still had to go on looking, because it seemed too simple to accept that life was an act of faith.

He remembered the exercise he had heard the Sufi master teaching while he was waiting for Veronika to come back to the piano: Simply look at a rose. What more was necessary?

Yet even after the experience of that deep meditation, even after having been brought so close to a vision of paradise, there they were, discussing, arguing, criticizing, and constructing theories.

His eyes met Mari's. She looked away, but Eduard was determined to put an end to that situation once and for all; he went over to her and took her by the arm.

"Stop it, Eduard."

He could say: "Come with me." But he didn't want to do so in front of all those people, who would be surprised at his forthright tone. That's why he preferred to kneel down and look beseechingly up at her.

The men and women laughed.

"You've become a saint for him, Mari," someone said. "It must have been yesterday's meditation."

But Eduard's years of silence had taught him to speak with his eyes; he was able to pour all his energies into them. Just as he was absolutely sure that Veronika had understood his tenderness and love, he knew that Mari would understand his despair, because he really needed her.

She resisted a little longer, then she got up and took him by the hand.

"Let's go for a walk," she said. "You're upset."

They went out into the garden again. As soon as they were at a safe distance, certain that no one could hear them, Eduard broke the silence.

"I've been in Villete for years," he said. "I've stopped being an embarrassment to my parents, I've set aside all my ambitions, but still the visions of paradise remain."

"I know," said Mari. "We've often talked about it, and I know what you're leading up to as well: It's time to leave."

Eduard glanced up at the sky; did Mari feel the same?

"And it's because of the girl," said Mari. "We've seen a lot of people die here, always when they least expected it, and usually after they'd entirely given up on life. But this is the first time we've seen it happening to a young, pretty, healthy person with so much to live for. Veronika is the only one who doesn't want to stay in Villete forever. And that makes us ask ourselves: What about us? What are we doing here?"

He nodded.

"Then, last night, I too asked myself what I was doing in this hospital. And I thought how very interesting to be down in the square, at the Three Bridges, in the marketplace opposite the theater, buying apples and talking about the weather. Obviously, I'd be struggling with a lot of other long-forgotten things, like unpaid bills, problems with neighbors, the ironic looks of people who don't understand me, solitude, my children's complaining. But all that is just part of life, I think; and the price you pay for having to deal with those minor problems is far less than the price you pay for not recognizing they're yours. I'm thinking of going over to my ex-husband's tonight, just to say thank you. What do you think?"

"I don't know. Do you think I should go to my parents' house too and say the same thing?"

"Possibly. Basically everything that happens in our life is our fault and ours alone. A lot of people go through the same difficulties we went through, and they react completely differently. We looked for the easiest way out: a separate reality."

Eduard knew that Mari was right.

"I feel like starting to live again, Eduard. I feel like making the mistakes I always wanted to make, but never had the courage to, facing up to the feelings of panic that might well come back, but whose presence will merely weary me, since I know I'm not going to die or faint because of them. I can make new friends and teach them how to be crazy too in order to be wise. I'll tell them not to follow the manual of good behavior but to discover their own lives, desires, adventures, and to *live*. I'll quote from Ecclesiastes to the Catholics, from the Koran to the Muslims, from the Torah to the Jews, from Aristotle to the atheists. I never want to be a lawyer again, but I can use my experience to give lectures about men and women who knew the truth about this existence of ours and whose writings can be summed up in one word: *Live.* If you live, God will live with you. If you refuse to run his risks, he'll retreat to that distant heaven and be merely a subject for philosophical speculation. Everyone knows this, but no one takes the first step, perhaps for fear of being called insane. At least, we haven't got that fear, Eduard. We've already been inmates of Villete."

"The only thing we can't do is run as candidates for president of the republic. The opposition would be sure to probe into our past."

Mari laughed and agreed.

"I'm tired of the life here. I don't know if I'll manage to overcome my fear, but I've had enough of the Fraternity, of this garden, of Villete, of pretending to be crazy."

"If I do it, will you?"

"You won't do it."

"I almost did, just a few moments ago."

"I don't know. I'm tired of all this, but I'm used to it too."

"When I came here, diagnosed as a schizophrenic, you spent days, months, talking to me and treating me as a human being. I was getting used to the life I'd decided to lead, to the other reality I'd created, but you wouldn't let me. I hated you, and now I love you. I want you to leave Villete, Mari, just as I left my separate universe."

Mari moved off without answering.

In the small and never-used library in Villete, Eduard didn't find the Koran or Aristotle or any of the other philosophers Mari had mentioned. He found instead the words of a poet:

> Then I said in my heart, As it happeneth to the fool
> so will it happen even to me. . . .
> Go thy way, eat thy bread with joy,
> and drink thy wine with a merry heart;
> for God hath already accepted thy works.
> Let thy garments be always white;
> and let not thy head lack ointment.
> Live joyfully with the wife whom thou lovest
> all the days of the life of thy vanity,
> which he hath given thee under the sun,
> all the days of thy vanity:
> for that is thy portion in life,
> and in thy labor wherein thou laborest under the sun . . .
> Walk in the ways of thine heart,
> and in the sight of thine eyes:
> but know thou, that for all these things
> God will bring thee into judgment.

"God will bring me into judgment," said Eduard out loud, "and I will say: "For a time in my life I stood looking at the wind, I forgot to sow, I did not live joyfully, I did not even drink the wine offered me. But one day, I judged myself ready, and I went back to work. I told men about my visions of paradise, as did Bosch, Van Gogh, Wagner, Beethoven, Einstein, and other madmen before me." Fine, let him say that I left hospital in order to avoid seeing a young girl dying; she will be there in heaven, and she will intercede for me."

"What are you saying?" said the man in charge of the library.

"I want to leave Villete," said Eduard, in a slightly louder voice than normal. "I've got things to do."

The librarian rang a bell, and a few moments later two nurses appeared.

"I want to leave," said Eduard again, agitated. "I'm fine, just let me talk to Dr. Igor."

But the two men already had hold of him, one on each arm. Eduard tried to free himself from the arms of the nurses, though he knew it was useless.

"You're having a bit of a crisis; now just keep calm," said one of them. "We'll take care of it."

Eduard started to struggle.

"Let me talk to Dr. Igor. I've got a lot to tell him, I'm sure he'll understand."

The men were already dragging him toward the ward.

"Let me go!" he was yelling. "Just let me talk for a minute."

The way to the ward was through the living room, and all the other inmates were gathered there. Eduard was struggling, and things were starting to look ugly.

"Let him go! He's crazy!"

Some laughed, others beat with their hands on chairs and tables.

"This is a mental hospital. No one here is obliged to behave the way you do."

One of the nurses whispered to the other: "We'd better give them a fright, otherwise the situation will get completely out of control."

"There's only one way."

"Dr. Igor won't like it."

"He'll like it even less if this gang of maniacs starts smashing up his beloved hospital."

Veronika woke up with a start, in a cold sweat. There was a terrible noise outside, and she needed silence to go on sleeping. But the racket continued.

Feeling slightly dizzy, she got out of bed and went into the living room, just in time to see Eduard being dragged off, while other nurses were rushing in, wielding syringes.

"What are you doing?" she screamed.

"Veronika!"

The schizophrenic had spoken to her. He had said her name. With a mixture of surprise and shame, she tried to approach, but one of the nurses stopped her.

"What are you doing? I'm not here because I'm crazy. You can't treat me like this."

She managed to push the nurse away, while the other inmates continued to shout and kick up what seemed to her a terrifying din. Should she go and find Dr. Igor and leave there at once?

"Veronika!"

He had said her name again. Making a superhuman effort, Eduard managed to break free from the two male nurses. Instead of running away, though, he stood there, motionless, just as he had the previous night. As if transfixed by a conjuring trick, everyone stopped, waiting for the next move.

One of the nurses came over again, but Eduard looked at him, summoning all his strength.

"I'll go with you. I know where you're taking me, and I know too that you want everyone else to know. Just wait a minute."

The nurse decided it was worth taking the risk; everything after all, seemed to have returned to normal.

"I think . . . I think you're important to me," said Eduard to Veronika.

"You can't speak. You don't live in this world, you don't know that my name's Veronika. You weren't with me last night; please, say you weren't there."

"I was."

She took his hand. The lunatics were shouting, applauding, making obscene remarks.

"Where are they taking you?"

"For some treatment."

"I'll come with you."

"It's not worth it. You'd just be frightened, even if I swear to you that it doesn't hurt, that you don't feel anything. And it's much better than sedatives because you recover your lucidity much more quickly."

Veronika didn't know what he was talking about. She regretted having taken his hand, she wanted to get away from there as soon as possible, to hide her shame, never again to see that man who had witnessed all that was most sordid in her, and who nevertheless continued to treat her with such tenderness.

But again she remembered Mari's words: She didn't need to explain her life to anyone, not even to the young man standing before her.

"I'll come with you."

The nurses thought it might be better like that. The schizophrenic no longer needed to be restrained; he was going of his own free will.

When they reached the ward, Eduard lay down on the bed. There were two other men waiting, with a strange machine and a bag containing strips of cloth.

Eduard turned to Veronika and asked her to sit down on the bed.

"In a few minutes the story will be all round Villete, and people will calm down again, because even the craziest of the insane feel fear. Only someone who has experienced this knows that it isn't as terrible as it seems."

The nurses listened to the conversation and didn't believe a word of what the schizophrenic was saying. It must hurt terribly, but then, who knows what goes on inside the head of a lunatic? The only sensible thing the young man had said was about fear: The story *would* soon be all round Villete and calm would swiftly be restored.

"You lay down too soon," said one of them.

Eduard got up again, and they spread a kind of rubber sheet beneath him.

"Now you can lie down."

He obeyed. He was perfectly calm, as if everything that was happening was absolutely routine.

The nurses tied some of the strips of cloth around Eduard's body and placed a piece of rubber in his mouth.

"It's so that he doesn't accidentally bite his tongue," said one of the men to Veronika, pleased to be able to give some technical information as well as a warning.

They placed the strange machine—not much larger than a shoe box, with a few buttons and three dials on it—on a chair by the bed. Two wires came out of the top part and were connected to what looked like earphones.

One of the nurses placed these "earphones" on Eduard's temples. The other seemed to be regulating the machine, twiddling some knobs, now to the right, now to the left. Although he couldn't speak because of the piece of rubber in his mouth, Eduard kept his eyes fixed on hers and seemed to be saying: "Don't worry, don't be afraid."

"It's set at 130 volts for 0.3 seconds," said the nurse controlling the machine. "Here goes."

He pressed a button and the machine buzzed. At that moment, Eduard's eyes glazed over, his body thrashed about on the bed with such fury that, but for the straps holding him down, he would have broken his spine.

"Stop it!" shouted Veronika.

"We have," said the nurse, removing the "headphones" from Eduard's temples. Even so, Eduard's body continued to writhe, his head rocking from side to side so violently that one of the men had to hold it still. The other nurse put the machine in a bag and sat down to smoke a cigarette.

The scene lasted a matter of moments. Eduard's body seemed to return to normal, but then the spasms recommenced, and the nurse had to redouble his efforts to keep Eduard's head still. After a while the contractions lessened, until they finally stopped altogether. Eduard's eyes were wide open, and one of the nurses closed them, as one does with the dead.

Then he removed the piece of rubber from Eduard's mouth, untied him, and put the strips of cloth in the bag along with the machine.

"The effects of electric shock treatment last about an hour," he said to the girl, who was no longer shouting and who seemed mesmerized by what she was seeing. "It's all right, he'll soon be back to normal, and he'll be calmer too."

As soon as the electric charge took effect, Eduard felt what he had experienced before: His normal vision gradually decreased, as if someone were closing a curtain, until everything disappeared. There was no pain or suffering, but he had seen other people being treated with electric shock, and he knew how awful it looked.

Eduard was at peace now. If, moments before, he had experienced the stirrings of a new emotion in his heart, if he had begun to understand that love was something other than what his parents gave him, the electric shock treatment—or electroconvulsive therapy (ECT), as the specialists preferred to call it—would certainly restore him to normality.

The main effect of ECT was to destroy short-term memory. There would be no nurturing of impossible dreams for Eduard. He could not continue looking forward to a future that did not exist; his thoughts must remain turned toward the past, or he would again begin wanting to return to life.

An hour later Zedka went into the ward, almost empty except for a bed where a young man was lying, and a chair, where a young woman was sitting.

When she got closer she saw that the young woman had been sick again, and that her bent head was lolling slightly to the right.

Zedka turned to call for help, but Veronika looked up.

"It's all right," she said. "I had another attack, but it's over now."

Zedka gently helped her up and led her to the toilet.

"It's a men's toilet," Veronika said.

"Don't worry, there's no one here."

She removed Veronika's filthy sweater, washed it, and placed it on the radiator. Then, she removed her own wool top, and gave it to Veronika.

"Keep it. I only came to say good-bye."

The girl seemed distant, as if she had lost all interest in life. Zedka led her back to the chair where she had been sitting.

"Eduard will wake up soon. He may have difficulty remembering what happened, but his memory will soon come back. Don't be frightened if he doesn't recognize you at first."

"I won't be," said Veronika, "because I don't even recognize myself."

Zedka pulled up a chair and sat down beside her. She had been in Villete so long it would cost her nothing to spend a few minutes longer keeping Veronika company.

"Do you remember when we first met? I told you a story to try to explain that the world is exactly as we see it. Everyone thought the king was mad, because he wanted to impose an order that no longer existed in the minds of his subjects.

"There are things in life, though, which, however we look at them, are valid for everyone. Like love, for example."

Zedka noticed a change in Veronika's eyes. She decided to go on.

"I would say that if someone only has a short time to live and decides to spend that time sitting beside a bed, watching a man sleeping, then that must be love. I'd go even further: if, during that time, that person has a heart attack, but sits on in silence, just so as to remain close to the man, I would say that such love had a lot of potential for growth."

"It might also be despair," said Veronika. "An attempt to prove that, after all, there are no reasons to continue battling away beneath the sun. I can't be in love with a man who lives in another world."

"We all live in our own world. But if you look up at the starry sky, you'll see that all the different worlds up there combine to form constellations, solar systems, galaxies."

Veronika got up and went over to Eduard. Tenderly she smoothed his hair. She was glad to have someone to talk to.

"A long time ago, when I was just a child, and my mother was forcing me to learn the piano, I said to myself that I would only be able to play it well when I was in love. Last night, for the first time in my life, I felt the notes leaving my fingers as if I had no control over what I was doing.

"A force was guiding me, constructing melodies and chords that I never even knew I could play. I gave myself to the piano because I had just given myself to this man, without him even touching a hair o' my head. I was not myself yesterday, not when I gave myself over to sex or when I played the piano. And yet I think I *was* myself." Veronika shook her head. "Nothing I'm saying makes any sense."

Zedka remembered her encounters in space with all those beings floating in different dimensions. She wanted to tell Veronika about it, but was afraid she might just confuse her even more.

"Before you say again that you're going to die, I want to tell you something. There are people who spend their entire lives searching for a moment like the one you had last night, but they never achieve it. That's why, if you were to die now, you would die with your heart full of love."

Zedka got up.

"You've got nothing to lose. Many people don't allow themselves to love, precisely because of that, because there are a lot of things at risk, a lot of future and a lot of past. In your case, there is only the present."

She went over and gave Veronika a kiss.

"If I stay here any longer, I won't leave at all. I'm cured of my depression, but in Villete, I've learned that there are other kinds of insanity. I want to carry those with me and begin to see life with my own eyes.

"When I came here, I was deeply depressed. Now I'm proud to say I'm insane. Outside I'll behave exactly like everyone else. I'll go shopping at the supermarket, I'll exchange trivialities with my friends, I'll waste precious time watching television. But I know that my soul is free and that I can dream and talk with other worlds that, before I came here, I didn't even imagine existed.

"I'm going to allow myself to do a few foolish things, just so that people can say: 'She's just been released from Villete.' But I know that my soul is complete, because my life has meaning. I'll be able to look at a sunset and believe that God is behind it. When someone irritates me, I'll tell them what I think of them, and I won't worry what they think of me, because everyone will say: 'She's just been released from Villete.'

"I'll look at men in the street, right in their eyes, and I won't feel guilty about feeling desired. But immediately after that, I'll go into a shop selling imported goods, buy the best wines my money can buy, and I'll drink that wine with the husband I adore because I want to laugh with him again.

"And, laughing, he'll say: 'You're crazy!' And I'll say: 'Of course I am, I was in Villete, remember! And madness freed me. Now, my dear husband, you must have a vacation every year, and make me climb some dangerous mountains, because I need to run the risk of being alive.'"

"People will say: 'She's just been released from Villete and now she's making her husband crazy too.' And he will realize they're right, and he'll thank God because our marriage is starting all over again and because we're both crazy, like those who first invented love."

Zedka left the ward, humming a tune Veronika had never heard before.

The day had proved exhausting but rewarding. Dr. Igor was trying to maintain the sangfroid and indifference of a scientist, but he could barely control his enthusiasm. The tests he was carrying out to find a cure for vitriol poisoning were yielding surprising results.

Y OU HAVEN'T got an appointment today," he said to Mari, who had come in without knocking.

"It won't take long. I'd just like to ask your opinion about something."

Today everyone just wants to ask my opinion, thought Dr. Igor, remembering the young girl's question about sex.

"Eduard has just been given electric shock treatment."

"Electroconvulsive therapy. Please use the correct name, otherwise it will look as if we're a mere band of barbarians." Dr. Igor tried to hide his surprise, but later he would go and find out who had made that decision. "And if you want my opinion on the subject, I must make it clear that ECT is not used today as it used to be."

"But it's dangerous."

"It used to be *very* dangerous; they didn't know the exact voltage to use, where precisely to place the electrodes, and a lot of people died of brain hemorrhages during treatment. But things have changed. Nowadays ECT is being used with far greater technical precision, and it has the advantage of provoking immediate amnesia, avoiding the chemical poisoning that comes with prolonged use of drugs. Read the psychiatric journals, and don't confuse ECT with the electric shock treatment used by South American torturers. Right; you've heard my opinion. Now I must get back to my work."

Mari didn't move.

"That isn't what I came to ask. I want to know if I can leave."

"You can leave whenever you want and come back whenever you want, because your husband has enough money to keep you in an expensive place like this. Perhaps you should ask me: 'Am I cured?' And my reply will be another question: 'Cured of what?' You'll say: 'Cured of my fear, of my panic attacks.' And I'll say, 'Well, Mari, you haven't actually suffered from that for the last three years.'."

"So I'm cured."

"Of course not. That wasn't what your illness was about. In the thesis I'm writing for the Slovenian Academy of Sciences"—Dr. Igor didn't want to go into any detail about Vitriol—"I'm trying to study so-called normal human behavior. A lot of doctors before me have done similar studies and reached the conclusion that normality is merely a matter of consensus; that is, a lot of people think something is right, and so that thing becomes right.

"Some things are governed by common sense. Putting buttons on the front of a shirt is a matter of logic, since it would be very difficult to button them up at the side, and impossible if they were at the back.

"Other things, however, become fixed because more and more people believe that's the way they should be. I'll give you two examples. Have you ever wondered why the keys on a typewriter are arranged in that particular order?"

"No, I haven't."

"We call it the QWERTY keyboard, because that's the order of the letters on the first row of keys. I once wondered why it was like that, and I found the answer: The first machine was invented by Christopher Sholes, in 1873, to improve on calligraphy, but there was a problem: If a person typed very fast, the keys got stuck together and stopped the machine from working. Then Sholes designed the QWERTY keyboard, *a keyboard that would oblige typists to type more slowly.*"

"I don't believe it."

"But it's true. It so happened that Remington—which made sewing machines as well as guns at the time—used the QWERTY keyboard for its first typewriters. That meant that more people were forced to learn that particular system, and more companies started to make those keyboards, until it became the only available model. To repeat: The keyboard on typewriters and computers was designed so that people would type more slowly, not more quickly, do you understand? If you changed the letters around, you wouldn't find anyone to buy your product."

When she saw a keyboard for the first time, Mari had wondered why the letters weren't in alphabetical order, but she had then promptly forgotten about it. She assumed it was simply the best layout for people to type quickly.

"Have you ever been to Florence?" asked Dr. Igor.

"No."

"You should go there; it's not far, for that is where you will find my second example. In the cathedral in Florence, there's a beautiful clock designed by Paolo Uccello in 1443. Now, the curious thing about this clock is that, although it keeps time like all other clocks, its hands go in the opposite direction to that of normal clocks."

"What's that got to do with my illness?"

"I'm just coming to that. When he made this clock, Paolo Uccello was not trying to be original: The fact is that, at the time, there were clocks like his as well as others with hands that went in the direction we're familiar with now. For some unknown reason, perhaps because the duke had a clock with hands that went in the direction we now think of as the "right" direction, that became the only direction, and Uccello's clock then seemed an aberration, a madness."

Dr. Igor paused, but he knew that Mari was following his reasoning.

"So, let's turn to your illness: Each human being is unique, each with their own qualities, instincts, forms of pleasure, and desire for adventure. However, society always imposes on us a collective way of behaving, and people never stop to wonder why they should behave like that. They just accept it, the way typists accepted the fact that the QWERTY keyboard was the best possible one. Have you ever met anyone in your entire life who asked why the hands of a clock should go in one particular direction and not in the other?"

"No."

"If someone were to ask, the response they'd get would probably be: 'You're crazy.' If they persisted, people would try to come up with a reason, but they'd soon change the subject, because there isn't a reason apart from the one I've just given you. So to go back to your question. What was it again?"

"Am I cured?"

"No. You're someone who is different, but who wants to be the same as everyone else. And that, in my view, is a serious illness."

"Is wanting to be different a serious illness?"

"It is if you force yourself to be the same as everyone else. It causes neuroses, psychoses, and paranoia. It's a distortion of nature, it goes against God's laws, for in all the world's woods and forests, he did not create a single leaf the same as another. But you think it's insane to be different, and that's why you chose to live in Villete, because everyone is different here, and so you appear to be the same as everyone else. Do you understand?"

Mari nodded.

"People go against nature because they lack the courage to be different, and then the organism starts to produce Vitriol, or bitterness, as this poison is more commonly known."

"What's Vitriol?"

Dr. Igor realized he had gone too far and decided to change the subject.

"That doesn't matter. What I mean is this: Everything indicates that you are not cured."

Mari had years of experience in law courts, and she decided to put them into practice right there and then. Her first tactic was to pretend to be in agreement with her adversary, only to draw him immediately into another line of argument.

"I agree. My reason for coming here was very concrete: I was getting panic attacks. My reason for staying was very abstract: I couldn't face the idea of a different way of life, with no job and no husband. I agree with you that I had lost the will to start a new life, a life I would have to get used to all over again. Further, I agree that in a mental hospital, even with its electric shocks—sorry, ECT, as you prefer to call it—rigid timetables, and occasional hysterical outbursts on the part of some inmates, the rules are easier to accept than the rules of a world that, as you say, does everything it can to conform.

"Then last night, I heard a woman playing the piano. She played superbly, in a way I've rarely heard before. As I was listening to the music, I thought of all those who had suffered in order to compose those sonatas, preludes, adagios: How foolish they must have been made to feel when they played their pieces—which were, after all, different—to those who held sway in the world of music then. I thought about the difficulties and humiliations involved in getting someone to fund an orchestra. I thought of the booing public who was not yet used to such harmonies.

"Worse than the composers' suffering, though, was the fact that the girl was playing the music with such soul because she knew she was going to die. And am I not going to die? Where is my soul that I might play the music of my own life with such enthusiasm?"

Dr. Igor was listening in silence. It seemed that all his ideas were beginning to bear fruit, but it was still too early to be sure.

"Where is my soul?" Mari asked again. "In my past. In what I wanted my life to be. I left my soul captive in that moment when I still had a house, a husband, a job I wanted to leave but never had the courage to.

"My soul was in my past. But today it's here, I can feel it again in my body, vibrant with enthusiasm. I don't know what to do. I only know that it's taken me three years to understand that life was pushing me in a direction I didn't want to go in."

"I think I can see some signs of improvement," said Dr. Igor.

"I don't need to ask if I can leave Villete. I can just walk through the door and never come back. But I needed to say all this to someone, and I'm saying it to you: The death of that young girl made me understand my own life."

"I think these signs of improvement are turning into something of a miraculous chain of healing," Dr. Igor said with a laugh. "What do you think you'll do?"

"I'll go to El Salvador and work with children there."

"There's no need to go so far away. Sarajevo is only about two hundred kilometers from here. The war may be over, but the problems continue."

"Then I'll go to Sarajevo."

Dr. Igor took a form from a drawer and carefully filled it in. Then he got up and accompanied Mari to the door.

"Good luck," he said, then immediately went back to his office and closed the door. He tried hard not to grow fond of his patients, but he never succeeded. Mari would be much missed in Villete.

When Eduard opened his eyes, the girl was still there. After his first electric shock sessions, he had had to struggle for a long time to remember what had happened; but then the therapeutic effect of the treatment lay precisely in that artificially induced partial amnesia which allowed the patient to forget the problems troubling him and to regain his calm.

THE MORE FREQUENTLY electric shock treatment was given however, the less enduring its effects; he recognized the girl at once.

"While you were sleeping, you said something about visions of paradise," she said, stroking his hair.

Visions of paradise? Yes, visions of paradise. Eduard looked at her. He wanted to tell her everything.

But at that moment, however, the nurse came in with a syringe.

"You've got to have this now," she said to Veronika. "Dr. Igor's orders."

"I've already had some today, and I don't want any more," she said. "What's more, I've no desire to leave here either. I refuse to obey any orders, any rules, and I won't be forced to do anything."

The nurse seemed used to this kind of reaction.

"Then I'm afraid we'll have to sedate you."

"I need to talk to you," said Eduard. "Have the injection."

Veronika rolled up the sleeve of her sweater, and the nurse injected her with the drug.

"There's a good girl," she said. "Now why don't the two of you leave this gloomy ward and go outside for a walk?"

"You're ashamed of what happened last night," said Eduard, while they were walking in the garden.

"I was, but now I'm proud. I want to know about these visions of paradise, because I came very close to having one myself."

"I need to look further, beyond the buildings of Villete," he said.

"Go on, then."

Eduard looked behind him, not at the walls of the wards or at the garden where the inmates were walking in silence, but at a street in another continent, in a land where it either rained in torrents or not at all.

Eduard could smell that land. It was the dry season; he could feel the dust in his nostrils, and the feeling gave him pleasure, because to smell the earth is to feel alive. He was riding an imported bicycle, he was seventeen, and had just left the American college in Brasília, where all the other diplomats' children studied.

H E HATED Brasília, but he loved the Brazilians. His father had been appointed Yugoslavian ambassador two years before, at a time when no one even dreamed of the violent division of their country. Milosevic was still in power; men and women lived with their differences and tried to find a harmony beyond regional conflicts.

His father's first posting was to Brazil. Eduard dreamed of beaches, carnival, soccer matches, and music, but they ended up in the Brazilian capital, far from the coast—a city created to provide shelter only to politicians, bureaucrats, diplomats, and to their children, who didn't quite know what to do, stuck in the middle of all that.

Eduard hated living there. He spent the day immersed in his studies, trying—but failing—to relate to his classmates, trying—but failing—to work up some interest in cars, the latest sneakers, and designer clothes, the only possible topics of conversation with the other young people.

Now and then, there would be a party, where the boys would get drunk on one side of the room, and the girls would feign indifference on the other. There were always drugs around, and Eduard had already experimented with almost all the possible varieties, not that he could get very excited about any of them; he either got too agitated or too sleepy and immediately lost interest in what was going on around him.

His family was concerned. They had to prepare him to follow in his father's footsteps, and although Eduard had almost all the necessary talents, a desire to study, good artistic taste, a facility with languages, an interest in politics, he lacked one essential quality for a diplomat: He found it difficult to talk to other people.

His parents took him to parties, told him to invite his school friends home and gave him a generous allowance, but Eduard rarely turned up with anyone. One day his mother asked him why he didn't bring his friends to lunch or supper.

"I know every brand of sneakers and I know the names of all the girls who are easy to get into bed. After that there's nothing left to talk to them about."

Then the Brazilian girl appeared on the scene. The ambassador and his wife felt better when their son began going out on dates and coming home late. No one knew exactly where she had come from, but one night, Eduard invited her home to supper. She was a well-brought-up girl, and his parents felt content; the boy had finally started to develop his talent for relating to other people. Moreover, they both thought—though neither actually said anything—that the girl's existence removed one great worry from their minds: Eduard clearly wasn't homosexual.

They treated Maria (that was her name) with all the consideration of future in-laws, even though they knew that in two years' time they would be transferred to another post, and they had not the slightest intention of letting their son marry someone from an exotic country. They had plans for him to meet a girl from a good family in France or Germany, who could be a dignified companion in the brilliant diplomatic career the ambassador was preparing for him.

Eduard, however, seemed more and more in love. Concerned, his mother went to talk to her husband.

"The art of diplomacy consists in keeping your opponent waiting," said the ambassador. "While you may never get over a first love affair, it always ends."

But Eduard seemed to have changed completely. He started bringing strange books home, he built a pyramid in his room, and, together with Maria, burned incense every night and spent hours staring at a strange design pinned to the wall. Eduard's marks at school began to get worse.

The mother didn't understand Portuguese, but she could see the book covers: crosses, bonfires, hanged witches, exotic symbols.

"Our son is reading some dangerous stuff."

"Dangerous? What's happening in the Balkans is dangerous," said the ambassador. "There are rumors that Slovenia wants independence, and that could lead us into war."

The mother, however, didn't care about politics; she wanted to know what was happening to her son.

"What about this mania for burning incense?"

"It's to disguise the smell of marijuana," said the ambassador. "Our son has had an excellent education; he can't possibly believe that those perfumed sticks draw down the spirits."

"My son involved in drugs?"

"It happens. I smoked marijuana too when I was young; people soon get bored with it. I did."

His wife felt proud and reassured. Her husband was an experienced man, he had entered the world of drugs and emerged unscathed. A man with such strength of will could control any situation.

One day Eduard asked if he could have a bicycle.

"We've got a chauffeur and a Mercedes Benz. Why do you want a bicycle?"

"To be more in touch with nature. Maria and I are going on a ten-day trip," he said. "There's a place near here with huge deposits of crystal, and Maria says they give off really positive energy."

His father and mother had been brought up under a Communist regime. To them crystals were merely a mineral product composed of certain atoms, and did not give off any kind of energy, either positive or negative. They did some research and discovered that these ideas about "crystal vibrations" were beginning to be fashionable.

If their son started talking about such things at official parties, he could appear ridiculous in the eyes of others. For the first time the ambassador acknowledged that the situation was becoming serious. Brasília was a city that lived on rumors, and as soon as his rivals at the embassy learned that Eduard believed in these primitive superstitions, they might think he had picked them up from his parents, and diplomacy, as well as being the art of waiting, was also the art of keeping up a façade of normality whatever the circumstances.

"My boy, this can't go on," said his father. "I have friends in the Foreign Office in Yugoslavia. You have a brilliant career as a diplomat ahead of you, and you've got to learn to face reality."

Eduard left the house and didn't come back that night. His parents phoned Maria's house, as well as all the mortuaries and hospitals in the city, to no avail. The mother lost her confidence in her husband's abilities as head of the family, however good he might be at negotiating with complete strangers.

The following day Eduard turned up, hungry and sleepy. He ate and went to his room, lit his incense sticks, said his mantras, and slept for the rest of that evening and night. When he woke up, a brand new bicycle was waiting for him.

"Go and see your crystals," said his mother. "I'll explain to your father."

And so, on that dry, dusty afternoon, Eduard cycled happily over to Maria's house. The city was so well designed (in the architects' opinion) or so badly designed (in Eduard's opinion), that there were almost no corners; he just kept straight on down a high speed lane, looking up at the sky full of rainless clouds, then he felt himself rising up at a tremendous speed toward the sky, only to plummet down again and land on the asphalt. Crash!

I've had an accident.

He tried to turn over, because his face was pressed against the asphalt, and realized he had no control over his own body. He heard the noise of cars braking, people talking in alarmed voices, someone approaching and trying to touch him, then a shout: "Don't move him! If anyone moves him, he could be crippled for life!"

The seconds passed slowly, and Eduard began to feel afraid. Unlike his parents, he believed in God and in the afterlife, but even so, it seemed grossly unfair to die at seventeen, staring at the asphalt, in a land not his own.

"Are you all right?" he heard someone say.

No, he wasn't all right; he couldn't move, but he couldn't say anything either. The worst thing was that he didn't lose consciousness; he knew exactly what was happening and what his situation was. Why didn't he faint? At precisely the moment when he was looking for God with such intensity, despite everything and everyone, God had no pity on him.

"The doctors are on their way," someone whispered to him, clutching his hand. "I don't know if you can hear me, but keep calm. It's nothing serious."

Yes, he could hear, he would have liked that person—a man—to keep on talking, to promise him that it was nothing serious, even though he was old enough to know that people only say that when the situation is very serious indeed. He thought about Maria, about the place where there were mountains of crystals full of positive energy, unlike Brasília, which had the highest concentration of negativity he had ever encountered in his meditations.

The seconds became minutes, people continued trying to comfort him, and for the first time since it all happened, he began to feel pain. A sharp pain that came from the center of his head and seemed to spread throughout his entire body.

"They're here," said the man who was holding his hand. "Tomorrow you'll be riding your bike again."

But the following day Eduard was in the hospital, with both his legs and one arm in casts, unable to leave for at least a month, and having to listen to his mother's nonstop sobbing, his father's anxious phone calls, and the doctor's reassurances, reiterated every five minutes, that the crucial twenty-four-hour period had passed, and there was no injury to the brain.

The family phoned the American Embassy, which never believed the diagnoses of the state hospitals and had its own sophisticated emergency service, along with a list of Brazilian doctors it considered capable of attending its own diplomats. Now and then, as part of a "good neighbor policy," it allowed these services to be used by other diplomats.

The Americans brought along their state-of-the-art machines, carried out a further barrage of tests and examinations, and reached the conclusion they always reach: The doctors in the state hospital had correctly evaluated the injuries and had taken the right decisions.

The doctors in the state hospital may have been good, but the programs on Brazilian television were as awful as they are anywhere else in the world, and Eduard had little to do. Maria's visits to the hospital become more and more infrequent; perhaps she had found someone else to go with her to the crystal mountains.

In contrast to his girlfriend's erratic behavior, the ambassador and his wife went to see him every day but refused to bring him the Portuguese books he had at home on the pretext that his father would soon be transferred; so there was no need to learn a language he would never have to use again. Eduard therefore contented himself with talking to the other patients, discussing football with the nurses, and devouring any magazines that fell into his hands.

Then one day a nurse brought him a book he had just been given, but that he judged "much too fat to actually read." And that was the moment that Eduard's life began to set him on a strange path, one that would lead him to Villete and to his withdrawal from reality, and that would distance him completely from all the things other boys his age would get up to in the years that followed.

The book was about visionaries whose ideas had shaken the world, people with their own vision of an earthly paradise, people who had spent their lives sharing their ideas with others. Jesus Christ was there, but so was Darwin and his theory that man was descended from the apes; Freud, affirming the importance of dreams; Columbus, pawning the queen's jewels in order to set off in search of a new continent; Marx, with his belief that everyone deserved the same opportunities.

And there were saints too, like Ignatius Loyola, a Basque soldier who had slept with many women and killed many enemies in numerous battles, until he was wounded at Pamplona and came to understand the universe from the bed where he lay convalescing. Teresa of Ávila, who wanted somehow to find a path to God, and who stumbled across it when she happened to walk down a corridor and pause to look at a painting. Anthony, who, weary of the life he was leading, decided to go into exile in the desert, where he spent ten years in the company of demons and was racked by every conceivable temptation. Francis of Assisi, a young man like himself, who was determined to talk to the birds and to turn his back on everything that his parents had planned for his life.

Having nothing better to do, he began to read the "fat book" that very afternoon. In the middle of the night, a nurse came in, asking if he needed help, since his was the only room with the light still on. Eduard waved her away, without even looking up from the book.

The men and women who shook the world were ordinary men and women, like him, like his father, like the girlfriend he knew he was losing. They were full of the same doubts and anxieties that all human beings experienced in their daily routine. They were people who had no special interest in religion or God, in expanding their minds or reaching a new level of consciousness, until one day they simply decided to change everything. The most interesting thing about the book was that it told how, in each of those lives, there was a single magical moment that made them set off in search of their own vision of Paradise.

They were people who had not allowed their lives to pass by unmarked, and who, to achieve what they wanted, had begged for alms or courted kings, used diplomacy or force, flouted laws or faced the wrath of the powers-that-be, but who had never given up, and were always able to see the advantages in any difficulty that presented itself.

The following day, Eduard handed over his gold watch to the nurse who had given him the book, and asked him to sell it, and, with the money, to buy all the books he could find on the same subject. There weren't any more. He tried reading the biographies of some of those visionaries, but they were always described as if they were someone chosen, inspired, and not an ordinary person who, like everyone else, had to fight to be allowed to say what he thought.

Eduard was so impressed by what he had read, that he seriously considered becoming a saint and using the accident as an opportunity to change the direction of his life. But he had two broken legs, he had not had a single vision while in hospital, he hadn't stopped by a painting that shook him to his very soul, he had no friends who would build him a chapel in the middle of the Brazilian plateau, and the deserts were all far away and bristling with political problems. There was, however, something he could do: he could learn to paint and try to show the world the visions those men and women had experienced.

When they removed the casts and he went back to the embassy, surrounded by all the care, kindness, and attention that the son of an ambassador could hope for from other diplomats, he asked his mother if he could enroll in a painting course.

His mother said that he had already missed a lot of classes at the American school and that he would have to make up for lost time. Eduard refused. He did not have the slightest desire to go on learning about geography and sciences; he wanted to be a painter. In an unguarded moment, he explained why:

"I want to paint visions of paradise."

His mother said nothing but promised to talk to her women friends and ascertain which was the best painting course available in the city.

When the ambassador came back from work that evening, he found her crying in her bedroom.

"Our son is insane," she said, her face streaming with tears. "The accident has affected his brain."

"Impossible!" the ambassador replied, indignant. "He was examined by doctors especially selected by the Americans."

His wife told him what her son had said.

"It's just youthful rebelliousness. Just you wait; everything will go back to normal, you'll see."

But this time waiting did no good at all, because Eduard was in a hurry to start living. Two days later, tired of marking time while his mother's friends deliberated, he decided to enroll himself in an art course. He started learning about color and perspective, but he also got to know people who never talked about sneakers or makes of car.

"He's living with artists!" said his mother tearfully to the ambassador.

"Oh, leave the boy alone," said the ambassador. "He'll soon get sick of it, like he did of his girlfriend, like he did of crystals, pyramids, incense, and marijuana."

But time passed, and Eduard's room became an improvised studio, full of paintings that made no sense at all to his parents: circles, exotic color combinations and primitive symbols all mixed up with people in attitudes of prayer.

Eduard, the solitary boy, who in his two years in Brazil had never once brought friends home, was now filling the house with strange people, all of them badly dressed and with untidy hair, who listened to horrible music at full blast—endlessly drinking and smoking and showing a complete disregard for basic good manners. One day the director of the American school called his mother.

"I think your son must be involved in drugs," she said. "His school marks are well below average, and if he goes on like this, we won't be able to renew his enrollment."

His mother went straight to the ambassador's office and told him what the director had said.

"You keep saying that with time, everything will go back to normal!" she screamed hysterically. "There's your crazy, drug-addict son, obviously suffering from some serious brain injury, and all you care about are cocktail parties and social gatherings."

"Keep your voice down," he said.

"No, I won't, and I never will again if you don't do something. The boy needs help, don't you see? Medical help. Do something!"

Concerned that the scene his wife was making might embarrass him in front of his staff, and worried that Eduard's interest in painting was lasting longer than expected, the ambassador, a practical man, who knew all the correct procedures, drew up a plan of attack.

First he phoned his colleague the American ambassador and asked politely if he could again make use of the embassy's medical facilities. His request was granted.

He went back to the accredited doctors, explained the situation, and asked them to go over all the tests they had made at the time. The doctors, fearing a lawsuit, did exactly as they were asked and concluded that the tests revealed nothing abnormal. Before the ambassador left they demanded that he sign a document exempting the American Embassy from any responsibility for sending him to them.

The ambassador immediately went to the hospital where Eduard had been a patient. He talked to the director, explained his son's problem, and asked that, under the pretext of a routine checkup, a blood test be done to see if there were any drugs in the boy's system.

They did a blood test, and no trace of drugs was found.

There remained the third and final stage of his strategy: talking to Eduard himself and finding out what was going on. Only when he was in possession of all the facts could he hope to make the correct decision.

Father and son sat down in the living room.

"Your mother's very worried about you," said the ambassador. "Your marks have gotten worse, and there's a danger that your place at the school won't be renewed."

"But my marks at art school have improved, Dad."

"I find your interest in art very pleasing, but you have your whole life ahead of you to do that. At the moment the main thing is to finish your secondary education, so that I can set you on the path to a diplomatic career."

Eduard thought long and hard before saying anything. He thought about the accident, about the book on visionaries, which had turned out to be only a pretext for finding his true vocation, and he thought about Maria, from whom he had never heard again. He hesitated for some time, but in the end, said: "Dad, I don't want to be a diplomat. I want to be a painter."

His father was prepared for that response and knew how to get round it.

"You will be a painter, but first finish your studies. We'll arrange for exhibitions in Belgrade, Zagreb, Ljubljana, and Sarajevo. I've got influence, I can help you a lot, but you must complete your studies."

"If I do that, I'll be choosing the easy route. I'll enter some faculty or other, get a degree in a subject that doesn't interest me but that will help me earn a living. Painting will just recede into the background, and I'll end up forgetting my vocation. I'll just have to find a way of earning money through my painting."

The ambassador was starting to get irritated.

"You've got everything, son, a family that loves you, a house, money, social position—but as you know, our country is going through a difficult time, there are rumors of civil war. Tomorrow I might not even be here to help you."

"I can help myself. Trust me. One day I'll paint a series entitled Visions of Paradise. It'll be a visual history of what men and women have previously experienced only in their hearts."

The ambassador praised his son's determination, drew the conversation to a close with a smile, and decided to give him another month; after all, diplomacy is also the art of postponing decisions until the problems resolve themselves.

A month passed, and Eduard continued to devote all his time to painting, to his strange friends and to that music apparently expressly designed to induce some psychological disorder. To make matters worse, he had been expelled from the American school for arguing with a teacher about the existence of saints.

Since the decision could be put off no longer, the ambassador made one last attempt and called his son in for a man-to-man talk.

"Eduard, you are now of an age to take responsibility for your own life. We've put up with this for as long as we could, but now you've got to forget all this nonsense about becoming a painter and give some direction to your career."

"But Dad, being a painter *is* giving a direction to my career."

"What about our love for you, all our efforts to give you a good education. You never used to be like this, and I can only assume that what's happening is some consequence of the accident."

"Look, I love you both more than anything or anyone else in the world."

The ambassador cleared his throat. He wasn't used to such outspoken expressions of affection.

"Then, in the name of the love you have for us, please, do as your mother wants. Just stop all this painting business for a while, get some friends who belong to the same social class as you and go back to your studies."

"You love me, Dad. You can't ask me to do that, because you've always set me a good example, fighting for the things you cared about. You can't want me to be a man with no will of my own."

"I said, 'In the name of love.' And I have never said that before, but I'm asking you now. For the love that you bear us, for the love we bear you, come home, and I don't just mean in the physical sense, but really. You're deceiving yourself, running away from reality.

"Ever since you were born, we've built up such dreams of how our lives would be. You're everything to us, our future and our past. Your grandfathers were civil servants, and I had to fight like a lion to enter the diplomatic service and make my way up the ladder. And I did all this just to create a space for you, to make things easier for you. I've still got the pen with which I signed my first document as an ambassador, and I lovingly saved it to pass on to you the day you did the same.

"Don't let us down, son. We won't live forever and we want to die in peace, knowing that we've set you on the right path in life.

"If you really love us, do as I ask. If you don't love us, then carry on as you are now."

Eduard sat for long hours staring up at the sky in Brasília, watching the clouds moving across the blue—beautiful clouds, but without a drop of rain in them to moisten the dry earth of the central Brazilian plateau. He was as empty as they were.

If he continued as he was, his mother would fade away with grief, his father would lose all enthusiasm for his career, and both would blame each other for failing in the upbringing of their beloved son. If he gave up his painting, the visions of paradise would never see the light of day, and nothing else in this world could ever give him the same feelings of joy and pleasure.

He looked around him, he saw his paintings, he remembered the love and meaning he had put into each brushstroke, and he found every one of his paintings mediocre. He was a fraud, he wanted something for which he had not been chosen, the price of which was his parents' disappointment.

Visions of paradise were for the chosen few, who appeared in books as heroes and martyrs to the faith in which they believed—people who knew from childhood what the world wanted of them; the so-called facts in that first book he had read were the inventions of a storyteller.

At suppertime, he told his parents that they were right; it was just a youthful dream; his enthusiasm for painting had passed. His parents were pleased, his mother wept with joy and embraced her son, and everything went back to normal.

That night the ambassador secretly commemorated his victory by opening a bottle of champagne, which he drank alone. When he went to bed, his wife—for the first time in many months—was already sleeping peacefully.

The following day they found Eduard's room in confusion, the paintings slashed, and the boy sitting in a corner, gazing up at the sky. His mother embraced him, told him how much she loved him, but Eduard didn't respond.

He wanted nothing more to do with love; he was fed up with the whole business. He had thought that he could just give up and follow his father's advice, but he had advanced too far in his work; he had crossed the abyss that separates a man from his dream, and now there was no going back.

He couldn't go forward or back. It was easier just to leave the stage.

Eduard stayed in Brazil for another five months, being treated by specialists, who diagnosed a rare form of schizophrenia, possibly the result of a bicycle accident. Then war broke out in Yugoslavia, and the ambassador was hastily recalled. It was too problematic for the family to look after Eduard, and the only way out was to leave him in the newly opened hospital of Villete.

By the time Eduard had finished telling his story, it was dark and they were both shivering with cold.

L ET's GO in," he said. "They'll be serving supper."

"Whenever we went to see my grandmother when I was a child, I was always fascinated by one particular painting in her house. It showed a woman—Our Lady, as Catholics call her—standing poised above the world, with her hands outstretched to the earth and with rays of light streaming from her fingertips.

What most intrigued me about the painting was that this lady was standing on a live snake. I said to my grandmother: 'Isn't she afraid of the snake? Won't it bite her on the foot and kill her with its poison?' "

My grandmother said: "According to the Bible, the snake brought good and evil to the earth, and she is keeping both good and evil in check with her love.'"

"What's that got to do with my story?"

"I've only known you a week, so it would be far too early for me to tell you that I love you, but since I probably won't live through the night, it would also be too late. But then, the great craziness of men and women is precisely that: love.

"You told me a love story. I honestly believe your parents wanted the best for you, but their love almost destroyed your life. If Our Lady, as she appeared in my grandmother's painting, was treading on a snake, that indicates that love has two faces."

"I see what you mean," said Eduard. "I provoked the nurses into giving me the electric shock treatment, because you get me all mixed up. I can't say for sure what I feel, and love has already destroyed me once."

"Don't be afraid. Today I asked Dr. Igor for permission to leave here and to choose a place where I can close my eyes forever. But when I saw you being held down by the nurses, I realized what it was I wanted to be looking at when I left this world: your face. And I decided not to leave.

"While you were sleeping off the effects of the electric shock treatment, I had another heart attack, and I thought my time had come. I looked at your face, and I tried to guess what your story was, and I prepared myself to die happy. But death didn't come, my heart survived yet again, perhaps because I'm still young."

He looked down.

"Don't be embarrassed about being loved. I'm not asking you for anything; just let me love you and play the piano again tonight, just once more, if I still have the strength to do it. In exchange I ask only one thing: If you hear anyone say that I'm dying, go straight to my ward. Let me have my wish."

Eduard remained silent for a long time, and Veronika thought he must have retreated once more into his separate world, from which he would not return for a long time.

Then he looked at the mountains beyond the walls of Villete and said: "If you want to leave, I can take you. Just give me time to grab a couple of jackets and some money. Then we'll go."

"It won't last long, Eduard. You do know that."

Eduard didn't reply. He went in and came back at once carrying two jackets.

"It will last an eternity, Veronika; longer than all the identical days and nights I've spent in here, constantly trying to forget those visions of paradise. And I almost did forget them, too, though it seems to me they're coming back.

"Come on, let's go. Crazy people do crazy things."

That night, when they were all gathered together for supper, the inmates noticed that four people were missing.

ZEDKA, WHO everyone knew had been released after a long period of treatment; Mari, who had probably gone to the movies, as she often did; and Eduard, who had perhaps not recovered from the electric shock treatment. When they thought this, all the inmates felt afraid, and they began their supper in silence.

Finally, the girl with green eyes and brown hair was missing. The one who they all knew would not see out the week.

No one spoke openly of death in Villete, but absences were noted, although everyone always tried to behave as if nothing had happened.

A rumor started to go from table to table. Some wept, because she had been so full of life and now she would be lying in the small mortuary behind the hospital. Only the most daring ever went there, even during daylight hours. It contained three marble tables, and there was generally a new body on one of them, covered with a sheet.

Everyone knew that tonight Veronika would be there. Those who were truly insane soon forgot the presence, during that week, of another guest, who sometimes disturbed everyone's sleep playing the piano. A few, when they heard the news, felt rather sad, especially the nurses who had been with Veronika during her time in the Intensive Care Unit, but the employees had been trained not to develop strong bonds with the patients, because some left, others died, and the great majority got steadily worse. Their sadness lasted a little longer, and then that too passed.

The vast majority of the inmates, however, heard the news, pretended to be shocked and sad, but actually felt relieved because once more the exterminating angel had passed over Villete, and they had been spared.

When the Fraternity got together after supper, one member of the group gave them a message: Mari had not gone to the movies, she had left, never to return, and had given him a note.

No ONE seemed to attach much importance to the matter: She had always seemed different, rather too crazy, incapable of adapting to the ideal situation in which they all lived in Villete.

'Mari never understood how happy we are here," said one of them. "We are friends with common interests, we have a routine, sometimes we go out on trips together, invite lecturers here to talk about important matters, then we discuss their ideas. Our life has reached a perfect equilibrium, something that many people outside would love to achieve."

'Not to mention the fact that in Villete we are protected from unemployment, the consequences of the war in Bosnia, from economic problems and violence," said another. "We have found harmony."

'Mari left me this note," said the one who had given them the news, holding up a sealed envelope. "She asked me to read it out loud, as if she were saying good-bye to us all."

The oldest member of the group opened the envelope and did as Mari had asked. He was tempted to stop halfway, but by then it was too late, and so he read to the end.

"When I was still a young lawyer, I read some poems by an English poet, and something he said impressed me greatly: 'Be like the fountain that overflows, not like the cistern that merely contains.' I always thought he was wrong. It was dangerous to overflow, because we might end up flooding areas occupied by our loved ones and drowning them with our love and enthusiasm. All my life I did my best to be a cistern, never going beyond the limits of my inner walls.

"Then, for some reason I will never understand, I began suffering from panic attacks. I became the kind of person I had fought so hard to avoid becoming: I became a fountain that overflowed and flooded everything around me. The result was my internment in Villete.

"After I was cured, I returned to the cistern and I met all of you. Thank you for your friendship, for your affection, and for many happy moments. We lived together like fish in an aquarium, contented because someone threw us food when we needed it, and we could, whenever we wanted to, see the world outside through the glass.

"But yesterday, because of a piano and a young woman who is probably dead by now, I learned something very important: Life inside is exactly the same as life outside. Both there and here, people gather together in groups; they build their walls and allow nothing strange to trouble their mediocre existences. They do things because they're used to doing them, they study useless subjects, they have fun because they're supposed to have fun, and the rest of the world can go hang—let them sort themselves out. At the very most, they watch the news on television—as we often did—as confirmation of their happiness in a world full of problems and injustices.

"What I'm saying is that the life of the Fraternity is exactly the same as the lives of almost everyone outside Villete, carefully avoiding all knowledge of what lies beyond the glass walls of the aquarium. For a long time it was comforting and useful, but people change, and now I'm off in search of adventure, even though I'm sixty-five and fully aware of all the limitations that age can bring. I'm going to Bosnia. There are people waiting for me there. Although they don't yet know me, and I don't know them. But I'm sure I can be useful, and the danger of an adventure is worth a thousand days of ease and comfort."

When he had finished reading the note, the members of the Fraternity all went to their rooms and wards, telling themselves that Mari had finally gone insane.

Eduard and Veronika chose the most expensive restaurant in Ljubljana, ordered the finest dishes, and got drunk on three bottles of 1988 wine, one of the best vintages of the century. During supper they did not once mention Villete or the past or the future.

I LIKE THAT story about the snake," he said, filling her glass for the *n*th time. "But your grandmother was too old to be able to interpret the story correctly."

"Have a little respect for my grandmother, please!" roared Veronika drunkenly, making everyone in the restaurant turn around.

"A toast to this young woman's grandmother!" said Eduard, jumping to his feet. "A toast to the grandmother of this madwoman sitting here before me, who is doubtless some escapee from Villete!"

People turned their attention back to their food, pretending that nothing was happening.

"A toast to my grandmother!" insisted Veronika.

The owner of the restaurant came to their table.

"Will you please behave!"

They became quiet for a few moments but soon resumed their loud talking, their nonsensical remarks, and inappropriate behavior. The owner of the restaurant went back to their table, told them they didn't need to pay the bill, but they had to leave that instant.

"Think of the money we'll save on that exorbitantly expensive wine," said Eduard. "Let's leave before this gentleman changes his mind."

But the man wasn't about to change his mind. He was already pulling at Veronika's chair, an apparently courteous gesture intended to get her out of the restaurant as quickly as possible.

They walked to the middle of the small square in the center of the city. Veronika looked up at her convent room and her drunkenness vanished. She remembered that soon she would die.

"Let's buy some more wine!" said Eduard.

There was a bar nearby. Eduard bought two bottles, and the two of them sat down and continued drinking.

"What's wrong with my grandmother's interpretation of the painting?" said Veronika.

Eduard was so drunk that he had to make an immense effort to remember what he had said in the restaurant, but he managed it.

"Your grandmother said that the woman was standing on the snake because love must master good and evil. It's a nice, romantic interpretation, but it's nothing to do with that. I've seen that image before, it's one of the visions of paradise I imagined painting. I used to wonder why they always depicted the Virgin like that."

"And why do they?"

"Because the Virgin equals female energy and is the mistress of the snake, which signifies wisdom. If you look at the ring Dr. Igor wears, you'll see that it bears the physician's symbol: two serpents coiled around a stick. Love is above wisdom, just as the Virgin is above the snake. For her everything is inspiration. She doesn't bother judging what is good and what evil."

"Do you know something else?" said Veronika. "The Virgin never took any notice of what others might think of her. Imagine having to explain to everyone that business about the Holy Ghost. She didn't explain anything, she just said: 'That's what happened.' And do you know what the others must have said?"

"Of course. That she was insane."

They both laughed. Veronika raised her glass.

"Congratulations. You should paint those visions of paradise rather than just talking about them."

"I'll begin with you," said Eduard.

Beside the small square there is a small hill. On top of the small hill there is a small castle. Veronika and Eduard trudged up the steep path, cursing and laughing, slipping on the ice, and complaining of exhaustion.

Beside the castle there is a gigantic yellow crane. To anyone coming to Ljubljana for the first time, the crane gives the impression that the castle is being restored and that work will soon be completed. The inhabitants of Ljubljana, however, know that the crane has been there for many years, although no one knows why. Veronika told Eduard that when children in kindergarten are asked to draw the castle of Ljubljana, they always include the crane in the drawing.

"Besides, the crane is much better preserved than the castle."

Eduard laughed.

"You should be dead by now," he said, still under the effects of alcohol, but with a flicker of fear in his voice. "Your heart shouldn't have survived that climb."

Veronika gave him a long, lingering kiss.

"Look at my face," she said. "Remember it with the eyes of your soul, so that you can reproduce it one day. If you like that can be your starting point, but you must go back to painting. That is my last request. Do you believe in God?"

"I do."

"Then you must swear by the God you believe in that you will paint me."

"I swear."

"And that after painting me, you will go on painting."

"I don't know if I can swear that."

"You can. And thank you for giving meaning to my life. I came into this world in order to go through everything I've gone through: attempted suicide, ruining my heart, meeting you, coming up to this castle, letting you engrave my face on your soul. That is the only reason I came into the world, to make you go back to the path you strayed from. Don't make me feel my life has been in vain."

"I don't know if it's too early or too late, but, just as you did with me, I want to tell you that I love you. You don't have to believe it, maybe it's just foolishness, a fantasy of mine."

Veronika put her arms around him and asked the God she did not believe in to take her at that very moment.

She closed her eyes and felt him doing the same. And a deep, dreamless sleep came upon her. Death was sweet; it smelled of wine and it stroked her hair.

Eduard felt someone prodding him in the shoulder. When he opened his eyes, day was breaking.

Y OU CAN go and shelter in the town hall, if you like," said the policeman. "You'll freeze if you stay here."

In a second Eduard remembered everything that had happened the previous night. There was a woman lying curled in his arms.

"She . . . she's dead."

But the woman moved and opened her eyes.

"What's going on?" asked Veronika.

"Nothing," said Eduard, helping her to her feet. "Or rather a miracle happened: another day of life."

As soon as Dr. Igor went into his consulting room and turned on the light—for day-light still arrived late and winter was dragging on far too long—a nurse knocked at his door.

T HINGS HAVE started early today, he said to himself.

It was going to be a difficult day because of the conversation he would have to have with Veronika. He had been building up to it all week, and had hardly slept a wink the previous night.

"I've got some troubling news," said the nurse. "Two of the inmates have disappeared: the ambassador's son and the girl with the heart problem."

"Honestly, you're a load of incompetents, you are; not that the security in this hospital has ever been up to much."

"It's just that no one's ever tried to escape before," said the nurse, frightened. "We didn't know it was possible."

"Get out of here! Now I'll have to prepare a report for the owners, notify the police, take steps. Tell everyone I'm not to be disturbed; these things take hours!"

The nurse left, looking pale, knowing that a large part of that major problem would land on his own shoulders, because that is how the powerful deal with the weak. He would doubtless be dismissed before the day was out.

Dr. Igor picked up a pad, put it on the table, and began making notes; then he changed his mind.

He switched off the light and sat in the office precariously lit by the incipient sunlight, and he smiled. It had worked.

In a while he would make the necessary notes, describing the only known cure for Vitriol: an awareness of life. And describing the medication he had used in his first major test on patients: an awareness of death.

Perhaps other forms of medication existed, but Dr. Igor had decided to center his thesis around the one he had had the opportunity to experiment with scientifically, thanks to a young woman who had, quite unwittingly, become part of his fate. She had been in a terrible state when she arrived, suffering from a severe overdose, nearly in a coma. She had hovered between life and death for nearly a week, just the amount of time he needed to come up with a brilliant idea for his experiment.

Everything depended on one thing: the girl's capacity to survive.

And she had, with no serious consequences, no irreversible health problems; if she looked after herself, she could live as long as or longer than him.

But Dr. Igor was the only one who knew this, just as he knew that failed suicides tend to repeat the attempt sooner or later. Why not use her as a guinea pig, to see if he could eliminate the Vitriol from her organism?

And so Dr. Igor had conceived his plan.

Using a drug known as Fenotal, he had managed to simulate the effects of heart attacks. For a week she had received injections of the drug, and she must have been very frightened, because she had time to think about death and to review her own life. In that way, according to Dr. Igor's thesis (the final chapter of his work would be entitled "An Awareness of Death Encourages Us to Live More Intensely') the girl had gone on to eliminate Vitriol completely from her organism, and would quite possibly never repeat her attempt at suicide.

He was supposed to see her today and tell her that, thanks to the injections, he had achieved a total reversal of her heart condition. Veronika's escape saved him the unpleasant experience of lying to her yet again.

What Dr. Igor had not counted on was the infectious nature of his cure for Vitriol poisoning. A lot of people in Villete had been frightened by their awareness of that slow, irreparable death. They must all have been thinking about what they were missing, forced to reevaluate their own lives.

Mari had come to him asking to be discharged. Other patients were asking for their cases to be reviewed. The position of the ambas-

sador's son was more worrisome, though, because he had simply disappeared, probably helping Veronika to escape.

Perhaps they're still together, he thought.

At any rate the ambassador's son knew where Villete was, if he
wanted to come back. Dr. Igor was too excited by the results to pay
much attention to minor details.

For a few moments he was assailed by another doubt: Sooner or
later Veronika would realize that she wasn't going to die of a heart
attack. She would probably go to a specialist who would tell her
that her heart was perfectly normal. She would decide that the doctor who had taken care of her in Villete was a complete incompetent; but then, all those who dare to research into forbidden subjects
require both a certain amount of courage and a good dose of incom-
prehension.

But what about the many days that she would have to live with the
fear of imminent death?

Dr. Igor pondered the arguments long and hard and decided that it
didn't really matter. She would consider each day a miracle—which
indeed it is, when you consider the number of unexpected things that
could happen in each second of our fragile existences.

He noticed that the sun's rays were growing stronger; at that hour the
inmates would be having breakfast. Soon his waiting room would be

full, the usual problems would arise, and it was best to start taking notes at once for his thesis.

Meticulously he began to write up his experiment with Veronika; he would leave the reports on the building's lack of security until later.

St. Bernadette's Day, 1998